THE RIGHT OF THE LINE

(ARK ROYAL, BOOK XIV)

CHRISTOPHER G. NUTTALL

ISBN: 9781099139253

Imprint: Independently pubished

Cover by Justin Adams
http://www.variastudios.com/

http://www.chrishanger.net
http://chrishanger.wordpress.com/
http://www.facebook.com/ChristopherGNuttall

All Comments Welcome!

DEAR READERS

There were a couple of times, over the last six months, that I was starting to wonder if this series was cursed. I start to write *Para Bellum*...and, as you might recall, I ended up spending six weeks in hospital. I start to write this book, *The Right of the Line*, and...well, the effects of radiotherapy stop me from writing for several weeks. In any case, this book has been delayed, for which I am truly sorry. I'm rather nervous to even start *plotting* the final trilogy of the overall series. <grin>.

I'm hoping that things will get better, from now on, but I cannot guarantee it.

Thanks for reading—and for your patience.

Christopher G. Nuttall
Edinburgh, 2019

CONTENTS

PROLOGUE

From: Admiral Tony Mulhouse, Strategic Planning Division
To: Admiral Sir John Naiser, First Space Lord
Classification: Top Secret, Eyes-Only FSL

ADMIRAL.

I MUST CONFESS that I was following the discussions concerning Amalgamation with a somewhat jaundiced eye. Any student of history knows that attempts to unite radically different countries is doomed to produce either an oppressive empire, or civil war and eventual fragmentation. The eventual downfall of the European Union—a well-meaning attempt to ensure peace, harmony and prosperity—stands as a warning to us all. We do not need to go far to see the remnants of the brutal ethnic conflicts that tore the continent apart and threatened to send us crashing back to a new Dark Age. I believed that Amalgamation will be utterly disastrous.

And yet, I have been forced to change my opinion.

My staff is still working on what little data we received from Second Falkirk before the flicker link went dead, but a number of issues have already become apparent. First and foremost, the virus is clearly not hampered by what *we* would call economic reality. We would love to be able to produce hundreds of thousands of long-range missiles, of course, but any proposal to do so would cause the Treasury to have a collective heart attack. They would say—and rightly so—that it would be a massive expenditure for very little immediate return, particularly given both their military limitations *and* the eternal political reality that health and education are generally regarded as more conductive to winning votes than defence. It was growing harder to secure the ring-fenced military budget before the new threat showed up and, sir, the simple truth is that too many MPs believe that *we* somehow provoked this conflict. They may understand that we cannot simply pick up our toys and go home—it only takes one to start a war, but two to end it—yet the discontent in Parliament will make it harder to secure an ever-growing military budget.

Second, and perhaps more serious, we may be unable to out-produce the virus even if we were granted an unlimited military budget. Our most extreme plans for war mobilisation may not be enough to stave off defeat, even if we are lucky enough to avoid serious problems with both civilian and military morale. It hasn't been *that* long since industrial action in a number of manufacturing nodes caused a major slowdown and we must be aware of the prospect of other strikes if ill-feeling should happen to spread. While strikes are technically illegal during wartime, the strikers may feel that they have nothing to lose—and that we cannot bring pressure to bear against them, as we would need them to go back to work as quickly as possible. A work slowdown would be harder to stop...and, once they got into the habit of demanding and receiving concessions, would be easy to repeat.

In short, we may have no choice but to push for a completely unprecedented Amalgamation.

I cannot say how this will work out in practice. We have worked closely with the Americans and the French over the past hundred years—and exercised regularly with Russia, China and the lesser spacefaring powers—but there is a vast difference between working together and actually sharing starships, bases and secrets. At heart, we are different nations. Can we unite in the face of a common foe? Or will our half-baked stumbling towards Amalgamation sow the seeds for yet another conflict?

I don't know, sir. But I know we must push forward now, before time runs out. We are facing an existential threat on an unimaginable scale. The long-term implications of Amalgamation will be of no concern if we don't *have* a long-term. There is no way we can guarantee the survival of humanity, even if we surrender. We literally *cannot* surrender without giving up everything. There will be things that walk and talk and look human, but they will not *be* human. The aliens *Invincible* discovered on Alien-3 are stark proof of the fate awaiting us if we lose this war.

I understand why so many people are opposed to Amalgamation. I would oppose it myself—I *did* oppose it myself. But right now, sir, those of us who are military men need to understand that our backs are firmly pressed against the wall. We have no choice but to proceed towards Amalgamation.

Thankfully, our counterparts should have the same understanding.

Tony.

PROLOGUE II

PRIVATE COLIN SHEPHERD rubbed his hands together as he stood in front of the gates, watching the steady stream of cars and buses as they passed through the outer security barrier and into the Permanent Joint Headquarters. He'd thought himself lucky to win the duty when Sergeant Rudbek had been handing out assignments, but he was starting to suspect it was a poisoned chalice. On one hand, all he really had to do was stand by the gates and look intimidating; on the other, it was cold, boring and hardly likely to look good on his resume. But then, he hadn't joined the Home Guard because he'd wanted to be a hero.

He allowed himself a tight smile as he swept his eyes over the cars. He'd barely scraped through school, ensuring he would almost certainly be conscripted into the army. The career counsellor had made it clear that the navy would probably not be interested in him, particularly as he didn't have any real qualifications, and there was very little hope of winning a coveted place at a technical college. Colin had cursed his luck—he had no particular inclination to get his arse shot off for king and country—and volunteered for the Home Guard. It had been a surprise when he'd been accepted without question, but the Home Guard was desperate for volunteers. They normally had to rely on conscription to fill the ranks.

And it isn't that bad being out here, he thought. The country had been on low-level alert since *Invincible's* first return from Alien-One, but nothing had actually happened. Colin found it hard to believe some of the wilder stories, even if they had government imprimaturs. Everyone knew the government lied. *There are some definite advantages to being in the Home Guard.*

He felt his smile grow wider as the line of cars slowly dwindled away. Guard duty on the outskirts of London was relatively safe, even if there *was* a war on. The bombardment was a thing of the past. Colin was entirely sure the Royal Navy would keep the new threat well away from the Solar System. He wouldn't have a chance to prove himself a hero, but it hardly mattered. Colin didn't want to *be* a hero. He just wanted to impress the girls with his uniform while waiting for his discharge. It was astonishing how many girls couldn't tell the difference between a combat infantryman and a guardsman. Or maybe they just didn't care.

A low rumble echoed through the air as a giant garbage truck drove down the street, followed by a pair of vans. Colin blinked in surprise, puzzled and alarmed. He'd been on guard duty outside PJHQ long enough to know that the garbage men never came on a Monday, certainly not to the military base. They shouldn't even have been allowed to get so close. The automated highways control system would have automatically barred any vehicle from entering the street unless it had permission…ice ran down his spine as he realised that something was badly wrong. A drill? Or a real emergency? He raised his rifle, shouting for the driver to stop. Instead, the driver gunned the engine and drove straight at the gates. Colin fired twice, but the truck kept moving. Colin had to throw himself out of the way—and straight into a trench—before the truck could knock him down. A moment later, there was a thunderous sound. Colin rolled over, his ears ringing. He couldn't hear anything.

He forced himself to stand, cursing himself under his breath. His rifle was missing…it took him a moment to realise that he must have dropped it when he'd dived into the trench. He drew his pistol from the holster as he forced himself to stand on wobbly legs, peering over the edge of the trench. The gates were gone, shattered beyond repair. And the other vans were moving forward, their doors already snapping open. Colin stared in horror, only slowly realising that this was no mere drill. PJHQ was under attack! His legs threatened to buckle as a stream of dogs, of all things, ran out of the vans and raced into the compound. Colin had only a moment to see the pouches the dogs were carrying before it was too late.

Fuck, he thought, numbly.

A man jumped out of the van, weapon already raised. Colin shot him twice, both bullets passing through the target's head. The man staggered, but didn't fall. Colin stared in disbelief. He'd hit the man twice! His brains were leaking out of his skull and yet he was still coming. Another man followed, then another…weapons flashing fire. Colin felt a sharp pain in his chest, despite the body armour. He'd been shot…

He fell back, crashing to the bottom of the trench. His pistol clattered to the concrete floor. Dogs leapt over his head, moving with an eerie silence that horrified him. Colin realised, in horror, that the stories he'd heard hadn't been exaggerated after all. It wasn't just *humans* who could be infected by the virus. The dogs could carry bombs—or worse—into the compound. They'd do a great deal of damage before they were shot down.

Colin looked up as a shadow fell over him. A man stood there, levelling a weapon at Colin's face. His expression was utterly blank, as if he had no feelings at all. Colin couldn't shake the impression that he was looking at something inhuman. The force animating the body was *very* far from human.

"No," he whispered. "I…"

But it was already too late.

CHAPTER ONE

CAPTAIN SIR STEPHEN SHIELDS felt out of place as he followed his brother into the COBRA conference room.

It wasn't the first time he'd been in a conference that was, technically, well above his pay grade. He was the youngest scion of an important family, related—directly or indirectly—to a great many important people. The Old Boys Network had seen to it that his rise through the ranks to starship command was smooth, without any of the bumps and bruises that would have destroyed a lesser career. Everyone expected him to—eventually—take his place amongst the leaders of his country. People opened doors for him even when—on the face of it—he was far beneath them.

But this…this was different.

He took his place amongst the wallflowers, the secretaries and aides who supported the cabinet ministers, and looked around the room. The bunker was miles below London, but it looked like a normal cabinet office, complete with a framed portrait of the king and his children hanging on the wooden walls. A small drinks cabinet sat in one corner, utterly untouched. The wallflowers were providing tea and coffee for their principals—Stephen was amused to note that *he* didn't rate coffee—but no alcohol. Stephen wondered, as the Prime Minister strode into the room, if there genuinely *was* anything in the cabinet. The government officials should know better than to drink on the job.

Although they've had a terrible shock, he thought, grimly. The first reports had arrived while they'd been driving to Whitehall. A few hours later, neither Stephen nor his brother would have been able to get through the streets without a police escort. *And there's little they can do but issue orders and wait for them to be carried out.*

He frowned, inwardly, as he met the First Space Lord's eyes. Admiral Sir John Naiser didn't look pleased to see Stephen, although the Admiral's staff would presumably have informed him Stephen had been invited to accompany his brother. Naiser had worked his way up the ranks without having a powerful family, although—as a legitimate war hero—he hadn't entirely been without assets of his own. Stephen wouldn't have blamed the older man for resenting his presence. It was a grim reminder that class and accidents of birth still counted in society. Naiser would never be amongst the greatest of the great and he knew it.

And he deserves better, Stephen thought. *He led the navy to victory in the last interstellar war.*

The Prime Minister sat down at the head of the table. "Gentlemen, be seated," he said. "This meeting is now in session."

Stephen took a breath. The Prime Minister looked to have aged twenty years in the space of a day. It was one thing to hear about disaster hundreds of light years away, but quite another to know that the war had come home with a vengeance. Bombings and shootings on the streets…it sounded as if hell itself had come to Britain. Stephen had hoped that the first reports had been exaggerated—they always were, in his experience—but the grim look on the Prime Minister's face suggested otherwise. The war had very definitely come home.

"Chief Constable," the Prime Minister said. "Please update us on the current…situation."

The Chief Constable didn't look pleased, Stephen noted. Andrew Middlebrow was a tall man, with a distinguished record, but he wouldn't have reached the very highest levels without a number of political connections. It would be easy for the poor man's patrons to drop him like a hot rock if they happened to need a scapegoat for the disaster. Middlebrow should be in his office, helping to coordinate the civil and military response, not briefing government officials deep under London. Stephen understood, though. A senior officer could issue orders, but he'd never be able to do anything for himself. All he could do was watch and wait while his subordinates dealt with the crisis on their own.

No wonder so many higher officers turn into micromanagers, Stephen thought, with a flicker of empathy. *It's the only way they can feel in control.*

Middlebrow stood at parade rest, clasping his beefy hands behind his back. "Yes, Prime Minister," he said. His voice was under tight control, suggesting that he was more than a little agitated. Normally, the briefing would be given by a junior officer. "Over the last two hours, there have been a series of attacks on military, police and government installations across the country. Preliminary reports from America and France suggest that they, too, have come under attack, although details are sparse. The attacks were closely-coordinated, almost all of them launched before our alert status could be raised."

He tapped a control, bringing up a holographic map of the country. Stephen leaned forward, feeling cold. A handful of red icons—mostly in or around London—glared at him. He knew very little about urban combat—he preferred to leave such operations to the groundpounders—but the display looked intimidating. London appeared to be surrounded by red icons. It was hard to recall that each of the attacks—individually—were nothing more than pinpricks. The country had barely been scratched.

"In almost all cases, the attackers were caught and killed before they could inflict major damage," Middlebrow said. "The most serious damage was done to a recruiting barracks in Slough, where a truck bomb was rammed through the gates and detonated on the parade ground. Other installations were barely damaged, although casualties were quite high. The attackers showed no concern for their own lives and managed to take

3

out a number of defenders before they were killed. In some cases, they were reported as continuing to fight until they were literally shot to pieces."

They were infected, Stephen thought. He shivered, inwardly. *The virus has reached Earth.*

"Our preliminary examinations of the dead bodies revealed the presence of the virus," Middlebrow said, echoing Stephen's thoughts. "Right now, we are attempting to trace them back to their point of infection and…"

"This isn't good enough," the Home Secretary snapped. "I thought we had defences in place to *stop* this…this kind of infection!"

"We took all rational precautions," Middlebrow said. "However, sir, the plain truth is that there are simply too many ways to smuggle something down to Earth that bypass most of our security checks. We have tightened things up as much as possible, but gaps remain. We may discover, for example, that a lone starship crewman was infected and…induced…to carry the virus through security. We'll have to backtrack the infected to figure it out."

"Fucking careless," the Home Secretary growled. "Prime Minister, I insist on an official inquiry…"

"After we have handled the current crisis, we will have time to reassess our safety precautions," the Prime Minister said. "Chief Constable, what are the odds of tracking down any surviving infected?"

Middlebrow winced. "Poor," he said. "We believed our testing regime was sufficient, but clearly we were wrong. The combination of blood tests and biological warfare sniffers needs to be reassessed. If they pass through a checkpoint, we'll catch them; if they don't…they may be able to hide out for quite some time. There are large swathes of the country with very limited security."

"So they could be…breeding…somewhere in Wales or Scotland or wherever," the Home Secretary said. "Is there *no* way we can find them?"

"We have deployed an extensive array of sensors," Middlebrow said. "And we have ordered civilians to return home and stay there. Anyone still moving at the end of the cut-off period will draw attention. The police force will investigate any signs of trouble."

"But we can't keep people inside forever," the Foreign Secretary said quietly. "They'll start to starve."

"And the economy will tumble," the Prime Minister added. "We can't keep the country in a state of emergency indefinitely."

"This is going to be worse than the Troubles," the Home Secretary predicted. "*Anyone* could be an enemy."

Stephen nodded in agreement. *Anyone* could be infected. Anyone... or *anything*. The police checkpoints were looking for humans, not dogs or cats or even mice. The xenospecialists had warned that the virus might be able to infect dogs and cats, although they *had* suggested that the animals couldn't host enough of the virus to make it a viable threat. Stephen hoped that was true, but it struck him as a classic example of wishful thinking. The virus could hardly be blind to the prospect of using smaller animals to spread itself. The only upside, as far as anyone could tell, was that insects couldn't become hosts. *That* would have made the virus unstoppable.

"And where did they get the weapons?" The Home Secretary glared around the room. "And the bombs?"

"Our preliminary assessment suggests that some of the weapons were legal, their owners presumably infected and turned against us." There was a hint of irritation in Middlebrow's voice. "And the bombs were all jury-rigged devices, the explosives put together from freely-available compounds. I have no doubt we'll eventually discover that shopkeepers and suppliers were infected and, again, forced to work against us."

"And the virus can turn our people against us so easily?" The Home Secretary sounded sceptical. "There's no way to resist?"

The Prime Minister glanced at the First Space Lord, who nodded. "There is considerable evidence, Home Secretary, that the virus is capable of both accessing and *using* the memories of its host. The host, to all intents and purposes, no longer exists. They are not held at gunpoint, they are not reconditioned...they are no longer who or what they were. They do not *choose* to betray us. They are not *us* any longer."

"Crap," the Home Secretary said. "There's nothing we can do about it?"

5

"We have taken precautions to prevent infection," the First Space Lord said, quietly. "But once the virus gets firmly established..."

It becomes impossible to stop, Stephen thought. He knew how infiltrations worked. The virus, he suspected, understood it intimately. Infiltrations and infections followed the same basic idea. The first thing an infection did was weaken the host's ability to fight, either by attacking the immune system or trying to gain control of the security services. *If we don't know that something is wrong, how can we stop it?*

"They're not good enough," the Home Secretary growled.

"There is little else we *can* do," the Chief Constable said. "We can expand the blood testing program—we have no choice, now we *know* the virus is loose on Earth. We can limit public transport in hopes of slowing any major outbreak..."

And that won't be easy, Stephen thought. *We shouldn't be thinking of this as a viral outbreak. We should be treating this as a biological attack. The virus is far more intelligent than we realised.*

He shivered. The Age of Unrest had seen a handful of biological attacks, all carried out by terrorists who had very little to lose. They'd taken advantage of advances in genetic bioengineering technology to attack their enemies... thankfully, the science hadn't been advanced enough for the engineered viruses to spread before they were detected and countered. A little more good luck for the attackers—and bad luck for the entire human race—and the entire planet might have been turned into a graveyard. And now...the virus was intelligent, combining a deep understanding of its own nature with a complete disregard for the lives of its hosts. It was easy to imagine it evading checkpoints and spreading itself over the entire planet.

"I'm sure the police have the matter well in hand," the Secretary of Defence said. "The question now is why...why now? Why launch the attacks now?"

"The attacks started shortly after the Battle of Falkirk," the First Space Lord said. "That *cannot* be a coincidence."

"And that means they have access to the flicker network," the Home Secretary said. "Or even the media."

And if the media is infected, Stephen mused, *could we tell the difference?*

"We told the media not to report on the battle," the Prime Minister said.

"But rumours would have spread anyway," the Home Secretary countered. "And..."

He took a breath. "How do we know that we were told the truth?"

The Prime Minister frowned. "What do you mean?"

"The virus can pose as a host, right?" The Home Secretary looked from face to face. "It wears a host's face, speaks with a host's voice...there's no way to tell if someone has been infected without a blood test. Prime Minister... how do we know that the entire MNF hasn't been infected?"

"The MNF understood the dangers," the First Space Lord said, quietly. "The virus *did* attempt to board a handful of ships, but...none of them were infected. Their crews took prompt action to remove the boarding parties before it was too late."

"And if they failed?"

"There were contingency plans," the First Space Lord said. "It would be difficult to subvert them."

"For someone from the outside, yes." The Home Secretary didn't sound convinced. "But what about someone on the *inside*? A single corrupt clerk in an office can do more damage—and hide it—than an entire team of burglars!"

"They would have to get inside first," the First Space Lord reminded him. "And, like I said, the MNF understood the dangers. They took precautions."

Stephen kept his face impassive. It was true that Admiral Weisskopf would have taken precautions, but it was also true that there was no way to know if the precautions had been completely successful. The Home Secretary was right, damn him. Sneaking onto a planet was far easier than boarding a starship—and Admiral Weisskopf had ordered regular blood tests—but there was no way to be entirely certain. They lived in an era when almost anything could be faked. There were talking heads on the nightly news that were almost certainly nothing more than computer-generated composites.

Why *couldn't* the virus have taken control of the flicker network and sent them misleading reports?

They managed to take control of Dezhnev *and send her against us,* he thought. *Why couldn't they do the same with an American battleship or two?*

He shook his head. *Dezhnev* and her crew hadn't known the dangers. They'd thought they were facing a conventional opponent...his lips twitched in grim amusement. The crew might not have realised they were facing an opponent at all. They'd had strict orders not to do *anything* that might be construed as hostile, anything that might spark off a third interstellar war with a mysterious alien race...they had very clear orders not to open fire unless there was a clear and present danger. It would be easy for the virus to take control of *Dezhnev* before the crew realised it was under attack. Stephen could imagine a dozen ways to do it.

It may not matter, he reminded himself. *The virus punched us right out of Falkirk. And now, it's on Earth.*

Stephen allowed none of his feelings to show as he surveyed the room. The First Space Lord looked calm and composed—he understood the realities of the situation—but the politicians seemed badly worried. They looked as if they were on the verge of panic. Stephen knew how hard it would be for the virus to work its way into the very heart of government or take control of the orbital defence systems, but the politicians didn't. They feared the worst. And they were all old enough to remember the Bombardment.

The Prime Minister's voice echoed in the silence. "There is no way we can *talk* to the virus," he said. "We have no choice but to press on."

"There has to be *some* way to make ourselves understood," the Foreign Secretary objected.

"The virus doesn't seem to think like us," the First Space Lord said. "And even if it did...why *should* it talk to us? It doesn't want to come to terms, it doesn't want surrender...it doesn't even want submission. We are locked in a war for survival, a war that has just come home. If we lose, we lose everything."

And that's the nub, Stephen thought. There had been no prospect of complete extermination during the First and Second World Wars. Humanity as a whole would not be wiped out by the conflict. But any war with an alien power put the survival of humanity itself at risk. The Tadpoles had killed millions of people during the Bombardment. God alone knew how many people would have died if they'd won the war. *The virus won't just defeat us, if it wins the war. It will destroy us.*

"So we keep fighting," the Prime Minister said. "And we tighten our precautions, once again."

"And then the virus will get around them, once again," the Home Secretary said. "Whatever we do, it will find a way to circumvent. We need to find a way to take the war into enemy space and *finish* it."

"The virus is a unique threat," the First Space Lord said. "And one that requires us to work closely with other nations to defeat. But it is not all-powerful. It has its limits. It can be beaten. We have not lost this war."

No, Stephen thought. He remembered the fleet of warships gathering in Alien-One. *But it may be too powerful for us to handle.*

"We lost a battle," the Prime Minister agreed. "But we have not lost the war."

"And our allies are coming," the Foreign Secretary said. "We are not alone."

"No," the Prime Minister said. "And *that* makes all the difference."

CHAPTER TWO

"I TRUST YOU FOUND THE MEETING to be interesting," the First Space Lord said. "It should have been an educational experience."

Stephen took a moment to organise his thoughts. The First Space Lord had caught his attention as soon as the COBRA meeting had come to an end, summoning him to the Admiralty once the roads were clear. Stephen had known better than to argue, even when his brother had demanded his attention. There was little to be gained by picking a fight with his uniformed superior. Besides, he could catch up with his brother later. The latest update from the BBC had made it clear that all non-essential flights to orbit had been suspended as long as the state of emergency remained in effect.

"It was...*interesting*," he said, finally. "I...permission to speak freely?"

"Granted," the First Space Lord said.

"I thought the politicians had to have military experience," Stephen said. "Or at least *some* kind of experience."

"The Secretary of Defence does have to have military experience," the First Space Lord said, calmly. "Everyone else...they don't *have* to have any relevant experience in the field to serve as a cabinet minister. They have staff to handle the practical details."

He looked as if he wanted to say something more, but stopped himself. Stephen understood, more than he cared to admit. The cabinet ministers were selected for political reasons, not because they were the best candidates for the job. They didn't *always* know how their departments worked, let alone what the people who were nominally under their command actually *did*. They tended to get blindsided by procedures and polices laid down by their predecessors they didn't realise hadn't been changed simply because there'd been a change in government. It wasn't easy for them to change anything, particularly when the civil service was opposed to change. The governing system made sure of it.

"They understand that the war needs to be fought," the First Space Lord said, briskly. "Right now, Captain, that is all that matters."

"Yes, sir," Stephen said.

"And the situation has become dire," the First Space Lord added. He pointed to a seat. "We have to decide how to proceed."

He took his seat behind the desk and keyed a switch. A holographic star chart appeared above his desk, the handful of alien-occupied systems glowing red against the green and blue of humanity's stars. Stephen felt his heart sink as he realised just how deeply the virus had sliced into the human sphere. Twelve colony worlds now lay within its grasp, just waiting to be infected. The colonists knew what to expect, but…Stephen doubted they could save themselves. Only a handful had any real defences, none of which were capable of standing off a major fleet. Their only hope was the virus deciding not to mop up the colonies while Earth and the major worlds were still untouched.

And it doesn't have to detach entire battle squadrons to bring most of those worlds to heel, Stephen thought. *A lone destroyer would be more than sufficient to smash the defences and infect the population.*

"We were able to re-establish contact with the MNF when it withdrew to UAS-4823," the First Space Lord said. "The virus was apparently able to take out the flicker station in Honshu, breaking our lines of communication. Admiral Weisskopf—or the person we think is Admiral Weisskopf—has sent a full report."

His lips twisted. Stephen understood. The odds of the virus being able to capture USS *Texas* and her crew intact were very low—it was far more likely that the ship would be destroyed in combat—but there was no way to be sure. The Home Secretary had had a point, when he'd raised concerns about just *who* was on the far end of the line. Maybe the man was being paranoid or…maybe he was right to be concerned. If the virus had managed to infect Admiral Weisskopf…Stephen shuddered. It didn't bear thinking about.

"We lost a third of the MNF outright," the First Space Lord said. "Another third is heavily damaged. Admiral Weisskopf made it clear that a number of ships were under tow. The remainder are low on ammunition. They will not be able to make a stand if the virus gives chase."

"And it probably absorbed navigational data from *Dezhnev* and her crew," Stephen said. "It won't have to waste time surveying the tramlines to pick out the route to Earth."

"Probably," the First Space Lord said. "*We* would certainly have drawn navigational data from a captured ship, if we had that level of access."

We wouldn't have risked sending her into battle, Stephen thought. A captured starship—a captured *alien* starship—was a prize beyond price. The Royal Navy was prepared to pay *millions* in prize money to the crew who brought home an intact alien ship, knowing that the value of the intelligence bonanza would be in the billions. It would take years, perhaps, to finish stripping the hull of valuable information. *Why did the virus risk us recapturing or destroying Dezhnev?*

He shook his head, dismissively. It wouldn't have taken *long* for the captured ship's datanodes to be downloaded into an alien datacore, not if the virus had access to the ship's command codes. There was no reason to assume the virus hadn't copied *everything* from *Dezhnev* before using her as a modified Trojan Horse. Anything else…he cursed the security nightmare under his breath. Anything else was just whistling in the dark. The virus owned and operated *starships*, for God's sake! It might be alien, but it couldn't be *that* alien.

The First Space Lord nodded to the hologram. "The remainder of the fleet is currently falling back on Zheng He, a Chinese colony and fleet base. The Chinese didn't have *that* long to turn the base into a fortress, but they've done enough to give us a *reasonable* chance of stalling the virus long enough for us to bring new weapons and starships online. We may not be able to win this war by outproducing the virus, Captain, but we may be able to develop new weapons and suchlike to tip the balance in our favour."

"Yes, sir," Stephen said. "I saw the projections."

"And absolutely none of them are remotely cheerful." The First Space Lord grimaced, as if he had bitten into something rotten. "The best-case projections give the virus a major production advantage over us—over *all* of us, British and Americans and everyone else put together. Their sheer willingness to deploy vast numbers of long-range missiles alone…well, let's just say we may be heavily outgunned. Our only real advantage is, I think, a certain degree of tactical flexibility and we may lose that if it absorbs more of our people."

"Perhaps, sir," Stephen said. "It's difficult to predict how their starships will react to any given situation. Sometimes they'll come boiling after us, the moment they catch a sniff of us; sometimes they'll just ignore us until we make ourselves impossible to ignore."

"And there's no way to know which choice they'll make until they do," the First Space Lord agreed. "They may also believe that they don't *need* to make any changes to their tactical doctrine."

Stephen nodded in grim agreement. He'd studied decision-making during his time at the academy and his instructors had pointed out *hundreds* of examples of human commanders making the same mistakes, time and time again, because they didn't face any personal consequences for their failure. They cared more about public relations—and the opinions of their superiors—than about the men under their command. It was easier and safer to send the men into the meatgrinder, time and time again, than to suggest ways to outflank the enemy and save lives. The virus might feel the same way. It might care as little for the loss of a single starship as Stephen cared for a single strand of hair.

And if what they're doing worked in every previous war they've fought, he told himself, *they may see no reason to change.*

"On the other hand, we can be reasonably sure they'll throw everything they have at Zheng He as soon as they realise that the MNF has stopped running," the First Space Lord said. "They already know the fleet has been badly weakened."

Stephen nodded. "They *must* know."

"Quite." The First Space Lord tapped a switch. "There have been a number of high-level discussions between senior military officers over the past few days. We were contemplating reinforcements for the MNF even before the virus launched its second offensive against Falkirk. *Invincible* and a number of other starships will be dispatched to Zheng He to back up the fleet and hold the line."

"Sir." Stephen took a breath and started again. "Sir, *Invincible* is in no condition to return to the front. Our hull plating has been badly damaged, our starfighter squadrons have been shot to ribbons…"

The First Space Lord held up a hand. "Captain, under normal circumstances, I'd be happy to give you, your ship and your crew a long period to recuperate. I'd even push for two-thirds of your crew to be reassigned to other ships while *Invincible* is put back together. But now…we are short on starships that can be rushed to the front. The politicians are unlikely to allow us to draw more ships from the home defence formations, particularly not now. We can only throw a handful of starships into the front line. *Invincible* is one of them."

Stephen swallowed, hard. "How long do we have?"

"The discussions are still underway, but I think you'll receive your formal orders by the end of the day." The First Space Lord frowned. "And I think you'll be told to depart within a week—ten days, at the most. Can your ship be readied in time?"

"There is no way we can return to full fighting trim in ten days," Stephen said, flatly. He forced himself to remember the last report from the engineers, after they'd surveyed the damage and planned the repairs. "If we had emergency priority, with repair work going on around the clock, we *might* be able to get up to eighty, perhaps ninety, percent of readiness. But that might be dangerously optimistic."

"Probably too optimistic," the First Space Lord said. He'd served a term in the shipyards, if Stephen recalled correctly. The *Vanguard* and *Invincible* classes had practically been his brainchildren. "But you *will* have emergency priority. I'll make sure you're assigned all the workers and supplies you need."

"That will be difficult," Stephen predicted. "Home Fleet will want…"

"Home Fleet will have to put up with it," the First Space Lord said. "We *must* keep the virus away from Earth, at all costs. If that means sending half-repaired ships into battle…"

He studied the holographic chart for a long moment. "Our allies are redeploying their ships to support us, Captain, but it will be several months before they can arrive in force. If we can hold the line that long, we should be able to get the remainder of our industrial base into full war production and start churning out new weapons. The boffins are *sure* they can come up with something to even the odds."

Stephen didn't bother to hide his scepticism. The boffins had been promising all kinds of technological advances for years, from long-range energy weapons that could slice through a starship like a hot knife through butter to forcefields that could protect a starship from a direct nuclear strike, but so far none of the advances had ever materialised. They'd inched forward slowly, only jumping forward when they had a piece of alien technology to reverse-engineer and put into mass production. There was no point in holding one's breath for a technological silver bullet. The virus would have to be stopped the old-fashioned way.

And we know it doesn't have access to super-advanced technology, either, he thought. It wasn't a particularly reassuring thought. *It just has more than enough starships to crush us by sheer weight of numbers.*

16

"There are some promising ideas," the First Space Lord said, calmly. "Quite a few technological advances seemed impossible until they became reality."

"Yes, sir," Stephen said.

"But there is a second concern," the First Space Lord added. "It is quite likely that the officer in command of the reinforcements will be a Russian."

Stephen blinked. "What? But…"

The First Space Lord nodded, curtly. "Believe me, I am aware of the political implications. There are too many unanswered questions surrounding *Dezhnev* and whatever orders she might have been given for me to feel happy about *any* of this. However, the Russians will be making the largest contribution. They practically *have* to be given the command."

"Sir." Stephen forced himself to calm down. "Can we trust them?"

"I trust them to know where their own best interests lie," the First Space Lord said. "They have nothing to gain and a great deal to lose by betraying humanity to *any* alien foe, particularly the virus. They're not going to be playing Vichy Russia when the virus doesn't *need* collaborators. The risks of working with them, Captain, are far exceeded by the dangers of *not* working with them. We need to leave the past in the past and work together to save humanity from destruction."

Stephen lowered his eyes. "Yes, sir."

"That said, you are to keep an eye out for trouble," the First Space Lord added. "And report to me if you sense *anything* out of kilter."

"Yes, sir." Stephen cursed under his breath. The orders would be difficult, if not impossible, to follow. "I'll keep an eye on them."

The First Space Lord smiled, briefly. "Do your best," he said. "Admiral Svetlana Zadornov is known for being competent, as well as a patriot. You can work with her."

"Yes, sir," Stephen said, again. "Shouldn't it be *Zadornova*?"

"I believe that Admiral Zadornov prefers the masculine form of her name," the First Space Lord said. "She is certainly never called Zadornova in official dispatches. And, given where she is, you can assume she's more than *merely* competent."

"She wouldn't have reached high rank without being extremely capable," Stephen agreed, calmly. It was unusual to encounter a woman in the Russian military, let alone one who held such a high rank. "And she *was* in the Battle of Earth."

"And received medals from all of the Great Powers," the First Space Lord said. "She was one of the first officers to receive the Star of Terra. There aren't many other officers, male or female, who have been honoured by the entire planet."

"Yes, sir," Stephen said. "I won't take her lightly."

"No," the First Space Lord agreed. "If nothing else, bear in mind she will be commanding a bigger ship."

Stephen had to smile. "Yes, sir."

"You will also be playing host to a starfighter squadron—perhaps more than one—from another nation," the First Space Lord added. "We're still smoothing out the details. The Germans have offered a starfighter squadron or two, but the French and Poles are throwing out objections and the Germans might wind up being reassigned to home defence duties instead. I'd hoped for an American squadron, but it looks like they're being reserved for their own ships. The Japanese are the only other prospects and *they* have colony worlds to defend, too."

"And there's little prospect of those worlds being ignored," Stephen mused. He studied the starchart for a moment, thinking fast. "Have we managed to draw anything from the captured datacores yet?"

"The boffins are still working on it." The First Space Lord looked displeased. "The current theory is that the virus stored astrographic information within its cells, rather than…well, anything *we* would recognise as a datacore. They haven't managed to pull anything *legible* from the captured ships. On the other hand"—he shrugged—"they might simply not have figured out how to work the system yet. Alien technology is always difficult to crack."

Stephen nodded. The Tadpoles might not have been human, but they'd been reasonably *humanoid*. Their computers had been different, yet they hadn't been *that* different. The virus, on the other hand, was completely alien. Who knew how a living virus *thought*? The boffins had been sure they'd crack the datacores, but how long would it take? And how would the boffins even know they'd succeeded?

Starcharts are understandable, he told himself firmly. *And we can pick them out by matching the data against our files.*

"I wish we didn't have to send you back into action so quickly," the First Space Lord said, grimly. "The exigencies of war demand it..."

"I understand," Stephen said. "There will be...*issues*...of course, but we will cope."

"And I'm sorry about the lack of shore leave for your crew," the First Space Lord added. "It won't do wonders for morale."

"No," Stephen agreed. "We knew what we were doing when we took the oath, sir. We'll cope."

He winced, inwardly. He didn't fear a mutiny—the Royal Navy hadn't suffered a mutiny for hundreds of years—but he knew what a lack of shore leave could do to a crew. They would start to suffer, start to slow down... too many experienced men and women would decline to re-enlist when their original terms of service came to an end. Better civvy street, they'd say, than the military. Civvy street wouldn't jerk them around and force them to remain on duty indefinitely...he shook his head. No one would be discharged during the war, not when trained officers and crew were desperately needed. They'd just have to suck it up.

And I'll just have to hope that they can cope, he told himself. *And that we can cope with any problems that might arise.*

"Very good, Captain," the First Space Lord said. "And good luck."

"Yes, sir."

CHAPTER THREE

"THERE ISN'T ANYTHING ON THE DATANET," Corporal Glen Hammersmith said. "The whole planet has gone quiet."

"Maybe they're all dead," Corporal Roger Tindal offered. "Or infected."

Captain Alice Campbell rubbed her eyes as she forced herself to throw off the last vestiges of sleep and get up. The shuttle flight shouldn't have been more than a couple of hours, but the emergency on Earth—whatever the hell it was—had forced the pilot to take a long detour before resuming his original course. Alice was no stranger to being told to hurry up and wait—or being ordered to fill out hundreds of forms, only to be told afterwards that half of them weren't necessary—but she had to admit there was something odd about *this* order. They were a *long* way from Earth. Whatever was happening on the surface couldn't have much to do with *them*.

Unless the virus really has infected the entire planet, she thought. She stood, gritting her teeth. Her body felt...strange, as if it wasn't completely *hers. It might have reached the homeworld before we knew what we were facing.*

She glanced at the displays, keeping her face under tight control. One showed an actress running from a monster, screaming her head off; the second was the live feed from the BBC, probably already hours out of date. She wondered, idly, which one was more realistic. The girl was wearing a dress that should have tripped her up a dozen times in the last few minutes, but the BBC wasn't known for detailed investigative reporting these days. It was probably repeating the government's talking points, whatever the hell they were. The crisis, whatever it was, had only just started. The government itself probably didn't know what its talking points were, yet. It would take hours, at least, for an official statement to emerge.

"The entire planet couldn't be infected," she said, finally. "Did they sound the system-wide alert?"

"No, Captain," Hammersmith said. "There doesn't seem to be any alert off Earth."

So far, Alice thought. They were two light-hours from Earth. The BBC's talking head had finished his babbling two hours ago. *They might have already sounded the alert for the rest of the solar system.*

She keyed a switch, bringing up the long-range sensors. The solar system looked normal. There were no vast fleets of alien starships crashing through the tramlines, no sudden silence as asteroid bases and industrial nodes shut down hastily to avoid being detected...she shook her head at the thought. The virus probably knew everything its unwilling hosts had known. It probably knew *precisely* where to find humanity's industrial nodes. A conventional foe would set out to destroy them, as Alice and her team had destroyed an alien shipyard months ago, but the virus might think it could take the shipyards intact instead. Alice had a terrible feeling that the virus might be right.

The intercom bleeped. "We've just received permission to approach the base," the pilot said, calmly. "We'll be docking in thirty minutes."

"He probably means thirty *hours*," Hammersmith stage-whispered.

"I heard that," the pilot said. He sounded more amused than indignant. He probably hadn't enjoyed the long flight either. "And they're very insistent on us docking as soon as possible."

"I'll go freshen up," Alice said. "You two...get ready."

She turned and made her way down to the washroom. It felt weird to have only three passengers in a shuttle designed for an entire company of marines, but there were some definite advantages. She splashed water on

her face, then peered at herself in the mirror. The tired-looking woman staring back at her was almost a stranger. She touched her close-cropped hair,
silently wondering why she hadn't had it permanently shaved after she'd
been told she could return to active duty. The marks on her pale skin were
a grim reminder of how hard she'd worked to rebuild muscle mass over the
last couple of weeks. No one would have blamed her for giving up, she'd
been told, but she knew that wasn't true. *She* would have blamed herself.

And then they summon me here, she thought, grimly. She'd thought she
was free of the doctors, free of their prodding as they tried to figure out why
she'd survived being infected; she'd thought she had her own life back...
although, she conceded with a wry smile, she'd chosen the wrong career if
she wanted *freedom. What on Earth do they want?*

She took a long breath, gathering herself. The orders had been clear.
She was to report to the asteroid base, bringing with her two men to serve
as an escort. Alice hadn't been sure what to make of it. She was hardly a
high-value target, hardly the sort of person to draw attention from would-
be kidnappers; she wasn't even a high-ranking military officer who might
have reasonably expected bodyguards. Who was going to threaten her?
And, if she was under arrest, they would have sent a platoon of redcaps to
escort her to jail. They wouldn't have asked her to pick her own guards...

A quiver ran through the shuttle. She put her thoughts aside as she
opened the hatch and made her way back to her seat. The display showed a
pair of starfighters falling into escort position, ready to engage if the shuttle
turned hostile. Alice rather suspected that the precaution was designed
to calm civilian nerves, rather than do anything effective. If someone had
sneaked a nuke onto the shuttle, there would be no way to detect it before the
shuttle docked and—by then—it would be too late. Alice had no doubt of it.

Tindal glanced at her as she sat down. "What do you think they
want, Captain?"

"Buggered if I know," Alice said. The BBC talking head was still blath-
ering about *something* that had happened in London. "I guess we'll find out
in a moment or two."

The shuttle rocked again, a low *thump* echoing through the craft as it docked. Alice was mildly surprised they hadn't landed in a proper shuttlebay, where it would be a great deal easier to unload the shuttle, but she supposed security was paramount. She stood as the gravity flickered, the shuttle's onboard field giving way to the base's, and made her way to the airlock. It was already hissing open. Alice wasn't too surprised to see that the hatch on the far side was firmly closed. An Earther could get sloppy if she wished, but someone who lived in space couldn't afford to play games. Space rarely gave anyone a second chance if they fucked up.

She walked down the tube, barely aware of the two men following. There was a long pause as the rear hatch closed—she heard it shut behind her—before the forward hatch hissed open. She wasn't remotely surprised to see a pair of armoured men, their weapons not *quite* pointing at the new-comers, in the featureless room beyond. They tested Hammersmith and Tindal quickly, then waved a pair of scanners over Alice before allowing the three of them through the *next* airlock. Alice doubted they were happy about simply allowing her to enter the base. She tested positive for the virus, even though it was dead.

Or, more accurately, it can't control me, she thought. She had nightmares, sometimes, when she thought it might still be able to influence her. If her mentality was changing, and all the standards she used to measure it were changing too, how would she *know* her mentality was changing? *It's still inside me.*

She looked around, interested, as they passed through the airlock. The room on the far side was a simple reception chamber, with everything from comfortable chairs and a drinks dispenser to a large display showing the latest updates from Earth. The tickertape was talking about bombings in Washington, New York and San Francisco. Two men were waiting for her, both wearing dark blue uniforms. She didn't know either of them, but she guessed they were xenospecialists. Who *else* would be interested in meeting her?

"Thank you for coming," the lead xenospecialist said. "I am Doctor Percival Adamson and this is Doctor Bendix."

"Charmed," Alice lied. The two doctors had the air of medical researchers, rather than *real* doctors or headshrinkers. They showed no reluctance to shake her hand as she introduced the two corporals. She guessed they knew they didn't have to be concerned about being infected, at least from her. "You *do* appreciate that you called me away from my duties…?"

"We do," Adamson said. "But we also feel that your duties are actually *here*."

Alice felt her heart sink. "You want me to join you here? I don't even know where *here* is!"

"This is Base Zero Alpha," Bendix said. He was a tall bald man, with pale skin that suggested he'd spent his entire life amongst the asteroids. "And we think you are uniquely placed to assist us."

And the rest of your crew, who are no doubt watching us from a distance, Alice thought, coldly. There would be limits to *just* how far they'd trust anyone. The black-ops community rarely showed its hand openly. *What do you want from me?*

"We have much to talk about," Adamson said. He gestured to the chairs. "Please, be seated. Can I fetch you a cup of tea? Or coffee?"

"Coffee would be good, thanks," Alice said. She glanced at her escort. "For you?"

"Tea, please," Hammersmith said, following her lead. "Roger?"

"Tea, please," Tindal said.

Alice sat down and watched as Adamson prepared the drinks with practiced ease. Whatever they wanted was going to be bad. She was morbidly certain of it. They wouldn't be plying her with tea and coffee if they *just* wanted to ask her a few questions. Hell, they could have just sent her an email if they'd thought of something that wasn't covered in her reports. Alice found it hard to imagine that there was *anything* she hadn't mentioned. She'd spent weeks putting together an outline of everything that had happened to her since the first infection.

She took the coffee from Adamson and sipped thoughtfully. The drink was milky, nowhere near as strong as she preferred. She opened her mouth to ask for something darker, then changed her mind. There was no point in pushing matters too far. Better to answer their questions and get out, before her superiors ordered her to stay. She cursed under her breath as Adamson sat down, balancing a mug of tea on his knee. She'd thought she was *done* with being a medical research subject.

"As you know, you and you alone are the only person to have endured a full-fledged infection and survived," Adamson said. "It was a remarkable achievement."

And, if we both know it, why are you taking us through it again? Alice sat up, straighter. *I know what happened. I was there.*

"So far, no one else has survived," Adamson continued. "A handful of minor infections were stopped in their tracks by prompt treatment, before the virus could make any permanent changes to their bodies, but otherwise…once the virus gets a solid foothold, it is only a matter of time before it overwhelms the brain and takes control. And then the only real solution is euthanasia."

Hammersmith leaned forward. "But you *did* save Captain Campbell, didn't you?"

"Yes, but the virus had not yet reached her brain," Adamson said. "We were able to kill it before it took complete control. The treatments…there is no way they could be used to kill the viral particles in a host's brain without killing the host, too."

"The operation would be a success, but the patient would die," Alice said. She took a sip of her coffee. "None of this is actually *new* to me."

"No," Adamson agreed. "But it does provide necessary context."

He paused, his eyes fixed on his teacup. "We were…intrigued by your report from Alien-3," he said. "You stated, specifically, that the infected aliens simply ignored you, even as they chased your comrades back to the shuttle. They took no notice of you."

"I recall," Alice said.

"We believe that your scent, for want of a better term, was permanently altered by the virus," Adamson said. "You were ignored because you smelled *right* to them. I think that, judging from our work here, you might have been ignored even if you were shooting and throwing grenades at them. It would take them some time to realise that you were a possible threat."

"Are you sure?" Alice didn't believe it. "I would be shooting at them, not...walking past with my hands by my sides. They would *have* to realise I was hostile."

"We think it depends on just how much of the virus's...ah, *brainpower* is involved," Adamson said. "If it isn't focused on the scene, it may not be able to realise—at least at first—that it has a problem."

"Like an elephant," Bendix said. "If you stamp on an elephant's foot, it takes the elephant some time to realise that it needs to say *ouch*."

"And then it stomps you into the ground," Alice muttered. She still didn't believe it. "I wouldn't care to try it."

"Our research here has been focused on finding ways to disrupt the virus's internal communications," Adamson explained. "We know—now—that it communicates through more than just *scent*. Each individual host breathes out one set of particles and breathes in another...in effect, the virus is a giant decentralised network."

"Just like the old internet," Tindal said.

"Exactly." Bendix sounded surprised. Alice reflected, rather sourly, that he'd probably thought that a soldier couldn't count to eleven without taking off his pants. "And, just like the old internet, we think it can be disrupted. We might even be able to infiltrate the network and turn the virus against itself. That, too, was a problem with the old internet."

"And you think you can take down the virus's communications." Alice met Adamson's eyes, evenly. "What does this have to do with me?"

Adamson looked embarrassed. "The changes in your scent are a limited form of inter-viral communication," he said. "You're basically telling the virus that you're friendly."

Alice's lips twitched. "I'm lying."

"Yeah, but we think the virus doesn't really have a concept of lying," Adamson said. He dropped his eyes. "I mean…not in the sense it can't lie to us, but in the sense it can't lie to itself. It doesn't seem to be able to realise that you're lying to it, at least as long as you don't force it to look at you directly…basically, you come across as truthful because it can't comprehend that you're lying."

"Until the penny drops," Alice said, coolly. "And then it will start getting paranoid about itself. It won't know if smaller subunits are telling the truth or lying."

"Not without a great deal more verification," Adamson agreed. "It would have to delay operations to verify that it is still in control before it resumed its advance."

"You still haven't explained why you want me here," Alice said. Her patience was nearly at an end. "What do you want?"

"We think we can expand upon your…scent," Adamson said. He looked at his hands. "You would be able to…ah, do more than merely assure your fellow infected that you're one of them. You would be able to issue commands. You could take control of some of the infected and turn them against the virus…"

Hammersmith snorted. "Just like Stellar Star in *Stellar Star and the Robotic Menace*…"

"Be quiet," Alice growled. The back of her neck felt hot as she turned back to the scientists. "Are you serious?"

"We think it should be possible," Adamson said. He sounded uncomfortable. "We have attempted to synthesise scent particles, but—so far—unsuccessfully. The pheromones are simply beyond our ability to produce, certainly not the subtle smells we require to influence the virus. It's a field of study that has not really been developed, for various reasons. The only people who took it seriously were perfumers, and they ran into legal trouble."

"I can imagine," Alice said, dryly. She'd heard about perfumes that were supposed to make the opposite sex attracted to you, but she'd never seen one. The claims had always struck her as typical advertiser bullshit.

A pheromone-based perfume that actually worked would be classed as a date-rape drug. "And what do you think I should tell them to do?"

"First, we should see if you can issue orders," Bendix said. "We *think* you should be able to trigger the pheromones, although we don't know for sure. We'll have to experiment. And then we can try and figure out how to issue more *complex* orders."

"I see," Alice said. The whole idea struck her as insane, but it was worth trying. Who knew? Perhaps she could find a way to infiltrate the virus and tear its communications network to shreds. Perhaps. "And when do you expect me to try? We can't go back to Alien-3 yet..."

"No." Adamson cut her off. "But we do have a number of infected humans here, the ones rescued from Alien-One. We thought you could try to command them, under controlled conditions."

And that's why you wanted me to have an escort, Alice thought. *You needed someone who could tell if it wasn't me who came back.*

Hammersmith blinked. "You have infected people *here*?"

"Under very tight security," Bendix assured him. "There's no way they can get to Earth."

"Hah," Tindal muttered.

"We'd blow up the base, rather than let them escape." Adamson stood. "Shall we go see them?"

"Yeah." Alice finished her coffee, wishing for something stronger. "I think we should."

CHAPTER FOUR

"IT'S LIKE A ZOO IN HERE," Hammersmith muttered, as they were led through a series of airlocks and into a darkened observation chamber. "But I've never seen a zoo so...*secure*."

Alice nodded, feeling uncomfortable as she peered around the chamber. The light was so low she could barely see, even though her eyesight was as perfect as genetic engineering and surgical enhancement could make it. The chamber was completely empty, the bulkheads utterly bare. There was nothing for the prisoners to use, if they somehow managed to smash through the walls and break into the chamber. She couldn't help thinking that the observers were just as much prisoners as the people in the next chamber. If the virus broke loose, it was quite possible that *none* of them would be permitted to leave.

"We keep biohazard protocols in place at all times," Adamson explained. "This entire subsection is completely isolated from the remainder of the base, save for a handful of datanet links that feed through a secure firewall and into an observation lounge on the far side of the walls. Everyone who goes into the inner section will go through a careful series of tests, just to prove their identity and verify that they're not infected. They have to wear protective gear as long as they're anywhere near the virus itself. If it is broken..."

His voice trailed off. Alice looked at him.

"And does it ever break?"

"They tore the protective garb off one unwary visitor," Adamson said. "I would have believed it impossible, if I had not seen it with my own eyes. We were fortunate to be able to yank him out and kill the infection before it was too late."

He indicated the far side of the chamber. The bulkhead was lightening… no, it was turning translucent. Alice leaned forward, feeling a shiver run down her spine as a cluster of humanoid figures came into view. They were human, as naked as she'd been on the day she was born, but…there was nothing *human* about them. They paced around the cage, heedless of their nakedness…she'd seen POWs in detention cages, yet they'd been human. The infected were…*different*.

That could have been me, she thought. *I could have ended up in a cage like this.*

A woman strode past the bulkhead, her bare breasts bobbing as she walked. None of the men paid any attention. Alice felt cold. The scene was utterly *wrong*. The men weren't ogling, or sneaking glances whenever they felt they could get away with it…they weren't even making a show of ignoring the women. They were just…she swallowed, hard. The virus had stripped everything from its victims. They didn't feel anything any longer.

Hammersmith sounded shaken. "What…what are you *doing* to them?"

"Right now, we're trying to learn from them." Bendix sounded cold, but Alice was sure she could hear a quiver. "The virus doesn't seem to quite understand the hosts. They are exercising constantly, and eating the food we give them, but they defecate wherever they wish and show no inclination to get dressed or take care of themselves in other respects. We think they're just waiting for orders."

"Orders which are never going to come," Adamson said. He looked at Alice. "Unless they come from you."

Alice swallowed, hard. "What do you want me to do?"

"Come with me," Adamson said. "Your companions can wait here."

"Captain?" Hammersmith turned away. "Should I…?"

"Stay here," Alice said. "And be ready to check that I'm me."

Adamson nodded as he led the way out the airlock and down a solid metal passageway. "I...after the last incident, it was decided that everyone who needed to go into the chamber would be wearing protective gear. We actually had to draw supplies from the biological warfare stockpiles, simply because"—he glanced back at her, a scowl on his face—"it never occurred to us that the virus would try to tear off our clothes. In hindsight, it should have done."

"Yes," Alice said, dryly. Desperate people could do desperate things. "I went through the biowarfare drills during training."

"Quite." Adamson stopped as they entered a sideroom. "You'll be going into the chamber alone, and naked. We think that, if you issue orders, they will be obeyed."

Alice stopped, dead. "You *think*?"

"You have been constantly monitored since you were infected," Adamson said. "We noticed that your local pheromones changed whenever you issued commands, something that rarely happened during the cruise."

"The deployment," Alice corrected, sharply. "You make it sound like I was taking an expensive vacation."

"In hindsight, it would have been better to put you in a command role." Adamson sounded irked. "We might have realised this earlier."

Alice shook her head, unsure of how she should be feeling. It seemed terribly speculative...and yet, she had the feeling they'd stumbled onto *something*. She just didn't know if it was anything they could actually *use*. The history of military research and development was strewn with brilliant pieces of kit that worked perfectly in the labs, but failed spectacularly when deployed in the field. Alice had no trouble thinking of a dozen things that could go wrong, all of which might end badly for her. She was skilled at unarmed combat, but the virus's hosts wouldn't care if they were hurt. She'd have to cripple or kill them to survive.

"We can try," she said. She looked at the other door. "Through there?"

"Yes," Adamson said. "Go through the door, get undressed, put your clothes in the cupboard and walk through the final door. You'll find an earpiece in the cabinet, one you can slot into your ear. Follow the instructions as you go."

Alice nodded, tersely. "Understood," she said. "I'm on my way."

She opened the door and walked into a small changing room. The walls were bare, save for a handful of cabinets, but she was sure there would be microscopic cameras everywhere. It wasn't the first time she'd been on a black-ops base. She would have been surprised if there weren't cameras in the toilets as well as the bedrooms. There were prisoners who were kept under less tight security. She scowled at the thought, then started to undress. She'd lost any sense of modesty when she'd joined the marines. It was hard to care about the watching eyes.

Time to move on, she thought, when she was naked. *Now...*

She stepped through the door, closing it firmly behind her. A recorded voice ordered her to keep moving, even as warm liquid splashed down from high above. Alice closed her eyes as she tasted something sharp and unpleasant in the water, something designed to cleanse her body of germs and pheromones. She wondered, grimly, if the water would kill her scent. It would be hard to issue any commands to the infected humans if they couldn't smell her. She kept walking, passing through a torrent of hot air. Her skin itched uncomfortably as it dried. It looked as though they didn't dare give her a towel.

The final door opened, revealing the confinement chamber. A gust of warm air brushed against her, bringing with it the indefinable scent of the infected. Alice braced herself as she stepped inside, half-expecting to be attacked on sight. The infected humans stopped their constant walking and turned to face her, their unblinking eyes staring at her... Alice couldn't keep from shuddering. She'd met Tadpoles and Vesy, both of whom were very alien, but the infected humans were utterly *inhuman*. It was hard to understand alien mentalities sometimes—she'd once heard that the Tadpoles cared nothing for their own children, something that bothered her more

34

than she cared to admit—yet...the virus was just too different to be easily understood. It was alien...

It wants to survive, she thought. It wasn't a comforting thought. The virus was too dangerous to let live. How could it be trusted? How could anyone talk to it, let alone dictate terms? *And its survival comes at the cost of our survival.*

A flicker of...*something* ran through the air. The infected were moving closer. Alice tensed, readying herself to fight. Her mind raced, considering tactics. It would be easy to hit the male infected in their groins, but would they even *notice*? She didn't know. She'd have to aim to cripple or kill and hope for the best. She stood straighter, bracing herself. What would happen if they managed to infect her?

"Stop," she ordered.

Another ripple ran through the warm air. The infected stopped, as if they'd run into a brick wall. Alice stared, suddenly realising that she hadn't expected the idea to work at all. The infected stared back at her, waiting for orders. She opened her mouth, her mind racing as she tried to figure out what was going on. Perhaps, just perhaps, the virus had never realised that someone could subvert its infection. It was like a mother leaving the house unlocked because she believed a child couldn't work the handle and open the door.

She closed her eyes, gathering herself. What should she tell them to do? What orders should she issue? What orders would they *understand*? Logically, she was encoding the orders within her altered pheromones...she shuddered, cursing the virus once again. She didn't understand what she was doing and that, she knew from bitter experience, could lead to something blowing up in her face. The virus presumably understood precisely how to issue orders. She was making it up as she went along.

"Turn your backs," she ordered. "And walk away."

The infected obeyed, turning slowly and walking until they hit the far bulkhead. They kept moving, as if they were trying to push their way *through* the bulkhead. Alice walked after them, feeling...*something* moving through the warm air. She stopped and closed her eyes again, trying to concentrate on the sensation. There was something there, alright; something warm and welcoming, something calling to her…she jerked back, hard. The virus was calling to her. It would have been easy, so easy, to just let go.

Adamson's voice echoed through the earpiece. "Alice? Are you alright?"

That's Captain to you, Alice thought, snidely. *Captain Campbell, not Alice.*

She felt a flicker of resentment. There were probably dozens, if not hundreds, of sensors turned on the confinement chamber. The watchers could probably monitor her emotional state from a distance, if they wished…she pushed the resentment down, hard. It was their bloody *duty* to monitor her emotional state and she knew it. Besides, she was probably the only person in the chamber *with* an emotional state. The infected were little more than robots. Or zombies.

"Alice?" Adamson sounded alarmed. "Should I send the team into the chamber?"

"No," Alice said. "I'm sorry. I think I was taken a little by surprise."

"I can send someone in if you want," Adamson said. "Or suit up myself…"

"I can handle it," Alice said, a little sharper than she'd intended. "Just give me a moment to consider."

She closed her eyes again, concentrating on a single command. *Come here.* The air seemed to shift around her—she felt, just for a second, as if she was in a swimming pool—as the infected stopped trying to walk through the bulkhead and turned towards her. She opened her eyes and shuddered. Their faces showed no trace of individuality. She thought she recognised a couple of them, but…she pushed that thought aside too. The men and women she'd known from the mission to the alien ship were dead. Their bodies were no longer theirs.

"The pheromone levels are rising," Adamson warned. "Are you coping?"

"I think so," Alice managed.

She bit her lip, tasting blood in her mouth. It was hard, harder than she'd realised, to send out silent commands. She'd always been good at multitasking, but the virus was clearly far superior…or, perhaps, not limited

36

by being trapped in a human body. She wondered, idly, how such an entity could *think*. It had to be spread across thousands—no, *billions*—of bodies. How could such a mentality even exist? She thought she understood, now, why the virus was so unconcerned about spending its bodies so casually. It had no reason to *be* concerned. It wasn't likely to run out of bodies in a hurry.

"It feels as though they're part of me, I think," she said. The infected started to walk around her. "But...I don't think this is an active group."

Adamson sounded worried. "How do you mean?"

"I mean there isn't enough of the virus to take control." Alice remembered the blobs she'd seen on the alien starship and scowled. "They're capable of following basic instructions, the commands encoded in the viral particles, but not of rising to sentience. My guess is that they were never intended to operate independently. They can spread themselves, and replicate, but not come up with their own plans."

"It might be harder to give orders to an active group." Adamson paused. "You'd better come out, if you don't mind."

Alice nodded, although part of her wanted to stay in the chamber. She wasn't sure why. The virus had abandoned its attempt to suck her into the groupmind...she had no *reason* to stay in the chamber. And yet...she had to fight to turn and walk through the airlock. Her legs felt stiff, as if she'd been in bed for weeks. There was a bit of her that really didn't want to leave.

It was trying to tempt me, she thought. *It couldn't absorb me by force, so it tried to convince me to surrender instead.*

She wasn't sure if it was deliberate or not—the virus hadn't shown any inclination to try to tempt anyone to allow themselves to be absorbed—but it hardly mattered. It had been tempting, for all the wrong reasons. She could have surrendered her individuality and found peace within the groupmind... she shook her head, sharply. It wouldn't have been *peace*. It would have been a living death. And yet, she'd found it tempting. She wondered, sourly, just how many people would have accepted if the virus had come in peace.

"If someone bioengineered you," she muttered as she passed through a shower of detergent, "they didn't miss a trick."

Adamson was waiting for her outside the changing room. "That was amazing," he said, as she emerged. "You gave us more raw data in two hours than we collected in months!"

"Great," Alice said. Had it really been two hours? She'd thought it had only been half an hour at most. "Are you sure I haven't been infected again?"

"Your blood chemistry hasn't changed," Adamson said. "And you won't be leaving here for another few hours, at the very least."

"Good, I suppose," Alice said. "What did you learn?"

"A little more about how the virus communicates," Adamson said. "And how we can use UV lights to disrupt it."

Alice felt a hot flash of anger. "We already *knew* that!"

"And how we might be able to mess it up by inserting pheromones of our own into the mix," Adamson said. "And how we might be able to get *you* into the mix..."

"Really?" Alice stopped and glared at him. "Do you realise just how limited I am, compared to the virus? How limited *any* of us are? These"—she held up her fingers—"are where my awareness stops. The virus is more aware of its surroundings than *any* of us. I can no more issue detailed commands than...than I can control someone with the force of my mind."

"But you can issue orders," Adamson said. "And the person who took the orders would know what to do, wouldn't they?"

"Yes," Alice said. It wasn't as if officers provided detailed orders when commanding their troops to attack. She'd met a handful of micromanagers in high office, but none of them had been quite that bad. "What good does *that* do?"

"Perhaps more than you might think," Adamson said. "For one thing, the viral pheromones must be universal. The virus has absorbed members of at least four alien species into its gestalt and it has been able to issue orders across the differing species' lines. I think the pheromones themselves must act as a form of universal translator, linked into the viral cells..."

"You *think*," Alice said.

38

"If it couldn't understand the hosts, it couldn't use their knowledge." Adamson let out a heavy sigh. "We haven't been able to design a neural link that allows…well, mind-reading, for want of a better term. Even what we have done—and we intend to use some of them to assist you—is not suitable for Tadpole use. What works for us would fry their brains. But the virus has somehow devised an *organic* solution to the problem. It has built an organic computer network. And we should be able to hack the network and tear it apart."

"If we can get inside," Alice said. She jerked a finger at the sealed airlock as her temper began to rise. "That isn't easy, mate. Those poor bastards back there? They're running on automatic, cut off from the mainstream and prevented from forming a groupmind of their own. We can do anything to them, if we want. But the main body of the virus? That's on starships and heavily defended worlds and…it's practically untouchable."

"I know," Adamson said. He sounded earnest. "But we believe it can be done. What you did today has opened up a whole series of possible approaches…it can be done. Given time, we can do anything."

"Hah," Alice said. She wasn't convinced. Every time she thought she'd beaten the virus, it managed to sneak its way back into her life. "We will see."

CHAPTER FIVE

"YOU'D BETTER GET OUT OF BED," a female voice said. "You've got a priority message."

Wing Commander Richard Redbird opened his eyes, unsure—just for a moment—where he was. It wasn't his cabin, and it wasn't the tiny little hotel room they'd found before being unceremoniously summoned back to the ship, it was…it was his *new* cabin, the one he'd been given when the former CAG had been hastily reassigned to another ship. He'd barely had a moment to move his carryall from his former cabin to the new one before he'd been plunged back into the maelstrom of rebuilding *Invincible's* squadrons—again.

"Fuck," he grumbled, as he pushed himself upright. Monica sat in his bed, her bare breasts bobbling invitingly. There was barely enough room for both of them. She looked on the verge of falling out and landing on the cold metal deck. "Who is it?"

"I don't know," Monica said, a little waspishly. "*I* don't have your fingerprints, do I?"

Richard scowled, then reached for the terminal. It was probably a good thing she *hadn't* tried to open the message. Her fingerprints might not have triggered alarms—depending on the message priority—but they *would* have been noticed. Some jobsworth who didn't have something better to do would realise that she'd been in his cabin and wonder why. It wouldn't take much imagination to draw the right conclusion. People made allowances for starfighter pilots, but he doubted they'd make one for Monica and himself. They were senior officers. They were meant to set a good example.

The message unlocked itself as soon as his fingers touched the terminal. It was short, straight and to the point. There would be a staff meeting at 1000 and he was invited. Richard let out a sigh as he glanced at the chronometer. Invited to attend? More like ordered to attend. Life had been a great deal simpler when he'd been a lowly starfighter pilot, rather than a squadron commander and CAG. He wished, sometimes, that he'd had the wit to decline the promotion when it had been offered. It wasn't as if starfighter pilots *often* climbed to the top of the ladder.

But the First Space Lord started his career as a fighter pilot, he reminded himself, as he sent a quick acknowledgement. *And now he's the master of the Royal Navy.*

Monica rubbed her eyes. "Good news?"

"A staff meeting," Richard grumbled. He was a CAG without starfighters or pilots to fly them. Most of *Invincible's* surviving pilots had been hastily reassigned when the carrier had limped back to Earth. Richard understood the need to share their experience as widely as possible, but it still galled him. He'd been lucky to keep Monica. "Perhaps they'll have something important to say."

"Perhaps," Monica agreed. "It might be good news."

Richard shrugged, watching as she stood and hurried towards the washroom. He couldn't believe it would be good news. There hadn't been any good news since they'd left Earth and that had been *months* ago. In theory, he was due to receive new starfighters and pilots at any time; in practice, every announcement of a new starfighter wing had been cancelled within the day. He understood the problem facing the Royal Navy—and the sudden need for experienced starfighter pilots to be deployed to the front lines—but it was still irritating as hell. How was he supposed to plan for their next deployment if they kept changing the rules?

And I might be reassigned at any moment, too, he thought. Truthfully, he was surprised he hadn't *already* been reassigned. He was a starfighter pilot first and foremost, a flyer with a string of kills to his credit. He wouldn't have minded if he'd been slotted into some junior flying officer's slot. The demotion wouldn't have bothered him in the slightest. He would have been more annoyed by the cut in pay. *Maybe they're just trying to decide where to send me.*

He stood, resisting the urge to walk to the washroom and join her under the shower. Whoever had designed the starship had given the CAG a private cabin, rather than forcing him to bed down with his pilots, but the washroom was barely large enough for a grown adult. There was no way they could share it, not without getting stuck in the tiny cubicle. His lips twitched at the thought—that would be hard to explain—before he felt a bitter pang of regret. No one, not even Monica, knew how tempted he'd been to simply walk off instead of returning to the ship. He knew he would be called a deserter, he knew he might well spend the rest of his life in prison, but...it might have been better than deploying once again. He'd watched helplessly as two separate wings of starfighters were blown away by the aliens. He didn't want to go through that again.

Then request reassignment somewhere else, he told himself. *You could push paper for a living instead.*

Monica emerged, wrapping a towel around herself. Richard felt another pang, a mixture of guilt and...and something he didn't care to look at too closely. They'd fallen into bed together six days ago, when they'd been on Earth. He still wasn't quite sure why he'd done it. Monica was pretty—she was striking, certainly—but she was his subordinate. They shouldn't have been anything more than friends, if that. People might make allowances for starfighter pilots on leave, but not pilots on duty. He knew he should have ended the affair as soon as they returned to the ship. But he hadn't. He'd needed her too much.

"I'll see you this afternoon," he said. "Hopefully, we should have some new figures to play with."

"Understood," Monica said. She didn't have many duties at the moment, either, leaving her at something of a loose end. "Good luck with the meeting."

Richard nodded as he walked past her and stepped into the shower. There were no water restrictions for senior officers, something that amused and annoyed him in equal measure. There was no *need* for water restrictions, even for the lowliest crewmen. But it was tradition and the Royal Navy was all *about* tradition. His lips curved into a thin smile as he turned on the water. He didn't mind the tradition about putting his body between his homeworld and an alien threat, but he drew the line at water conservation measures. It wasn't as if *Invincible* couldn't capture a comet!

He basked under the water as long as he dared, then grabbed a towel and dried himself before stepping back into the cabin. Monica was gone, for better or worse. He hoped she hadn't been seen as she left the compartment. Nothing moved faster than scuttlebutt, even on a giant assault carrier. If someone *had* seen her leave, it would be all around the ship by the end of the day. And then...it would only be a matter of time before the senior officers heard the news.

Although they might not pay any attention to the babble, he thought, as he pulled on his tunic and inspected himself in the mirror. His uniform looked impeccable, but his eyes were dark and shadowed through lack of sleep. *By the time the rumour reaches their ears, it will have grown out of all proportion.*

Richard smiled at the thought as he picked up his terminal and opened his inbox. There was a whole string of emails, none of which seemed particularly urgent. A couple looked to have already been superseded before he'd even had a chance to read them. He swallowed a curse as he slipped his terminal onto his belt and headed for the hatch. His life would be a great deal easier if the strategic planning officers on Nelson Base would make up their minds *before* sending him advance orders. He simply didn't have the time to constantly prepare to receive new starfighters and their pilots who didn't even make it to the hangar deck before they were reassigned.

He stepped through the hatch and strode up the long corridor towards the conference room, passing a trio of jogging marines and a handful of dockyard workers on the way. The ship was still being patched together after the *last* encounter with the aliens, something that made him fairly certain that *he* would be reassigned sooner or later. *Invincible* was a powerful ship—and the Royal Navy wasn't about to scrap her—but it would be months before she could return to the front line. There was no point in assigning starfighters to a ship that couldn't even serve as a glorified hangar. He scowled at the thought. Clearly, some idiot on Nelson Base hadn't got the memo. They were still moving starfighters around the system like pieces on a chessboard.

"Ah, Commander Redbird," Commander Daniel Newcomb said, as Richard entered the conference room. "Take a seat, please. And wait."

"Yes, sir," Richard said.

He stepped past Newcomb and took a seat, trying to relax. The XO was clearly worried about *something*. Rumour had it that the XO had been offered—and refused—command of his own starship, although Richard didn't believe it. Very few officers would *refuse* a command, particularly when doing so practically *guaranteed* that the Royal Navy wouldn't offer him another one. Better to command a garbage scow than be permanently denied a shot at the captain's chair. No, the XO wasn't being reassigned. He would be gone by now if someone had offered him his own ship.

Richard leaned back in his chair, accepted a cup of coffee from the steward and forced himself to watch as the room steadily filled with officers. Lieutenant-Commander David Arthur, the tactical officer; Chief Engineer Theodore Rutgers, looking as if he hadn't slept a wink for the last week; Major Henry Parkinson, Royal Marines...the XO had summoned every departmental head on the ship. Richard took a sip of his coffee, gritting his teeth against the sudden feeling of acid in his stomach. This was no mere meeting, he decided; this was *serious*. They hadn't held a formal conference since...since *Invincible* had left the shipyard for the first time.

"Captain on deck," Newcomb said, sharply.

"Remain seated," Captain Shields said. He strode into the room, waving Major Parkinson back into his chair. "We have much to discuss."

45

Richard nodded, tersely. Captain Shields looked as if he hadn't slept either…where had he been? The last Richard had heard, Captain Shields had been recalled to Earth to brief the First Space Lord personally. Richard didn't envy him. Captain Shields was very well connected—something Richard envied—but that wouldn't always work in his favour. An aristocratic officer could expect more surveillance than someone who'd worked his way up from midshipman to captain or even admiral. His family would drop him like a hot rock if he let the side down.

Captain Shields sat down. "You may not have heard yet—the government has been trying to keep word from spreading—but, twenty-four hours ago, there were a series of terrorist attacks on Earth. A number of military and civil locations were attacked by armed insurgents. So far, the investigations have barely begun"—he held up a hand to forestall questions—"but it is clear that the virus was directly involved. The attackers were all infected and, presumably, no longer in control of themselves."

Shit, Richard thought.

"There's no *presumably* about it," Major Parkinson rumbled. "They were enslaved from the moment they were infected."

"How the hell did they get down to Earth?" Newcomb sounded as if he didn't want to believe it. "We have all the orbital towers and spaceports locked down tight."

"We don't know," Captain Shields said. "And we don't have time for speculation. The worse news is, practically simultaneously, there was another attack on Falkirk. This one was successful."

Richard felt his stomach twist as he realised the implications. If the MNF had been defeated—or destroyed—the virus would have a clear path to Earth. Even if it hadn't been destroyed, the virus would have access to dozens of lightly-defended colony worlds…they wouldn't stand a chance when the virus took control of the high orbitals. There were contingency plans, he was sure, for the colonists to go underground, but…how could they hope to hold out when the virus could twist their own people against them? The entire population might as well be composed of traitors.

46

"They couldn't have taken out the entire fleet," Arthur said. "The MNF is—was—the most powerful fleet short of Earth itself."

"The fleet is falling back," Captain Shields said. "And we're going to meet them."

"Captain…" Chief Engineer Theodore Rutgers swallowed hard and started again. "Captain, with all due respect, we are not remotely *ready* to leave spacedock, let alone return to the front lines. It will take months to carry out even the most essential of repairs."

Newcomb smiled, humourlessly. "And how long will it *really* take you?"

Rutgers was too tired to dissemble. "Commander, *months* is an optimistic estimate. We took one hell of a beating and…"

Captain Shields held up a hand. "I'm aware of our condition," he said. "And so is the Admiralty. They are, however, determined to put us back on the front lines."

Richard felt his heart sink. *They hate us.*

"We will have first call on *everything*," the captain added. "Everything the shipyard has is ours, if we need it. We can take whatever we need, from supplies to dockyard workers. We have a blank cheque, as long as we are ready for deployment in a week or so."

"Fuck." Rutgers looked at the table. "Captain…it won't be easy."

"I know." Captain Shields scowled. "But we have to do it."

Rutgers shook his head slowly. "Give me an hour and I can draw up a basic plan of attack," he said. "The most important issues can be tackled fairly quickly, if they let us cannibalise a couple of half-built ships. But…we won't be at full fighting trim. At best, we'll be at eighty percent…"

"Which means we'll all be flogged if the Adjutant General's Corps bothers to carry out an inspection," Newcomb said. "Or are all the petty little safety regulations being put aside in times of war?"

"Yes," Captain Shields said, flatly. His voice was utterly toneless. "No one is expecting miracles, Commander. They just want us on the front lines as quickly as possible."

They are expecting miracles, Richard thought.

Captain Shields met Richard's eyes. "We're going to be assigned new starfighters and pilots," he said, curtly. "You'll get a fuller breakdown within the hour, once they've finalised the deployments, but it looks as if you'll be getting pilots from Europe as well as Britain and the Commonwealth. I trust that won't be a problem?"

"It shouldn't be a problem, sir," Richard said. He kept his face impassive. There would be all sorts of minor problems, the kind of issues that were normally sorted out during the shakedown cruise. This time, they'd be going to war without working the kinks out first. "I think we can handle it."

"Good," Captain Shields said. "Let me know if there are any major issues that need to be smoothed out."

Just me, Richard thought. "Yes, sir."

"Major Parkinson, you'll be keeping most of your detachment," Captain Shields said. "I want you and your men to run security at all access points. *No one* is to get onto this ship without having their blood tested, repeatedly. I don't know how the virus managed to get to Earth without being detected, but I don't want it repeating the same feat here."

"Yes, sir," Parkinson said.

"Captain, we cannot afford to have our work impeded," Rutgers said. "There will be a *lot* of engineers coming in and out of the ship at all times."

"We'll just have to cope," Captain Shields said. "We have to assume the worst, at least until we *know* how the virus got to Earth."

And we might never know, Richard thought. The virus couldn't have slipped through the orbital checkpoints, could it? He thought the checks were infallible, but...what if he was wrong? *The virus might have found a way to get through without setting off all kinds of alarms.*

"We'll do our best, Captain," Rutgers said. The engineer looked worried. "But I caution you that any disruption is going to have the most disruptive effects."

"Deal with it," Newcomb growled. The XO crossed his arms over his chest. "There's more at stake here than *us*."

"True, Mr. XO," Captain Shields agreed. He looked from officer to officer. "I know it won't be easy. I know we will not be departing with a full load. I know we may take grievous damage in our next engagement because repairs weren't carried out properly. But we have no choice. If the virus can't be stopped…"

Richard nodded, shortly. He'd seen the projections, both civil and military. They were uncomfortable viewing. The virus might be unstoppable if it gained a solid foothold in human space. And then…he shuddered. There would be no resistance, no insurgency against alien masters. Independent thought wouldn't even be a memory. Humanity would simply cease to exist. It would be the end.

And that means we have to fight, he thought, numbly. No wonder the Admiralty was so keen to get *Invincible* back to the front lines. There was no other choice. *Better to die fighting than to be infected and absorbed.*

"I expect each and every one of you to do your utmost to prepare for departure on schedule," the captain said. "We'll get some rest when we're on the way. Dismissed."

CHAPTER SIX

"I THOUGHT YOU SAID you couldn't read my mind," Alice grumbled.

She glared at herself in the mirror. It wasn't the first time she'd had an EEG scan—she'd had her brainwaves monitored during advanced training—but she had to admit that Doctor Bendix's scanner was hellishly intimidating. It felt oddly heavy against her bare scalp. The sensors attached to her chest and the handful of holographic displays, blinking constantly, made it worse. She couldn't escape the feeling that they were probing her very thoughts themselves.

"Technically, we can't," Doctor Bendix said. He was examining one of the displays, stroking his chin thoughtfully. "But we *can* make some educated guesses about what you're thinking and feeling at any given time."

Alice glanced at him. "Right now, I'm feeling homicidal," she said. "Does *that* show up on your monitors?"

"I can see your irritation, even anger," Bendix said. "But you're not about to lose control."

"If you say so," Alice said. She resisted the urge to unleash her anger. "What are you trying to do?"

Bendix gave her a faint smile. "Right now, we're attempting to determine how you alter your scent," he said. "If we can figure out how you're doing it, we should be able to duplicate it. Or trigger it in the other infected…"

51

"Eat curried eggs," Hammersmith said. He was standing by the hatch, looking terribly out of place. "Or go out on the town for a night of kebabs and curry. That always changes *my* scent."

"I know." Alice snorted at the weak joke. "Believe me, I know."

"I don't think that will be much help," Bendix said, stiffly. "We have to figure out how you release command pheromones."

"You want to devise a stink bomb," Alice said. "Or something along those lines."

"Quite," Bendix agreed. "It might make it impossible for the virus to coordinate its efforts if the pheromone channel is completely jammed up."

"I won't shower for a week," Hammersmith offered. "And then you can throw me into the arms of the enemy."

"That would be *everyone*, if you don't shower for a day," Tindal jibed. "Just imagine the scene. Where is the stink bomb? He got strangled by his own bleeping side!"

"It has to be the right kind of stench," Bendix said. He took one last look at the displays and stepped back. "Alice? If you'd like to issue a command...?"

Alice gathered herself. "*Stop!*"

There was a pause. "Interesting," Bendix said. "There was relatively little brainwave activity, but the pheromones spiked anyway."

"Are you saying she's stupid?" Hammersmith said. "Or that she just doesn't think..."

Alice scowled at him. "Just you wait."

Bendix ignored the byplay. "When you walk and talk, you do it without thinking."

"Definitely," Tindal said. "We *had* noticed Hammersmith says things without thinking."

"You may think about what you're doing," Bendix said, "but you're not thinking about *how* you're doing it. You don't have to tell your legs how to move when you walk, for example, and you don't have to concentrate on *how* you talk to talk. Your body does it for you."

"And we don't know how we do it," Alice said. She tried to put it into words. "Like...like you don't have any trouble breathing when you're not *thinking* about breathing, but if you start thinking about it you have to force yourself to take breaths."

"Pretty much, yes," Bendix said. "The virus has modified your body. You seem to have acquired new organs *and* a control system, but you don't know how you use it."

"I didn't even know I *had* it until I came here," Alice said. "All I knew was that it had altered my scent in some way."

"Yeah." Bendix returned his attention to the displays. "Give us another command."

"*Walk forward*," Alice barked.

"A little more activity on *that* one, I fancy," Bendix said. "We *may* be able to duplicate it."

"And then what?" Alice's head was itching. It was all she could do to keep from lifting the helmet and scratching her scalp. "What can you *do* with it?"

"Simulate the unconscious reaction," Bendix said. "And then we can use it to turn the other infected into pheromone factories."

"I see," Alice said. "How? In small words, please."

Bendix waved a hand at the displays. "Basically, we copy what you do and transfer it to one of the other infected," he said. "And then we simulate the reaction in their bodies."

"That sounds a little ominous," Alice said.

"It is." Bendix didn't look at her. "We can use the technology to trigger someone's pain receptors, for example, or make them aroused beyond all restraint. It has been done, from time to time. The technology is kept under very close control."

Alice frowned. "Do you use this to *torture* people?"

"Not in the sense you mean," Bendix said. "But we have used the technology, at times, to inspect someone's *nerves*. Tiny jolts of pain can show us what, if anything, is wrong with the victim's nervous system. And...we have had some success with other applications."

"I don't think I want to know," Alice said. She'd been taught to respect the rules of war, if only out of simple pragmatism. It would be hard to blame the enemy for mistreating prisoners if enemy personnel were mistreated when they were taken captive. "And I hope this will help you find a way to defeat the virus."

Bendix nodded. "We think it will," he said. "Now…"

It felt like hours before he finally consented to allow Alice to remove the helmet and change back into her uniform. Alice felt as if she'd been put through the wringer, even though she hadn't really *done* very much. Basic commands, it seemed, were stronger—and produced more pheromones— than more complex commands. Indeed, the more complex the command, the harder it was for her to produce *any* pheromones. She was starting to suspect that there were layers to inter-viral communication that were completely beyond her ability to perceive.

"Or maybe there are subtle points we are unable to detect, yet," Bendix said. "The virus was never allowed to take full control of you."

Alice nodded, shortly. "I used to own a terminal that wasn't…well, it wasn't *mine*. My grandmother had bought it for me, but she locked out the higher command functions before handing it over. I couldn't access the higher levels until I was older. There was no way I could customise it for me."

"An interesting comparison," Bendix said. "And quite a good one."

He shrugged. "We will manage to unlock the higher levels eventually," he said. "It's just a matter of time."

"Yes." Alice felt her stomach rumble. "Is there something to eat around here?"

"I'll show you to the cafe," Bendix said. "And then we can decide what to do next."

"I have to report back to my ship," Alice said. "Do you need anything else from me?"

Bendix said nothing for a long moment. "I don't know," he admitted. He opened the hatch and led them down the corridor. "We're in uncharted territory here."

Alice winced, inwardly. She wanted to go back to the ship, to rejoin the marines and…she'd *earned* it, damn it. She'd earned it *twice*. But she also knew her duty. If she was best suited to play the role of experimental animal, she needed to play it. She caught herself before letting out a heavy sigh. She didn't *want* to be an experimental animal. She wanted to get out of the asteroid base before someone could suggest she stayed.

"Hey, Doc," Tindal said. "Do you think you could stimulate arousal in men and women alike?"

"It's fairly easy." Bendix didn't seem surprised by the question. "Arousal is one of the simplest emotions to simulate."

Tindal grinned. "So you could ensure that I stayed hard all night long?"

Alice rolled her eyes. There were times when she thought that none of the marines had really grown up, although she supposed it shouldn't have surprised her. Every time they deployed, they knew there was a risk they wouldn't be coming back. It was rare for a marine to marry, let alone form permanent attachments outside the squad. A certain degree of horseplay was expected, even encouraged. It helped blow off steam.

"I didn't know that was a problem," Hammersmith teased.

"It could be done," Bendix said. "Genital stimulators have been used in various…ah, *clinics* for the last few decades. *However*, you would rapidly start to suffer from physical side effects. You don't want to know the details."

"None of us want to hear the details," Alice said, sharply. "And no, you don't want one for yourself."

"Not until you're old and gray," Hammersmith chimed in.

Bendix led them into a small compartment and nodded towards the vending machines. "Take what you want," he said. "Doctor Adamson should join us in a moment or two."

"Glad to hear it," Alice said. She understood why the base was largely empty, but it was starting to creep her out. "And then…what?"

"We'll see," Bendix said, vaguely.

Alice eyed him, then turned to the vending machine and ordered a mug of coffee. It tasted foul, but she'd had worse. Another machine offered everything from ration bars to cheeseburgers. They would probably be reconstituted, she decided as she ordered one, but it didn't matter. She'd learnt, long ago, not to worry about where food came from, particularly in space. It was safe to eat. That was all that mattered.

And Granddad ensured I wasn't too squeamish, Alice recalled. Growing up on a farm had left her with no illusions. The roast beef she'd eaten the night before she'd gone to boarding school had come from a cow, not the supermarket. *He never let me get too prissy about what I ate.*

Her lips twitched. She honestly didn't understand how some of her fellow boarders had managed to tie their shoelaces in the morning. How could they *not* know where food came from? Mankind needed food to *live*. Even if someone managed to eat a strictly vegetarian diet, they still had to kill plants to get their food. The poor girls had been so ignorant of the realities of life, they'd practically needed minders. Alice hadn't envied the tutors at all.

She looked up as Doctor Adamson entered the compartment. "We've learnt a great deal from you," he said. "And we could learn a great deal more."

"I don't know how," Alice said, feeling her heart sink. "I've done everything I can, but…the virus didn't give me an operations manual."

"We know," Doctor Adamson said. "The problem, I suspect, is that the virus normally builds up command structures within the victim's body. Yours were smashed during treatment and, so far, they haven't managed to reconstitute themselves."

Alice tensed. "I thought the infection was dead. Dead and gone."

"We think so, too," Doctor Adamson said. "And you were tested regularly, just in case. There's no sign of the structures trying to rebuild themselves. However…we have to be careful."

"I know," Alice said.

"They're probably capable of manipulating pheromones to a far greater extent than you," Adamson added. "You simply lack the control systems to *really* make use of your new organs."

"That could be a problem," Alice said, dryly. "Do you think you can convince the poor bastards down there"—she jabbed a finger at the bulkhead—"to emit the kind of pheromones you need?"

"We don't know," Adamson said.

"We *can* use implants to control someone's body," Bendix said. "But it is hard to do it *convincingly*. Outside remote control is practically impossible, unless we have a breakthrough. I don't think we can turn one of the infected into anything more than a basic pheromone factory."

You're talking about living people, Alice thought. *Humans.*

She shuddered. She *couldn't* allow herself to start thinking of the infected as *human*. Once the infection took control, they were dead. Dead...yet alive. She knew just how lucky she'd been to escape the virus's control. Everyone else...euthanasia might be the only logical response. No, it *was* the only logical response. She had to clasp her hands to keep them from shaking. It was monstrous. And yet, it was the *only* choice. What good was a Conduct After Capture course if the POWs could simply be infected, then restrained until the infection took control of their bodies?

We can't even trust ourselves to keep secrets, she thought. *Anyone can be turned into a traitor once they've been infected.*

"We will find out," Bendix said. "And then we will know."

"For the moment, we don't think you have anything further to offer us," Adamson said. "And your...ability to issue commands might be useful elsewhere."

"If I happen to stumble across an isolated group of infected," Alice said. It was clever of the scientists to concede the possibility, but she had no illusions about how hard it would be to turn the concept into reality. Once she started issuing orders, the virus would *notice* her. "I might end up being killed out of hand."

"You're welcome to stay," Bendix said. "We don't have *many* guests here."

Alice made a face. "How many people are watching us through the sensor nodes?"

"Thousands," Adamson said. He didn't seem too worried, even though he *had* to know that the entire base would be under observation. There would be no privacy anywhere within the rocky shell. "They won't be in any danger if something goes badly wrong."

"True." Alice allowed herself a moment of respect. If something went wrong—if the virus got loose—the base would be nuked. Adamson and Bendix would be dead before the virus could take over their bodies. She wondered, suddenly, just how many layers of security she hadn't been allowed to see. "I'd sooner go back to the ship."

"Just try not to get killed," Bendix said. "We might have a use for you later."

If they let me go back to the ship, Alice thought. *They might decide I'd be better off elsewhere.*

"We won't let her get killed," Tindal said. He munched his burger thoughtfully. "And she won't let us get killed either."

"We have been working on a few modified stinkers," Adamson said. "Given a few days, we *should* be able to produce enough pheromones to stop the infected in their tracks. But we don't think it will last very long."

"No," Bendix agreed. "Not on a planetary surface, anyway. The pheromones appear quite sensitive to local weather conditions."

"Then perhaps we should concentrate on plunging a planet into a new ice age," Hammersmith said. "Wasn't there that concept of…ah, terraforming Venus by blocking out the sun?"

"It was a little more complex than that," Adamson said. "And merely reducing the planet's temperature wouldn't be enough to stop the virus. We'd need to find a counter-virus, something that can drive the virus out of its hosts."

"And then the hosts die, because they don't have brains any longer," Alice said. She'd seen the autopsies. The infected weren't under mind control. They literally didn't have *minds*. If the virus were to be removed, if its control structures were to be smashed, the host would collapse and die. "We would be committing genocide."

She took a breath. "And the hell of it is that we might not have a choice."

"No," Bendix agreed. "We might not."

Alice took a sip of her coffee. Years ago, back when humanity had *known* it was the only intelligent race in the universe, people had speculated that aliens might be so *alien* that they were literally incomprehensible. There would be war, simply because the galaxy wasn't big enough for humanity *and* a completely unpredictable alien race. How could it be otherwise when there was no hope of communications, of finding common ground? And yet, when humanity *had* encountered aliens, they had found ways to talk...

She shook her head. The virus was different. It wasn't interested in political power, it wasn't interested in trade...it merely wanted to absorb every other life form into its gestalt. How did one talk to it? How could one convince the virus that it *needed* to talk? She'd been as close as anyone to touching the virus's mind and *she* didn't have any idea how it could be brought to the negotiating table. Hell, she didn't even know if the virus had any concept of diplomacy. It was simply too inhuman, too *alien*, to understand.

It can infect our bodies and puppet them well enough to fool people long enough to carry out attacks, she thought. *And yet, it can't talk to us...*

"We'll keep in touch," Adamson said. "And if you have any ideas, feel free to forward them to us."

"I will," Alice said. "And you let us know if you come up with anything useful."

"It may not be possible," Bendix said. "Security, you know."

Alice nodded, tartly. She'd seen the BBC's broadcasts. They hadn't *lied*, not exactly, but they'd certainly kept some of the more disturbing facts from the public at large. Alice wasn't sure how she felt about that. She'd met more than a few civilians who panicked at nothing—her sister was a prime example—but others were far more capable. Besides, it might be good for the civilians to be a little concerned, to keep their eyes out for signs of infection. The virus wasn't going to be beaten by the military alone.

And the Home Guard might start shooting people on suspicion of infection, she thought, grimly. She'd trained alongside the Home Guard. They were enthusiastic, but inexperienced. *And then all hell will break loose.*

"I know," she said, putting the thought aside. "Just get it to us as quickly as you can."

CHAPTER SEVEN

"WELL, THEY'RE *FINALLY* ON THEIR WAY," Richard said, as he and Monica walked down to the flight deck. "They should be landing in ten minutes."

Monica nodded. "I've got the bunks ready for them," she said. "Germans and Italians and Americans...oh, my."

"We should count ourselves lucky to get the Americans," Richard said. The Royal Navy and the United States Navy regularly exchanged starfighter squadrons. They used the same equipment, spoke the same language... the Germans and the Italians used the same starfighters, but would they speak the same language? The last thing he needed was a communications breakdown in the middle of an engagement. "I don't know the first thing about the Germans and Italians..."

"Well, Germans come from Germany and Italians come from Italy," Monica said. She grinned as he gave her a sharp look. "Beyond that, I don't know. They do meet the basic requirements, don't they?"

"Yeah." Richard had read the files carefully. "They're qualified, but beyond that...I don't know how they'll fit in."

"We'll see," Monica said. She paused as they stepped through a hatch into the observation dome. "And they'll be just as eager to make this work, won't they?"

Richard nodded. Germany and Italy had been hit hard during the Age of Unrest, hard enough to completely discredit their pre-war governments and do a *lot* of economic and structural damage. They'd been lucky their neighbours hadn't been willing to exert the effort to keep them down, although it had been a close-run thing. Eastern Europe had historical reasons to be nervous of a strong Germany. If they hadn't been equally worried about the Russians, they might have allied with the French to keep the Germans down. Even so, it had taken both Germany and Italy a long time to build up a presence in space and they were still far behind the Great Powers.

Although that may be about to change, Richard mused. *The Great Powers are the ones who bear the brunt of the interstellar wars.*

He leaned forward as the first starfighter flew into the flight deck and landed neatly on the metal surface. The Americans weren't trying to show off, something that suggested a reassuring degree of experience. Only an idiot would try to show off when he was landing on a carrier, particularly an unfamiliar carrier. The Americans hadn't built anything like *Invincible* for themselves.

And they may not have to build any, if the Amalgamation goes as planned, Richard thought, wryly. *We'll all be part of the same space navy.*

"Interesting," Monica mused. "They're definitely an experienced bunch of pilots, but I'd say they were a little rusty."

"Reservists, according to their files," Richard said. "The Yanks didn't recall them until the first Battle of Falkirk."

"Surprising," Monica said. Her voice hardened. "Or perhaps it isn't *so* surprising."

Richard winced. Rumour had it that *Invincible* and the remainder of the task force—a task force that only existed on paper, so far—was going to be thrown to the lions to buy time for Earth to assemble its defences. It was hard to argue with that assessment, particularly as they were receiving pilots who were either reservists or inexperienced graduates. He scowled as the next set of starfighters settled on the landing pad. If they *were* being sent to sell their lives dearly, more experienced officers and pilots would make the battle a more costly encounter for the enemy. If...

"Go tell the Yanks to assemble in the briefing compartment," he ordered. "I'll join you when the rest of the pilots have landed."

"Yes, sir," Monica said.

Richard barely heard her. He was watching the Germans as they landed with a smooth confidence that belied Germany's lack of a dedicated fleet carrier. The Germans *had* hastily turned a handful of freighters into escort carriers, if the files were to be believed, but Richard knew through bitter experience that escort carrier operations had very little in common with *fleet* carrier deployments. He wondered, idly, if the Germans had borrowed a French carrier before the war had broken out. The French were the only ones who might help the Germans, in exchange for later considerations...

Or maybe they just did it in simulators, he mused, as the Italian and British starfighters landed. They looked wobbly, but resolute. *This might be their first time on a real carrier.*

He put the thought aside for later consideration as he turned and walked back through the hatch, down towards the briefing room. It wasn't going to be *easy* dealing with starfighter pilots from three different nations, even though...he shook his head, dismissively. He didn't have a choice. He'd hoped to get three British squadrons instead of just two, but they simply weren't available. The shortage of trained personnel was so acute that he couldn't even dig up a spare squadron leader or CAG from somewhere. It would have been nice to lose *one* of his two hats.

The briefing compartment was full to bursting when he walked in the door, the newly-graduated pilots bullshitting about how many hours they'd flown and how many enemy starfighters they'd blown out of space while the older pilots indulgently listened. Richard studied the latter for a long moment, wondering how many of them would be trouble. It was never easy to call up the reserves, if only because they had to leave their jobs at a moment's notice. The Americans had more reservists, he'd been told, than the Royal

Navy, but he would be surprised if they didn't have similar problems. It was astonishing how many businesses were held together by combat vets.

Monica whistled, loudly. "Commander on deck!"

Silence fell. The pilots hastily scrambled to their feet. Richard allowed his eyes to wander over them, silently noting who wore their uniforms properly and who had allowed themselves to be a little slapdash. The latter was often a sign of a lack of attention to detail, suggesting the pilot might be careless in combat. Richard winced, inwardly, to note how many of those that there were. It wasn't going to be easy to iron out the kinks before they had to go into combat.

"Be seated," he ordered, curtly.

He took a moment to allow them to sit, then continued. "First, welcome onboard HMS *Invincible*. For those of you who don't know me"—as far as he knew, *none* of the newcomers knew him—"I am Wing Commander Richard Redbird, currently serving as both Commander Air Group and Squadron Leader A. This will be somewhat unwieldy in combat, but we seem to have no choice. We will therefore learn to cope."

"Damn right," someone muttered.

Richard ignored the interjection. "We have orders to leave this system and deploy to the front lines in a week, ten days at the most. The ship is currently *crammed* with shipyard workers who have been drafted in from all over the system to get us ready to leave on time. You, fortunately, will not be involved with repairing the ship. Instead"—he allowed the word to hang in the air for a few seconds—"you will be training extensively, training as you have never done before. By the time we leave, I want us to be *ready* to work together to kick enemy arse. I want you to make them sorry they ever *heard* of us.

"Those of you who have previous experience, before you left your respective services, are going to help the maggots learn. We don't have time to hold your hands. Yes, I know; hardly any of you have experience on a ship like this. Deal with it. If you have problems, I expect you to cope with them like mature adults. If not…believe me, I will be your worst fucking nightmare. We simply don't have time to mess around. We don't have time."

Richard made a show of checking his watch. "It is now 1345. I want you—all of you—in the simulators at 1445. Get your bunks, get some coffee, have a shower, take a shit…do whatever you have to do, as long as you are in your simulators by 1445. Any questions?"

He waited, but there were none. "Very good," he said. "One other thing. If you have anything—and I mean *anything*—that happens to be forbidden by Royal Navy regulations, which you can download on your terminals if you aren't already familiar with them, get rid of it. Put it in the bins or sell it to the yard dogs, no questions asked. I don't care, as long as it isn't with you when we depart. Whatever it is, get rid of it.

"Squadron leaders, stay behind. Everyone else, dismissed."

"Follow the blue lines to your bunks," Monica said, as the pilots rose. "First come, first served."

Richard allowed himself to relax as the pilots filed out of the compartment. They looked a little subdued, now that he'd made his speech. He hoped that would last, at least until they went through the first set of training simulations. Richard had designed them himself, carefully crafting the engagement to give the enemy a set of unexpected advantages. Anyone who went into battle with a cocky faith that they couldn't lose was in for an awful shock.

Better they die a thousand simulated deaths than die once, for real, he told himself. It was hard not to escape the sense of *déjà vu*. Hadn't he given the same lecture before? How many of those pilots who'd listened to him, back then, had died? *No matter what I tell them, no matter what I say, some of them are going to die.*

He gritted his teeth, then turned to face the squadron leaders. He hadn't had anything like enough time to do more than skim their files, but he'd learnt enough. Lieutenant-Colonel Darren Vargas and Lieutenant-Colonel Tyrone Leif commanded the two American squadrons, one USMC rather than USN. Richard hoped *that* wouldn't be a problem. The British Army and the Royal Marines worked closely together, but the United States Marine Corps was practically a second army in its own right. Beside them, Lieutenant-Colonel Johannes Fritsch represented the Germans and Colonel Francesca Bernardello represented the Italians. She looked surprisingly young, for someone who was a full colonel, although Richard knew better than to assume that meant she'd had an unfair advantage over her peers. Most starfighter pilots were young.

"Thank you for staying," he said, shortly. "I don't have much time, so we'll have a more formal gathering later...perhaps when we're halfway to our destination. Until then...do any of you have any real concerns over our current plan?"

"Train, train and train again," Vargas said. He was a big black man, so dark that Richard found it hard to look him in the eye. "I like the way you think."

"Our pilots will not," Leif predicted, cheerfully. "But they have to be ready to go at a moment's notice."

"If we're attacked here, we're fucked anyway," Vargas pointed out.

"We can still fight," Francesca said. She met Richard's eyes. "My only concern is that it was a long flight from Luna Base Thirty to *Invincible*. My crews need a chance to stretch their legs."

"They'll have it." Richard nodded in understanding. Four hours in a starfighter cockpit wasn't fun, even if the pilots *weren't* being shot at. "And your planes will be ready to fly again shortly."

"I assume we will be carrying out live-fire exercises," Fritsch said. His accent was so thick that Richard could barely understand him. "We brought drones for target practice."

"We may have to wait," Richard said. He nodded towards the display. "We're in the middle of the shipyard complex. I doubt they'd let us launch starfighters *here*."

"Then we fly out of the shipyard complex and exercise there," Fritsch growled. "There's no substitute for live-fire exercises. Sir."

"No," Richard agreed. He promised himself, silently, that he'd hunt down whoever had assigned Fritsch to *Invincible* and make him very sorry. Fritsch had the makings of a good officer—Richard could hardly disagree with his assessment of life-fire exercises—but his accent was too thick. He'd have to lose it. "But right now, we may not be able to do more than a handful of launches."

"Cheer up," Vargas said. "In all of our emergency drills, they always leave out the emergency. We'll learn the hard way."

"We will certainly be running scramble exercises," Richard agreed. "But, right now, actually launching our starfighters will have to wait."

"Bah," Fritsch muttered.

"We don't have a choice, do we?" Francesca's voice was firm. "And besides, we will have time to practice during the voyage."

"I certainly hope so," Richard said. The captain *might* want the ship to remain unnoticed as she passed through Terra Nova and headed to Falkirk—or wherever the unified command authority intended for humanity to make her stand—but it was unlikely. It would do nothing for morale if they sneaked through a star system that had been human right from the day it had been discovered. "If nothing else, we can run a few drills before we jump through the first tramline."

"That would be good." Fritsch sounded relieved. "My pilots do not have enough experience in carrier operations."

"They'll be ready in a few weeks," Leif said.

"Yeah," Vargas said. "Do you know where we're going yet?"

"No." Richard shook his head. "Captain Shields may know, but he hasn't bothered to confide in me."

"Odd," Francesca said. "Is it a state secret or something?"

"It may be," Monica pointed out. "In the last two alien wars, we didn't have to worry about spies. Here…a handful of infected people in the right place would let the virus keep track of us. We might even have an infected bastard on our ship."

"You checked our blood." Francesca rubbed her wrist. "But I take your point."

"We go where we're sent," Richard said. He took a moment to check their reactions, then continued. "I won't—I don't—have time to handle all the CAG duties. Ideally, one or more of you would be training to take my place, just in case something happened, but we don't have time for that either. I need you to handle your squadrons without reference to me. If there are any minor issues, I expect you to handle them yourselves."

Vargas grinned. "Excellent. A blank cheque for mayhem!"

"You'll be too tired for mayhem," Leif predicted. "My pilots, on the other hand, are used to sleeping uncomfortably."

"Just because *you* jarheads think that it isn't a proper bed unless you're lying in a muddy trench with some bastard dropping rocks on you…"

Richard cleared his throat. "Jokes aside, behave yourselves. Or we will all be for the high jump."

"Yes, sir," Leif said.

"And now that's settled, you can get your carryalls to your bunks," Richard said. "I'll see you all in the simulators."

"Where we will whoop ET's ass," Vargas said.

Richard smiled. He doubted it. The programming he'd done would teach them all a lesson about being cocky. "We'll see," he said. "Dismissed."

Monica stayed behind as the others left. "Interesting bunch," she commented. "You read their files?"

"Just the highlights," Richard said. "You?"

"Fritsch has a chip on his shoulder, I'm not sure why," Monica said. "But he's extremely competent, so his government gave him squadron command and sent him to us. Francesca is the daughter of a powerful Italian businessman, but…she was a test pilot and an aerobatic flyer before she was called up. She wouldn't have been in the aerobatic team unless she was extremely good."

Richard nodded. The Red Arrows—the greatest aerobatic display team in the solar system—were perfectionists. No one, regardless of their connections, was allowed to join the team unless they were *brilliant* flyers. He couldn't imagine that it would be any different in Italy. If nothing else, anyone who *wasn't* extremely good trying to perform the stunts would probably wind up dead. Francesca might look good on a recruiting poster—Richard had a feeling she probably *was* on a recruiting poster somewhere—but she wouldn't have survived the aerobatic stunts if she wasn't a good pilot too.

Which doesn't mean she's a good squadron commander, he reminded himself. *I'll have to keep an eye on them.*

"We'll see," he said. He felt a sudden wave of tiredness and groaned, inwardly. He'd been running himself ragged since they'd been told they would be deploying in a week. "Any other thoughts?"

"You should probably groom either Wallace or O'Brian as a replacement squadron leader, just in case you have to take on more of the CAG duties," Monica said. "Wallace is the better flyer, if the files are to be believed, but O'Brian has better people skills. And family connections in Northern Ireland."

"We'll see how they perform in the simulators," Richard said. He resisted the urge to sit down, if only because he wasn't sure he could stand up again. "You go get ready. I'll see you in thirty minutes."

"Yes, sir," Monica said.

She left, the hatch hissing closed behind her. Richard felt himself sag, as if he simply didn't have the energy to carry on. 1410? It felt like 2400, time he really should be in bed. How long had it been since he'd slept properly? He honestly wasn't sure. Months, perhaps. Too many people had died under his watch for him to feel anything but a numb tiredness that threatened to overcome him. Too many...

He opened his belt pouch and removed the injector tab. It wasn't a good idea to use stims, not really. He knew, all too well, just how easy it was to become dependent on them. And yet, he didn't have a choice. The next week was going to be frantic. He couldn't afford to rest.

I'll stop when we're on our way, he thought. *And that will be the end.*

Quite calmly, he pushed the tab against his skin and pressed the trigger.

CHAPTER EIGHT

"RUSSIAN COMMAND, SIR?"

Stephen winced at Newcomb's tone. It was very far from diplomatic, the sort of comment that should—that could—only be made in private. The Admiralty and the Foreign Office would be outraged to hear that it had been made at all. And yet, he didn't disagree with his XO. There were too many question marks over Russia, dating back all the way to the First Interstellar War, for *anyone* to be happy under Russian command.

"So it would seem," he said, finally. The message had been brutally clear. Admiral Svetlana Zadornov, former commanding officer of RFS *Brezhnev*—the first *Brezhnev*—had been assigned to command Task Force Resolute. "And I doubt the Admiralty is interested in hearing any complaints."

"No, sir," Newcomb said. "But can we trust the Russians to behave themselves?"

Stephen shrugged. "There are issues I'm not at liberty to discuss," he said, grimly. "But, right now, I think we can trust the Russians to know where their best interests lie."

He looked up at the holographic starchart. The latest set of updates from the MNF had warned that the virus was steadily advancing towards Zheng He, detaching a handful of smaller formations to deal with the colony worlds on either side of the main advance. Stephen liked to think that the colonies would delay the virus, at least for a few weeks, but he had to admit it was unlikely. The colonies had almost no military significance. They wouldn't delay the virus any longer than it took for the virus to land troops and begin the infection.

Or they might simply blow the orbital facilities into dust and then leave the colony for later attention, he thought. The virus might be alien, but he dared not assume that it wouldn't understand military logic. There was nothing to be gained by absorbing the colonies when the remainder of the human sphere was hastily girding itself for war. *No, it will come straight at us until it runs into a force powerful enough to stop it.*

He frowned. The updates had made it clear that Task Force Resolute was a task force in name only. On paper, it was powerful enough to overwhelm a well-defended system; in practice, only three carriers and one battleship had been assigned to the fleet. The remaining forty starships were a mixture of cruisers, destroyers, and a couple of experimental units that had never been put into mass production. Stephen had his doubts about how well the fleet could function as a single unit. Their communications networks and datanets were designed to be compatible—the First Interstellar War had taught humanity the importance of ensuring that they could link their datanets across national boundaries—but only a handful of captains had operated in a multinational formation before the war. There wouldn't need to be malice to cause problems.

Of course not, he told himself, sourly. *Who needs malice when you have simple inexperience paired with a desperate need for haste?*

"It doesn't matter right now," he said. He sat back in his chair, silently dismissing the issue with a wave of his hand. "Where do we stand for meeting our departure date?"

"Better than I expected," Newcomb said. "The engineers are confident that they can replace the damaged components and weld the armour back into place before the deadline. We've made a bunch of enemies, sir, but we should be ready to depart on time."

Stephen had to smile. "I received a whole string of complaints from Commander Davis," he said. "He'll just have to cope."

"Yes, sir," Newcomb said. "How badly did we impact on *his* deadline?"

"A couple of months, at least," Stephen said. He sobered. "Let's just hope the virus doesn't reach Earth before Commander Davis is ready to launch *his* ship."

He looked down at his hands, feeling a pang of guilt. They'd had no choice, but to cannibalise fusion cores, heavy weapons and datanet processors from the half-completed HMS *Furious*. They hadn't had a choice... which hadn't stopped the shipyard crews from bitching and moaning about what it had done to their schedules. Stephen didn't blame them for being pissed. Starships weren't thrown together like Lego models. Commander Davis and his crews would have to revise their production plans on the fly, pushing ahead with some aspects of the work while delaying others until replacement fusion cores could arrive. There was no way they'd meet *their* deadline.

And some asshole in Nelson Base will probably make snide comments about their competence when they fail to meet their deadline, Stephen thought, coldly. *Furious* had already been delayed once, while the designers absorbed the lessons from *Invincible's* shakedown cruise and made adjustments to *Furious*. *They'll say the delay came from incompetence rather than military necessity.*

"I'm sure they'll have the ship ready to fly and fight," Newcomb said. "Overall, we should meet the deadline. Our real problem, however, is that our rear ablative armour will be weakened. There isn't anything we can do about that without replacing the entire section and *that* would take weeks."

"And a handful of lucky hits there would cripple us," Stephen mused. "Even one, if it hit the weakest point."

"Yes, sir," Newcomb said. "Theo thinks he can bolt on extra armour, but it won't stand up to more than one or two shots at most. *And* it would attract attention."

Stephen winced. "And then the enemy would know where to aim."

"Yes, sir."

"If they didn't already know," Stephen added, after a moment. "Who *doesn't* know to aim for the drive section if they want to cripple the ship?"

He shook his head in irritation. The designers had done their work well, but they'd run up against a number of practical limits. Every critical system on the ship was heavily protected, save for the drive section. It was as strongly armoured as human ingenuity could devise, but the rear section couldn't be covered in armour without rendering the drive field useless. And, unlike the forward drive nodes, there was no way to hide the drive section either. The structure would draw fire as soon as the enemy drew within engagement range.

"We don't have a choice, sir," Newcomb said. "If we want to meet our deadline, we have to accept that we'll be flying with weakened armour."

"I know," Stephen said, tiredly. He'd worked the problem dozens of times, trying to figure out a solution that satisfied everyone, but there wasn't one. *No one* had managed to devise more than a temporary solution. "Order the engineers to install the extra armour. We'll take the risk of drawing fire."

"Yes, sir," Newcomb said.

He didn't sound happy. Stephen didn't blame him for that either. No one in their right mind would take a poorly-armoured ship into combat, not unless there was no other choice. The lessons of the First Interstellar War, where lightly-armoured fleet carriers had been chopped apart by plasma weapons with casual ease, were sealed into the Royal Navy's collective memory. There had been great advances since then—*Invincible* and her sisters could have won the Battle of New Russia effortlessly, if they'd somehow fallen back in time—but it would be a long time before the scars faded. What good was heavy armour if there was no time to install it?

Stephen changed the subject. "And the remainder of the ship?"

"We've managed to repair most of the internal damage," Newcomb assured him. "We did hit some snags because of the need to keep the internal security locks in place, but...the engineers assure me we should have everything ready before we meet the deadline. There may be some issues, once we set out..."

He shrugged. "We can probably fix those during the voyage."

"Good," Stephen said. "And the crew?"

"Morale is low, but I'm keeping them too busy to grumble." Newcomb smiled, rather thinly. "There's a lot of worried people on the ship, crewmen concerned about their families and friends on Earth. The BBC isn't helping, I think."

"Probably not," Stephen agreed. The BBC's updates were long on scare-mongering and short on actual *news*. It was easy to lose trust in reporters and the media when one didn't have it in the first place. God knew the military updates weren't very informative either. "Is there anyone we should be concerned about?"

"Everyone," Newcomb said, flatly. "There aren't many crewmen who *don't* have families on Earth."

"No," Stephen agreed. "And there isn't much we can do about it either."

He scowled. The government, in its wisdom, had ordered large chunks of the national datanet to be shut down. He could see the logic—the infected might be using the datanet to communicate—but he could also see the downside. In the absence of proper information, rumours would spread rapidly...and panic would follow in their wake. There were already reports of innocent people being shot on suspicion of being infected. God alone knew how *that* would work out.

"No, sir," Newcomb said. "Have you been privy to any...private updates?"

"Nothing particularly detailed," Stephen said. Duncan *had* sent him an email, but Stephen hadn't had the time to read it. It hadn't been marked urgent. "They still don't know how the virus got down to the surface."

"They probably captured a RockRat miner and worked from there," Newcomb said. "A RockRat could lead them to a smuggler crew and eventually a passage down to Earth without any of those pesky security checks."

"Perhaps," Stephen said. "But..."

He shook his head. It was possible, although he found it hard to believe. RockRats might be anarchists, unwilling or unable to subordinate themselves to the Belt Alliance—let alone the Great Powers—but they were also extremely competent. They had to be. Space was an unforgiving environment, a place where the slightest mistake could spell disaster. A RockRat was about the *least* likely person to neglect basic safety precautions.

"Or maybe they managed a suborbital insertion without being noticed," he said, after a moment. "There's enough debris in orbit that they *might* have been able to make a stealth insertion without triggering the alarms."

"There's a lot of sensor platforms in orbit," Newcomb pointed out. "It's hard to imagine them managing to land without being detected and blown out of space."

"True." Stephen nodded. If the orbital platforms detected an illicit landing, they'd fire first and ask questions later. "We may never know."

But we have to know, he thought. *Or else we might never feel safe again.*

"I'll push the Admiralty for permission to update the crew," he said, instead. "But, right now, very few people know *anything*."

"Yes, sir," Newcomb said. "Hopefully, things will get better when we're underway."

Stephen nodded, grimly. It had been a long time—nearly two hundred years—since the Troubles, when terrorists and wreckers had targeted military families in a desperate bid to destroy morale. They'd paid a steep price for their crimes—and so had a vast number of innocents, he acknowledged grimly—but the damage had lingered. *This* war was going to be worse. There was no point in retaliatory killings when the targets wouldn't even *notice*.

"Let us hope so," he said. "What about the foreigners?"

"No troubles as yet, but the CAG informs me that they have yet to do anything more than eat, sleep and run simulations," Newcomb said. "Poor Redbird has had them in the simulators from dawn till dusk."

"Ouch," Stephen said. "And how are they getting along?"

"They're doing about as well as can be expected, he says." Newcomb shrugged. "But the shipyard CO refused permission to carry out live-fire drills."

"And we can't override him," Stephen mused. "We'll just have to make up for them during transit."

"Yes, sir." Newcomb consulted his datapad. "Thankfully, they fly the same basic starfighters as us. Their logistic requirements are practically identical to ours. We shouldn't have any problems supporting them. The only real problem is that a couple of pilots don't speak perfect English, but we're working on that."

"Ouch," Stephen said. It was rare to encounter a spacer who *didn't* speak English. "Is it likely to cause problems in combat?"

"The CAG is confident that most of the issues can be worked out," Newcomb said. "And if they're not...we can probably cope with any problems, as long as the pilots stay in their national formations."

"Good," Stephen said. He rubbed his eyes. "Are there any other issues?"

"Nothing serious enough to bring to your attention," Newcomb said. "There was some minor grumbling over shore leave being cancelled, but the senior chiefs took care of it."

"We might have to do something about that," Stephen said. He considered it for a moment, but nothing came to mind. There wasn't anything he *could* do, short of sending the crew on shore leave...and that was obviously impossible. "Maybe we should send for a NAAFI ship."

"They want to get out of the hull and stretch their legs, sir," Newcomb said. "A NAAFI ship won't cut it."

"I know," Stephen said. "Particularly as a NAAFI ship won't bring them what they want."

"They also know what's at stake," Newcomb added. "It won't be *that* hard to keep them focused."

"They're not *machines*," Stephen pointed out. "And even machines wear out if you work them too hard."

He studied his desk for a long moment, trying to think of *something*. A military force couldn't remain on alert forever, no matter what the politicians and media claimed. A constant state of alert—of high activity with no end in sight—would wear them down as surely as a steady series of engagements. Tiredness would start to seep in, leading to a constant stream of mistakes... some which would be life-threatening. It would only take *one* mistake to lead to utter disaster…he shook his head. He'd just have to make sure that the crew had a chance to rest during transit. But it wouldn't be good enough.

Of course not, he thought, dryly. *How can they relax properly when they might be called to action at any moment?*

"Keep me informed," he said. Another update blinked up in front of him. Two starships had been withdrawn from the task force roster, with only one—so far—earmarked as a replacement. "And keep an eye on crew morale. If we can do something about it…"

"Yes, sir," Newcomb said. "You *could* push for the prize money to be paid out now."

"I could," Stephen said. The Admiralty hadn't quibbled over the prize money, but the Treasury was balking. He had been preparing himself to lodge an official protest when the virus had started its terrorist campaign. "But where would they spend it?"

"It would give them hope for the future," Newcomb said. "And that might be just what they need."

"True," Stephen agreed. "Very true."

He smiled, thinly. "Dismissed."

Newcomb saluted, then left the ready room. Stephen watched him go, then tapped a command into his terminal. His steward entered a moment later, carrying a mug of coffee and a plate of sandwiches. Stephen frowned— he didn't feel like eating—but there was no point in arguing. The poor woman had orders to make sure her captain ate properly at all times.

"Thank you," he said, as she put the plate on his desk and withdrew as silently as she'd come. "I'll eat them soon."

He glanced at the sandwiches, picked one at random and started to eat while studying the readiness reports. *Invincible* was slowly coming to life, although his departmental heads hadn't hesitated to point out issues that might—*might*—turn into serious problems during the voyage. Stephen scowled, cursing the virus under his breath. He'd known commanding offi- cers who'd objected to reading anything that smacked of negativity, but he'd never seen the point of it himself. Better to plan for the worst and hope for the best than ignore a problem in the hope it would go away. If his officers were concerned about something, he needed to be concerned about it, too…

Even if I have to ignore it, he thought, sourly. He hated to leave a potential problem alone—it was the sort of thing that led to disaster, under normal circumstances—but there was no choice. *We simply don't have the time to fix everything.*

He reached for another sandwich, tapping a switch to bring up the live feed from the starfighter simulators. Commander Redbird had outdone himself, Stephen noted; he'd crafted simulations *designed* to knock the fighter pilot arrogance out of anyone who hadn't realised that they were not invincible. The early engagements looked to have been utterly disastrous, with the entire wing being practically wiped out time and time again. It was only now that the stats were steadily starting to improve.

"And the virus isn't *that* good," Stephen muttered. The simulated enemy starfighters were impossibly fast, flown by pilots with improbable aiming skills. "Unless they've been hiding some *real* high-tech from us…"

He gritted his teeth. It was quite possible that the virus *was* hiding something from them, intentionally or otherwise. Stephen had seen it deploy starships that would have been outdated fifty years ago, alongside ships that could match the best warships humanity could produce. Who knew what it had yet to send into battle? It might have overwhelmed a far more advanced race on the other side of its territory…hell, humanity didn't even know just how much space it actually *controlled*. There were so many unanswered questions that Stephen couldn't help feeling that they were jumping into the unknown…

"But we don't have a choice," he told himself. He forced himself to put his concerns aside and concentrate on preparing his ship for war. "We have to fight."

CHAPTER NINE

"YOU FOLKS HAD BETTER GET COMFORTABLE," the pilot called. "There's a line of shuttles and shit waiting to dock."

Alice blinked in surprise. "On *Invincible*?"

"That's right," the pilot confirmed. "And the line is moving pretty damn slowly."

"They're probably testing everyone for the virus, again," Hammersmith muttered. He looked disgustingly fresh for someone who had only managed to catch a few hours of sleep during the flight. Beside him, Tindal was snoring gently. "Or...*something.*"

"Probably," Alice said. "We'll just have to wait."

She leaned back in her uncomfortable seat and brought up the live feed from the shuttle's external sensors. The shipyard was, as always, a teeming hive of activity...but, this time, the activity seemed to be concentrated on *Invincible*. Hundreds of shuttles, worker bees and mobile shipyard modules hovered around the giant carrier, while thousands of dockyard workers in suits crawled over her hull. A giant metal hexagon was steadily being steered towards the rear of the starship. It took her a moment to realise it was a piece of armour. The captain was clearly determined to get his ship ready to deploy as quickly as possible.

"There's a convoy being assembled," Hammersmith pointed out. "Perhaps we're going to be escorting her."

"Perhaps," Alice said. The freighters looked as if they'd been designed in the belt, rather than one of the national or corporate shipyards, but that hardly mattered during wartime. The Belters were in danger too. Her lips thinned in cold dislike. Her wretched father had joined the Belters, after he'd been unfrozen. The Belters either didn't know about his past or simply didn't care. "But they wouldn't assign a damaged assault carrier to protect a convoy."

"She can still fight," Hammersmith said. "*We* can still fight."

"Not in a real engagement," Alice said, firmly. "And how would *we* be able to bring our strength to bear?"

The shuttle quivered, slightly. "We've just moved up in line," the pilot said. "We'll be docking in twenty minutes or thereabouts."

"Hurry up and wait," Hammersmith said. The shuttle quivered again. "Do you think we'll be reassigned?"

Alice shrugged. It hadn't been *that* long since they'd returned from their *last* deployment. It wasn't uncommon for marine units to be reassigned if their mothership had to return to the shipyards, but they would normally receive a period of shore leave first. She sighed, inwardly, at the thought. There was little point in *her* being given shore leave. Where would she go? God knew she probably wouldn't be allowed to enter the orbital towers or take a shuttle down to Earth. She wouldn't even be allowed to visit Sin City.

Not that I'd want to go in any case, she told herself, firmly. *I'd sooner take a tour of the lunar surface then waste a few hours in Sin City.*

She forced herself to wait as the shuttle inched towards the starship, trying to control her impatience. Hammersmith was right. "Hurry up and wait" had been part of the military life for thousands of years. There was nothing she could do to speed things up, so she might as well take advantage of the time to relax. There would be another challenge soon enough.

And I still don't know what's going to happen to me afterwards, she thought, as she keyed her terminal. There *still* weren't any updates from Earth, just bland platitudes that probably spread panic. She hadn't even heard anything from her sister! *They've probably put a block on outgoing messages from Earth.*

"Here we are," the pilot said. The shuttle hummed to life. "We've just been assigned a docking port."

"Goody," Alice said. She put her terminal in her carryall, then poked Tindal. "Wake up!"

Tindal jerked awake. "Fire! Plague! Martians!"

"We're only docking," Hammersmith said. "Quit messing around."

"Oh," Tindal said. The gravity field flickered, just for a moment. "That's worse."

"Yeah," Hammersmith said. "I'm sure the Major will have kept careful note of all the press-ups you didn't do."

"I knew it." Tindal stood and grabbed his carryall as a low *thud* echoed through the shuttlecraft. "The Major hates my guts."

"I doubt it," Alice said. She took a long breath. "And if you say that in front of him, you'll be for the high jump."

She turned towards the hatch as it hissed open, revealing a decontamination chamber. Alice sighed, then motioned for the two men to go ahead of her. *They* wouldn't have any problem with the blood tests, while she... she shook her head in irritation. The virus in her bloodstream was dead, but it would still set off alarms. She supposed she should be grateful she hadn't been reassigned. *Invincible's* crew might understand what had happened to her, but hardly anyone else would give her the benefit of the doubt. They'd shoot her the moment they saw the blood results, convinced they were doing the right thing. The hell of it was that they might well be *doing the right thing.*

A pair of doctors in full protective gear materialised as she stepped through the hatch, one pressing a sensor against her neck while the other waved a device she didn't recognise over her chest. Alice gritted her teeth as the pressure intensified, but said nothing. The doctors were only doing their jobs. She covered her eyes as the light grew brighter, killing any free-floating viral particles that might have accompanied her through the hatch.

The doctors shrugged, then dismissed her with a wave. Alice told herself, firmly, she should be glad they weren't carrying out a *full* decontamination procedure. *That* wouldn't be fun.

Major Parkinson met her as she stepped through the inner hatch. "Alice? Welcome home."

"Thank you, sir," Alice said, feeling her heart sink. He outranked her. She should go to him, not him to her. That he'd come to welcome her personally was probably bad news. She wondered, sourly, what it would be. Was she being reassigned? Or simply being benched until the doctors performed more checks? Or medically discharged? "What's the bad news?"

The major didn't smile. "Come with me."

Alice slung her carryall over her shoulder and followed him through a maze of metal corridors. She knew the ship like the back of her hand, but the constant stream of strangers performing repair works practically everywhere she looked confused her. She'd been led to expect that *Invincible* would be repaired over the next six months, not...she frowned, feeling cold. It looked as if the entire dockyard workforce was working desperately to ready *Invincible* for deployment. Her eyes narrowed as she spotted a pair of starfighter pilots who clearly weren't British. It *definitely* looked as if they were going back to the war.

Major Parkinson led her through the hatch into Marine Country and right down the corridor into his office. Alice felt the cold sensation in her chest steadily growing worse. Normally, she would have a chance to reclaim her bunk and stow her carryall in her locker before taking her place in the duty roster. Unless, of course, she was in trouble...she shook her head, mentally. Major Parkinson was hardly the sort of man to let the grass grow under his feet. If she was in trouble, she'd know about it. She certainly hadn't done anything to merit a chewing out before she'd left the ship.

"Take a seat," Parkinson ordered. He took a pair of mugs from the dispenser and passed one to her. "Cheers."

"Cheers," Alice echoed. The coffee was military-grade, strong enough to keep her awake for hours. It tasted vile, but she didn't care. "Major… what is going on?"

"I received an interesting set of orders concerning you," Parkinson said. "Can you *really* control the infected?"

Alice resisted the urge to threaten Adamson and Bendix with grievous bodily harm, if she ever saw them again. It was their *duty*, damn them, to report what they'd found. She was mildly surprised they'd even let her go. But then…

"In a manner of speaking," she said. She briefly ran through what had happened during her absence. "I can give orders, sir, but not very *complex* orders."

"So you're perfectly qualified for command rank." Parkinson didn't smile at his weak joke. "And you actually have to be *there* to give orders?"

"They have to be able to smell me," Alice said. "And they can't be allowed a chance to actually *think* about their orders."

"A Downing Street Drill," Parkinson mused.

Alice nodded. It wasn't uncommon for Special Forces soldiers to be tested just to see how far they'd go before they questioned their orders, if only to keep them from following instructions that ended with the assassination of the Prime Minister. A rogue officer in the right place could do a great deal of damage if his men followed orders without question. It still galled MI5 and the other investigative agencies that they hadn't figured out just who had ordered Sir Charles Hanover assassinated, let alone who'd done the deed. Alice rather suspected that his cabinet had been involved. An authoritarian leader tended to become a liability long before he realised he had to go…

She was woolgathering. She cursed her lack of discipline and dragged her attention back to her superior. Parkinson was waiting patiently, his expression unreadable. She winced, inwardly. He should be chewing her out for not paying attention to him. She would have preferred a lecture to forbearance. Forbearance almost certainly meant she wasn't going to like what he had to say.

"For the moment, you are being held in reserve," Parkinson said. "I've been told that you're unique. If we get a chance to put you in a place where you can issue orders, we'll take it...but otherwise, your life will be preserved."

"Sir," Alice said. "I...with all due respect, I understand the dangers..."

"I know," Parkinson said. "And if you weren't so unique, I'd put you back on the duty roster without a second thought. You've earned your place here. But you're suddenly more than *just* a Royal Marine. You're a unique asset that has to be held in reserve until we have a chance to inflict maximum damage on the enemy."

"Yes, sir," Alice said, stiffly. There was nothing to be gained by arguing. Parkinson was only following orders. "What do you want me to do?"

"For the moment, you'll effectively be on detached duty," Parkinson said. "I've had the guest cabin prepared for you. You can stay there with a close-protection detail..."

"Sir," Alice protested. "I don't *need* protection."

"You might," Parkinson said. "First, if the virus realises what you can do, you'll be targeted at once. It cannot be *that* alien. It will see you as a threat and try to remove you. Second...there are people who will *also* see you as a threat. You may find yourself targeted by humans too."

"On this ship?" Alice met his eyes. "Am I in *real* danger?"

"You could be." Parkinson looked back at her, evenly. "People don't need much of an excuse to panic, do they? They won't look at the evidence, they won't give a damn about the doctors clearing you, they won't even take your record into account. And if they start to blame you for something... you're fucked."

"Yes, sir," Alice said, reluctantly. "I take your point."

She fought to keep the disappointment and anger off her face. Being wounded was one thing—she could fight her way back onto active duty if she was badly wounded in combat—but this? How was she supposed to recover from *this*? How could she ever serve in combat again after being nothing more than a helpless principal, the person who had to be protected at all costs? She felt a moment of grim amusement at the irony. How often had *she* complained about the principal when *she'd* been on close-protection duty? And now, *she* was the principal.

At least I know how to handle myself, she thought. *And I know not to do things that will put lives at risk.*

"I know it isn't where you want to be," Parkinson said. "But it is where we *need* you to be."

And would you say that to a male trooper? Alice knew she was being unfair, but she couldn't help herself. How many times had she had to assert herself because her fellow recruits hadn't taken her seriously? God! It was harder to assert herself against the ones who wanted to help her, rather than the sexist bastards. At least the latter didn't try to hide their dislike. *Or would you let him go straight back to active duty? And tell him to shut the fuck up if he bitched about his condition?*

She put her emotions under tight control. "I understand, sir. I will do my duty."

"That's all we ask," Parkinson said. "And you may make the difference between life and death."

"Yes, sir," Alice said. "And...are we deploying somewhere?"

Parkinson looked vaguely surprised by the question. "Yes. You can get the full details from the datanet, but the long and short of it is that we're being redeployed within the week. The virus has begun its offensive."

"...Shit," Alice said. That explained why the scientists had been so accommodating. "I didn't know."

"Most of the civvies don't know, not yet," Parkinson said. "Be careful what you tell them."

"Yes, sir," Alice said. It was an odd thing for him to say. When would *she* get to meet a civilian? "I'll watch my tongue."

"Dismissed," Parkinson said. "We'll catch up tomorrow."

Alice saluted and left the room, walking down to the guest cabin. It was small, probably too small for anyone who hadn't served in the military, but it was luxury incarnate to her. The bed was *hers*. She didn't have to hot bunk with someone who had filthy night habits or worse…she sighed as she dropped her carryall on the bed. The cabin was also *very* secure, with only one hatch and no access to the tubes. She couldn't help thinking that it could easily be turned into a cell—or a trap. Only one way in meant there was only one way out.

You're being paranoid, she told herself, stiffly. *There's no reason to fear attack.*

She sat down on the bunk and pressed her fingers against the terminal. It came to life, displaying a handful of priority messages. She skimmed through them quickly, noting that the attacks on Earth had clearly been coordinated with the Battle of Falkirk. It seemed unlikely that the timing was a coincidence. She shook her head in bitter despair. No wonder her superiors were keen to put her to work as…as an alien controller, rather than a marine. They were desperate. She didn't have access to fleet deployments—she didn't have anything like that level of clearance—but she could make some educated guesses. There was very little between Falkirk and the inner worlds. If the virus managed to gain a secure foothold, it might be difficult—if not impossible—to stop it from overrunning the remainder of the Human Sphere.

And no messages from Jeanette, she mused. She would have been more concerned if one of the updates hadn't noted that all messages from Earth were being held in a buffer until the state of emergency was lifted. *I wonder…*

She frowned as a new message appeared in her inbox. A personal message…her eyes narrowed, concerned. There was no one who might send her a personal message, except for Jeanette. But her sister was on the other side of the datanet buffer. The header insisted that it had come from the task force… she frowned. Who in the task force would send *her* a personal message?

Maybe it's spam, she thought, as she opened the message. *And someone is looking at fines and jail time…*

Her mouth dropped open as she saw the sender. Alan Campbell. It couldn't be…She swallowed hard, all the bitter resentments and hatreds bubbling up from the back of her mind as she checked the message details. There was no mistake. Alan Campbell, Master of the *Flying Cuttlefish*... Alan Campbell, father of Jeanette and Alice Campbell...Alan Campbell, the murderer of his wife, the man who'd left his daughters without either a father or a mother...

No, she thought. *What's* he *doing here?*

Her fingers were suddenly numb. She forced them to work, flicking through the message header to check the details. The *Flying Cuttlefish* had been assigned to the task force, apparently...she wanted to scream in rage. Her father was a murderer, her father was a monster, her father was...she knew, she had to admit, that he was also a legitimate war hero, but...

"Fuck it," she said. Jeanette *might* be able to forgive their father, but Alice never could. The bastard had killed their mother. "Just..."

She caught herself, a moment before she slammed her fist into the keyboard. What did the bastard sperm donor want? She glanced at the message, realised he was asking for a meeting, and shook her head, firmly. She was damned if she was going to meet him. She wanted to bury a knife in his heart and...she wondered, despite herself, if she could get away with it. If the government needed her, the government could cover up the crime. She could do it...

And the Major—and everyone else—would be disappointed in me, Alice thought. She found it hard to care, even though she knew she *should*. *And I wouldn't have a place here any longer.*

Pushing the thought aside, she stood. The gym should be clear right now, unless schedules had changed. She wanted to pound a punching bag into dust...

...And, if she imagined she was beating her father into a pulp, that was no one's business, but hers.

CHAPTER TEN

ADMIRAL SVETLANA ZADORNOV knew, without false modesty, that she'd been lucky to reach command rank, let alone survive both internal and external enemies until she had reached flag rank in the Russian Navy. It was rare for a woman to join the navy and rarer still for her to request assignment to actual starships, instead of a comfortable position in the military bureaucracy where she could combine work with marrying and giving birth to the next generation of Russians. Indeed, Svetlana was fairly certain she wouldn't have been allowed to reach command rank if she hadn't been barren, something that had limited her value to her family. There weren't many times that she regretted it. Better to risk her skin for the *Rodina* than spend the rest of her life as a brood mare.

Although they probably get more mileage out of me being a war hero, Svetlana thought, as she sat in her ready room. *There aren't many international heroes who are still on the fleet lists.*

She smiled, coldly. RFS *Brezhnev*—the second *Brezhnev*—was a fleet carrier, named for her old command. The first *Brezhnev* had fought in the Battle of Earth, then been destroyed during a brief encounter with an enemy raiding party shortly before the end of the war, thankfully some time after Svetlana herself had been promoted into carrier command. She still missed the old ship, even though she hadn't looked back at the time. She'd taken one of the worst crews in the fleet and turned them into a *proper* crew. And they'd rewarded her during the battle...

Her lips thinned as she studied the display. Two hundred years of interstellar expansion had come to a sudden end when the first of a series of alien enemies had come boiling out of nowhere to challenge the human race. Humanity had barely had any time to recover from the *first* war before the second began, followed rapidly by the third. Svetlana had heard American and British officers bemoaning the endless series of threats, asking why no alien race ever seemed to come in peace, but Svetlana had never understood it. The universe was red in tooth and claw. There was no *right* to anything, no right to even *life* itself, that could not be taken away. The Americans and the British could allow themselves to believe that the universe was *just*, if they wished; Mother Russia had never allowed her children the same freedom. It didn't matter who was in the right, legally or morally. All that mattered was strength and the will to use it. It was a lesson Svetlana had learned herself, time and time again. She had never been allowed to rest on her laurels.

She smiled, coldly, at the thought. She'd been underestimated when she'd joined the navy. Too many of her fellow cadets—and her training officers—had been unable to look past her breasts. But now...who was laughing now? She was a patient woman, with a vindictive streak a mile wide. The instructor who'd threatened to fail her unless she *serviced* him— she grimaced at the thought—was spending the rest of his life in Siberia. And he was doing something a *lot* more useful than merely counting trees.

Her intercom bleeped. Her aide's voice echoed in the quiet room. "Admiral, I have established a link to HMS *Invincible*. Their captain is waiting to speak to you."

"Put him through," Svetlana said. "And then secure the line."

"Yes, Admiral."

She leaned forward as Captain Shields materialised in front of her. Technically, she should have invited him to visit her ship in person, rather than send a holographic representation, but neither of them had the time. The British had been a little cagey about *just* how much damage *Invincible* had taken during her last deployment, but Svetlana was very good at reading between the lines. She just hoped they'd reach their destination and link up with the MNF before the shit hit the fan, again. The politics could destroy her as effectively as an alien missile.

The problem with climbing so high, she reflected wryly, *is that it's a very long way to fall.*

"Captain Shields," she said, banishing the thought. "Thank you for coming."

"Thank you for inviting me," Captain Shields said.

Svetlana studied him for a long moment. He was tall, lanky rather than muscular, with short blond hair a shade too bright to be natural and a neatly-trimmed goatee. She couldn't help thinking he looked weak, compared to her brothers and cousins; she recalled, from his file, that he was an aristocrat, a man who'd been given his command because of his blood rather than his competence. But that meant nothing, she reminded herself sharply. Svetlana wouldn't have climbed so high if *she* didn't have powerful relatives, including one who sat on the Politburo itself. And no one had seriously pushed for Captain Shields to be removed from command, even after the disastrous First Contact with the virus.

But he couldn't have done a better job, Svetlana thought. Hindsight was generally clearer than foresight, but...without knowing about the virus, without understanding the true nature of the threat, there had been little else that could have been done. *He took every precaution we could imagine. It's just that our imagination was so profoundly inadequate.*

"It is my intention to depart on schedule, even if we don't get all the ships we were promised," Svetlana said, stiffly. The British, French and Americans had all promised warships that had unaccountably failed to materialise. There was no point in carrying out fleet exercises when the number of ships assigned to the fleet changed with every passing hour. "Can you and your ship make the deadline?"

"I believe so," Captain Shields said. "Barring unanticipated problems, we should be able to depart as planned."

And that is a slightly more mealy-mouthed answer than I would have liked, Svetlana thought, amused. *But I should be grateful you're not telling me what you think I want to hear.*

She felt a flicker of annoyance at a bad habit she'd never quite been able to break. A Russian officer would have promised her the sun, the moon and the world itself if he thought it was what she wanted. But then, it wasn't uncommon for the same officer to then look for scapegoats if he couldn't *give* her what she wanted. Too many Russian leaders had threatened punishment for failing to meet impossible deadlines, rather than offering rewards for good performance. And when those officers—and scientists—had failed to meet the deadlines, they'd been executed...depriving Russia of their services. Who knew how much had been lost because of a merciless response to predictable failure?

"Good," she said. She tapped a switch, forwarding him a document. "I'll be splitting the task force into three subunits. Resolute One will be under my personal command; Resolute Two will be yours; Resolute Three will be under American command, once the Americans finally decide which flag officer they're throwing to the wolves. Each subunit will be built around a fleet carrier, giving us options for both offense and defence."

"Understood, Admiral," Shields said. His eyes peered at something outside the range of the holographic scanner. "You intend for us to take the offensive?"

"Ideally, I'd like to get the task force to Zheng He in one piece," Svetlana said. "But afterwards...yes, I feel we should find a way to take the offensive. A little aggressive raiding up towards Falkirk, perhaps even Alien-One, will knock the virus off balance and give us time to assemble our fleets."

She smiled to herself. Her training officers had once told her that no one went wrong by constantly planning ways to take the offensive, even when there was more to be gained by holding a defensive line than attacking enemy targets in an engagement that might be costly even to the victors. And she *liked* the idea of going on the offensive, of taking her ships into enemy territory and making *them* panic for once. She had always regretted that her duties during the Second Interstellar War had kept her from the operation that had ended the war.

"The virus may not care," Shields cautioned. "And we still know nothing about just how many ships it actually deploys."

"All the more reason to keep it off balance," Svetlana said. "We cannot give it time to bring its full might to bear against us."

She smiled, inwardly. She agreed with his concern, although she knew better than to admit it where her superiors—or political enemies—might hear her. In the past, Russia had been able to use an immense superiority in men and materiel to grind the enemy down—tactical sophistication had been very much a hit-and-miss affair, when simplicity was the key to victory—but now...it took years to build a fleet carrier. She couldn't afford to throw Russian starships into a meat grinder when they were, effectively, irreplaceable.

And yet, that would be seen as an act of cowardice, she thought, curtly. *They'd prefer me to get a lot of men killed rather than withdraw from a battle I couldn't win.*

"We will start our exercises once we depart," she said, calmly. "I want both simulated and live-fire drills, despite the costs. We need to fight as a unit."

"Agreed," Captain Shields said.

"Make no mistake," Svetlana said. "This is not a pleasure cruise. I will not be hosting dinners"—she thought she saw a flicker of approval on his face—"and we will not be exchanging visits. Instead, we will be working to prepare for combat."

"Easy training, hard mission," Captain Shields quoted. "Hard training, easy mission."

"Better to get the bugs out before the enemy takes advantage of them," Svetlana agreed, calmly. She leaned back in her chair. "Do you have any concerns you want to raise?"

"Merely a concern about the enemy ships bypassing Zheng He and attacking further into the Human Sphere," Captain Shields said. "We *know* they somehow managed to reach Earth."

Svetlana frowned. "And we still have no idea how they got to the surface," she said. "There were no attacks in Russia, but that doesn't mean the virus isn't *there*."

She frowned. A handful of her uncle's political enemies had pointed out that the virus was unlikely to survive in Russia. It needed hot and wet atmospheres to thrive, not a bitterly cold environment. Svetlana had disagreed, reminding them that Britain was hardly a tropical country; the virus might not have been able to spread through the atmosphere, but the infected had still been able to carry out their mission. The virus could remain active in a person's body, even if they couldn't spread it by coughing and breathing. It wouldn't care about the temperature outside as long as the host body was alive.

"We'll proceed with care," she said, "and keep flanking units in place at all times."

Her eyes narrowed. "And are you *sure* that your ship isn't infected?"

Captain Shields looked back at her, evenly. "We decontaminated the ship thoroughly, once we returned to Sol. The crew was tested, time and time again. The virus was simply never offered the chance to infect and subvert a crewman before he could be tested. No one was infected."

"But you cannot be absolutely sure," Svetlana mused. She'd seen the reports. The virus was apparently capable of making bodies for itself. Absurd shambling blobs, to human eyes, but bodies nonetheless. Her imagination provided a whole series of grim images, of tiny alien creatures slipping into the tubes while the starship's crew was distracted by their larger cousins. "What if you're wrong?"

"We do tests regularly," Captain Shields said. "We are fairly sure we're secure."

"I hope you're right," Svetlana said. The FSB had gone nuts, trying to locate anyone who might have been infected before they had a chance to spread the infection. She supposed she should be grateful. A combination of her family's influence and the FSB's distraction had ensured that she hadn't been assigned a personal *zampolit*. "And what about Captain Campbell?"

"I have been *assured* that she doesn't carry *active* viral material within her bloodstream," Captain Shields said. He spoke with a hint of irritation, as if he'd answered the question before. "And we are keeping her under close watch. If that changes—if there are any reasons to suspect that she has been...subverted—we will obviously take steps."

The FSB would have killed her and burnt the body, just to be sure, Svetlana mused. She'd read the briefing papers very carefully, but they'd left her unsure if the British had come up with a workable concept or if they were clutching at straws. *They wouldn't have risked turning her into a weapon.*

She pushed the thought to one side. She had no qualms about killing the enemies of the *Rodina*—and she wouldn't waste her time mourning traitors—but she was reluctant to penalise someone who hadn't committed a crime. No one had known, back then, about the virus...and even if they had known, it might have been impossible to take precautions. The poor bastards had been prisoners! The virus could have simply infected them and that would be that.

"Keep a very close eye on her," she ordered. She took a long breath. "We'll speak again, before departure. Until then...inform me if anything changes."

"Yes, Admiral," Captain Shields said.

His projection vanished. Svetlana kept her face impassive. The British officer had been cooperative, but...she sighed, inwardly. The briefing had made it clear that she had to be careful, that she had to be in command, that she had to be *seen* to be in command...and that, most importantly of all, she could not *lose*. Mother Russia didn't just demand success, she *needed* success. Svetlana wouldn't have been given her command if there had been any more qualified candidate.

She leaned back in the chair, taking a moment to gather herself. She was a national hero as well as an international hero, but she knew as well as anyone just how fickle the public could become if she failed. They wouldn't have the chance to judge her properly, let alone make up their own minds. They'd…they'd be told what to think by their betters. Her lips twitched as she remembered the absurd gyrations the propagandists had gone through when they'd tried to present her to the public. Svetlana was a military hero… no, a *heroine*…a heroine who'd defied the role laid down for her by convention and law…she snickered, remembering how the wretched bastards had tied themselves in knots. They could hardly say they *disapproved* of her military career, but they couldn't exactly approve of her leaving her feminine calling either. No wonder they'd gone a little mad. Svetlana had read reports claiming that she'd not only beaten the Tadpoles on her own, as if she hadn't had a starship under her feet, but defeated the Lord High Tadpole himself in single-combat.

And the fact that there isn't a Lord High Tadpole isn't allowed to get in the way of a good story, Svetlana thought. It had its amusing side—and its useful side—but, on the whole, she just found it irritating. *How many people actually believe the crap those assholes shat out?*

She dismissed the thought with a shrug. It didn't matter. All that mattered was winning and making herself—and, by extension, Russia—look good. And if that meant taking the credit for someone else's work, she'd do it. It wasn't honourable, but there was no time for honour.

Because if the truth comes out, she thought as she walked to the hatch, *our days might be numbered.*

• • •

Stephen stepped back from the holographic projection, feeling—for the first time since he'd heard the news—a glimmer of optimism. Admiral Zadornov was clearly competent as well as practical, something that was definitely a relief after dealing with too many officers who couldn't find their fly buttons without a map and a dedicated navigator. She might be Russian—and *very* well-connected, if her file was to be believed—but that didn't mean she was bad at her job. Indeed, she was a genuine international hero.

And she wants to go on the offensive, Stephen thought. Admiral Zadornov was hardly alone in wanting to take the offensive—Stephen couldn't help thinking that Lord Nelson would have approved—but too many people were only concerned with stemming the alien onslaught, rather than launching an offensive of their own. *And if she's right...*

He shook his head. If only the virus was predictable! He didn't know—no one knew—which way the virus would jump, if pressed. It was easy enough to guess what a human would do, or one of the allied races, but...the virus might do nothing. It might halt its offensive. Or it might alter its plans and drive straight at Earth. There was simply no way to know.

And it doesn't care about the lives of its people, he thought, morbidly. It took months to train a naval crewman...years, really, for them to learn everything they needed to know. The virus, on the other hand, was really a single entity. It didn't need months to train before it went to war. *We can kill a hundred of them for every one of ours and still lose the war.*

Stephen sat down, then shook his head. There was no point in fretting over what couldn't be changed, not now. They were committed. All they could do was hope for the best...

...And prepare, whatever it took, for the worst.

CHAPTER ELEVEN

THE ENEMY STARFIGHTER appeared out of nowhere.

Richard swallowed a curse and yanked his starfighter to one side as a hail of plasma bolts tore through the space he'd been a second ago. The enemy pilot was good, damn him. He twisted on his axis, trying to bring his plasma guns to bear on Richard's starfighter as Richard rolled out of control. *The bastard probably set his guns on automatic,* Richard thought as he struggled to regain control. It was hard to pull up just enough to take a clear shot before it was too late. A plasma bolt slapped his drive field as the enemy craft exploded into a ball of flame.

"Nice shot," Monica called.

"Concentrate on your flying," Richard snapped back. A dozen—no, a *hundred*—alien starfighters were materialising, flying out of an asteroid belt that looked like something from an unrealistic movie. "Don't give them time to overwhelm us."

The alien starfighters closed, impossibly fast. Richard snapped orders as the wing reassembled, bracing themselves for impact. They'd been caught on the hop, but they reacted well, forming up into a defensive formation as the enemy craft opened fire. Richard bit down a curse as plasma bolts burned through space and tore into his starfighters. The pilots slipped into evasive patterns—he'd been amused to discover that every other space navy had its own version of the drunken pilot manoeuvre—and returned fire. A handful of enemy starfighters vanished from the display as human blasts struck home. But they just kept coming.

They can afford to spend themselves freely to bring down just one or two of our pilots, he thought grimly, as one of the German flyers exploded into a fireball that was rapidly extinguished by vacuum. *And there's no way we can afford to trade one-for-one without running out of pilots.*

He gritted his teeth as he saw an emergency beacon glittering in the display, only to be silenced by an enemy plasma bolt. The pilot had been lucky to eject—it was commonly acknowledged that the ejection seats were designed more for PR than actual use—but her luck had run out seconds later. Data from the earlier engagements had made it clear that the virus targeted emergency beacons as well as communications platforms and recon drones, although it was unclear if it was picking off helpless pilots as part of its strategic vision or if it was just targeting anything that happened to be putting out radio noise. Richard had heard that Nazi pilots during the Battle of Britain had been encouraged to shoot British pilots who bailed out of their aircraft, just to ensure that those pilots weren't simply given a new aircraft and sent back into the fight, but there was no way to know if the virus had bothered to give the issue any actual *thought*. It was impossible to tell if it *knew* the human pilots were a dwindling resource. It certainly didn't have any trouble churning out new pilots…

It must know, Richard thought. He picked off an enemy starfighter with practiced skill, then diverted another from killing an American pilot. *It could have interrogated the people it infected and drained them of everything they know.*

"They're pressing our flanks hard." Fritsch sounded worried. "We can't take these losses."

"No," Richard agreed. Another swarm of alien starfighters emerged from the asteroid field and headed straight for the fight. "I think we've worn out our welcome."

"I'll say," Francesca Bernardello said. She sounded reassuringly calm. A former test pilot would be used to far worse situations. "I haven't had such an unwelcoming reception since I took my childhood friends to meet my aunt."

"Hah," Richard said. "All ships, fall back on the fleet. I say again..."

He swallowed another curse as the alien starfighters pressed their advantage, firing thousands of plasma bolts at the retreating human craft. The odds of any single bolt finding a target were very low—the starfighters were tiny against the immense vastness of space—but the virus could afford to spend them freely. Rear-mounted guns shot back as the human starfighters started to run, but their targeting was far from accurate. Richard allowed himself a cold smile as two alien starfighters were picked off. The gods of the umpire computers were with them today...

Or perhaps not, he thought, as the alien starfighters accelerated. Someone had set the pursuit speed firmly on *impossible. They're going to catch up with us.*

"Damn," Monica said, mildly. "We're not going to make it back to the flak guns, are we?"

"We'll see," Richard said. The alien starfighters closed rapidly, firing as they came. He'd made a mistake, he realised grimly. He should have pressed into the asteroid field or even stood his ground, rather than retreating. They were too far from the fleet to rely on the starships to cover their retreat. "I think..."

His controls locked. The display dimmed, the tactical outline covered by a pair of red-edged words. GAME OVER. Richard silently promised himself—again—that he'd hunt down the bastard who thought that was funny and show him what made *Richard* laugh. His mouthpiece suddenly felt heavy in his mouth, the constant chatter from his earpiece dimmed. He sighed as he watched the rest of the engagement, command constantly moving down the ladder as the alien starfighters wiped out the remaining senior officers. They'd definitely been caught with their pants down and...

I got caught with my pants down, he thought. His lips twitched as he remembered his first instructor, who'd pointed out—graphically—just how badly he'd let himself be sodomised during his first practice flight. The cadets had made bets on just how long it would be before the wanker had a heart attack—Richard didn't think there'd been a single person who actually *liked* the instructor—but he'd had a point. *We simply aren't ready for a real engagement.*

He rubbed his eyes as the remaining pilots were blown out of space. They were good, better than he'd feared, but they weren't a coherent team. Not yet. They'd do well against real aliens, he hoped—the simulated enemies were faster and more accurate than *real* enemies—but they still had their weaknesses. Richard sighed, then pushed back the canopy. He felt so tired and drawn that it was all he could do to stand up and clamber out of the simulator. His legs threatened to collapse the moment he touched the deck. He had to fight to remain upright as the remainder of the simulators emptied. He didn't dare show any signs of weakness. He'd been pushing himself too hard over the last few days.

Shower, he thought. *And then bed.*

He dismissed the thought with a scowl. He was sweaty and smelly, but he didn't have *time* for a shower. He didn't want to admit it, yet...he had to admit he was getting a little old for starfighter operations. A normal career path would have seen him moved upwards, into operations or command, or simply transferred to the reserves, allowing him to return to civilian life. He wondered, absently, if he could somehow get himself busted back down to Flying Officer, then told himself not to be stupid. It was rare for someone to be demoted *that* far down the ladder. It was far more likely that he'd be transferred to an asteroid base in the middle of nowhere and told to stay there. It was almost tempting.

But I wouldn't get to fly starfighters, he thought.

"Briefing compartment, five minutes," he said, once the pilots were assembled. "Move it."

He smiled, thinly, as the pilots hurried through the hatch. Most of them would be heading for the washrooms, if they had any sense. Pilots could urinate in the cockpit—it was one of the little details mysteriously left out of the recruiting brochures—but no one *liked* to use the bags. Far too many pilots remembered the stories about how aircraft and starfighters had crashed while the pilots were fiddling with the tubes. The jokes were appalling, but there was a serious point to them. Better to go while they were on the carrier than in the midst of a fight.

The compartment emptied rapidly. He waited until the pilots were gone, then reached into his pocket and dug out the stim. The plastic injector felt soft against his hand, as if it belonged in a children's playset. Richard hesitated before pressing the tab against his bare skin and pushing hard. There was a brief, uncomfortable sensation—he'd been told the tabs had been deliberately designed to be unpleasant—followed by a rush of energy. The world seemed *sharper*, all of a sudden. It was an illusion—he *knew* it was an illusion—but it was hard not to feel as if he was finally *awake*. He gritted his teeth. He'd wean himself off the stims as soon as the ship was underway. He had no choice.

He took a deep shuddering breath, then forced himself to stand upright and walk through the hatch. The constant humming of the carrier's drives pervaded the air as soon as he left the simulator chamber. It felt new and strange, even hostile. He told himself, firmly, not to be silly. The drives needed to be tuned before *Invincible* left the shipyard. A drive failure was bad at any time, but he hated to think what would happen if the drives failed in the heat of battle. Or even in a transit system, without even a stage-one colony within reach. The Royal Navy would be dreadfully embarrassed if her first assault carrier had to be towed home…

And if the virus spots us, we won't have time to go home, he thought, morbidly. A carrier that could neither fly nor fight would be a sitting duck. *We'll be blown out of space before we realise we're under attack.*

The pilots were chatting to each other—too loudly for his peace of mind—as he strode into the briefing compartment. It was good to see that the various national contingents were breaking down into a single unit, although he'd decided—it felt like an eternity ago—that they would have to keep flying in their national squadrons, just to limit the prospect of a misunderstanding in the heat of battle. He wanted to think the simulations

105

had exposed their weaknesses, giving him time to address them before they were pitched into a *real* battle, but he knew better than to believe it. The simulations weren't real. Everyone *knew* they weren't real. And *that* made it harder for the pilots to take them seriously.

Particularly as we won't be dodging through asteroid belts or trying to put a torpedo down a tiny exhaust shaft so we can blow up a moon-sized starship, he thought, fighting down a sudden urge to giggle. *That never happens in the real world.*

He took the stand and studied the pilots as they quietened. It definitely looked as if a handful of international friendships—and relationships—had formed, although he found it hard to imagine that any of the newcomers had had *time* to do more than eat, sleep and fly endless missions in the simulators. He made a mental note to keep an eye on the situation—he'd have to say something if the relationships started to impinge upon professionalism—and tapped the podium for attention. The last of the chatter died away as the pilots looked at him. Richard felt a spasm of guilt. They were so *young.*

"Well," he said. "That was certainly an interesting disaster, wasn't it?"

There was a low mutter of agreement. He wondered, sourly, just how many of them blamed *him* for the disaster. Richard *had* set the simulator parameters after all, although he'd randomised as much as possible to ensure that *he* was caught by surprise as much as any of his pilots. The system wasn't perfect, but it worked. It helped that they finally had *real* data to plug into the simulators.

"So," Richard continued, after a moment. "What went wrong?"

"We lost," an American pilot said.

Richard had to smile. "Specifics?"

The American didn't lack confidence. "Specifically, sir, we should have stayed closer to the carrier or pushed our way into the asteroid field," he said. "If we'd taken out the enemy base, we might have been able to give the bastards something else to think about."

"Perhaps." Richard kept his face expressionless. It would have worked, in the real world. There were hard limits to how many starfighters could be

based on a carrier, let alone a makeshift asteroid base. But, in the simulator…
he shook his head. The pilots didn't realise it, but they'd been deliberately
sent into a no-win situation. The simulated aliens had an unlimited number
of starfighters at their disposal. "Anything else?"

"We lost cohesion as soon as the senior officers were taken out,"
Francesca Bernardello said, stiffly. "The chain of command was shot to hell."

"That's something we're going to have to work on," Richard agreed,
calmly. "But we may not have the time to do it properly."

"We may need to harmonise pilot training," Darren Vargas said. "Even
a tiny difference can prove fatal."

"Particularly when we're trying to reorganise our squadrons on the
fly," Richard said. It would have been a great deal easier if his command
consisted solely of British pilots, who would have undergone identical training before deployment even if it was the first time they'd flown together,
but…he shrugged. It couldn't be helped. "We're going to have to scramble
the squadrons together randomly and see what happens."

"Which won't be particularly realistic," Fritsch said.

You have no idea, Richard thought, numbly. How many times had *he* had
to reorganise a rapidly-dwindling number of starfighters? Too many…and,
every time, unit efficiency had fallen sharply. They would have improved,
if they'd been given *time. Every bloody simulated reorganisation leaves out the
bloody reorganisation.*

"We have no choice," Monica said, sharply. "Unless you actually *want*
to start shooting down our own pilots…"

A faint chuckle ran through the compartment at the weak joke. Richard
didn't think it was particularly funny. His head was starting to ache in a
manner that suggested he *really* hadn't had enough sleep. He needed to go
to bed, but he was too keyed up to rest. And besides, he simply didn't have
the time. His fingers were already reaching for another stim before he managed to stop himself. He'd already taken far too many for his own good.

"I don't think it will be necessary," he managed. "Instead, we'll start practicing reorganisation tomorrow. And we'll establish new chains of command."

"Ouch," someone muttered.

Richard couldn't disagree. Technically, there was a clear chain of command from the Squadron Leader right down to the lowliest Flying Officer. On paper, there should be no trouble identifying who was in command at any given moment. But, in the heat of battle, it wasn't so easy. The person who took command—who needed to take command—might not be the person who, by the book, *should* be in command. Richard was all too aware of the potential for confusion at the worst possible time. God knew it had happened, time and time again, during the previous interstellar wars. He'd studied the records. The person who *should* be in command sometimes didn't even realise he *was* in command until it was too late.

"We'll practice," he said, although he doubted the simulations would do more than demonstrate the problem. There were just too many ways things could go spectacularly wrong. "And now…"

He glanced around the compartment. The youngsters were looking revoltingly bright-eyed and bushy-tailed, but the older pilots were clearly feeling worn down by the endless simulations. He didn't blame them. Starfighter flying was a young man's game. The stats spoke for themselves. The older pilots were steadily losing their edge.

"Get some grub…and rest," he ordered. He glanced at the chronometer. It was 1700. "We'll resume regular exercises tomorrow. Dismissed."

He turned as the pilots started to hurry through the hatch and blinked in surprise as he saw Commander Daniel Newcomb leaning against the bulkhead. When had *he* entered the compartment? Richard felt his heart sink in dismay, and fought to keep his face impassive. There had been a time when he would have *noticed*, surely. It wasn't as if the XO was a latecomer who was trying desperately to remain unnoticed…

"Commander," he said. It was hard to keep his voice even. "What can I do for you?"

"We'll be departing tomorrow," the XO said. "Or so we have been told."

Richard nodded. The departure date had been moved forward, then put back, and *then* moved forward again so often that he'd privately decided not to take anything for granted until the fleet actually left the solar system. He guessed there was probably yet another update lurking in his inbox. He hadn't had time to check.

The XO leaned forward. "Are we ready to fight?"

Are the starfighters ready to fight? Richard had no trouble understanding what he was *really* being asked. *And what about their pilots?*

"They're better than I've told them," he said, after a moment. He hadn't had time to write proper reports. Thankfully, neither Captain Shields nor his XO had been inclined to complain about the lack. "There are a handful of issues that need to be solved, but we probably don't have time."

"There isn't time for a proper work-up," Newcomb agreed. He sounded contemplative. "But they can fight?"

Richard felt his legs threatening to buckle. He forced himself to stand straighter. "Yes, sir," he said. "They can fight."

CHAPTER TWELVE

"I THINK THE AMERICANS are overcompensating for something," Commander Newcomb said wryly, as they stood on the bridge and watched the task force assemble. "Just how big *is* that ship?"

Stephen had to smile. USS *George Washington* was easily the largest fleet carrier the human race had managed to put into space, larger and more powerful than anything deployed by any of humanity's friends or foes. She carried six wings of starfighters and mounted enough weapons to be a serious threat to anything she encountered, although neither the Americans nor anyone else had solved the problem of constructing a carrier that could also go toe-to-toe with a battleship. Stephen was inclined to think that the Americans had copied *Invincible's* plans and scaled her up a little.

"Big enough to make us look like a minnow," he said, although it wasn't really true. "And visible enough to draw attention from all over the system."

He scowled. He'd never really agreed with the strategists who insisted that the Royal Navy needed to constantly scale up its carriers. The *Theodore Smith* class was barely a decade old, and the planners were already designing its replacements. But Stephen himself wasn't so sure. The larger the carrier, the bigger the target...and the larger the hole in the line of battle if the carrier were to be taken out. A single *Theodore Smith* cost nearly three times as much as a single *Invincible*, giving the Royal Navy more flexibility...it was a simple truth, he reflected, that a carrier could only be in one place at once. Better to have three ships than one...

"The *Overcompensator* class," Newcomb said. "We should have time to test ourselves against her."

"It would be interesting," Stephen agreed. *George Washington* had just been launched. He would be astonished if *something* didn't go wrong during her maiden voyage. The whole idea of a shakedown cruise was to find and fix any problems before the carrier had to go into battle. The Americans were taking one hell of a gamble. "We're still doing repairs, and *they* don't even know their ship yet."

He shook his head. If he'd been in command of the fleet, *he* would have protested the assignment. It was impossible to predict what would go wrong with a newly-launched starship—or when. And *Washington* was the first of her class. Her crew hadn't had the chance to serve on a similar ship. Simple inexperience would lead to all sorts of problems...he put the thought aside. It wasn't his place to lodge protests. Admiral Zadornov was probably grateful to have the American ship. On paper, at least, *Washington* nearly doubled the starfighters assigned to her fleet.

"Never mind," he said. He allowed his voice to harden. "Mr. XO. Are we ready to depart?"

Newcomb's face darkened. "As ready as we can be, Captain," he said. "And better than I'd feared."

Stephen nodded, curtly. It wasn't the ringing endorsement he'd wanted, but no experienced officer could have given one...not when there were still too many issues that required a long stay in a shipyard to fix. *Invincible* was ready to depart, on paper, but...he forced himself to keep his face impassive. Some of the problems could be fixed while they were underway. Others... would just have to be compensated for, as best as they could. The war had taken a desperate turn. It was hard to think of his ship as expendable, let alone the remaining carriers and battleships assigned to the task force, but they were...as long as they bought time for Earth to reinforce her defences and bring new weapons and starships online. And for help to arrive from the allied powers...

"Very good," he said, finally. "Are there any major issues?"

"The lower aft armour is noticeably weak," Newcomb said. "And there's nothing we can do about it."

"Save for coating the plates with dummy armour and hoping the enemy fires dummy torpedoes at it," Stephen said, wryly. The joke had been out-dated well before the human race had begun the conquest of space. "A shame we don't have time to make the *entire* hull look weak."

"No, sir," Newcomb agreed. "But that would probably draw fire."

"We won't *ever* not draw fire," Stephen pointed out. Anyone who knew *anything* about naval tactics would target the carriers first. It was page one of the tactical manual. And there was no sign that the virus disagreed. "Unless *Washington* and *Brezhnev* draw their attention."

"They probably will," Newcomb predicted.

Lieutenant Thomas Morse cleared his throat. "Captain, signal from the flag," he said. "The fleet is to depart in ten minutes, mark."

"Understood," Stephen said. He glanced at the display. "Mr. XO, are the remaining shipyard personnel off the ship?"

"Yes, sir," Newcomb said. "A handful *did* volunteer to stay, but I made sure they were counted off the ship."

Stephen nodded. "A shame we couldn't have taken them with us," he said. "But they're needed here."

He grimaced. It was easy to look down on military personnel who *weren't* starship crew, or starfighter pilots, or even groundpounders. They hadn't volunteered to put themselves on the firing line. But...some of them were nothing more than useless oxygen thieves, but others were vitally important. A trained shipyard worker was more essential to the war effort, Stephen knew, than a random starship crewman. He would do more for the Royal Navy on his shipyard than on a starship. But there was no glory in serving in the rear...

It doesn't matter, he told himself, sharply. *The needs of the service come first.*

"And they probably wouldn't bother with a court martial if we kidnapped them," Newcomb said. "They'd just put us out the nearest airlock the moment they realised what we'd done."

"Quite," Stephen agreed. "It sounds like the plot of a bad novel."

"Or a worse *Stellar Star* episode," Newcomb said.

Stephen turned his attention back to the display. The three carriers were at the centre of the formation, with *Invincible* taking point. Someone would probably make snide remarks about Admiral Zadornov not putting herself in danger, but Stephen knew better. *Brezhnev* wasn't in any less danger than *Invincible*. It wasn't as if they were separated by a few thousand light years. On an interplanetary scale, it wouldn't take more than a few seconds for starfighters—or missiles—to fly from *Invincible* to *Brezhnev*.

And anyone attacking us would have to break through the screen, he thought. The smaller ships had been carefully deployed to ensure that no one could sneak up on the fleet without being detected, with a reserve held near the carriers to cut off anyone who tried to punch through and engage the bigger ships. *We would have plenty of time to launch starfighters before they landed on top of us.*

He leaned back in his chair, contemplating the possibilities. They hadn't had anything like as much time for drills as he'd hoped—*Invincible* and *Washington* weren't the only ships that were being hastily readied for deployments—but they'd worked their way through a handful of simulations. There was no hiding the fleet, if the enemy got a sniff of their presence... he scowled, knowing his concerns had been overruled by higher authority. *He* would have preferred to remain under cloak at all times, but...he shook his head. The Admiralty—or its senior officers—had insisted that human starships should not be seen sneaking around in human space. It suggested a lack of security.

It isn't as if anyone would see us if we were under cloak. Stephen smiled at the thought, then sobered. *And we dare not assume that the virus hadn't sneaked a ship or two through the tramlines already.*

"Captain," Morse said. "Signal from the flag. It's time to leave."

Stephen nodded, curtly. "Helm, take us out as planned," he ordered. A shiver ran down his spine. They'd tested everything—they'd powered up the drives long enough to glide out of the shipyard—but something could still go wrong. "And then hold us in formation."

"Aye, Captain."

The humming of the drives grew louder as they powered up. Stephen tapped his console, bringing up the live feed from the drive nodes. They'd been tuned, he'd been assured, but there just hadn't been the *time* to ensure that they were in perfect harmony. Military-grade technology was designed to allow some leeway—the carrier was capable of flying and fighting with half her nodes shot out—yet…a disharmonic *now* would put additional wear and tear on the drive nodes, something that would come back to haunt them when they went into battle. The irony made him scowl. They finally had a blank cheque to requisition whatever they wanted without having to convince the bureaucrats the expense was actually necessary, but—away from Earth—they couldn't *get* it. There was no way they'd be able to replace a failed node once they left the inner worlds behind.

And we'd have problems doing it anyway, he reminded himself. *It wouldn't be easy to replace a drive node while we were underway.*

"The fleet is moving into formation," Lieutenant Sonia Michelle reported. The helmswoman sounded edgy, as if she were nervous about the risk of colliding with another starship. It was hard for one ship to accidentally ram another, but the danger could never be entirely discounted. "All systems are optimal."

So far, Stephen thought. He would almost have been happier if problems *had* developed. It might have been possible to fix them and catch up with the fleet if they developed before they made the first jump. *But we haven't brought the drives to full power yet.*

He forced himself to relax as the fleet picked up speed, heading for the nearest tramline. A handful of civilian ships were holding position just outside the shipyard's security zone…reporters, he guessed. Or Belters, keeping a wary eye on the fleet. The political situation had grown more poisonous in the last few days, according to the updates from Duncan. Too many accusations of infection—or, worse, open treason—had been hurled in the last few days, with very little in the way of actual *proof*. Stephen hoped it wouldn't turn into something more than angry shouting. Humanity couldn't hope to beat the virus if the situation dissolved into actual civil war.

Maybe that's the real danger. It was a perverse thought, but he contemplated it anyway. There were so many isolated asteroid settlements, from religious communes to tiny mining stations and corporate fiefdoms, that no one could be sure the virus was gone. *We can test for the virus, we can capture or kill any poor infected bastard we can find, yet we can never be entirely sure we wiped them all out.*

The drive hum grew louder, just for a handful of seconds, then faded back into the background. Stephen glanced at the live feed—the power curves were well within acceptable limits—and forced himself to relax. Again. The engineering crew would have sounded the alert if something had gone *seriously* wrong. Instead...he sighed inwardly. He was going to be on edge for hours, if not days. No naval officer was unaware of just how unforgiving space could be, how easy it was to make an innocent mistake that snowballed into utter disaster. And all he could do was keep his guard up, be wary of anything that might start the snowball rolling...and hope for the best.

"Captain." Newcomb's voice broke into Stephen's thoughts. "All departments have checked in. They are all operating within acceptable parameters."

"Good," Stephen said. He studied the display for a long moment. "And our final messages?"

"They're held in the buffer, ready for transmission," Newcomb said. "The tradition lives."

Stephen had to smile. A few short years ago, the final transmissions—the last messages a starship would send before it crossed the tramlines and fell out of contact with Earth—had been a vital part of the navy's traditions, a symbolic cord-cutting when the full weight of power and responsibility fell on a commanding officer like the hammer of God. But now, with the flicker network, it was no longer necessary. A message that would once have taken weeks, if not months, to reach its destination could be there in a few short hours. The boffins were even promising that real-time conversations would be possible within the next few decades...

"The tradition lives," he echoed. It was important to remember that they would still be hundreds of light years from Earth. Hopefully, the Admiralty would remember it too. If they started to micromanage...*that* was going to be a problem in the next few years. He was morbidly sure of it. "Transmit the messages when we reach the tramline."

"Aye, sir."

Stephen forced himself to wait as the fleet crawled towards the tramline, the formation slowly tightening as the flagship issued orders. A civilian would have said the formation was sloppy, Stephen suspected, but it hardly mattered. No one in their right mind would risk a tight formation when they might be plunged into battle at any moment. The risk of a collision would grow considerably higher if the entire fleet had to take evasive action at a moment's notice.

He keyed the display, bringing up the long-range sensors. The solar system hummed with activity, from tiny mining ships prospecting within the asteroid field to giant colonist-carriers transporting vast numbers of people from Earth to their new homeworld. Stephen rather suspected that interest in colonisation had declined over the past few months, as people realised that a stage-one colony world would be almost defenceless if the virus came knocking. The old certainties—that colonists could go underground and hide until their planet was liberated—no longer applied.

And yet, anyone who manages to get in on the ground floor is sure to bequeath a strong estate to his descendants, Stephen thought. *The rewards for paying one's own way to a colony world are huge.*

Sure, his own thoughts answered. *If you live long enough to claim them.*

He pushed the thought aside as his sensors picked up a handful of military ships leaving Earth. It looked as if they were going to Mars, although it was impossible to be sure. The Red Planet wasn't heavily defended—Mars had become a backwater when the tramlines had been discovered—but the virus would have great difficulty establishing a presence on the planet. And yet…the analysts had pointed out, time and time again, that the virus didn't need to care about cost-benefit assessments. It could afford to spend all the time it liked infecting and absorbing Mars.

And it probably knows better than to risk leaving Mars alone, Stephen thought. *The planet might not be an industrial powerhouse, but it isn't completely harmless.*

"Captain," Sonia said. "We are approaching the tramline."

"Signal from the flag," Morse added. "Lead elements are to jump when they cross the tramline. We're to follow on command."

"Understood," Stephen said. "Follow the Admiral's lead."

He braced himself as the tramline grew closer. It was unlikely, according to all the tactical manuals, that there would be an ambush on the other side of the tramline. They were deep within human space, with heavy reinforcements only a few short hours away. It was hard to imagine any *human* strategist proposing such an operation, still less any tactical officer taking the suggestion seriously. Any power strong enough to mount a deep strike mission without risking unacceptable losses wouldn't *need* to. Still, it was best to be careful. No one *really* knew how many ships the virus could afford to lose.

The Tadpoles hit Earth, he reminded himself. *But they thought they held an unbeatable tactical advantage.*

He sucked in his breath. It was hard to believe that a major enemy fleet could have slipped through the defence line and taken up position at Terra Nova, but it was easy to consider a number of possible scenarios. None of them were particularly viable, from a human point of view, yet…there was no way to predict what the *virus* would do. It *had* to know that it needed to take out the human navies to win, didn't it? The Royal Navy didn't have *that* many ships in reserve. It wouldn't take *that* many major losses to cripple the navy and render further resistance futile.

Not that it matters, he thought, as the seconds ticked away. *We can't come to any sort of accommodation with the virus. It would be better to turn our own worlds into radioactive nightmares.*

The timer reached zero. The first ships vanished from the display. Stephen tensed, his eyes slipping to the timer. The ships had standing orders to scan for possible threats, then send a courier back while they secured the far side of the tramline. It shouldn't take long...he was aware, terrifyingly aware, of every passing second. If there *was* a hostile force on the far side, waiting for them, it might *just* have been able to take out the lead elements before they could reverse course and escape. It might...

A yellow icon blinked back into existence. It turned blue a second later.

"Captain," Morse said. It was easy to hear the relief in his voice. "Signal from the flag. The emergence zone is clear. We're to proceed as planned."

"Take us through," Stephen ordered. He allowed himself to relax, just a little. He'd faced the virus too often to be entirely sanguine. There might well be a cloaked ship trailing the fleet from a safe distance. "And then set course for the next tramline."

"Yes, sir," Sonia said. "Jumping...*now.*"

CHAPTER THIRTEEN

ALICE BROODED.

It wasn't something she *should* be doing, she knew. She'd never been particularly introspective, at least until she'd recovered from the first infection. In hindsight, a little more introspection—and forethought—would have kept her from getting into trouble so often at school, although she rather suspected that introspection wasn't considered a desirable trait in a Royal Marine. How many people would throw themselves into a firefight if they had time to think about all the many horrible ways it could go wrong?

She glared down at the latest message from her father, wondering—again—why he thought he had *any* claim on her. She was his daughter, but…he'd murdered her mother. She would have found it easier to forgive a man who had abused her, she thought, rather than a man who had robbed her of both mother and father in a single catastrophic act. He could have filed for divorce, in the certain knowledge the courts would have sided with him. People did *not* cheat on deployed military officers. It was socially unacceptable. It was simply Not Done. Alice's mother would have been an instant pariah…

But at least she would be alive, Alice thought. *And we wouldn't have had to stay with our grandparents.*

She paced the tiny cabin, cursing under her breath. She had never *liked* being still, let alone being forced to wait on the sidelines while others did the work. She hadn't been *ordered* to stay in the cabin, but she was still—technically—on detached duty. She'd been told that she was a mission-critical package, a person who was supposed to be escorted and protected by the marines…a person who could not be allowed to take care of themselves. She muttered a whole string of curses as she remembered the people *she'd* escorted, once upon a time. Who did they think *she* was? The Prime Minister?

The Prime Minister cannot influence alien behaviour, she reminded herself, rather sarcastically. There was a good chance that her life was *more* important than the Prime Minister's. She understood the logic, just as she understood the military necessity. God knew she would have probably made the same decisions herself, if things had been reversed. But it wasn't easy to bear. *Am I just going to stay here until I get to play?*

The terminal *pinged*. She felt a surge of hope as she tapped the screen, which rapidly faded as yet *another* message from her father appeared in her inbox. She clenched her fists, somehow—barely—resisting the impulse to put a fist through the device. Perhaps…perhaps he intended to start a new career as a datanet spammer. She couldn't think of anyone *else* who would have sent so many messages when the lack of a reply should have been more than enough proof that the recipient wasn't interested.

Damn him, she thought.

She sat back on the bed, tiredly. She'd forced herself to look into her father's post-war life, if only to make sure he wasn't in a position to bring pressure to bear on her or her superiors. It hadn't made encouraging reading. Her father had somehow inveigled his way into a Belter polyamorous marriage—the mere *thought* was sickening—and worked his way up to command his own freighter. It was hard to believe that a man who'd murdered his own *wife* could command anything, even himself, but…her thoughts ran in circles. The Belters kept their own law and enforced their own justice instead of relying on planetside courts. Perhaps murdering one's wife was socially acceptable amongst the Belters. Or…she cursed, once again. Maybe they saw the *wife* as the villain because she'd gone behind her husband's back, rather than openly entering a polyamorous relationship. Who knew?

Her wristcom bleeped. "Captain," Patterson said. "Report to Bay One. Immediately."

"Yes, sir," Alice said.

She jumped up and headed to the hatch. *Captain.* That was a joke. Technically, she had the rank...but she didn't have the duties to go with it. She'd been effectively beached. Her record was going to be a nightmare. God knew how she'd be paid. She made a mental note to look into it, then decided it didn't matter. They hadn't *formally* beached her, which meant she should be paid the standard rate. They'd certainly have some problems arguing otherwise if the matter reached a court.

Marine Country was crowded as she hurried down the corridor, glancing from side to side. A dozen marines were working out in the gym while others slept or studied the records from *Invincible's* last voyage. She stepped to one side to allow a platoon to jog past, their leader snapping off a salute without ever breaking stride. She didn't recognise the bootnecks following him. They had to be newly-assigned to the ship. Her heart twisted as she finally admitted, deep inside, that she would never be a normal marine again. There was no way she could ever return to the ranks.

"She's an alien," someone whispered.

Alice felt the back of her neck grow warm in embarrassment. She wanted to swing around and confront the speaker, just as she'd confronted the girls who'd taunted her at boarding school. Slamming her fist into their noses had been very satisfying, even if it *had* earned her an encounter with the headmistress's cane. But it would be a sign of weakness now, one she could not abide. She forced herself to ignore it as she made her way down to Bay One. A handful of marines were waiting for her.

"We just opened the crates," Patterson said. He held up something that looked a practice grenade. "What do you make of these?"

"They look like gas grenades, sir," Alice said. They'd always struck her as slightly absurd, although there was nothing funny about inhaling a lungful of tear gas. "What are they?"

"Stink bombs," Corporal Glen Hammersmith announced, cheerfully. "I feel like a kid again."

"Again?" Tindal smirked. "I have it on good authority you lied about your age when you signed up."

Hammersmith ignored him. "They're stink bombs," he said. "Someone farted into a bottle and..."

"That will do." Patterson spoke mildly, but there was enough command in his voice to make the younger man shut up. "Officially, these are Type-One Pheromone Dispensers. Unofficially, they're...well, *stink bombs*. They're designed to dispense pheromones in all directions."

"I see," Alice said. "The researchers managed to produce something workable?"

"We don't know." Patterson passed her the practice grenade. "The briefing notes weren't very clear."

Alice nodded, sourly. There was nothing particularly complex about stink bombs. They were really little more than a handful of chemicals which were either smelly on their own or produced a bad stench when combined. Schoolchildren could produce them in chemistry labs...she'd heard the stories, although she'd never seen it done. The stink bombs could be produced, then put in storage until they were needed. A pheromone bomb, on the other hand...she hefted the grenade in her hand, thoughtfully. It was difficult to say just how long the pheromones would actually *last*.

"They should work, if the pheromones remain active," she said. The grenade *looked* like a small aerosol, right down to the colour and weight. "But we don't know how long they'll survive in these containers."

"That's the problem," Patterson said. "We cannot afford to go into battle relying on weapons we know to be unpredictable."

Alice nodded in agreement. It was a basic rule of thumb that a device that worked perfectly in the laboratory wouldn't work properly in the field.

There were all sorts of issues that would only become apparent when the new weapon was actually tested in realistic conditions. Normally, the grenades would be tested extensively before being issued to troops who might reasonably expect to go into combat. It was astonishing just how often a minor—and overlooked—factor could make the difference between a successful lab test and a complete disaster in the field.

"The theory is solid." Alice hated to defend boffins, none of whom had ever seen a muddy battlefield, but it had to be said. "The pheromones should trigger a cascade reaction in alien atmospheres. In practice...the results might be a little mixed."

"We might be better off simply venting the atmosphere and watching the aliens freeze to death," Tindal said. "The weapon doesn't seem *that* workable."

"And we have to test it," Alice mused. She had no doubt the weapon *would* have been tested against the infected prisoners, but *that* was hardly a battlefield test. The virus wouldn't be fighting back. "We have to know if it works."

A marine captain, someone she didn't recognise, stepped forward. "It strikes me as a waste of time. Sir."

Patterson glanced back at him. "Captain Anders, I understand your reasoning. But we have to *know* if the pheromone grenades work in battlefield conditions."

"Even a harmless smoke grenade can cause confusion if tossed into a bunker," Alice pointed out. Captain Anders? She'd never heard of a Captain Anders. Newly promoted then, at a guess. She would probably have heard his name, even if they hadn't actually met, if he'd been longer in his rank. "And a few moments of confusion could make the difference between success and failure."

"Yes, but waiting to see if the grenades actually work could *also* make the difference between success and failure," Anders countered. "*Their* success and *our* failure." He snorted, rudely. "How do these things even *work*?"

"When they detonate, the grenades soak the area in alien pheromones." Alice took a breath. "In theory, the pheromones—the very *strong* pheromones—will trigger off a reaction, spreading the pheromones through the air. The infected will actually relay the command onwards to their *fellow* infected. And it will take them some time to realise that it's a false command. Indeed, in a sense, it won't *be* a false command."

"Like an email with all the proper security headers and suchlike," Hammersmith put in, wryly. "Or an order with all the correct command codes attached."

Anders gave him a quelling look. "Yes, but we would question an order to surrender if we received it," he pointed out. "Or a command to remove our armour and strip naked in the middle of the battlefield. Common sense *alone* would ensure it."

"We have common sense?" Patterson smiled. "Why was I not informed?"

"The virus isn't human." Alice took a breath. "It is a single entity spread across millions of bodies. Its *thinking* isn't human. It can no more question a pheromone burst than your rifle could question your decision to fire, even if it's a negligent discharge. *You* might be in the wrong, Captain. Your rifle would *not* be."

"There are risks," Patterson said, flatly. "If there is anyone here who wanted a nice safe life...he's fucked anyway."

Alice had to laugh, although it wasn't funny. Her father's generation had grown up in a nice safe world. The only people who'd seen the elephant were the ones who'd joined the army and been deployed to the security zone. The Royal Navy hadn't seen real action in decades. Now...Earth had been bombarded, uncounted millions of civilians had died, and the virus was running loose. There was no safe space any longer. Really—realistically— the world had never been safe. The military had just never been allowed to believe otherwise.

"Yes, sir," Anders said. "However, I must question the value of these... stink bombs. Venting the ship"—he nodded to Tindal—"would be a far better option."

Tindal made a face. "Can these things affect us?"

"No," Alice said. "To us, they're just stink bombs."

"Even to you?" Anders eyed her, suspiciously. "Could *you* be influenced by these *stinks*?"

Alice felt her temper begin to fray. "I can no more be affected by these devices, *Captain*, than you could have a period. I may *look* like an alien, as far as their senses are concerned, but I do not have the command structures that can—that will—respond to the pheromones. I am immune to them. I can no more read them than I can be influenced by them."

"Are you sure?" Anders glared at her. "You might not *know* you were being influenced."

"I'm sure," Alice said. "The doctors checked and checked again…"

"She has been cleared for active duty," Patterson said. "If she wasn't so…vital, right now, she would be your senior officer."

Anders reddened. "With all due respect, sir, we don't *know* if she can be trusted."

Patterson met his eyes, evenly. "*Captain* Campbell was never actually under alien control," he said. "She was rescued and treated in time to prevent the virus from getting its hooks into her. She then volunteered for a dangerous and experimental medical procedure which destroyed the alien cells beyond repair, allowing her to return to the ship. During her second cruise, she was kept under close supervision and monitored constantly. There was no sign—not even the merest hint—that she was in any way compromised. We have no reason to disbelieve the doctors when they say she's safe."

Alice allowed herself a smile. "If I was under alien control, Captain, would I have taken part in a mission to wreck an alien shipyard?"

Anders snorted, but said nothing.

"We'll be testing the weapon as soon as possible," Patterson said. "However, we will plan on the assumption that they will not be effective in combat."

"Yes, sir," Alice said.

"We'll start tomorrow," Patterson said. "Alice, stay with me. Jon—everyone else—dismissed."

Alice let out a long breath as the compartment slowly cleared. "I take it he doesn't like me?"

"He was on the ground when the virus hit Stonehouse Barracks," Patterson said. "I debriefed him myself, when he was deployed up here. There was no warning at all before the shooting started, he said; no hint of trouble before all hell broke loose. The virus's puppets did their job to perfection."

"And now he's taking it out on me," Alice said. She didn't blame Anders for being paranoid, particularly after his garrison had been attacked, but there were limits. "The hell of it is that he might have a point. We don't *know* how these weapons will work in the field."

"No," Patterson agreed. "But we won't know until we try."

He took the practice grenade back and put it in the case. "Your thoughts?"

"There shouldn't be any need for specialised training," Alice said. She took the papers he offered her and ran her eye down the text. It was painfully obvious that the writer hadn't been a marine—his style was neither brusque nor concise—but it *looked* as though the grenades should function like standard *gas* grenades. "We can just lob them into enemy positions and follow up with explosives if the stink bombs don't work."

Patterson looked pained. "They'll all be calling them *stink bombs* after today," he predicted, sourly. "And then people will stop taking them seriously."

"That will stop after they're deployed, sir," Alice said. "And if they work."

"If they work," Patterson agreed. He closed the case and sat on it. "Do you have any other concerns?"

"No, sir," Alice said. She wanted to ask—to *demand*—to return to active duty, but she knew it was pointless. "I just can't wait to test them in the field."

"No more *personal* concerns?" Patterson cocked his head. "Nothing you want to discuss with a friend, instead of a CO?"

Alice tensed. There was only one thing she might have wanted to discuss and that was…she shivered. Had her *father* contacted Patterson? It was none of his goddamned business, but…if he'd somehow brought pressure to bear on Patterson, it had *become* his business. Or…had one of the monitors alerted him to the endless stream of messages? She wasn't naïve enough to think she wasn't being monitored. Anders wouldn't be the only one who had quiet doubts about her, doubts that couldn't be quelled by any means known to mankind. She'd heard the stories. There had been traitors who had passed an entire stream of lie detector tests because they hadn't *known* they were traitors. They'd believed—they'd honestly believed—they were loyal citizens. But the conditioning they'd been given said otherwise…

"No, sir," she said, finally.

Patterson studied her thoughtfully. "You're still receiving messages from your father."

Alice coloured. "I have no interest in speaking to him. Sir."

"I don't blame you," Patterson said. "And no"—he held up a hand—"I have no intention of *forcing* you to talk to him."

"Sir." Alice paused, unsure what to say. She knew how to accept praise or take a reprimand, but this was different. It was personal. "With all due respect, my private communications are none of your business."

"I tend to agree," Patterson said. His bluntness was almost refreshing. "But not everyone *does*, where you're concerned."

Of course not, Alice thought, sourly. She knew the score. *I had no expectation of privacy from the moment I put the uniform on.*

He straightened. "Talk to him or don't, as you see fit. But it might be better for you—and him—to get some sort of closure before it's too late. My father and I…we didn't talk for a long time. He wasn't the best of men and…I thought myself well rid of him. And then, he died in the war. And there are times…"

The alarms howled. "Shit!"

"Battlestations," Alice said. Her fingers checked her service weapon, automatically. She didn't have a combat station, not now, but she had no intention of sitting around doing nothing. "We're under attack!"

CHAPTER FOURTEEN

"WHAT DO WE HAVE?"

Stephen had been half-asleep in his Ready Room when the alarms began to howl. He'd rolled off the sofa, grabbed his uniform jacket and hurried onto the bridge almost before the XO called him. He hadn't expected to contact the enemy somewhere between Earth and Zheng He, but the possibility couldn't be ruled out. The media seemed to assume that the tramlines were impassable barriers—and he had a feeling that some politicians felt the same way—but anyone who knew anything about deep-space operations knew better. The concept of fortifying the tramlines was nothing more than an impractical joke.

"Seven contacts, three definitely alien," Lieutenant-Commander David Arthur said, as Stephen took his seat. "They're cloaked, but we caught them when they crossed the picket line."

"Too close for comfort," Commander Daniel Newcomb said.

"Oh yes, by far," Stephen agreed. He took his chair and studied the display. "Our status?"

Newcomb didn't have to look at his console. "The CSP is ready to redeploy on your command, sir," he said. "Ready and reserve starfighters are preparing for launch now. All weapons and tactical sensors are standing by."

"They know we've seen them, sir," Arthur said. "The picket swept an active sensor over them."

Pity, Stephen thought, although it couldn't be helped. Newcomb was right. The red icons on the display were too close for comfort. He frowned, unsure what the virus had in mind. The fleet wasn't *trying* to hide its presence. If the virus had wanted to merely keep an eye on the human ships, it could have deployed a single starship to shadow the fleet from a safe distance. Instead, the enemy starships were closing the range rapidly. It wouldn't be long before they were in missile range. *What the hell are they doing?*

His mind raced. The enemy was badly outnumbered and outgunned, as far as he knew. Did they have something new and deadly up their sleeves? Something that would tip the balance of power firmly in their favour? Or did the virus think there was no hope of escape? Or...did it have enough ships to sacrifice a handful just to gather intelligence? There could be more ships, lurking in the endless darkness of interplanetary space. The ships they'd seen might be nothing more than the tip of the iceberg.

And we may never know, Stephen thought.

"Signal from the flag, sir." Lieutenant Thomas Morse sounded excited. "We're to intercept the enemy ships and destroy them."

Stephen nodded. "Launch the ready starfighters," he ordered. For once, there was no shortage of starfighter cover. There was no way to know if the enemy had starfighters too—it didn't *look* as if they'd brought a fleet carrier to the party—but it was hard to believe that they had *many*. None of the sensor contacts looked particularly large. "The CSP is to cover the antishipping strikes."

"Aye, sir."

Stephen leaned back in his chair, feeling the frustrations and fears of the last few weeks slowly drain away. Action was always chancy—he knew it was quite possible that *Invincible* might be blown out of space every time he took his ship into battle—but at least he was doing something. He wasn't sitting on his ass, dealing with paperwork or reading reports of disasters hundreds of light years from Earth. He was going to make the virus sorry it had ever sent ships into human space.

"Our escorts are to flank us," he added, after a moment. A low quiver ran through *Invincible* as she picked up speed. "And prepare to fend off kamikaze attacks."

"Aye, sir."

The display updated rapidly. Seven contacts, four of them very definitely oversized cruisers and a fifth almost certainly a converted freighter. A carrier, probably. He tried to calculate the number of starfighters that the virus could have crammed into the ship's hull, but drew a blank. The virus's nature made it impossible to even *guess* at the figures. It was quite possible that it hadn't bothered to provide more than basic life support for the warm bodies manning its ships. Stephen had served on a converted freighter, back at the start of his career. It hadn't been a comfortable experience—the ship had been so cramped that none of the officers had had enough room to swing a cat—but it was luxury incarnate compared to an alien ship. Stephen had read the reports. The virus didn't seem to give a damn about basic comforts.

And they're still closing on us, he thought, grimly. The alien ships were coming closer, boring towards the centre of the formation. *What are they doing?*

He felt his expression darken. If the virus managed to ram a cruiser into *Invincible* or one of the other carriers...it would be a worthwhile trade. The virus wouldn't care that it had lost a cruiser, but humanity? Stephen knew, better than most, just how badly the Royal Navy had been sapped over the last two decades. There were newer and better carriers on the drawing board, ships that might turn the tide of the war...if they were ever produced. But if the navy couldn't keep the virus from reaching Earth...

"Sir," Newcomb said. "The starfighters are on their way."

"Understood," Stephen said.

• • •

Wing Commander Richard Redbird felt alert—too alert—as his starfighter was catapulted out the launch tube and into space. His eyesight was a little *too* sharp, his breathing a little *too* ragged…he cursed under his breath as his thoughts started to wander, bringing them back under control with the discipline of years in a cockpit. He'd taken the stim only a few minutes ago, barely long enough for it to take effect. He hadn't seen any choice. He'd been tired and cranky after hours of simulations, even *before* the alarms started to howl. He certainly hadn't been in any state to encounter the enemy.

"Gosh," someone said. "This environment is *frightfully* unrealistic."

"As you were." Richard felt a hot flash of anger. Pilots might joke that *real* space was boring, compared to the elaborate asteroid fields and supernovas of *simulated* space, but the enemy ships out there were very real. They didn't have time for stupid jokes. "Form up in squadrons and prepare to attack."

Richard glanced at the live feed from the sensor pickets and frowned. Seven ships…the cruisers were probably *covered* in anti-starfighter weapons, if he was any judge. The virus clearly believed in quantity over quality. He didn't blame it. The virus was smart enough to know that it couldn't match humanity when it came to flying starfighters, so it had decided to swamp the human pilots with hundreds of starfighters and uncounted hundreds of thousands of plasma bolts instead. Getting into torpedo range was going to be a nightmare. The odds of any single plasma bolt hitting his starfighter were very low, but there were a *lot* of plasma bolts…

He bit his lip hard, tasting blood in his mouth. He couldn't afford to let his mind wander, not now. The enemy ships were getting closer, their sensor cloaks stripped away as they passed through the inner picket line. Four large cruisers, two freighters and one ship that looked…*odd*. He couldn't help remembering some of the old interplanetary exploration ships, built in the days before fusion cores and artificial gravity. They'd been strange too, compared to modern ships. The drive section had been kept well away from the rest of the hull.

"It looks like a survey mission," Monica said. "And they're coming right at us."

"They probably want to know what we can throw at them," Richard said. He eyed the alien freighters, feeling a flicker of puzzlement. If they were carriers, surely they should be launching their starfighters by now. The human starfighters were closing the range with terrifying speed. "We won't let them get much closer."

Alerts flashed up in front of him. He almost panicked, his hands twitching uncomfortably, as red icons flared to life. The freighters were launching starfighters...no, they were launching *missiles*. Richard stared, unable to believe his eyes. He'd heard of the arsenal ship concept, back in basic training, but he'd never actually *seen* one. No one had been able to make it work. Missiles were too expensive—and too vulnerable to countermeasures—to be expended so freely. He felt his heart pounding as more and more missiles appeared on the display, the number steadily climbing upwards at a terrifying rate. No human admiral would ever fire missiles so freely. It was unlikely that any commander would have so many missiles on hand.

It took him longer than it should have done to issue the right orders. "Engage the missiles as they come into range," he snapped. "And then form up to engage the enemy ships."

He listened to the responses as the range closed with alarming speed. No *sane* enemy would waste a shipkiller missile on a cloud of starfighters, but accidents happened. Or...he told himself, firmly, that it was unlikely that the enemy intended to use nuclear warheads to wipe out the starfighters. It might be theoretically possible, but the starships behind the starfighters made far more tempting targets. Even the virus had to agree—surely—that taking out a carrier was more important than killing a handful of starfighters. If nothing else, stranded pilots would die in interstellar space when their life support ran out.

His guns started to pound as the missiles swept closer, passing through the starfighter formation and boring onwards towards the carriers. Dozens were picked off, but dozens more flashed in and out of range before they could be engaged and destroyed. Richard swallowed another curse as he glanced at their drives, knowing there was no way they could reverse course themselves and engage the missiles again before it was too late. Missiles didn't have to worry about flesh and blood pilots. They were easily the fastest things in space.

But the gunners will see them coming, Richard told himself. No one had managed to find a way to hide a missile drive. The incoming wave of death might as well have sent a message to announce its arrival. *And the ships will take them out before they slam home.*

He snapped out orders as the squadrons regrouped, leading them towards the nearest alien ship. The cruiser opened fire, just as he'd predicted—it looked as if every last inch of the alien hull was covered in plasma weapons—but its targeting was shitty. Richard glanced at the two arsenal ships—they weren't making any attempt to break off, even though they'd shot their bolt—and dismissed them. They wouldn't get close enough to the human ships to be dangerous. The cruisers were the real problem.

Sweat trickled down his back as the range closed. Alarms howled as plasma bolts flashed by his ship, a handful coming so close that he could practically see them with the naked eye. He corkscrewed in, twisting the starfighter from side to side in hopes of making his position completely unpredictable. The enemy computers *had* to be trying to guess where he'd be, quickly enough to put a plasma bolt in the same place. And then, he was suddenly within torpedo range...

"Fire," he ordered. A dozen starfighters had followed him down, flying through the plasma storm...he tried not to think about the ones who hadn't made it. He didn't know who had lived and who had died. He didn't want to know their names. "I say again, *fire.*"

The starfighter jerked as he volley-fired his torpedoes straight at the alien ship, then evaded a plasma bolt that came within bare metres of his hull. He blinked in surprise, unsure—in his addled state—precisely *what* was surprising. It took him long seconds to realise that the aliens, in defiance of all previous behaviour, were *still* trying to kill the starfighters, rather than engaging the incoming missiles. He heard one of his pilots cry out in horror, her voice silenced by a direct hit. He'd put them through hundreds of simulations, but somehow he'd missed *that*. He tried not to think about the implications as the alien starship shuddered under his blows, falling out of formation a second before it blew up. Spectacularly. The virus couldn't have enough cruisers to trade them for starfighters...could it?

No, he told himself. *It must have been a glitch, or...*

He considered the problem as he issued orders, reforming the squadrons. The virus must have known that its ships wouldn't survive the engagement, once it had realised they'd been detected. There was no point in trying to keep them alive for a few seconds more when they could take out a few more human starfighters. In the short term, trading cruisers for starfighters was a mug's game. In the long term, it might prove decisive. He didn't want to, but he glanced at the overall report anyway. Five starfighters were gone. They wouldn't be replaced in a hurry.

"I think we got them." Monica sounded inhumanly cheerful. "Good shooting, everyone."

"Yeah." Richard cleared his throat and started again. "Very good shooting, everyone."

· · ·

"Impressive," Newcomb said. He sounded as if *impressive* wasn't the word he would have chosen. "That's a *lot* of missiles."

"And they're all coming towards us," Stephen said. The starfighters had barely put a dent in their number. "Tactical, the point defence is to engage as soon as the missiles enter range."

"Aye, sir."

Stephen took a long breath. It wasn't the first time he'd been on the receiving end of more missiles than any human commander would dare to fire—he shuddered to think what the Treasury would say about spending so much money for so little—but it was the first time he'd seen it in a minor skirmish. It boded ill for the future. There was no way *Invincible* and her consorts could reply in kind, certainly not against so few enemy ships. The virus's starships had been wiped out, but they might just have sold their lives dearly.

They must have depleted their stockpiles over the last few months, he told himself. He wanted to believe it. He desperately wanted to believe it. But he knew better. The virus couldn't be *that* alien. It wouldn't have expended so many missiles if it didn't have thousands more in reserve. *How many do they have if they're spending them so freely?*

He watched, calmly, as the missiles swept through the defence perimeter. The escorts opened fire, picking off hundreds of missiles. *They* didn't seem to have been targeted, leaving them free to cover *Invincible*. Stephen wasn't surprised. A handful of destroyers were worthless compared to the escort carrier. The virus would gain more by crippling *Invincible* than by wiping out a hundred destroyers. And yet, as more and more missiles vanished from the display, it grew harder to believe that the virus was *sane*. There *had* to be a point of diminishing returns...didn't there?

The point defence went live, filling space with hundreds of plasma bolts. Stephen kept his face under tight control as more and more missiles died, each one targeted for destruction long before it entered range. Unlike starfighters, missiles tended to follow predictable courses. They were small targets—it still took several plasma bolts to *guarantee* a hit, when plasma bolts were notoriously inaccurate—but they were rapidly worn down. None survived to hit the carrier.

Stephen *heard* a sigh of relief echoing around the bridge as the last of the missiles vanished from the display. The virus had shot everything at them—including the kitchen sink, part of his mind whispered—and lost. Whatever it had had in mind, it had failed. Or had it? The display was empty, but that didn't mean there wasn't another ship somewhere out there, watching them. Stephen could easily imagine a cloaked watcher taking careful note of how the human ships had responded to the brief attack. The next time, the virus would know more about *Invincible's* point defence. It might be able to get a missile—or a whole swarm of missiles—through the defences next time.

And that makes sense, if one has the missiles to spare, Stephen thought. He'd seen the projections, studied the tactical simulations...but he hadn't been prepared for the real thing. Not really. The aliens had fired thousands of missiles in defence of their shipyards, yet...that was different. He'd thought of it as a desperation ploy, not SOP. *If they have millions of missiles on hand, expending a few hundred just to test the waters might be an effective practice.*

"Launch another cluster of recon drones," he ordered. If there *was* a watcher out there, they might as well try to make life difficult for him. "And then recall the starfighters. I want one rearmed squadron ready to launch in twenty minutes."

"Aye, Captain," Arthur said.

Stephen leaned back in his chair, knowing that the brief engagement was only the beginning. They were still deep in human space...they should have been safe. The thought was immensely frustrating. They should have had more time, damn it. But they couldn't count on anything now. If a roving fleet of alien ships had attacked them *here*...

It was possible, he supposed, that they'd simply gotten unlucky. The fleet wasn't trying to hide its passage. The virus could have seen them coming and planned a brief ambush. But that was whistling in the dark. If there was one alien task force prowling though human space, there would be others. Nowhere was safe.

And if they take out the shipyards, we're screwed, he thought. *That would be the end of everything.*

CHAPTER FIFTEEN

RICHARD'S HANDS STARTED SHAKING the moment his starfighter landed on the deck. He stared at them, as if they were weirdly fascinating, as the starfighter was hastily moved through the tubes and into the hangar. His hands no longer felt as if they were *part* of him, as if they were something he'd put on for the occasion and could take off whenever he wanted. He felt…he wasn't sure *how* he felt. His body was drenched in sweat, his tunic clinging to his skin…he shuddered as he heard the cockpit being unlatched from the outside. He knew he should be worried—normally, a pilot would open the hatch from the inside—but it was hard to care. He just wanted to sit and stare at his hands.

Move, he told himself, firmly.

It was hard, so hard, to get any traction. His body felt like a lump of useless flesh. He knew he could move, he knew he could climb out of the cockpit and drop down to the hangar deck, but it was hard to motivate himself. There was a bit of him that felt completely disconnected from the world around him, that no longer gave a damn about the consequences. He'd used too many stims in the last few days. The world felt dull and dead.

The cockpit opened. "Sir?"

Richard forced himself to look up. A pale face peered down at him. A *worried* face…it took him a moment to realise the deckhand was female.

She was pretty, in a way, but she'd cut her hair short and dressed like a man…he told himself, once again, that his mind was wandering. He stilled his hands with an effort, and slowly started to unbuckle himself from the harness. He was damned if he was going to ask her for help. *That* would be far too revealing.

"Sir?" The deckhand sounded worried too, damn her. "Do you need help?"

"I'm getting too old for this shit," Richard muttered. He brushed away her proffered hand, instead forcing himself to stand up on his own. His legs felt like sacks of potatoes. Mouldy potatoes. He wanted to take another stim, but he didn't dare. "I'm coming."

He staggered out of the cockpit and carefully clambered down to the deck. The metal seemed to shift under his feet, forcing him to grab hold of the starfighter to steady himself. It wasn't the first time he'd landed slightly the worse for wear, after hours in the cockpit, but…he shook his head in frustration. He really *was* getting too old for this. His eyes swept the hangar deck, noting the number of pilots grinning like idiots and swapping lies about plasma bolts that had come far too close to wiping them out of existence. The poor bastards felt like vets now, he reminded himself. They'd been bloodied. But they hadn't faced enemy starfighters yet.

The deckhand gave him an odd look. "Was it bad out there?"

"Yeah," Richard managed. "It was bad out there."

He forced himself to walk towards the hatch, trusting in the deck crew to ready his starfighter for the next mission. Captain Shields had ordered a starfighter squadron to be ready for immediate launch…Richard silently thanked all the gods he'd ever heard of that *his* squadron hadn't been chosen for *that* duty. He might have to take his ship out again at a moment's notice, but at least he'd have a few minutes to take a stim or do *something* to force himself to feel better. He didn't dare fly without one, not now. The mere thought made his hands start to shake again. He wanted—he needed—to hit the rack and get a few hours of sleep.

Monica met him at the hatch. "That could have been a lot worse."

"Yes," Richard said.

Sweat poured down his back. His emotions were spinning out of control. Five pilots were dead, but he didn't know them. It was almost a relief, even though he *knew* he should be worried about attrition. He couldn't afford to lose anyone. And yet...he didn't know who he'd lost. They weren't quite *real* to him. He knew there was something wrong with that attitude, but...

Monica eyed him, concerned. Richard winced, inwardly. If there was anyone who might realise that something was wrong with him, it was Monica. She'd known him for...it felt like years. It was strange to realise that it had barely been a year or so. He wondered, briefly, what would happen if he went to the doctor and asked to be put on sick leave. The doctor might agree, but...Richard shook his head. There was no replacement waiting in the wings, no one who could take his place. And he refused to seek leave when it meant abandoning his pilots. *That* would be the ultimate failure.

He almost stopped—dead—when he realised she'd led him to the briefing room. He'd forgotten...he glared at her back as she walked into the compartment, struggling to resist the urge to turn and run. A debriefing... of *course* there would be a fucking debriefing. His thoughts ran in circles, remembering the days when debriefing had meant something very different. It might be almost preferable to *the* debriefing. His lips twitched. A giggle almost escaped. Captain Shields would have a lot to say about the *other* kind of debriefing, none of it good. Starfighter pilots had a lot of latitude, but not *that* much.

The pilots still looked cheerful as he strode into the briefing room. Richard felt a surge of hatred, mingled with envy and a grim awareness that their cheer would soon be gone. It wouldn't be long before it dawned on them, if it hadn't already, that five of their comrades were gone. They would never be seen again. Richard would have to clear out their lockers, box up their possessions and...he bit his lip, once again. He would do it. He would carry out his duty until he could carry it out no longer. He would *not* let his people down.

He tapped the podium for attention. "That was our first real engagement," he said. The pilots looked back at him, their expressions sobering

143

as they realised what it meant. They'd popped their cherries, alright. It was the morning after now. "We were lucky."

A low murmur ran through the compartment. Richard ignored it.

"There were no enemy starfighters," he said. "We don't know why."

"They could be off trashing Earth right now," someone said. "Or…"

Richard glared him into silence and continued. "We lost five of our fellows breaking through their point defence," he said. "Five pilots are dead… and more will follow. It would have been a great deal harder if we'd faced enemy starfighters. I will be saying that time and time again. It would have been a great deal harder if we'd faced enemy starfighters."

He wondered, morbidly, how many of his pilots would *truly* get it. They felt themselves invincible. The deaths might shake them, or they might not. Richard had lost count of how many of the youngsters had died simulated deaths. The simulations were good, almost *too* good. It was easy to come to believe that death meant nothing more than restarting the simulation.

"We will discuss the engagement endlessly tomorrow," he added. "By then, the tactical staff will have analysed everything we did. They'll tell us, with the benefit of hindsight, everything we did wrong. Until then…those of you assigned to the reserve, go get some sleep. The rest of you, grab a shower and wait in the ready room. We could be attacked again at any moment."

He took a moment to survey the room. It was sinking in now, he saw. The confident faces were slowly darkening as they realised—finally—that anyone could die. Richard found himself wondering who would be the *next* to die. An American? A German? An Italian? Or perhaps one of his own pilots? He kicked himself, mentally, a second later. They were *all* his pilots. He had to take care of them.

His hands started to shake again. He clasped them behind his back.

"If you have questions, we'll address them later," he concluded. "Dismissed."

Monica caught his eye as the compartment emptied. "What now?"

Richard glanced at the duty roster. Technically, Vargas was the duty officer, but Vargas and his squadron were sitting in the launch tubes, ready to catapult themselves into space at a moment's notice. Someone else would have to command the ready fighters. Monica? She was the best candidate. He knew he couldn't take command himself.

"You'll take command of the ready fighters," he said. "I need to catch some sleep."

"A good idea," Monica said, tonelessly. "You look terrible."

"Probably," Richard said. He tried to smile. He had the feeling it looked more like a grimace. "I'll see you later."

"Later," Monica echoed.

Richard nodded, then forced himself to turn and stumble down the corridor to his tiny cabin. It was growing harder and harder to think clearly... no, he knew he *wasn't* thinking clearly. His mind kept going back to the warnings attached to packets of military-grade stimulants. In theory, they could be used constantly; in practice...it wasn't advised. The long-term effects could be disastrous. Addiction was the least of them. He shuddered, remembering the drug rehabilitation clinics he'd been told about at school. The addicts were treated like criminals. They even had permanent blots on their records.

And they weren't endangering anyone but themselves, he told himself as he opened the hatch and stepped inside. *They were still treated for drug abuse.*

He sighed as he lay down on the bed. He wanted—he needed—another stim. He could feel the craving gnawing at him, insisting—demanding—that he take another. And another. He cursed his own mistake as he closed his eyes. One stim was harmless. Two...three...they were probably harmless too. But how many had he taken? He didn't know. He didn't want to know.

His body was tired. His mind even more so. But it still felt like hours before he finally fell asleep.

• • •

"A fascinating engagement," Admiral Zadornov said, as her holoimage sipped a glass of tea. "And really quite revealing."

Stephen took a sip of his own tea. "Yes, Admiral," he said. "If they were prepared to arm a relatively small squadron with so many missiles..."

He didn't have to finish the sentence. He'd read the reports from the tactical analysts. They might have used five words where one would do, and added so many caveats that it was sometimes hard to follow their logic, but in general they agreed with his conclusions. The human race was in deep shit.

"They might well have been trying to close the range when we spotted them," he said, quietly. "Or they might have been trying to gather intelligence."

"My spooks"—Svetlana smiled, coldly—"think it was the latter. The virus has every interest in knowing what reinforcements are being sent up the chain. And how we might react to threats."

She studied her tea thoughtfully. "Any *normal* enemy would have learned a great deal from our reaction," she mused. "But what did the virus learn?"

"We have to assume the worst," Stephen said. "They might well have figured out the gaps in our defences. We came very close to taking a direct hit or two."

He took another sip of his tea. It was standard operating procedure, in peacetime, to deny potential enemies any insights into the full capabilities of military technology. It wasn't uncommon for a cloaked ship to be spotted, then ignored as long as it didn't move closer...in hopes of convincing the ship's crew that they hadn't been detected at all. There were ships and technologies, Stephen knew, that had never been shown to humanity's alien allies. He believed—quite firmly—that the aliens, allied or not, did the same. It was never easy to forge ties with non-human races. Who knew what incident would lead to another war?

But such niceties couldn't be tolerated in wartime. Someone was probably going to argue—Stephen was *sure* someone would argue—that he should have let his ship be hit a couple of times, rather than reveal the full capabilities of his point defence weapons and sensor arrays. It was the kind of absurd concept he'd expect from an armchair admiral, the kind of idiot who'd assume there was long-term advantage to be gained from short-term vulnerability. Stephen knew better. A single hit in the wrong place might cripple—or destroy—his ship. *Invincible* was tough, but not *that* tough. He wouldn't risk taking a hit if there was any other alternative. No sane commanding officer would do otherwise.

"And they may be able to take advantage of what they learned," Svetlana said. "Of course, it would be hard to tell what they *already* know…"

"Unfortunately true," Stephen agreed. "They've had plenty of opportunities to watch our hardware in operation."

And someone will argue that we showed them something they didn't already know, his thoughts added. Backbiting was disturbingly common in government. *And no one will ever be able to prove otherwise.*

Svetlana waved her hand, dismissing the subject. "We will continue on our course to Zheng He," she said. "It is unfortunate that we cannot pick up speed."

"Yes, Admiral," Stephen agreed. The warships could move faster, if they were prepared to leave the freighters behind. They couldn't take the risk. "We may arrive, only to discover that the system is already under attack."

"Or fallen," Svetlana said. "But there's nothing we can do about it."

Stephen allowed himself a moment of admiration. He'd met admirals who fretted endlessly about matters that were out of their hands, issues that couldn't be changed no matter what they did. Their tendency to micromanage was driven by a fear of losing control, control they'd never really had. Svetlana, on the other hand, didn't seem inclined to waste time worrying about things she couldn't change. There was no way to speed up without paying an unacceptable price and that was the end of it.

And someone will say she made the wrong call, if it blows up in our face, Stephen thought, grimly. *There's always someone willing to nitpick from hundreds of light years away.*

He winced, inwardly. The First Interstellar War had forced the Admiralty to do something outsider observers had considered impossible: change tactics in a hurry. The Bombardment of Earth had done a great deal of damage, but it had also focused a few minds. But the Anglo-Indian War had been fought on a very small scale, while the Second Interstellar War had taken place far from Earth. Humanity's very existence had never been under threat. Now...now the virus had taken the war right into humanity's very body. The handful of attacks on Earth might be signs of a far greater threat.

"We proceed," Svetlana said. "*Invincible* and her escorts will stay on point, for the moment. If you detect any further alien contacts, engage at once. We'll try to deny them any further intelligence."

"We could cloak," Stephen pointed out. "Or try to conceal at least *some* of our strength."

Svetlana looked impassive. "It would cause confusion and delay," she said. "And half the freighters can't cloak."

And someone would probably accuse us of trying to lure the virus into attacking, Stephen mused. *It wouldn't be a bad idea if we were sure of victory.*

"No, we keep it simple," Svetlana said. "And we push on at best possible speed."

"Understood, Admiral," Stephen said. He wasn't sure it was the right decision, given the potential options on the table, but he understood her reasoning. "If we spot the bastards, we'll give them hell."

"Make sure you do," Svetlana said. "I want them to know we won't stop fighting."

She raised a hand in dismissal, then tapped her wristcom. Her holoimage vanished. Stephen nodded to himself as he turned his attention to the endless series of reports. His ship had performed well, with a minor handful of exceptions. None of them were a surprise. Two sensor nodes—hastily replaced before their departure—had failed in combat and had to be replaced again. The engineers weren't sure *why* they had failed, but promised they'd find out once the fleet was back underway. A tactical officer had added a note about starfighter performance, warning that the pilots hadn't been quite up to scratch...

Which isn't too surprising, Stephen thought. He made a mental note to read the report later, along with the debriefings from the flight deck. *We all got flatfooted by those missile ships.*

He checked the rest of the reports, then stood. There was nothing particularly urgent in his inbox, just...more and more reports. His time would
be better spent inspecting his ship, after a brief nap. Paperwork could wait.
He checked the status display—there was no sign of any more alien ships
within sensor range—and walked to the sofa. A quick nap and then...it felt
wrong to be napping when they might be attacked again at any moment,
but there was no choice. He needed to be rested when the next attack began.

The virus knows we're coming, he thought. If he'd had any doubts, the
brief engagement had laid them to rest. The virus had had plenty of time
to send a message back to its forward bases before commencing the attack.
And it has more than enough time to prepare a proper welcome.

CHAPTER SIXTEEN

"THIS IS FUCKING RIDICULOUS," Captain Jon Anders said. "Just... *look* at it!"

Alice resisted the urge to point out that Anders, like every other senior officer onboard ship, had been offered a chance to comment on the design before the engineers had started to turn the concept into reality. The Royal Marines knew better than to allow designers without combat experience to start work on hardware without input from the men who'd have to take it into combat. She had to admit that the breaching pod was an experimental hodgepodge—and quite unlike anything else the marines had deployed over the years—but it was still the best solution to their problems. Or, at least, the best solution to their problems so far.

"It could be worse," she said. "It could be a giant passenger shuttle that would be visible from the moment it launches right until it gets blown into dust."

"Yes, I suppose it could," Anders snapped. "But *this* is a disaster waiting to happen."

Alice shrugged. The engineers had taken a standard worker bee, the type of tiny maintenance craft that could be found in any shipyard, and turned it into a conical landing craft designed to land on an enemy hull, burn its way into the interior and allow the marines to flood inside before they could be stopped. The official version would be much neater, she was sure, but the one in front of her would do. It would get her and a handful of escorts onto an alien ship...assuming, of course, that they didn't get spotted on approach and blown out of space.

And we won't have to wear armour or protective suits, she thought. *There won't be a moment when we are exposed to vacuum.*

"I seem to recall that *every* new idea was greeted with howls of outrage from the traditionalists," she said, sweetly. "If they had their way, we'd still be swimming in the sea instead of evolving legs and walking on dry land."

Anders jabbed a finger at the landing craft. "And what will happen if this...this piece of shit gets sighted before it manages to land on an alien ship?"

"We die." Alice took a breath. "What happens when a standard assault shuttle gets spotted on approach too?"

"At least the passengers might have a chance to live," Anders pointed out. "*You* will be dead."

Alice looked back at him, evenly. "I am aware of the dangers, Jon. But can you see any alternative?"

Anders glared. "You are going to be walking onto an alien ship wearing fuck-all and you expect to survive? You expect to take control? What next? I have boobs, you must obey?"

"I smell nice, you must obey." Alice put rigid controls on her temper. It wouldn't do to assault a fellow marine, particularly an officer. There were too many senior men who disliked the idea of female marines for her to take the risk. Besides, she had to set a good example for the men. "If this works, we wind up with an alien ship. And more prize money."

"And if this fails, you wind up dead." Anders didn't sound convinced. "And that will be the end of you."

Alice wondered, briefly, what would happen if she decked him. Technically, she was on detached duty...which wouldn't stop Major Parkinson from chewing them *both* out for brawling like common squaddies. Or drunken spacers on leave. Maybe she could convince him to get in the ring with her. God knew marine officers were not allowed to let their skills fade, once they reached high rank. They were expected to keep fit as long as there was a chance they might lead troops into combat.

"I know the risks," she said. "I *told* you I know the risks. And I ask, again. Do you have a better idea?"

"No," Anders said. "But I don't like the thought of throwing away lives, either."

Even my life? Alice rather doubted it. *You might be happier if I died in that landing craft.*

She pushed the thought to one side. There was no point in disputing the simple fact that their plan *was* risky. There was nothing they could do to mitigate the risk. Anders was right about that, if nothing else. She would be unarmoured—effectively unprotected—if the landing craft sprung a leak. The thought made her snort. Her instructors had always based their emergency decompression training on having the right equipment close at hand. If the trainees didn't, they'd pointed out, they were dead.

"If you don't have the right gear within reach, and if you don't know how to use it," they'd said, "take your last seconds to bend over and kiss your ass goodbye."

"It should work," she said. "And if it doesn't..."

"Madness," Anders said. "This whole scheme is madness."

Alice felt her temper begin to crack. "Do you have a better idea? Really? Because, as far as I can see, all you're doing is whining about something that might *save* lives."

"Something that hasn't been properly tested," Anders said.

"We're testing it now," Alice said. "This isn't a tank on Salisbury Plain. How the *fuck* are we meant to test this under anything like realistic conditions?"

She met his eyes. "A few seconds should be enough to tell us if it works or not," she added, curtly. "If it doesn't work, we proceed with storming the ship the old-fashioned way."

"And you'll be dead." Anders shook his head. "The whole plan is suicide."

Alice blinked in surprise. Anders was no coward. He had a long and honourable record. He wouldn't have been promoted if he hadn't impressed his sergeants along with his direct superiors. There was no reason to believe that he was lacking in moral fibre. And yet, he was opposing something that might save lives? She shook her head a moment later. She'd done enough work with experimental gadgets to know that something would normally go wrong before the kinks were worked out. Testing something new in a combat zone was always a gamble. Risk was one thing. Unnecessary risk was quite another.

"I know the dangers," she said, firmly. "And if it fails, it fails."

She glanced inside the landing pod, noting how the engineers had based the interior on a starfighter cockpit. The occupants would be held firmly until the craft had burned its way into the enemy ship, at which point they'd be hurled down the shaft and...straight into an alien environment. The thought made her shiver, even though it wouldn't be the first time she'd boarded an alien ship. There was no way to know what they'd encounter until it was too late.

And if all our guesses about the interior are wrong, she reminded herself, *this whole scheme might not get off the ground.*

It was a worrying thought. One of the boffins she'd met during her debriefings at the biological warfare research lab had compared the virus to a hermit crab. It didn't make anything for itself. It didn't have a style, from the blocky and functional starships that humanity produced to the weirdly melted designs favoured by the Tadpoles; it merely took over captured ships and converted them to its cause. The ship they'd captured on their previous mission had been dissected, piece by piece. The boffins had concluded that the virus had infected the ship almost as much as it had infected the crew. In theory, Alice's pheromones could spread through the ship without hindrance. In practice...

Well, that's something we're going to have to find out, she mused. *If the virus realises what I'm doing, it may have time to devise countermeasures.*

154

"Well, good luck," Anders said. "If I were in command, you'd never be allowed to do this."

"Good thing you're not in command," Alice said, stiffly. She was fairly sure that Anders would have refused to accept her, even if she'd never been infected. "We'll start training tomorrow."

"Yes," Anders said. "You asked for volunteers?"

"Eventually," Alice said. She'd intended to go alone, but Major Parkinson had vetoed that idea. He'd insisted that she needed an escort, one that could cover her long enough to start pumping out pheromones. "And I had more than I could handle."

Anders made a face. "And are you sure you can handle it?"

"We'll find out," Alice said. She grinned at him. "I need to brush up on my unarmed combat training. You want to meet me in the ring?"

"I suppose I don't have a choice." Anders gave her a nasty look. "See you in ten?"

"Yeah," Alice said. She'd trapped him. If he declined her challenge, he'd look like a coward; if he accepted it, it would be *de facto* admission that she *was* his equal. She felt her grin widen at the thought. If Anders wanted to hold back in the ring, she'd make him eat a couple of his teeth. "I'll be there."

She watched him go, then turned back to the landing craft. It was a gamble—Anders was right about that, damn him—but one she had to take. There was little else she could do. She wouldn't be returning to the ranks, not now. She knew, technically, that she should report back to the biological warfare lab and offer them her services, but she couldn't stand the thought. She wanted to be doing something, not sitting around like a schoolgirl who had an excuse note to keep her out of sports. She wanted...

At least I proved myself, she thought as she headed for the hatch. Before her, there had been no female Royal Marines. Now, at least, anyone who wanted to follow in her footsteps would find it a little easier. A little. Male or female, commando training was punishing beyond belief. She had never seriously considered SAS Selection. Breaking *that* barrier might have been beyond her. *They can't say I failed because of a lack of moral fibre in myself.*

She walked down the corridor and into the training compartment, feeling a flicker of dismay as she realised they had an audience. Major Parkinson and a couple of marines were watching as Anders set up the ring, his face grim. Alice wondered, briefly, just what they'd said to each other before she'd arrived. Major Parkinson was old enough to know that some disputes needed to be settled physically, but he wouldn't be pleased if one managed to render the other unfit for duty. There were few things modern medicine couldn't cure—her heart twisted as she remembered that the virus was one of those things—but none of them could afford to spend a few days in sickbay. Captain Shields would not be pleased.

Major Parkinson nodded to the ring. Alice took a moment to gather herself, then stepped over the line. There were no ropes. She hadn't seen them outside formal boxing rings for inter-military contests, when the Royal Marines would compete with the Paras and SAS for the military title. Combatants were meant to be careful not to step across the line… or to let themselves be thrown across it. She'd been told it was meant to promote spatial awareness, but she had a feeling the *real* reason was to give someone a chance to back out if they felt they were overmatched. *That* would be embarrassing.

Of course, being punched out of the ring would also be embarrassing, she thought. *He's probably stronger than me…*

She dropped into a combat stance and assessed her opponent. Anders was nowhere near as big as some of the soldiers she'd seen—an artilleryman she'd met once had been *huge*—but he was strong and wiry. Fast too, unless she missed her guess. He would have been training alongside his men for months, ever since he got promoted. He might not be a martial artist—someone who set out to win awards as well as combat qualifications—but he wouldn't be a slouch either. Of course not. He was a marine.

Major Parkinson blew a whistle. Alice waited, curious to see if Anders would make the first move. If he didn't like the idea of women in combat, he might hesitate to hit her…she felt her lips twist at the thought. She was a *marine*, damn it. If she hadn't been able to stand the thought of being hit, she wouldn't have put herself in a position where she *could*—no, *would*—be hit. Her instructors hadn't hesitated to put her through hell, trying to force her to quit. She was damned if she was letting him treat her like a shrinking violet now.

And I don't want him to wind up looking like an ungallant fool either, Alice thought. She'd met too many men who thought they had to protect women. Perhaps she would have taken that more seriously if her father hadn't been such an asshole. *Protect* was sometimes nothing more than *control. I don't want to undermine him…*

She lunged forward, snapping out a wicked punch. Anders darted back, evading her blow, then hurled himself at her. Alice dodged, refusing to grapple with someone who was almost certainly stronger and fitter than her. She might lose, but she wasn't going to lose by having him push her out of the ring. Losing was one thing; looking like an idiot was quite another. She saw a faint smile cross his face, a second before he threw a punch of his own. Alice evaded it with an effort, trying to jab through his defences. Only an idiot would willingly *take* a punch on the assumption he'd survive the impact. She'd seen too many badly-done fight scenes to have any respect for their producers.

Anders closed with her again, trying to pummel her. Alice dodged, watching for an opening and throwing a punch as soon as she saw one. Anders twisted, grunting in pain as she struck his arm. Alice darted forward, only to realise—too late—she'd made a mistake. Anders struck her side, hard. Alice staggered, forcing herself back. Anders hesitated, then pushed forward again. Alice aimed a kick at his groin. It would have gotten her sent off, if she'd done it at school, but Anders merely twisted. Her foot struck his bottom.

Someone cheered, loudly. "She kicked his ass!"

"Silence," Major Parkinson ordered.

Anders let out an odd sound—it took Alice a moment to realise that he was trying not to laugh—and waited. Alice glared at him, readying herself. She was in pain, but she'd been in pain before. She hadn't been hurt that badly. It wouldn't take *that* long to recover. Anders scowled, then advanced slowly and warily. Alice felt a flicker of sympathy. He wanted to win, but he'd lose respect if he didn't beat her fairly. She might gain more credit from a vicious defence than he would for an easy victory.

He leaned back, just for a second, then came at her again. Alice twisted, then closed herself, their hands and feet snapping back and forth as they fought. She heard the sound of spectators exchanging bets, the odds rising and falling as...a blow struck her shoulder, sending her crashing to the deck. She rolled over to avoid a sharp kick, bracing herself for another. It never came. Instead, Major Parkinson blew his whistle. The cheers and boos from the spectators came to an abrupt end.

Alice blinked. *What?*

She looked down, feeling her cheeks heat. She'd rolled over the line. Technically, she'd lost. Technically. Anders looked as irked as she felt, although she wasn't sure why. He hadn't won completely, but...he hadn't lost respect either. And she'd left a nasty mark on his cheek. Anders shrugged, then held out a hand. Alice hesitated before taking it and allowing him to help her to her feet. She didn't have any hard feelings towards him, at least. She was more annoyed at herself.

"An interesting fight," Major Parkinson said. He dismissed the spectators, driving them out of the compartment before continuing. "I trust you two will work together in the future. Properly."

"Yes, sir," Anders said.

"Yes, sir," Alice echoed. She wondered, again, what Anders had told Major Parkinson before they'd started the fight. A grudge match? It wouldn't be the first time, even though it was technically against regulations. It was astonishing how many problems were quietly settled through fisticuffs. "If you don't mind, I need a shower."

"And both of you are to get checked out by the medics," Major Parkinson said. It was an order, however phrased. She knew better than to ignore it. "And I expect this to be the end of the matter."

Alice nodded, then headed for the hatch. Her body was aching, with pains in a dozen places, but she felt good. She'd lost, yet…it had been her mistake. She hadn't been pounded to within an inch of her life. Anders was probably relieved. There had been no easy way for him to win without looking bad. She felt a pang of annoyance, mingled with amusement. She'd met worse people at school. There had been a boy who'd been so intent on touching her inappropriately that he'd dropped his guard. She still smiled when she thought about it.

She stepped into her cabin and frowned as she saw her terminal. There was another message from her father, just waiting for her. She stared at it for a long moment, then reached out to delete it. Whatever he had to say, she didn't want to hear it. And yet…

Maybe I'll talk to him soon, she thought. She drew back her hand. This time, she'd keep the message. She'd look at it later, when she had time. *And then I'll see what he has to say.*

CHAPTER SEVENTEEN

"JUMP COMPLETED, SIR," Lieutenant Sonia Michelle reported.

"Local space is clear," Lieutenant-Commander David Arthur added. "We appear to be alone."

Stephen sucked in his breath. He hadn't *expected* to be ambushed, the moment *Invincible* and her escorts jumped into Zheng He, but he'd had the feeling they were being followed ever since the first brief engagement. There had been a handful of sensor ghosts, all too far away to be chased down and positively identified…the fleet had stayed on alert for weeks, even though nothing had happened. He couldn't help feeling as though they were wearing themselves down even before they went into battle.

"Send a formal signal to System Command," he ordered. "Inform them that we have arrived."

"Aye, sir," Lieutenant Thomas Morse said.

Stephen watched, grimly, as the display started to fill with icons. Zheng He had been a going concern for nearly forty years, the colony established well before the First Interstellar War. The Chinese had struck lucky, he admitted wryly. Their first survey had suggested that Zheng He was on the end of a tramline chain, but—after the First Interstellar War—it had become clear that there were three *more* tramlines within the system. They'd had the inside track on developing them, through both possession of Zheng He and a surprising amount of military muscle. It might have led to conflict if the tramline chain had been the only one open for further expansion.

He felt his expression darken as he silently compared the sensor readings to what he'd seen the *last* time he'd passed through Zheng He. There were only a handful of asteroid miners—*visible* asteroid miners, he reminded himself—moving through the asteroid field, probably mining raw materials for the mobile shipyards and factory ships. The remainder would have been withdrawn, he was sure, or gone into hiding for the duration. The Chinese had been in the middle of developing the asteroid belt when the new threat had materialised. It had to be frustrating to have to shut down operations at a moment's notice, but it was better than the alternative. The powered-down facilities and ships might survive long enough for the system to be liberated, if the virus attacked. Stephen—and everyone else—knew that it was only a matter of time until the virus did just that.

And it won't have had any trouble downloading and interpreting data from captured datacores, he thought, grimly. Spacers had strict orders to wipe and destroy datacores if there was a chance of them falling into enemy hands, but he knew better than to assume they'd *all* been destroyed. *Dezhnev* alone could have told the virus *precisely* where to send its invasion fleets. *They already know where to find the MNF when they want to resume the offensive.*

Newcomb stepped up beside him. "The remainder of the fleet has jumped," he said, quietly. "We have arrived."

"Pity there won't be any time for shore leave," Stephen muttered back. The crew had been worked hard over the last few weeks. The combination of constant maintenance and repair work—and going to battlestations the moment they picked up the slightest *hint* of enemy contact—had taken a toll. He was all too aware that the crew might be becoming blasé about potential threats. The sensors had cried *wolf* so often, it was hard to remember that there were *real* wolves about. "I'm surprised the virus hadn't attacked the system already."

"It has to be bringing up supplies and reinforcements." Newcomb sounded thoughtful. "Even if it doesn't have to *pay* for warship hulls and missiles and whatever else it wants to bring to the party, it still has to drag them all the way from its forward bases to…well, *here*."

"True," Stephen agreed. "And it *did* take months to launch its first offensive after it knew there was something to attack."

He scowled at the thought. His critics had charged him with *starting* an interstellar war. He'd done everything right, according to the book, but… that hadn't been enough to silence *everyone*. The virus wasn't interested in talking—and it didn't look as if it *could* be diplomatic even if it wanted to be—yet…his family's enemies hadn't stopped making political hay out of the whole affair. He supposed he should be grateful. If the virus had launched an immediate offensive, it would have been a great deal easier for his enemies to portray the virus as responding to unprovoked aggression.

And it might have outrun its logistics if it tried, Stephen reminded himself. *That might not have worked out too badly for us, in the short run.*

"Captain," Morse said. "The MNF has responded to our signal. They're welcoming us to Zheng He."

Newcomb cleared his throat. "Nothing from System Command?"

"Not yet, sir," Morse said. "System Command may have been shut down for the duration."

Probably, Stephen thought.

He felt a moment of sympathy for the colonists. Zheng He was reasonably well-developed, for a colony world that was only forty years old. It was quite possible the administrators had ordered everyone to go to ground, at least until the crisis was over. He wondered, grimly, just how many colonists would die even if there wasn't an invasion. The Chinese would have done everything in their power to make the colony self-sufficient—no one wanted to be hauling grain across hundreds of light years—but it wouldn't be easy to keep farming the land while trying to hide from watching sensors. Humanity's orbital sensors were extremely good. Stephen had seen them track individuals trying to sneak out of the Security Zone. He dared not assume that the virus's sensors were any less capable. It might be impossible for the colonists to hide for long.

We'll do our best to keep the colony safe, he told himself. *But our best might not be good enough.*

"Signal from the flag, sir," Morse said. "We're to rendezvous with the MNF as quickly as possible."

Stephen nodded. "Helm, plot a least-time course."

"Aye, sir," Lieutenant Sonia Michelle said. Her fingers danced over her console. "We will link up with the MNF in five hours."

Newcomb glanced at his commander. "Quickly enough to prevent them from throwing an offensive through the tramline?"

Stephen shrugged. There were now two major human formations in the system. The virus *could* mount an immediate offensive, in hopes of smashing one formation before the two fleets could combine into one, but the timing would be tricky. There were few *human* commanders who would bet everything on such a risky gamble, if only because the attacking fleet might be unable to disengage in time to escape the *second* fleet. But would the virus take the risk? He mulled it over for a long moment, then shrugged again. There was nothing they could do to minimise the risk. If the virus attacked, it attacked.

He sat back in his command chair and contemplated the tactical situation. The MNF wasn't in close orbit around Zheng He itself, somewhat to his surprise. Instead, it was positioned to block any offensive that might come through the tramline and either head towards the planet or drive onwards to Earth. The handful of orbital industrial nodes orbiting Zheng He might well be important to the colony's continued growth, but—compared to the warships—completely expendable. Judging from their reduced energy emissions, Stephen rather suspected they were being shut down. The MNF would have orders to retreat, if faced with overwhelming force, rather than dying bravely in defence of Zheng He. There was no point in trying to keep the nodes active when they—like the asteroid miners—could be preserved for the post-war world.

Or used to support a resistance, if we lose, Stephen thought. It was possible to conceal an entire civilisation in an asteroid belt, with a little effort. The

Chinese government might be reluctant to try—the more repressive governments had discovered that giving so much autonomy to the asteroid Belters could be dangerous—but the colonists might have other ideas. *Something of humanity might survive in space if the virus overwhelms the planets.*

He put the thought aside as the hours ticked away, the MNF slowly growing larger on the display. It had once been the most powerful formation the human race had deployed, but now…he felt the bridge go quiet as the realities of war sank in once again. Thirty powerful ships—cruisers, battleships, fleet carriers—were gone, wiped from existence. Others were badly damaged, their power emissions so low that—under other circumstances—they would have been scrapped. Worker bees and drones buzzed around them, doing everything they could to patch up armour, emplace new weapons and repair the damage before the enemy ran them down again. Stephen knew, with a certainty that no longer surprised him, that they were running out of time. The virus wanted—*needed*—to take Zheng He as quickly as possible.

And we still don't know where the other tramlines lead, Stephen thought. The Chinese hadn't surveyed the new tramline chains, not yet. It might be too late now. *The attack could come at us from anywhere.*

"Their starfighter formations are a mess," Newcomb commented, quietly. "They're not deploying anything like enough fighters to cover themselves."

"They were shot to pieces in the brief engagement," Stephen said. He could imagine the chaos that had gripped the fleet. The carefully-ordered formations would have been shattered, forced to reconstitute themselves at a moment's notice. Lines between national squadrons would have been erased, putting pilots from a dozen different nations into scratch formations that were completely unprepared for battle. "And they probably couldn't have drawn more from Zheng He."

"A shame the Chinese didn't build a bigger naval base," Newcomb said. He made an odd little sound. "We would have objected, wouldn't we?"

"Score one for Amalgamation," Stephen said.

He didn't relax—not completely—until the two fleets finally combined into one. The two datanets linked together, following an extensive exchange of security codes to ensure that neither fleet had been infected and compromised. Stephen wasn't entirely sure he trusted the protocols—he was grimly aware that the virus could make a mockery out of security protocols, simply by infecting people who knew how to bypass them—but there was no alternative. They couldn't board the MNF and check *everyone* for the virus, not now.

They knew the dangers, Stephen reminded himself. *They won't have let themselves be infected.*

"Signal from the flag, sir," Morse said. "Admiral Zadornov requests that you join her for a conference call."

"Understood." Stephen stood. "Mr. XO, you have the bridge."

"Aye, sir," Newcomb said. "I have the bridge."

Stephen nodded, then strode through the hatch into his ready room. Admiral Zadornov's staff were already setting up the holoconference, hazy figures blurring in and out of existence as security handshakes were exchanged and secure laser links established. He took his seat, silently accepted a cup of tea from his steward and waited. It seemed like forever before a handful of blurry figures finally snapped into existence. Stephen sucked in his breath as Admiral Weisskopf appeared in front of him. The dark-skinned American looked as if he'd been through hell. His fleet had been shot to pieces and forced to retreat, leaving uncounted thousands of civilian colonists to their fate.

He had no choice, Stephen thought. He'd seen the contingency plans, the ones that had been devised before humanity understood the full power and horror of the virus. Admiral Weisskopf had had strict orders to preserve his fleet, even if it meant abandoning colonists to a fate worse than death. But it couldn't have sat well with him. *And even if he comes to terms with what he did, someone will say it could have been different.*

"Admiral," Weisskopf said. He sounded tired and worn. "And Captain... Stephen. Good to see you again."

"Likewise," Stephen said.

"We need a status update," Admiral Zadornov said. "How many of your ships can fly or fight?"

Admiral Weisskopf looked pained. "Right now, roughly a third of my ships are in no condition to fight anything more dangerous than an unarmed freighter. They could be repaired, with a proper shipyard, but"—he shrugged, elaborately—"we have to send them home. The remainder are better off, particularly if you can cover us long enough to make some essential repairs, yet…we're short on starfighters and quite a few other things. The base here simply doesn't have the facilities to support us."

"We brought emergency supplies," Svetlana said, briskly. "My staff will be in touch. We can start distributing them as soon as we work out a proper schedule."

"We have one," Admiral Weisskopf said. "We worked it out once we knew you were coming."

Svetlana nodded in approval. "Then we can start distribution at once," she said. "Right now, however, I need to know your intentions."

"Intentions?" Admiral Weisskopf chuckled, humourlessly. "My current intention is to repair my fleet, hopefully before the bastards launch another attack. Before you arrived, we knew—I knew—that we were screwed. I'm surprised they didn't finish us before you got here."

He took a moment to centre himself. "The administrators wish to evacuate as many colonists as possible. I intend to detach my damaged ships, cram them to the gunwales with refugees and send them back up the chain. It won't be a very comfortable voyage, but at least they'll be out of the firing line."

"Unless they run into alien raiders," Stephen said. "We were briefly attacked on the way here."

"It can't be helped," Admiral Weisskopf said. "The colony was…ah, a *planned* colony. It cannot go underground easily, not without condemning a sizable chunk of the population to starve. They never anticipated needing to face such a threat."

"No one did," Stephen said.

Svetlana nodded. "In that case, we'll begin evacuation at once."

"The majority of the evacuees are already ready," Admiral Weisskopf confirmed. "They just need shuttles and marine escorts. Conditions downstairs...are not good. The administrators fear they might lose control."

"Unsurprising." Svetlana's face was completely unreadable. "I suppose the real question—now—is which of us is really in command?"

"I haven't been given any specific orders," Admiral Weisskopf said.

And you might be recalled to Earth at any moment, Stephen added, silently. *There will be people looking for scapegoats...*

He kept his face under tight control. Technically, Admiral Weisskopf was senior to Svetlana; practically, Admiral Weisskopf had lost a major battle. It was hard enough to convince major governments to put their forces under someone else's command at the best of times, let alone after the prospective commanding officer had failed to cover himself with glory. The only officer to transcend national interests had been Theodore Smith, and *he'd* died in the First Interstellar War. And he'd only ever commanded a small task force.

"Very well," Svetlana said. "Once the evacuees are packed away, I intend to start a policy of aggressive raiding up towards Alien-One. We need time. The more we can delay their next offensive, the better. Do you have any objection?"

"No." Admiral Weisskopf smiled, slightly. "Anything that can buy us time is welcome."

Stephen leaned forward. "Did you attempt to monitor their operations?"

"They've been moving forward slowly, establishing positions on the far side of the tramline," Admiral Weisskopf said. "So far, they haven't mounted any major raids on this system. We think—we *think*—that they've outrun their logistics chain, but we don't know for sure. I simply didn't have the numbers to test the theory."

"The timing is unfortunate," Svetlana agreed. "If we'd been here earlier"—she shook her head—"it doesn't matter. Hopefully, we can put some stress on their logistics and hold them at bay long enough for reinforcements to arrive. And then we can start thinking about taking the offensive ourselves."

"Making them react to us for a change." Admiral Weisskopf bared his teeth. "That would be *very* satisfactory."

"Yes, sir," Stephen said.

"But, right now, our priority is to hold Zheng He," Svetlana added. "Our raids will be designed to minimise our exposure."

She smiled at Stephen. "*Invincible* will take the lead, of course."

"Yes, Admiral," Stephen said. "We will be honoured."

"We will also draw up contingency plans for when they attack the system," Admiral Weisskopf stated. "They will give us a very hard time, given half the chance. We cannot afford another long-range missile engagement."

"No," Svetlana agreed. "However, we do have very good point defence. We can—we will—make it very difficult for them to slam a missile into our ships."

"That's what I thought," Admiral Weisskopf said, flatly. "And they fired so many missiles that they managed to get a handful through the defences and hit their targets. If they manage to combine decoy drones and ECM with their missiles…"

"Or if they start using missiles as antistarfighter weapons," Stephen added. "We may find ourselves at a serious disadvantage."

"Then it is all the more important that we take the offensive as quickly as possible," Svetlana said. "As soon as the colonists are evacuated, we will start raiding their systems. And, when this system is heavily reinforced, we can start punching our way up to Alien-One. It has to be a key system."

"Perhaps," Stephen agreed. Alien-One was heavily defended. The combined might of every human—and allied—navy would find it a very hard target. "It must be. But we don't know how many key systems the virus has."

"Then we will deprive the bastards of at least *one*," Svetlana said. "We can win. We just have to hold on long enough to win."

"Damn straight," Admiral Weisskopf said.

CHAPTER EIGHTEEN

"IT LOOKS JUST LIKE ANY COLONY WORLD," Corporal Glen Hammersmith commented, as the shuttle flew towards Zheng He's spaceport. "I was expecting something a little more...*exotic*."

"You might have to wait another fifty years," Alice said. There *were* a handful of classically Chinese buildings at the heart of the colony, according to the briefing notes, but the vast majority of structures were either prefabricated barracks that had been produced on Earth or simple wood or brick houses that had been built locally. "It takes time for a colony world to develop a style of its own."

She keyed the sensors, studying the live feed. The Chinese had designed and built a single large city, rather than hundreds of tiny settlements that would—eventually—be linked into a much larger colony. Zheng He City was surrounded by farms and a handful of factories, giving the colony world every appearance of success, but she couldn't help thinking that it was actually terrifyingly *fragile*. A single KEW would be more than enough to shatter the colony beyond easy repair. She wondered, as the shuttle dropped towards the landing pad, if the colony administrators were really prison officers. It wasn't uncommon for the more repressive governments to keep their colonies under tight control. They feared that the colonists would—eventually—seek independence. But, in keeping the colonists under control,

171

the administrators were ensuring the explosion—when it came—would be considerably worse.

But if they give the colonists too much independence now, the colonists might be reluctant to repay the mother country later, she reminded herself. The issue of just *what* to do with colonists who wanted more local control had plagued every country that had established a colony world. *They have to find a way to strike the balance…*

She dismissed the thought as the shuttle touched down, checking her rifle and stunner with the ease of long practice. The briefing had made it clear that the embarking process shouldn't take that long—the administrators had already prepared the colonists for departure—but she knew better than to take that for granted. People would panic, people would want to leave ahead of schedule…or they'd want to stay, trusting in their skills to keep them alive when—if—the virus occupied the high orbitals. Personally, Alice would have understood—and perhaps even joined—the latter. It was never easy to give up a life and become dependent on charity, even if she had trusted the government to take care of the refugees. Alice remembered, all too well, the chaos that had followed the bombardment. The government hadn't *meant* to starve anyone, or deprive them of medical care—and security—but the damage had been so extensive that untold hundreds of thousands had suffered and died anyway.

"Here we go," Corporal Roger Tindal said. "Watch your backs."

The hatch slammed open. Alice jumped up and led the way to the hatch, taking her first breath of alien air as she jogged out of the shuttle. The air was warm, with a faint taste of something strange…she flinched, just for a second, before remembering the virus hadn't had a chance to establish itself on Zheng He. It wasn't a threat; it was just the world's distinctive smell. The wind shifted slightly, blowing a hint of burning hydrocarbons towards the marines. The Chinese had struck oil, she recalled from the briefing notes. It was uncommon to use petrol-fuelled vehicles on a colony world—electric vehicles were much more efficient—but she supposed the settlers had their reasons. It was much easier to produce and repair the more primitive designs, even if they did pollute the atmosphere. No doubt the settlers intended to replace them once the colony was firmly established.

Alice heard sergeants shouting orders as more shuttles landed, some unloading marines and others readying themselves to receive evacuees. She glanced from side to side, finally spotting the command post hastily being established in a large hangar. A handful of officers were setting up terminals on folding tables, barking orders as if they expected to receive incoming fire at any moment. Her lips twitched with amusement. Major Parkinson had pointed out that it was an excellent opportunity to practice deploying a large number of marines to a planetary surface, without having to deal with incoming fire or the overconfidence that came with *knowing* it was just an exercise. She couldn't help wondering what the Chinese made of it.

They're probably hopelessly confused, she thought. *Everyone* looked confused. Junior officers, NCOs and enlisted men were gathering along the edge of the spaceport, while senior officers from a dozen different nations were hastily trying to organise the different contingents into a coherent force. *We never planned to have to operate as a joint force, let alone deploy to a planetary surface.*

"Captain Campbell, reporting," she said, as she spotted Major Parkinson studying a map of the city. "Sir?"

Major Parkinson looked relieved to see her. "Take your squad to the evacuation camp here"—he tapped the map—"and escort the evacuees to the shuttles. They can go first."

"Yes, sir," Alice said. "Who are they, sir?"

"The administrators and their families," Major Parkinson said. "For some reason"—his face twisted in disgust—"they put themselves at the top of the list."

Alice nodded, curtly. She wasn't surprised. Bureaucrats were the same no matter where they were. She nodded to her squad, then led them out of the spaceport and down towards the evacuation camp. It looked as if someone had converted a transit barracks into a temporary home, although there was a permanence about the structure that surprised her. Transit barracks were, by their very nature, temporary. Most colonist administrators wanted—needed—to get the newcomers out to their final destinations as quickly as possible.

She felt her unease grow worse as she peered further down the road, into the city itself. It looked deserted—there wasn't anyone on the streets, as far as she could tell—but her combat instincts were tingling. Something was badly wrong. She gritted her teeth as she stopped outside the evacuation centre, noting how the guards looked jumpy. It was only a matter of time until they shot someone. She made a mental note never to turn her back on them. She didn't want to be shot in the back by someone who was nominally on her side.

And if they knew what I was carrying, she thought darkly, *they'd probably feel entirely justified in shooting me.*

An administrator appeared out of a side door. "Thank you for coming," he said. He gave her an odd look, as if she wasn't quite what he'd expected. "Did you bring buses? Or trucks?"

"No," Alice said, curtly. "The evacuees are going to have to walk to the spaceport."

The administrator looked shocked. Alice felt her patience rapidly dwindling. The spaceport wasn't *that* far away. It would take longer to load the evacuees into trucks, even assuming she'd *brought* trucks, than it would to have them walk all the way to the spaceport. She silently calculated the distance in her head and smiled. It was barely two kilometres.

"Now," Alice said. "Please."

"But they have all their belongings with them," the administrator protested. "They need..."

Alice swallowed the impulse to haul off and deck him. "We don't have room for anything other than the evacuees themselves," she said, sharply. God! What was so important that it was worth wasting time and risking lives? She would make an exception for a child's toy, but not for...the family jewels. "And if they are not heading up the road in ten minutes, they'll be bumped to the bottom of the evacuation list."

"I'll talk to your commanding officer," the administrator said. "I'll…"

"Get them moving, now," Alice said. "Or I'll turn around and leave you all behind."

Something of her anger must have shown in her face, for the administrator wilted and turned away from her. There was a long moment as he shouted orders into the barracks—Alice wished, just for a moment, that she knew how to speak the language—and then the evacuees started filing out. Alice rolled her eyes as she silently noted the number of men, women and children. The men, at least, could have joined the colonial militia or done *something* useful…couldn't they? Some of them cast resentful glares at her, as if *she* were the reason they had to leave their homeworld. Others—the children, mainly—looked terrified. They didn't understand what was going on, but they didn't like it.

"Leave your luggage behind," she snapped at an elderly man who was carrying a large rucksack. "If you take it to the shuttle, it will be dumped."

The man looked oddly relieved, just for a second, as he dropped the rucksack on the concrete ground. Alice heard *something* smash inside, perhaps a piece of china…she felt a flicker of pity as a middle-aged woman started berating the man for breaking something. She glared the woman into silence, resisting the urge to point out that the china—or whatever it had been—was lost anyway. It was unlikely they'd be able to recover anything from the colony after the war.

The virus might just blow up the buildings from orbit and move on to the next target, she thought, as she watched the line heading up the road. *There won't be enough people left to attract its attention.*

She shuddered, keeping her face carefully blank. Children cried, teenage boys and girls whined to their mothers…they wouldn't have lasted a day at *her* boarding school, not with that sort of attitude. She wondered, absently, why they hadn't done a day of work in their lives, then shrugged. It wasn't her problem. She glanced into the barracks once the administrator had pronounced them empty, snorting at just how *much* luggage had been piled into a corner. She'd *thought* there were too few refugees…

"Captain," Hammersmith said. "Do you hear...?"

Alice's head snapped up. Someone was shouting in Chinese, behind them. She turned, just in time to see the streets suddenly come alive with people. The evacuees were screaming, starting to run...she saw a middle-aged man knocking down a little girl as he fled the growing mob. Alice blanched as her team lifted their weapons, realising just how badly they'd screwed up. They were caught in the open—they were *all* caught in the open—unable even to seek cover without leaving the evacuees to be torn to shreds. She cursed openly, remembering just how many soldiers had been killed by mobs. It wasn't a good way to die.

"STOP," she shouted, knowing it was useless. The mob might not be *able* to stop. The people at the back would keep pushing forward, even if the people at the front had other ideas. She saw a young man fall, only to be trampled by his former friends. She hoped he'd survive, but she doubted it. "STOP OR BE FIRED UPON."

She lifted her rifle and fired a handful of warning shots over the mob's head. Nothing happened. The mob didn't stop. She glanced at her team, then lifted her stunner. They were meant to do nothing more than stun, but a stunned body could still be trampled. She knew, from grim experience, that a stun bolt could *kill* someone with a heart condition or...she shook her head. The only other option was firing bullets straight into the crowd. She shuddered to think how many people would die if she did.

And I don't even blame them for rioting, she thought, grimly. *I'd riot too if my leaders were putting their possessions ahead of me...*

"Fire at will," she ordered, grimly.

The stunner had always felt slightly unnatural to her. There was no recoil, just a faint sensation...so faint that, in all honesty, she'd always wondered if she was imagining it. Bodies started to crumple, falling to the ground; others fell as they tripped over the bodies, hitting the concrete hard enough to hurt. Alice cursed as she realised that many of the stunned bodies were shielding the people behind them from the stun bolts. Bullets would go through flesh and bone like a knife through butter, but a stun bolt? It hit one body and stopped.

She unhooked a gas grenade from her belt and hurled it into the crowd, shouting out a warning and snapping her mask into place a second later. The crowd seemed to waver, just for a second, as the grenade exploded, blowing clouds of smoke in all directions. She braced herself, half-expecting the crowd to snap masks or even wet clothes into place—she'd heard horror stories of mobs that came prepared for non-lethal warfare—but instead it started to come apart. Hundreds of bodies hit the ground, shuddering, coughing and vomiting helplessly. Others fled back to the city, clearly intending to hide before it was too late. She wondered, grimly, what would happen to them. The Chinese authorities wouldn't be very kind.

No one is, these days, she thought.

"Fuck," Hammersmith said, flatly. He wiped his forehead as the wind slowly dispelled the smoke. "I thought they were ready for us."

"They probably thought they were doomed whatever they did," Alice said. "And they wanted a chance to get back at the bastards who abandoned them."

She looked over her shoulder. The evacuees were running now, save for a handful who'd fallen and couldn't get up. A flicker of contempt ran through her. The bastards hadn't even tried to stop and save their families from the mob. But then, she supposed, they might not even have noticed they'd lost someone. She'd seen that before, back on Earth. It was sometimes hard to know someone was missing until it was too late.

"What now?" Hammersmith asked. "Do we carry the bastards to the shuttles?"

"Yeah." Alice glanced into the city. "And then we have to figure out what to do with the others."

She keyed her communicator, informing Major Parkinson of the incident, then started to check the stunned bodies. Most of them seemed to be fine—or they would be, once the effects of the stunners wore off—but a couple were dead and several more were choking as their twitching bodies tried to vomit. She winced as she helped them into the recovery position, silently relieved to see a pair of trucks heading down from the spaceport. They could carry the stunned bodies to the shuttles and toss them inside before they had a chance to wake. It wasn't going to be pleasant—she had a feeling the CO would want to keep them on the planet until the remainder of the population was evacuated—but it couldn't be helped. She tried not to think about the ones who would never wake up.

"Good work," Major Parkinson said, once the trucks had carried her and her team back to the spaceport. The evacuees were being helped onto the shuttles—one took off as she watched—their faces grim as they contemplated everything they were leaving behind. "It could have been worse."

"It will be, if we ever have to evacuate a bigger population," Alice said. Zheng He was tiny, her population practically non-existent compared to Britannia or New Washington or Terra Nova. "It's taking us nearly all of our lift capacity to evacuate a few hundred thousand people. What's it going to be like if we have to evacuate New Destiny or Garland?"

"Bad," Major Parkinson said. "We couldn't even begin to make a dent in the numbers. But that doesn't mean we don't have to try to get civilians out of the firing line."

Alice kept her thoughts to herself. The colonists were totally unprepared for life on a starship, particularly a damaged warship that was in no condition to fight, manned by a skeleton crew who simply didn't have the time or supplies to look after a panicky mob of evacuees. God alone knew what was going to happen if the convoy came under attack. She doubted the battered warships could put up much of a fight.

But the only other option is leaving them here, she thought, morbidly. *And if we do that, the virus will get them.*

"We'll get the rest of the poor bastards off the planet, then leave ourselves," Major Parkinson said. He made it sound easy. It would be, if everyone cooperated. "And then we can take the offensive."

Alice looked up. "We're hitting back?"

"Scuttlebutt says the Admiral is planning something," Major Parkinson said. "And you might have a chance to strut your stuff."

"Or get my ass blown off, sir," Alice said. She smiled, thinly. "How do you know it will be *us* taking the offensive?"

"Who else?" Major Parkinson smiled. "What other carrier is so suited to mounting a limited offensive?"

"Yes, sir."

Major Parkinson shrugged. "You and your team can reinforce the gates," he said. "I want to clear the entire city by tomorrow. After that…anyone who wants to stay can take their chances, as far as I'm concerned. The colony administrators can file complaints later, if anyone survives."

"Yes, sir," Alice said. She remembered the evacuees complaining about being forced to leave their possessions behind and groaned. Some people were just selfish wankers. "I'm sure they'll be complaining about us."

"If they have a chance," Major Parkinson said. "Their government isn't going to be very happy about what happened here, is it?"

Alice thought about it. "Poor bastards."

"Quite," Major Parkinson agreed. "Poor bastards."

CHAPTER NINETEEN

"BOSS, I NEED TO PISS!"

"Go in the bag, for fuck's sake," Richard said. The patrol had been boring, but he was experienced enough to know that boring was *good*. An encounter with the enemy might not be boring, yet it might also be lethal. He would have enjoyed the flight more if he hadn't had to put up with banter and dumb jokes from his pilots. "And keep the channel clear unless you have something to contribute."

He glared at his display, silently daring the pilot to say something—anything—that would give Richard a legitimate excuse for tearing the poor bastard a new arsehole. It had been too long since Richard had taken a stim, too long since he'd felt the surge of energy...his fingers twitched, as if they wanted to pluck the injector tab from his utility belt and press it against his bare skin. He wanted it...he told himself, firmly, that he couldn't have it, not now. A patrol was no time to be distracted, either by banter or semi-illicit drugs. He would be in deep shit if he lost control so far from *Invincible*.

His eyes found the carrier, holding position on the edge of the formation. The last few days had been hectic, with thousands of personnel transferred from the damaged and crippled ships to more spaceworthy vessels. Richard had forced himself to listen to their stories, from the usual bullshit about missiles and plasma bolts they'd seen with their naked eyes to more accurate descriptions of how the engagement had gone. Some of the newer pilots had sobered up—a lot—after they'd heard the stories from Second Falkirk. The virus had kicked humanity's arse. It was sheer luck that the MNF had been able to extract its surviving ships before the entire fleet was wiped out.

And we have to hold position here until we're ready to take the offensive, he thought. He would have killed for a week of shore leave, for him and his pilots, but it wasn't going to happen. The only people left on Zheng He now were a handful of colonists who'd decided to stay behind, against orders. *It isn't as if there's a resort we can go to now.*

He smiled, rather faintly, at the thought. They hadn't seen a single enemy ship since the brief engagement a few weeks ago—unless the handful of sensor ghosts they'd picked up had been more than *just* ghosts—but the operational tempo hadn't faltered. He and his pilots were in danger of overworking themselves through endless training sessions, both real and simulated, although he knew they should be grateful they weren't *really* being shot at. His fingers twitched again, reminding him that he wanted—he wanted, not needed—a stim. It wouldn't be long before tiredness started to lead to mistakes and mistakes started to lead to disasters...he shook his head, savagely. His mind was starting to wander again. He'd zoned out. God knew what would happen if he zoned out in the middle of an engagement...

Ping! Richard jerked up, feeling as if he'd just shot himself with a wickedly-effective stimulant. There was something out there, a sensor flicker that might—that just might—be *real*. His display updated rapidly, suggesting a handful of possible vectors. The intruder—if it was an intruder—was far too close for comfort. It was already close enough to gather intelligence on the fleet's dispositions. Richard hated to think what an imaginative enemy could do with such information. A massive missile strike might be the least of it.

"Form up on me," he ordered. He tapped a command, updating the remainder of the CSP. They'd have to hold the line while his squadron moved to investigate. "Watch your sensors carefully. If you get a sniff of something, alert us at once."

"Apart from myself, you mean?" Flying Officer Kelvin Hameln was already convinced he was the squadron joker. "It was a mistake to have beans for dinner…"

"And maintain radio silence, otherwise," Richard snapped, although he knew it was probably pointless. A passive sensor could detect and track a starfighter from halfway across the system. "We don't want to give them any more data!"

He kept a wary eye on his sensor readouts as he led the squadron away from the fleet. The contact had been brief, but long enough—*just* long enough—for him to get a solid idea of the mystery craft's course and speed. Not, he reminded himself, that that meant anything. A prowling starship under heavy stealth—or cloaked—would be sure to alter course regularly, even if it didn't know it had been detected. And if it thought it *had* been detected—and the flight of starfighters heading towards its position was a dead giveaway—it would either try to escape or go for broke. Richard tensed as the range closed. If there was something out there…

"Contact," Flying Officer Susan Ruben said. A red icon appeared on the display. "One ship, unknown class."

"Shit," Richard said. He'd hoped it *was* a sensor glitch. A contact—a real contact—meant trouble. "I'm going in for a closer look. The remainder of the squadron is to hold position and wait for orders."

His sensors bleeped an alert as he closed the range. The alien starship was still trying to hide, but it had to know it had been detected by now. An alarm sounded as the ship decloaked, the red icon blurring for a seconds before resolving into a destroyer-sized starship. Richard swallowed a curse as the enemy ship twisted, angling towards the fleet. There was a moment when he thought it was going to charge, just like the previous ships had done, before it spat out a hail of missiles at the carriers.

"All fighters, form up on me," Richard ordered. The destroyer was turning away, picking up speed as it headed away from the fleet. Richard silently ran through the vectors in his head. They'd get one shot at the bastard before they put too much distance between themselves and *Invincible*. Their life support packs were dangerously low. "Prepare to engage."

The missiles sliced through his squadron and roared towards the fleet. A handful of pilots opened fire, but Richard's immediate assessment suggested none of them had scored a hit. *That* was odd. The missiles were fast, faster than starfighters, but they couldn't outrun a computer-targeted plasma bolt. Richard put it away for later consideration as the squadron lanced towards the enemy destroyer, evading a handful of plasma bolts as the destroyer fought for its life. There was no way it could outrun a starfighter, but the intelligence directing the craft had no intention of giving up so easily. Richard would have admired it if he hadn't known how dangerous it could be.

This is war to the knife, he thought, as he led the squadron into torpedo range. The destroyer was fighting desperately now, filling space with hundreds of plasma bolts. *Either we exterminate the virus, or it exterminates us.*

"Fire on my command," he ordered. The range closed until he was almost *touching* the enemy hull. "Fire!"

His starfighter jerked as he launched his torpedoes. He yanked the craft to one side, determined that he wouldn't offer the bastard an easy target if the virus put hurting the human race ahead of simple self-preservation. Four other starfighters followed him in, firing their torpedoes then spinning into evasive manoeuvres. The enemy destroyer seemed to shudder as the torpedoes punched home, explosions pockmarking its hull before it lost hull integrity and blew up. Richard checked his scope automatically, looking for signs the crew had managed to get to the lifepods before it was too late, but saw nothing. The virus didn't give a damn about its host bodies. They were...disposable.

"We got him," Hameln carolled. "I want to paint him on my hull!"

"Later," Richard snapped. "Right now, we have to get back to the ship."

And brace ourselves for the next attack, he thought. *It won't be long in coming.*

• • •

"They've crammed all kinds of penetrator aids into their warheads, Admiral," Commander Steven White said. The American's holoimage twitched uncomfortably. "As near as we can make out, they're using a number of different forms of ECM to make it harder to accurately track their missiles. We know they're there, we know their rough location, but it isn't enough to let us *hit* them. The only way to take them out is to fill space with plasma bolts…"

"As if we were facing starfighters, not missiles," Admiral Weisskopf growled.

"Yes, sir," White said. "In the time it takes us to shoot one missile out of space, two or three more have broken through our defences."

"Brilliant," Stephen said, sarcastically. "They came very close to slamming a missile into *Invincible*."

"It will get worse," White predicted. "The more they learn about our countermeasures, the more they can improve their systems to…ah, counter the countermeasures and…"

"Keep raiding the system," Admiral Weisskopf said, cutting him off. "We can't go on like this."

Stephen nodded. The virus seemed disinclined—for the moment—to launch a full-scale invasion of the system, but the handful of pinprick raids were doing more than enough damage. They were steadily wearing down morale and readiness, while hampering plans to evacuate the planet and dismantle what remained of the system's industrial base. The hit the virus had scored on one of the industrial nodes had thrown all of the plans out of shape.

"No, we can't." Admiral Zadornov's image leaned forward. Her voice was very cold. "I propose we move up our plan to send *Invincible* into enemy territory. Captain Shields, when can your ship depart?"

"Two hours, if you let me recall the marine detachments and prioritise their departure from the planet," Stephen said. He would have preferred to recall the marines sooner, but the remaining evacuees had priority. "We are as close to ready now as we can reasonably expect."

"We'll also be stripping a carrier from the fleet," Admiral Weisskopf warned. It had the air of a *pro forma* protest, rather than a serious objection. "We're already short on fighter cover."

"We're converting some of the freighters into makeshift carriers," Svetlana reminded him, although she didn't sound particularly enthusiastic. "At the very least, we'll have more hangar space."

Stephen scowled, but there was no point in objecting when he didn't have a better idea. They simply didn't have the tools, facilities or manpower to do a *real* carrier conversion. The best they could do, with what they had on hand, was to carve out a very basic flight deck that would both launch and recover the starfighters. Stephen had seen the simulations. The converted carriers would work fine until they drew enemy attention. They never lasted very long after they were targeted by hostile starfighters. There was no way they could even defend themselves.

"I'll dispatch the cripples this afternoon, then," Admiral Weisskopf said. "We'll be using drones in hopes of convincing any unfriendly eyes that they haven't been allowed to leave—yet. If the analysts are right, the virus won't question it."

"If," Stephen said. He had his doubts. The *virus* might approve the use of cripples to draw and absorb fire—it was the sort of cold pragmatism he had come to expect from the wholly alien entity—but it had also absorbed a number of human minds. It had to know that humanity would hesitate to throw away a crippled ship—and her crew—if there was any other alternative. "It depends on what it managed to learn from us."

"It may not understand what it learnt," Svetlana pointed out. "No matter how many times people tried to explain what it is like to be human to our alien allies, they never got it. We didn't really understand them either."

Stephen nodded. He could understand, intellectually, that the Tadpoles sired hundreds of children and accepted the ones who survived to adulthood, but emotionally...? It was horrific. A parent who casually killed their own child was a monster. The idea that parents could just throw their children into the wild and expect them to grow up was impossible to accept. But it worked for the Tadpoles. No doubt they found human reproduction to be just as incomprehensible.

"We have to try," Admiral Weisskopf said. He smiled, rather grimly. "And if we fool them into believing that we're stronger than we are, so much the better."

"Make it work harder to ready an assault force to take the system," Stephen said. "It's hard to believe that it would choose to bypass us."

"Quite," Admiral Weisskopf said. "If nothing else, we could raid merry hell out of their supply lines if they left us in their rear."

Svetlana nodded. "Captain Shields, recall your men. You have orders to raid the enemy logistics chain at your discretion, with the sole proviso that you are not to travel more than three jumps into enemy territory. I'll send formal written orders before you depart."

"Understood, Admiral," Stephen said. He felt his heart leap, even though he would be jumping out of the frying pan and straight into the fire. Independent command, again! "If we cruise through the three systems between Zheng He and Falkirk, we should find *something* to kill before we return home."

"And be careful when you do," Admiral Weisskopf warned. There was a hint of pessimism in his voice. "We might lose the system while you're gone."

Stephen nodded. It was a valid point, all the more important because of what had been lost after Second Falkirk. "The flicker network is gone, isn't it? And we were just getting used to *having* it."

"Unfortunate," Admiral Weisskopf said. His lips twitched. "And yes, it is."

"Yes, sir," Stephen agreed. On one hand, the loss of the flicker network meant that it would be difficult for him and his crew to be micromanaged by someone hundreds of light years away; on the other, it meant they'd have no way to know what might be happening *behind* them. He hadn't known, during the mission into enemy space, that Falkirk had been attacked until they'd flown right into the ongoing battle. "If we're operating alone, we'll just have to wing it."

"I can't spare any escorts," Svetlana said. "I'm sorry."

"I understand," Stephen said. He didn't blame her. The fleet was critically weak in small ships, even destroyers and frigates. Svetlana needed to hold them back to cover her fleet carriers. "*Invincible* was designed for solo operations."

"A mistake, perhaps," Admiral Weisskopf said. "But one that might have paid off for you."

Stephen shrugged. "We can talk about the advantages and disadvantages of her class later," he said. There were strong arguments for and against assault carriers, all of which were being tested in fire. If humanity survived, he had no doubt the *next* generation of carriers would incorporate a great many lessons from his experience. "Right now, all that matters is winning the war."

"Agreed," Svetlana said. For a moment, her face turned hard and cold. "Good luck, Captain."

"Aye," Admiral Weisskopf agreed. "Give them hell."

Stephen watched the holoimages vanish, then tapped his wristcom. "Mr. XO, our departure date has been moved up. Recall the marines from the surface, then inform the crew that we will be departing in two hours."

"Aye, sir," Newcomb said. He sounded confident. The planning for the operation had already been completed. "Our destination?"

Stephen allowed himself a smile. "Enemy space."

"Yes, sir."

He checked his terminal, glanced at a handful of messages that could wait until they returned from enemy-held space, then finished his tea and stood. A low quiver ran through the ship as the drive powered up, *Invincible* seemingly pulsing with excitement at the thought of returning to her original function. She was designed to take the war to the enemy, not to serve as part of a bigger fleet or escort a convoy...no matter how important the convoy was to the war. Stephen touched his desk lightly, feeling the quivering growing stronger. His ship was eager to depart.

Smiling, he walked through the hatch and onto the bridge. His crew had prepared for departure already, but the bridge was still a hive of activity as they made the final preparations. They knew—now—that they'd be leaving in just under two hours. He nodded to his XO, then surveyed the bridge. The crew knew they'd be flying into danger—they knew that some of them, or all of them, might not come back—but they were responding with admirable calm. He was proud of them.

And a siege mentality was starting to set in, he thought, as he nodded to his XO. *The mere thought of taking the offensive has done wonders.*

He took his chair and watched the display update. The CSP and marines were recalled, a handful of drones deployed in hopes of convincing any watching eyes that *Invincible* had remained with the fleet…Stephen wasn't sure if it would work, but it was worth a try. The fleet had been redeploying regularly, ships cloaking and decloaking constantly to confuse the enemy… if it worked, the virus might think nothing of *Invincible's* departure. Or… would it even notice at all? Would it even care?

"Don't care was made to care," he said.

Newcomb glanced at him. "Captain?"

"No matter," Stephen said. "Are we ready to depart?"

"Aye, Captain," Newcomb said. "We're ready."

"Tactical, engage the cloak," Stephen ordered. The light dimmed, automatically. He felt a surge of excitement. "Helm, set course for the tramline."

"Aye, Captain."

CHAPTER TWENTY

THERE WAS NO REASON TO FEEL any difference between Zheng He and Margo. There was no reason to think that one star system felt different from the other, as if a star system had a *feel* at all. And yet, the moment *Invincible* jumped through the tramline into Margo, Stephen felt as if he was being watched. He braced himself, half-expecting missiles to start slamming into his ship before his crew had a chance to see their opponent…seconds ticked away and nothing materialised. The display was clear.

"Jump completed, Captain," Lieutenant Sonia Michelle said.

"Local space is clear," Lieutenant Alison Adams said. The sensor officer worked her console for a long moment. "I'm not picking up any radio noise from Margo."

That's hardly surprising, Stephen thought. *The virus has had plenty of time to silence all opposition.*

"The cloak is engaged," Lieutenant-Commander David Arthur reported. "We appear to be free and clear."

Unless someone saw the cloak flicker when we jumped through the tramline, Stephen thought grimly. The odds against it were staggeringly high, but it was—theoretically—possible. He'd been careful to ensure that *Invincible* stayed well away from a least-time course to the tramline, to minimise the risk of detection, yet there was no way to be sure. They might wind up playing a game of cat-and-mouse with a cloaked watcher, without ever being entirely sure that there *was* a watcher. *We have to hope for the best and prepare for the worst.*

"Tactical, deploy sensor platforms," he ordered. "And watch—carefully—for the slightest hint of noise."

"Aye, Captain."

Stephen leaned forward, keeping his face impassive as the display slowly filled with blue icons. Margo itself was a dead world, one that resembled Mars more than Venus; the settlers had started a terraforming program, but it would be many centuries before a human could breathe the planet's air without a mask. The handful of tiny colonies should have had time to go underground, but there was no way to *know*. They knew better than to risk breaking radio silence, particularly if they didn't have any reason to think there was anyone who would pick up the signals. Anyone *friendly*, at least. The virus wouldn't hesitate to drop rocks on the colonies if it picked up a hint of their existence.

And they might not be able to survive underground, not long enough for us to liberate the system, Stephen reminded himself. Margo was too rough a world to attract any of the Great Powers. The settlers were religious dissidents, without the resources they needed to make their world self-sufficient. *They may not survive without supplies from outside.*

He frowned as a red icon snapped into existence, a lone starship traversing the system. A handful of projected vectors formed around the enemy ship—the *presumed* enemy ship. It was unlikely that anyone *other* than the virus would be crossing the system openly, but there *might* be stragglers from the MNF. Stephen watched the vectors get harder, suggesting that the mystery ship had come directly from Falkirk. It was hard to remember, sometimes, that the vectors were pretty much meaningless. The mystery ship could have changed course at any time before she'd been detected.

It had to come from somewhere, Stephen thought. He quietly plotted out an intercept course, then dismissed the thought. There was no way *Invincible* could ambush the alien ship unless her crew obligingly altered course or slowed down. He'd have been more than a little suspicious if they *did*. *And that somewhere has to be Alien-One.*

"Deploy two drones to follow the enemy ship," he ordered. He didn't dare take *Invincible* too far from the tramline until he had a rough idea of the enemy's positions. Margo had fallen weeks ago. It was unlikely that the virus had pulled its fleets back to Falkirk, not when it needed to maintain the pressure on Zheng He. "And watch carefully for enemy bases."

"Aye, sir."

Stephen felt sweat on his back as the hours ticked by, more and more data steadily flowing into the display. There were a handful of faint radio sources now, all completely incomprehensible. One analyst likened the signals to an extremely complex computer code, suggesting that the virus might be using the radio signals to link its different subgroups together. Stephen made a mental note to use ECM to disrupt the signals, when push came to shove, but he doubted it would be *that* effective. The virus would probably use lasers to coordinate its ships when the fighting started in earnest. Stephen knew that datanets had been knocked down, in the past, but it had almost always happened when command starships had been blown out of space. It was vanishingly rare for a command datanet to be hacked from the outside.

We learnt that lesson the hard way, he reminded himself. It had been centuries since the last of the rogue hackers had been tracked down and executed, during the Troubles, but the scars they'd left still cast a long shadow over humanity. *And the virus might have learnt the same lesson during its early expansion...*

He considered the problem for a long moment. The xenospecialists were still unsure if the virus was a natural development, yet another sign that evolution didn't always favour the humanoid form, or if it was a weapon a mystery race had developed for unknown reasons...only to lose control, their weapon turning on them before launching itself into space to conquer the galaxy. Stephen himself had no particular horse in the race, although he preferred to think that the virus might be natural. It was hard to imagine a race stupid enough to design something as complex as the virus without taking precautions to ensure they didn't lose control. But the virus was fantastically complex, evolving at a terrifying rate to absorb and integrate host bodies from a dozen different biochemistries. Perhaps it had simply evolved past the safeguards and destroyed its creators.

New icons flared to life in front of him. "Captain," Arthur said. "I'm picking up a cluster of ships holding position near the tramline."

Stephen silently calculated the vectors in his head. The alien ships were in position to block anything that came through the tramline on a least-time course to Margo and Falkirk. It was a valid precaution, but anyone who knew anything about the realities of interstellar travel also knew that it was pointless. Evading the alien fleet would be easy. *Invincible* had done it and *she* hadn't even known the alien ships were *there*. And yet…he felt his expression darken as the alien fleet slowly took on shape and form. Battleships, carriers, cruisers…a formidable force, but nowhere near as powerful as the fleet that had driven the MNF out of Falkirk. It looked more like a blocking force than anything else, albeit one on a larger scale than anything the Royal Navy could reasonably deploy. That, Stephen noted grimly, was something that might have to change.

We can't hope to out-produce the virus, he reminded himself. *We'll have to keep researching new technologies and hoping that we discover a silver bullet.*

He gritted his teeth. He'd studied enough military history to know that *real* silver bullets—a weapon that would instantly make all previous weapons obsolete—were very rare. Even when one side had possessed a formidable advantage in research and development, it was still hard—if not impossible—to come up with a war-winner. And there was always the danger of discovering—too late—that the new weapon came with drawbacks of its own. The magnificent fleet carriers from the era before the First Interstellar War hadn't stood a chance when they'd been pitted against an enemy with plasma weapons and stealthed starfighters. They'd been too thin-skinned to survive…

"Only a handful of the ships are at combat readiness," Arthur said. "The remainder appear to be powered down."

"They must have the same limitations *we* have," Newcomb commented. "The wear and tear on their equipment must be something to behold."

"Perhaps," Stephen mused. "It's good to know that they do have some limitations."

His face twisted. It was a basic reality of interstellar war that *no* ship and crew could remain on alert indefinitely. The crews got tired of constant drills, while sensor nodes and starship components wore out…sooner or later, *something* would fail. The virus might not give a damn about its host bodies, but it had to be aware of their limitations. He briefly considered an attack, only to dismiss the thought as suicidal a second later. There was no hope of getting into striking range before the enemy ships powered up and launched starfighters. Their deployments were right out of the tactical manual…nothing particularly imaginative, but they didn't *have* to be imaginative. The virus understood the tactical realities as well as he did.

Close enough to the tramline to be sure of detecting a rushed attack, he mused, *yet too far away to allow us to catch them with their pants down.*

"Deploy a flight of drones to monitor their positions," he ordered. "And then shift a second flight of drones towards the other tramline."

"Aye, Captain."

Newcomb caught his eye. "Captain…what's happened to the rest of their fleet?"

"Good question," Stephen said. A shiver of unease ran down his spine. He would be happier if he knew where the missing ships were, although he supposed he'd change his mind if the answer turned out to be *behind him*. *Invincible* was tough, but the virus had destroyed *battleships* when it had forced its way into Falkirk. "And I wish I had an answer."

He scowled as he turned his attention back to the display. Newcomb was right. *Hundreds* of enemy warships were missing. It was possible, he supposed, that they had been powered down so completely that they were effectively undetectable…possible, but unlikely. And yet, if they weren't in Margo, where *were* they? Holding position in Falkirk? Or snapping up the human colonies that had been left high and dry? He doubted it. None of the colonies were particularly well-defended. A single gunboat would be enough to smash all resistance and begin the infection.

"We have to find them," he said, bluntly. "But we have another mission here."

"Yes, sir," Newcomb said.

Stephen cleared his throat. There was no point in waiting any longer. "Helm, set course for Tramline Two. Best possible speed."

"Aye, Captain."

The hours ticked by slowly. Stephen stayed on the bridge until the end of his shift, then retreated to his ready room for a few fitful hours of sleep. He could *feel* oppressive silence spreading through his ship, his crew speaking in whispers even though they *knew* the virus couldn't hear them. It felt as if a single dropped pot or burst of loud music would be enough to bring the wrath of God Himself down on them. Stephen could barely keep himself from whispering, too. It felt as if they were mice, being watched by an unseen cat...

We've done this before, he reminded himself. *Invincible* had sneaked through a dozen enemy-held star systems, some so heavily defended that he wouldn't care to attack them without half the Royal Navy behind him. The odds of being detected were low, as long as they were careful. *We can do it again.*

He felt tired and worn when his alarm bleeped, as if he'd only slept for a few seconds. It was hard to believe, when he checked the chronometer, that six hours had passed. He glanced at the status display as his steward brought him a mug of coffee and some breakfast, silently reassuring himself nothing had happened while he was asleep. *Invincible* had picked up a handful of additional contacts, two holding position near the planet itself. It didn't bode well for the colonists. They'd have problems monitoring local space unless they powered up active sensors, which would draw the virus's attention and get them smashed flat...

"Just living here didn't bode well for the colonists either," Stephen muttered. The coffee tasted foul, but it jerked him awake. "There isn't even a gas giant to provide a handy source of fuel."

His wristcom bleeped. "Captain, we're detecting a small number of enemy ships in transit between the two tramlines," Newcomb said. He sounded disgustingly fresh for someone who couldn't have had more than a couple of hours of sleep…if he'd had any at all. "They appear to be a supply convoy."

Stephen sat upright. "How many escorts?"

"We're picking up four destroyers and what *might* be either a small carrier or another arsenal ship," Newcomb said. "The freighters themselves might be armed, of course."

"And one or more of them might be a converted carrier," Stephen mused. The Royal Navy had used the same trick itself, back in the First Interstellar War. A flotilla of enemy raiders would charge an apparently undefended convoy, only to discover—too late—that one of the freighters was actually a small carrier. "They presumably studied our tactical manuals."

Or came up with the trick themselves, he added, silently. The virus *needed* to grapple with the realities of interstellar logistics. It couldn't allow raiders like *Invincible* to pillage its supply lines with impunity. *We're not the first spacefaring race the virus encountered.*

"Alter course to intercept, then deploy additional probes to ensure that there are no other alien ships within range," Stephen ordered. He keyed the terminal, assessing the vector calculations for himself. It would take hours for the enemy warships near the tramline to become aware of the raid, let alone do something about it, but it was quite possible that the virus had *other* ships in position to intercept. "And then ready the crew for action."

"Aye, Captain," Newcomb said. His voice was calm, but Stephen could hear the excitement underneath. "We will reach engagement range in two hours."

Stephen closed the link, then hurried into the washroom for a quick shower before donning a fresh uniform and making his way onto the bridge.

The silence was gone, replaced with the thrill of anticipation. He had to smile. It wasn't the first time his crew had gone to war—they'd tested themselves against the virus long ago—and they *knew* they could handle combat. They might encounter something bigger than them, something powerful enough to blow *Invincible* out of space, but combat itself wouldn't overwhelm them. None of *his* crew would freeze under pressure.

"We *could* try and take one of the ships intact," Newcomb suggested, diffidently. "It might tell us something useful."

"And bring in a great deal of prize money," Stephen agreed. It *was* tempting. The more insights they had into the virus, the better. And the crew would love to have extra spending money when they returned home. "But they'll come haring after us the moment they realise what we're doing."

He shook his head. "Too risky. We're already too exposed out here."

"Yes, sir," Newcomb said.

Stephen took his seat and studied the alien formation. Four destroyers and an unknown ship, the latter a complete unknown. A small carrier? It was possible, he supposed. He didn't *think* it was a missile-carrier, unless the virus had deliberately designed it as a one-shot weapon. It struck Stephen as a bit wasteful, although he could see the logic. An arsenal ship would be targeted as soon as it was identified. Better to spit out the missiles in one giant volley and retreat, rather than have the missiles taken out along with the ship...

"Inform the CAG," he said. "His starfighters are to make a stealthy approach to the target ships."

"Aye, sir," Newcomb said. He paused, just for a second. "All squadrons?"

Stephen nodded. There was no point in holding anything back, not now. One pass to obliterate the warships, another to smash the freighters... and then a hasty retreat back into cloak. They'd have plenty of time to put themselves beyond all hope of detection before the enemy warships arrived, with blood in their eye. If, of course, the enemy warships *were* deployed. It was quite possible that the virus would realise that the situation was beyond recovery and leave the convoy to its fate.

No human officer would feel comfortable making such a call, Stephen thought, as the first starfighters appeared on the display. *They wouldn't want to abandon the freighters to certain destruction, even though cold logic would suggest that the freighters were doomed whatever the officer did. But the virus isn't human.*

He swallowed hard, feeling the weight of command descending on his shoulders. He'd made his call...and now, all he could do was watch as the starfighters glided towards their enemies. Their icons were dim, warning him that the craft were almost completely powered down. A handful of vectors formed beside them, a grim reminder that even their exact *positions* could only be estimated after the first few minutes. So far, there was no hint that the enemy had noticed them, but that would change. The convoy wasn't trying to hide. Its ships were running active sensor sweeps. It was only a matter of time before they realised they were under attack.

And they'll definitely notice when the starfighters power up their drives, he told himself, coldly. Starfighters were too small to carry cloaking devices. There would be no hope of concealment as the starfighters slipped onto attack vectors. A civilian-grade passive sensor would have no trouble seeing a flight of starfighters in such close proximity. *And then...*

The display flashed red. "They *see* them," Newcomb said. A rush of excitement ran around the bridge. "They're targeting the starfighters now."

"Order the starfighters to engage at will, then power up our drives and weapons," Stephen ordered, calmly. "Prepare to attack!"

CHAPTER TWENTY-ONE

RICHARD FELT…SLUGGISH.

It wasn't just that he was floating in the inky darkness of space, completely disconnected from the squadrons that were meant to be under his command…without even a *sense* of movement as his starfighter plunged through space at a speed unimaginable to groundhogs and reporters. It was…he tried to think clearly, but his mind refused to function properly. His hands weren't shaking, not any longer. They were dead weight, as if he was trapped in a lumpish piece of meat that no longer responded to his commands. The whole scene felt like a nightmare, a nightmare in which he couldn't run or fight or do *anything* to evade the terrible fate he *knew* was behind him. It was impossible…

Alerts sounded. His display flashed to life. "Attack," a voice snapped. "All squadrons, attack!"

Richard tried to grit his teeth, but nothing happened. His starfighter was powering up—he could *feel* the gravity field shifting as the drive field came online—yet it was all he could do to sit up. His body felt tired, too tired to sleep…he had to *think* to force his fingers to reach for his pouch. He knew—he *knew*—the dangers of using stims on a battlefield, but he had no choice. His fingers fumbled their way into the pouch—he almost panicked as they almost dropped the tab on the deck—and pressed the tab against his bare skin. There was a hiss, followed by a sudden rush of energy. The world seemed to snap into focus. Someone was yammering at him.

"Commander?" Monica. It was Monica. "Richard? Can you hear me?"

"I can hear you," Richard confirmed. God! How long had she been shouting at him? "My power-up had to reboot."

He cursed under his breath as he took control of the starfighter. It was a plausible excuse—pieces of technology failed all the time—but he wasn't sure if she would believe it. He wasn't sure if *anyone* would believe it. He should have taken the stim hours ago, to give time for the edge to wear off before he went into combat, but there hadn't been any way to time it properly. Instead...the timing had been shitty and he'd almost collapsed. He forced his mind to focus, concentrating on the enemy ships. The freighters were slowly altering course, as if they had a hope of evading the starfighters. He almost laughed with glee. The starfighters could spot the freighters an hour's head start—and three drive nodes into the bargain—and they'd still run the freighters down before they had a chance to break contact and go doggo.

"Form up on me," he ordered. "Prepare to engage."

He felt himself smile, a cold predatory smile. An enemy destroyer was advancing forward, putting itself between the starfighters and their prey. It wouldn't have been a bad tactic, normally, but right now it was utterly futile. *Invincible* was right behind her starfighters, her plasma weapons already targeting the destroyer. There was no way in hell the enemy ship would survive long enough to give the freighters a chance to escape. He tapped his console, designating the enemy ship as the target before leading his starfighters straight towards the destroyer. Space started to fill with plasma bolts, but Richard barely noticed. In his hyped-up state, they seemed to be moving in slow motion. It was easy to evade them, even when they threatened to brush against his drive field. He had to fight to keep himself from carolling with joy as the range closed rapidly. It was all he could do to fire his torpedoes when he entered attack range. He wanted—he needed—to fly so close to the alien ship that he could have reached out and touched her hull.

"Torpedoes away," he snapped. "I say again, torpedoes away!"

He smiled, thinly, as four of his subordinates launched their torpedoes too. The analysts had speculated that the virus had decided to prioritise taking out human starfighters, rather than defending its own ships, but the enemy destroyer clearly hadn't got the memo. Or, Richard decided, it was rather more likely that the analysts were full of shit. The virus *couldn't* have enough warships that it could afford to trade destroyers and cruisers for a handful of tiny starfighters. If it did, it would have pushed its way to Earth by now. The enemy destroyer was fighting desperately to survive, ignoring the retreating starfighters as it targeted their torpedoes. But it was a fight it was doomed to lose.

"Scratch one destroyer," someone shouted. "I *got* the bastard!"

"*Someone* got him," Richard corrected.

He chuckled, feeling oddly amused. *He* might have got the destroyer. They'd have to study the records, after the battle, to determine who had really struck the fatal blow. He'd be surprised if they didn't end up sharing the kill. Destroyers were smaller than fleet carriers, but a single torpedo hit was rarely enough to kill them. A combination of hits, however, would set off a chain reaction that was almost always fatal. Nothing smaller than a battleship could survive.

"Form up on me," he ordered. He checked the status display, quickly assessing the overall situation. The four enemy destroyers had been blown to hell, while the mystery starship was altering course and trying to evade contact. It might have succeeded in evading *Invincible*, Richard told himself as he altered course, but it didn't have a hope of escaping the starfighters. "Prepare to engage the enemy."

He listened to the acknowledgements as the squadron reformed around him and flashed towards the enemy ship. She wasn't shooting, somewhat to his surprise. The odds of hitting anything might be low, but they'd be precisely *zero* if the enemy ship wasn't shooting at all. What *was* it? A transport? A military-grade freighter? Or…what? A carrier would have launched her fighters by now, surely. There was nothing to be gained by holding them back, not when the carrier herself might be taken out at any moment. He was almost relieved when the enemy ship finally opened fire. At least it was doing *something*...

Maybe it's their version of a survey ship, he thought. Survey ships were built on warship hulls, with armour and weapons, but they were designed more to evade any potential foes than engage them in combat. *Or maybe they just threw an experimental ship into the line of battle.*

He put the thought to one side, then keyed his console. "Follow me in," he ordered. "Let's kill the bastard!"

• • •

"The enemy warships have been destroyed," Newcomb reported. "The starfighters did well."

"Good," Stephen said. The enemy freighters were trying to scatter, but it was already too late. "Accelerate to flank speed, fire as you bear."

"Aye, Captain," Sonia said.

"Engaging the enemy...now," Arthur added.

Stephen felt a low vibration running through the hull as *Invincible's* main guns opened fire, hammering the closest enemy freighter into a wreck before she finally lost hull integrity and exploded. Arthur didn't wait for orders, shifting fire automatically to the next target. The secondary guns opened fire as additional targets came into range, tearing their way through freighters that barely had enough armour to stand up to one or two shots. A pair of freighters altered course, as if they had realised they couldn't escape and intended to ram *Invincible* before they were destroyed, but they didn't stand a chance. They were vaporised before they could get anywhere near their target.

If they were humans, we would accept their surrender, Stephen thought. *But they're not human. They literally cannot surrender.*

He felt a flicker of guilt, which he ruthlessly quashed. The freighters might be harmless—only three of them were armed, with weapons that might as well be water pistols if they were fired at *Invincible*—but they carried supplies that would make the enemy ships within the system far more dangerous if they had a chance to reach their destination. Every destroyed enemy freighter made it harder for the virus to supply its forces, winning time for Earth to ready its defences and humanity's allies to arrive. It felt as if he was stamping on ants, but…he shook his head. There was no room for scruples when the only two options were victory, or death. *Anything* was justified if the only alternative was extinction.

And it makes you wonder just what the war will do to us, he thought. The Troubles had done a great deal of damage, more than anyone cared to admit. They'd done what they needed to do to survive, to preserve Britain as an independent society, but…what had it done to them? He'd read the journals of men who'd fought in the wars. They'd slowly discarded their…*decency*… as the fires of war burned ever hotter. *What sort of monsters were they?*

"The final freighter has been destroyed," Newcomb said. "I…"

He broke off as red icons flared to life. "Captain," Morse said. "Sensors are picking up a major enemy fleet on approach vector. They're coming from Tramline Two!"

Stephen nodded, curtly. A planned ambush? No, the timing was too poor. Bad luck, more like. The enemy had been running reinforcements to the system, probably hoping to increase the pressure on Zheng He…*Invincible* had simply been unlucky. But not *that* unlucky. The enemy ships weren't in range to catch her, not before she broke contact and escaped.

"I think we've outstayed our welcome," he said. "Recall starfighters. Helm, alter course. Tactical, deploy ECM drones. Let them waste their time chasing down the drones while we beat feet back to the tramline."

"Aye, Captain," Arthur said.

"And deploy a pair of recon drones towards the new arrivals," Stephen said. He glanced at the live feed, wondering when—if—the *original* alien fleet was going to make a move. They *shouldn't* know—yet—that the convoy had been attacked. "Let's see what's bearing down on us."

"Aye, Captain."

"The starfighters are returning now," Newcomb said. "They sound pleased with themselves."

"They should be," Stephen said.

He smiled, grimly, as the alien ships started to pick up speed. They were trying hard, but there was no way they were going to be able to run his ship down and destroy her before he broke contact. They wouldn't even get close enough to see through the decoys before it was too late. He kept a wary eye on the long-range sensors, just in case they were being driven into a trap, but very few tactical officers would want to risk everything on such a complex manoeuvre. The Royal Navy had learnt—the hard way, in some cases—to keep operational deployments and combat tactics as simple as possible.

And they won't even get into missile range, unless they've designed even-longer-range missiles, he thought. *They have to know they don't have a hope of catching us.*

"Captain," Lieutenant Alison Adams said. "There's an...*odd*...ship in the alien fleet."

"Odd?" Stephen looked up. "What is it?"

"She's about twice the size of a battleship, but...she's odd." An image of an alien ship appeared on the display. "My first thought was that they'd simply scaled up a battleship, but there are a number of oddities. I can't be sure, sir..."

"I understand," Stephen said. "What *can* you tell me about her?"

"She's *crammed* with sensors," Alison said. "And studded with point defence...percentage-wise, she's got more than a fleet carrier. But she doesn't seem to have any offensive weapons, as far as I can tell. No heavy plasma turrets, no missile tubes..."

"As far as you can tell," Newcomb said. "From this distance, we're lucky we can see *anything*."

"Yes, sir," Alison said. "But, if she was merely an oversized battleship, surely they would have run into the law of diminishing returns."

"Maybe," Stephen mused. It *was* an odd design. He'd watched a designer scale up a fleet carrier once, then point out all the flaws with the design.

Battleships were cruder than fleet carriers, but Alison was right. At some point, the ship would just become a grossly-inefficient mass…and an easy target. "But they wouldn't have built her unless they thought they knew what they were doing."

"A real *Overcompensator* class," Newcomb joked.

Stephen shrugged. The virus had been in space for centuries. It—or whoever had created it—had probably made all the mistakes that newly-spacefaring civilisations made when designing spacecraft and starships for the first time, made them and *learned* from them. And the virus didn't seem to have the common human belief that bigger was always better. Even as a missile carrier, the enemy battleship made no sense.

"Keep an eye on her," he ordered. "Maybe she'll do something to show us what she can do."

He leaned back in his command chair as the starfighters landed, the cloaking device engaging seconds later. The virus would have great difficulty tracking his ship, even if it was smart enough to see through the decoys at once. It didn't matter, he told himself. By the time the virus's fleet entered starfighter range, *his* ship would be well away. The enemy would have *real* problems tracking them down before it was too late.

"The enemy fleet is not altering course," Alison said, after a moment. "It doesn't seem to have a solid lock on us."

"Good," Stephen said. There was no way they could *attack* the fleet, but at least they could keep an eye on it. "How many of those ships have we seen before?"

Alison worked her console for a long moment. "Unsure, sir. I think four or five of the ships fought at Second Falkirk, sir, but it's hard to be sure. The records are not good."

"Understood," Stephen said.

He forced himself to relax as the alien ships continued on their course towards Tramline One, clearly intending to rendezvous with the original fleet. And then…even fresh, the virus didn't have enough firepower to punch its way into Zheng He and smash the MNF to a bloody pulp. It had to know it, too. And yet, the mere presence of the fleet would be enough to keep eyes focused on Margo. The virus might be up to something else, relying on the fleet to divert humanity's attention. It had become a great deal easier to coordinate operations over light years in the last decade...

Although only an idiot would gamble on such a chancy operation, Stephen thought. *Too many fancy plans have come apart because someone tried to be clever.*

"Captain," Newcomb said. "Where do we go from here?"

Stephen hesitated. They *could* sneak through Tramline Two themselves, heading up the chain towards Falkirk—and even Alien-One. A string of pinprick raids in its rear might convince the virus to divert ships to hunt *Invincible* down, buying time for Earth to organise its defences. But, at the same time, the MNF had to be warned about the fleet on the far side of the tramline. The Admirals *had* to know the virus was gathering its strength for another push forward. They might even consider a raid on Margo, just to make sure the virus had other things to worry about. Even a handful of minor attacks would keep the virus busy...

...If they knew there was a window of opportunity. If.

He scowled. He *liked* independent command. He liked having one ship—*just* one ship—under his command. He knew, all too well, he wouldn't be allowed to remain a captain indefinitely. The Royal Navy would offer him a promotion—the family name would make sure of that, unless he screwed up so badly he was transferred to a mining colony on the other side of explored space—and he would be unable to decline. He'd be moved up the ranks, but he'd never command again. No Admiral had ever commanded a ship as well as a fleet. It simply wasn't practical. He *wanted* to head further up the tramline, to remain out of contact with the MNF...

...But he knew his duty.

"Set course for the tramline," Stephen ordered. "We'll jump back to Zheng He and inform the Admirals of what happened here, then return to the offensive."

"Aye, Captain," Newcomb said.

And someone will probably say I ran away, Stephen thought, sardonically. *Whatever I do, there will be people who say that I made the wrong choice.*

He pushed the thought aside as *Invincible* picked up speed. It wouldn't take *that* long to return to Zheng He, report to the Admirals and receive their orders. And they *had* hurt the virus. A handful of freighters that could barely shoot back...it was a cheap victory, but one that might have a colossal impact on the war.

And if I tell myself that again and again, he thought, *I might even come to believe it.*

It felt like hours before they finally approached the tramline, keeping a wary eye out for tiny sensor distortions that might hint at the presence of a cloaked ship. But there were none. Local space was quiet. Stephen didn't feel reassured. Everything had gone perfectly—well, almost perfectly—and it worried him. He would almost have been happier if they'd been chased to the tramline by a small fleet of alien ships. It would have been hazardous—his lips quirked at the absurd thought—but at least the penny would have dropped. It was better than waiting for it to fall...

An alarm sounded as soon as they crossed the tramline. "Captain, I'm picking up an emergency alert," Morse snapped. "A Code Blue!"

Stephen blinked. "Battlestations," he snapped. A Code Blue? "Set Condition One throughout the ship!"

"Aye, sir," Newcomb said.

CHAPTER TWENTY-TWO

"CONDITION ONE IS SET throughout the ship," Newcomb said. "We're ready."

"Communications, alert System Command to our return," Stephen ordered. There didn't appear to be an actual *battle* going on, but it was impossible to be sure. The light-speed delay could be covering up a full-scale engagement. "Helm, take us into the system."

"Aye, Captain."

Stephen forced himself to think as he waited for a response. A Code Blue meant only one thing, now. A starship—a *human* starship, one reported missing or lost—had reappeared in the system. And that meant...it was possible, he admitted privately, that the ship had simply lost contact with the rest of the MNF during the engagement, but they had to assume the worst. *Dezhnev* had done a great deal of damage, when she'd been used to sneak an attack force into engagement range at Falkirk. Stephen hated to think what another infected starship could do at Zheng He.

We haven't had anything like enough time to fortify the system, he thought, numbly. There was an entire fleet massing on the far side of the tramline. *If the virus is willing to take the losses, it can take the system.*

He glanced at Newcomb as more and more information flowed into the display. It didn't *look* as though a battle was going on, although the MNF had moved into a force-protection deployment that would have saddened Nelson, Cunningham or any of the other admirals who'd made their name through aggressive tactics and a determination never to admit defeat in the face of the enemy. It was a formation that practically surrendered the initiative, although it did have some advantages. The enemy would have to close with the formation or risk leaving a powerful fleet in their rear.

"They're not evacuating the system," Newcomb said, quietly.

"No," Stephen agreed. He'd seen the contingency plans. It didn't look as if any of them were being put into action. "The threat, if there is a threat, cannot appear too big."

He puzzled over the mystery as they waited for contact. The virus *had* used *Dezhnev* as a Trojan Horse, but it *had* to know that tactic would never work twice. There were a dozen plans for inspecting any ship that went missing, only to reappear later. No ship that had lost contact with her fellows would be allowed inside the defence perimeter until she was inspected from top to bottom…and, if she powered up her weapons, she would be unceremoniously blown out of space. Stephen disliked the idea of firing on a friendly ship, but he knew there was no choice. The infected would probably be relieved, if something of the original personality still lived on in the host body. They wouldn't be unwilling traitors any longer.

"Captain," Morse said. "I have an update from System Command. Sir… it's *Raleigh*!"

Newcomb started. "Does it think we're idiots? First *Dezhnev* and now *Raleigh*?"

Stephen glanced at him. HMS *Raleigh* had split off from the main body of Task Force Drake, shortly before *Invincible* and her remaining cohorts had headed up the tramline chain to Alien-Five. He'd wondered at her absence, when it became clear that *Raleigh* had neither waited for *Invincible* nor headed straight to Falkirk herself, but there had been no way to know what had become of her. A survey ship was hardly an assault carrier, let alone a battleship. Captain Hashing and his crew might have died in an unexplored alien system, their fates a mystery to everyone they'd left behind. He'd long since given up hope of seeing *Raleigh* again.

And yet, here she was.

"Orders from System Command, sir," Morse said. "We're to intercept and…assess…*Raleigh* for any signs of contamination. If she is infected, we're to blow her out of space."

Stephen tapped the display. *Raleigh* was holding station several light minutes from the planet…in fact, looking at the vector, *Raleigh* appeared to have popped out of one of the unexplored tramlines, rather than sneaking her way through Falkirk and Margo to reach Zheng He. He keyed his console, bringing up the forwarded message packet. So far, *Raleigh* had cooperated with every order she'd received. System Command seemed torn between dispatching the marines or launching an immediate attack.

This enemy doesn't just wear our faces, Stephen thought, grimly. *It can pretend to be us, for a while. And it knows precisely how to fool us.*

"Helm, intercept course," he ordered. "Tactical, monitor *Raleigh* closely as soon as we get into range. She is *not* to be given a chance to do any damage."

"Aye, sir," Arthur said.

"It can't be the *real* Hashing, can it?" Newcomb looked worried. "They've been gone for months!"

"*Raleigh* was designed for long-term operations," Stephen said, slowly. He'd never considered transferring to survey operations—and his family probably wouldn't have let him—but he'd studied *Raleigh* and her sisters when she'd been placed under his command. If there were any starships that could have endured such a long voyage without returning home, it was the survey ships. They had more redundancies worked into their systems than a fleet carrier. "And she came out of the wrong tramline."

"And they could be lulling us into a false sense of security," Newcomb pointed out. "We have to be very careful."

"Very careful," Stephen agreed. He allowed his eyes to linger on *Raleigh's* icon. The range was closing steadily. Soon, they would *know*. "Order the marines to prepare to board."

And hope to hell, his thoughts added silently, *that I'm not sending them to their deaths.*

• • •

"You know," Hammersmith said, "we *could* have boarded one of the alien freighters."

"And then been blown to pieces when that fleet turned up," Alice snapped. She was sweating inside her suit, all too aware that she might be walking into a trap. If *Raleigh* was infected, the marines were going to die. Or worse. She didn't fear death, only being infected—again. It was the thought—the fear—that kept her up at night. "What good is money if you can't fucking spend it?"

She turned her attention to the live feed from the sensors as the shuttle slid towards *Raleigh*. The survey crew had done as they were told, powering down everything apart from life support...it should have reassured her, but it didn't. There were all kinds of weapons that wouldn't show up on a sensor sweep until someone pulled the trigger. She could feel an *itching* at the back of her skull, a mocking reminder that she would never be fully at ease with herself again. And yet, it wasn't strong enough for her to sound the alarm. She was half-convinced she was imagining it.

Most girls get gaslighted by shitty boyfriends, she thought. *I'm the only one who manages to gaslight herself.*

"They're opening the hatch," the pilot called. "Are you ready?"

"Won't you come into my parlour, said the spider to the fly," Tindal said. "Yummy cakes and..."

"That will do," Alice said. She checked her weapons automatically as a dull *thump* echoed through the shuttle. They'd docked. "Stay on alert, but *don't* fire unless you have no other choice."

The hatch hissed open, revealing a perfectly normal airlock. Alice tensed, half-expecting the environmental sensors to start screaming in horror. The itching behind her eyes grew stronger, slowly turning into a pounding headache. She had to take a deep breath to keep herself from grunting in pain, reminding herself—again—she'd been through worse. The inner hatch hissed open—someone must have overridden the safety protocols—and revealed the starship's interior. Alice risked a glance at the sensors. The air was clean, for a given value of *clean*. The atmospheric scrubbers had to be on their last legs, she noted, but at least there were no traces of the virus.

She forced herself to walk forward, through the hatch. A pair of men waited for her, both conspicuously unarmed. Alice let out a breath she hadn't realised she'd been holding. It had been uncommon, prior to the war, for officers and crewmen to carry weapons on duty, but now…standing orders said that everyone had to be armed. Several of the marines could have been blasted down before they even knew they were under attack. The virus wouldn't have gained much—*Invincible* could blow *Raleigh* into dust without raising a sweat—but it would have made the human race more paranoid. In the long run, it might even have come out ahead.

"I need to test your blood," she said. She produced a sampler from her belt and held it out to the leader. "And then we have to search your entire ship."

"I understand," the leader said. He didn't seem too surprised. "Here."

Alice tested him, letting out another breath when the sampler confirmed that he was uninfected. His companion was equally clean. Alice muttered a brief report into her mouthpiece, then directed the two men into the shuttle. The entire ship would have to be evacuated, just to make sure they'd checked and rechecked everyone. She just hoped the virus hadn't found a new way to be sneaky. Her position was precarious enough as it was.

It might have figured out how to condition people, rather than turn them into host-bodies, she thought, as another shuttle docked at the lower hatch. *We might have problems catching them before they do us some damage.*

The feeling of unease didn't go away until the entire crew—three hundred men and women, starship crewmen and survey specialists—were carefully checked and the entire ship was searched from top to bottom. *Raleigh* felt oddly comfortable, compared to *Invincible*; Alice couldn't help thinking that the lowliest crewman on the survey ship had more space to call his own than *she'd* ever had as a marine, at least before she'd become infected. There were dozens of minor luxuries, things she would never have expected on a military ship. But then, *Raleigh* wasn't a purely military ship. A sizable percentage of her crew were civilians.

"The ship appears to be clean, sir," she said, once the search was completed. *Raleigh* wasn't designed to make life hard for boarders, thankfully. She was fairly sure they'd swept everywhere, from the bridge to the maintenance tubes. "There's no hint of the virus's presence. But they've been gone a long time."

"Yeah." Major Patterson sounded concerned. "And we don't know what they've been doing."

He snorted. "Download a complete copy of their command datacore, then power down the rest of the ship. The brass can decide what to do with her."

And her crew, Alice thought. She knew, better than anyone, just how tricky the virus could be. A paranoid mind would want to keep *Raleigh's* crew locked up indefinitely, just in case the virus had managed to circumvent the blood and atmospheric tests. *What the hell are we going to do with them?*

She put it out of her mind. It wasn't her problem.

• • •

"I'm sorry we can't meet in person," Stephen said. "After *Dezhnev*...we have to take a few precautions."

"I couldn't believe it when they told us," Captain Vandal Hashing said. "I knew the virus was powerful, but to drive us out of Falkirk and..."

He shook his head. "You've got my logs, so I'll give you the basic overview. We headed into alien-controlled space and moved through five tramlines, having to double-back a couple of times when we discovered that the tramline chains came to an end. Some systems were quite heavily industrialised, I might add. I think a couple actually had intelligent life of their own before the virus arrived. Now, of course, the virus is the only living thing in the system, at least as far as we know."

"It's quite likely," Stephen agreed.

Hashing nodded. "They caught a sniff of us in one system and chased us through three successive tramlines. I thought I'd dodged them twice, but they kept coming. Eventually, I followed an unexplored tramline chain and broke contact...we didn't dare try to reverse course. Our projections hinted that we *should* find a chain that took us back to the Human Sphere, so we kept going. Eventually, we popped into Zheng He."

"And nearly got blown away by trigger-happy defenders." Stephen glanced at the report on his terminal. The WebHeads had studied the copied datacore carefully and come to the conclusion that it *couldn't* have been faked. No one could fake a starship's records, not unless they had *years* to spare. It certainly *looked* as if *Raleigh* had had a lucky escape. "I wish I knew I could trust you."

Hashing showed a flicker of anger. "Sir...I do understand, but my crew..."

"Will be taken care of," Stephen said. He found the anger a little reassuring, but...would the *virus* know he'd find it reassuring. The doctors swore blind that Hashing and his crew weren't infected, yet...he didn't want to take chances. "And thank you."

"You're welcome," Hashing said, dryly. "We did our duty, did we not? Give the bastards hell."

His holoimage vanished. Stephen frowned, studying the report again. A tramline chain—a largely unexplored tramline chain—that ran all the way to Alien-One. Did the virus know it existed? It was impossible to be sure. *Raleigh* had broken contact with the virus's ships before she'd adjusted course for Zheng He...Hashing had taken one hell of a gamble. He might well have run into a dead end and been forced to reverse course, adding months to his voyage as well as greatly increasing the risk of detection. He could have even given the virus a backdoor into Zheng He...or further afield, letting it bypass the MNF altogether. And yet, the gamble had paid off. The opportunity *had* to be exploited.

He keyed his terminal. "Communications, get me a secure link to Admiral Zadornov."

"Aye, Captain."

Stephen poured himself a cup of tea and waited. It might take some time for Svetlana to respond. She had too many responsibilities to respond immediately to his call. But her holoimage materialised in just under five minutes.

"Captain," Svetlana said. "I was just reading the report from your boarding parties."

"There's no reason to believe that the crew was infected," Stephen said. "Or subverted in any other way."

"Apparently not," Svetlana agreed. "Although it *is* possible that they could have been conditioned."

"They would still have had to fake their records," Stephen pointed out. "*And* repair any damage to their ship without leaving the slightest *hint* of repair work on their hull."

"Which could be done, with a shipyard and willing cooperation." Svetlana frowned. "We don't *know* the ship came through Tramline Four. None of our long-range sensors can prove or disprove it. We didn't even know she was there until she announced her presence."

"The data is solid," Stephen insisted. "And it would not be *easy* to rewrite chunks of the ship's automatic records system without leaving very visible traces behind."

"Perhaps," Svetlana said. "But the history of communications is *strewn* with codes and encryption systems that were completely unbreakable until they weren't. We cannot afford to take the risk that they're lying to us."

"They've been checked thoroughly too," Stephen said. "They have no dangerous markers in their blood. And, if they're telling the truth, we have a backdoor into their space that we can use to take the virus by surprise."

"If." Svetlana said nothing for a long moment. "If they're telling the truth...yes, you're right. We could put an offensive force into Alien-One without them having a clue that it's coming. If..."

She met his eyes. "And how many ships would we have to detach from Zheng He to make the operation workable?"

Stephen knew the answer. "Too many."

"Yes." Svetlana scowled. "I share your eagerness to go on the offensive. And yes, I think we should hit them back, as hard as we can. But...right now, our priority is to keep the virus from punching its way into this system and driving us out. We cannot afford to detach a sizable body of ships, Captain, and send them so far away that they will be out of touch with the rest of the formation for weeks, if not months. The risk of utter disaster is too great."

"Yes, Admiral," Stephen said. He didn't like it, but he understood the logic. "Might I suggest, therefore, that we take steps to verify the data? A handful of ships could probe up to Alien-One, proving that the tramline chain actually exists. If so, we can take the offensive when our reinforcements finally arrive. Or mount a stealth strike on Alien-One, if the Admiralty is disinclined to consider the operation. Let the virus respond to us for a change."

Svetlana smiled. "And which ship do you have in mind for the mission?"

Stephen didn't bother to dissemble. "My ship and crew *do* have considerable experience in enemy space, Admiral."

"Indeed they do," Svetlana said, dryly. She smiled. It made her look like a predator eying her prey. "Very well. Have your people talk to my people. I want a proposal for the operation on my desk by the end of the day. Unless something changes, you can plan to leave in a week or so."

Giving you enough time to consider raiding Margo, Stephen thought. There hadn't been time to assess the results of *Invincible's* last trip into enemy territory. *Or to overcome your paranoia about Captain Hashing and his crew.*

"I'll see to it personally, Admiral," he said. "If the chain does exist, we might be able to knock the virus right back..."

"If," Svetlana said. She sounded interested, but wary. "And if you want to skin the fox, first you have to *catch* it."

CHAPTER TWENTY-THREE

"AND SO, WATCH YOUR BACK," Richard concluded. The pilots watched him with varying levels of attention. "The virus can and *will* take advantage of the slightest weakness."

He rubbed his forehead as he dismissed the pilots. The rumours that they were going on the offensive—or at least doing *something* more interesting than orbiting Zheng He and preparing for the inevitable attack—hadn't been confirmed, but he'd heard enough to make him certain there *would* be a deployment. *Invincible's* fighters had been spared the punishing CSP duties inflicted on the other carriers; instead, they'd been ordered to study the records and drill until they could fly their starfighters in their sleep. Richard felt his legs quiver as the last of the pilots left the briefing compartment. It was all he could do to stagger down the corridor to his cabin. He didn't need sleep. He needed a stim.

The hatch hissed open. He stumbled through and headed straight for the cabinet, fingers fumbling at the latch. It took him two tries to open it and find the packet of stims, half-hidden behind a handful of private possessions. He'd never really bothered to bring anything truly *personal* with him, as he moved from duty station to duty station. A starfighter pilot might not only be transferred at very short notice, often without time to do more than grab the bare minimum of supplies, but return from a battle only to discover that his mothership had been vaporised. He pressed the tab against his neck and pushed the trigger. There was a sharp *twang* of pain, followed by a rush of energy. Richard almost sagged in relief. *That* was more like it.

"Richard," a female voice said. "What the hell are you doing?"

Richard jumped and spun around, one hand dropping to the weapon he wasn't carrying. He'd never seen the *point* of carrying a pistol while on duty, certainly not when *Invincible* was surrounded by hundreds of friendly warships. It was unlikely that *he* would be called upon to repel boarders... his mind caught up with his panicked thoughts. Monica was standing by the hatch, arms crossed under her breasts. She looked beautiful, but angry. Very angry.

Monica took a step forward. The hatch hissed closed behind her. Richard stared, unsure how she'd managed to sneak up on him. Had he been so far out of it that he hadn't noticed her standing by the hatch? He certainly hadn't bothered to check the hatch was closed before he dug out the stims. He'd never expected...he felt a rush of embarrassment, mingled with an odd kind of relief. Monica *did* have a standing invitation to visit his quarters whenever she liked. She hadn't broken any of the navy's unspoken regulations...he laughed at himself a moment later. That was the least of his worries.

"I knew there was something wrong," Monica said. She sounded angry, although the anger was directed more at herself than him. "You've been taking stims, haven't you?"

"Yes," Richard said. There was no point in trying to deny it. "I have it under control."

Monica's eyes sharpened. "You nearly blanked out in Margo, didn't you? I checked the flight logs. Your starfighter didn't need to reboot the flash-wake sequence, did it?"

Richard glared at her. "You've been accessing *my* flight logs?"

A hot rush of anger burned through him. It felt like a violation of his privacy...and God knew there was little privacy to be found on a starship. He might have a cabin of his own, but...it still wasn't very private. He'd spent long enough in various barracks to know that privacy was practically non-existent. The only consolation was that the starfighter pilots had a long tradition of pretending they didn't see certain things.

"I'm a squadron leader," Monica reminded him, as if he'd forgotten. "I *do* have clearance to access flight logs."

"Yes, but…" Richard found it hard to put his thoughts into words. His mouth was terrifyingly dry. "You don't have the right…"

"I have the duty," Monica said. She shook her head slowly. "The other pilots don't know you so well, Richard, but I've known you for years. I've fucking gone to *bed* with you! I know you and I know something is wrong."

"I can handle it," Richard repeated.

"Really?" Monica met his eyes, daring him to disagree. "Just like those idiot druggies can handle it?"

Richard flinched. He knew—everyone knew—that there was a tiny subculture of people who'd dropped out of the mainstream, choosing to seek consolation in drink and illegal drugs…homeless, often abusers and abused…tolerated by society, as long as they stayed out of sight. Everyone knew someone who knew someone who'd fallen into the underclass and never emerged; a boy who let himself become addicted to drugs or electronic stimulation, a girl who fell into the clutches of a sex gang…someone who couldn't muster the strength to seek help and escape. It was a horror story lurking under the reassuring lies civilisation told itself. The idea of becoming one of them was unthinkable.

"I knew a girl at school who thought she could handle it," Monica said. "And you know what? She fell off the rails and got expelled, when they found the pills in her trunk. And *she* wasn't in command of seventy-odd starfighter pilots and their ships!"

"Seventy-two," Richard corrected, absently. "I…"

Monica cut him off. "How long have you been taking stims?"

Richard had to think about it. "Since…since we got back to the ship," he said, finally. "It was the only way to keep going."

"You've been taking them for months." Monica sounded stunned. "You're an addict."

"I'm not an addict," Richard protested.

"That's what Claire said," Monica snapped. "She kept trying to tell us that, time and time again. She said she could quit any time she liked! And what happened? She just kept taking the pills, searching for that elusive high, until it was too late."

"Stims are not drugs," Richard said.

"No," Monica agreed. "They don't give you pleasure. But your body can become dependent on them...your body *has* become dependent on them. That's why we're not supposed to take the bloody things for more than three days in a row. Didn't you read the fucking warnings?"

Richard stalked over to the bed and sat down. "I didn't have a choice."

"Yes, you bloody did." Monica softened her voice. "I know, it wasn't a good time for you. It wasn't a good time for any of us. But you can't deal with a problem by medicating it into going away. It just gives you *more* problems."

She paused, as if she was calculating something. "If you took one stim a day, ever since we left Earth...you *have* to be utterly dependent on them by now. I'm surprised you held up as long as you did."

"Thanks," Richard said, sourly. "It hasn't dulled my effectiveness."

"You walked right past me," Monica said. "You didn't see me. I could have been stark *naked* and you would have walked right past me."

Richard couldn't help himself. He giggled. "It wouldn't be the first time I've pretended not to see something."

"Yeah." Monica took a long breath. "There are lots of things we pretend not to see, aren't there. The pilot who has a quick wank in his bunk, the pilot who needs to shit when there are no private bathrooms...the tattoos and porn stashes and lots of other things that are technically against regulations, but don't impede efficiency. And yes, the handful of pilots who wind up sleeping together. We turn a blind eye to them."

She met his eyes. "I can't turn a blind eye to this."

"I know," Richard said. "I would have reported myself if I hadn't been *needed*."

"There are six squadron leaders attached to this ship." Monica didn't sound convinced. He didn't really blame her. "Any one of them could have taken over your duties, with one of their subordinates moving up to take over theirs. We do a shitload of cross-training just to make sure we have someone who *can* take over if their superior officer gets blown into stardust. You are not irreplaceable."

"Now," Richard said. He reached under the bed and found a bottle of water. "There wasn't anyone who could take my place back then."

"No," Monica agreed. "But do you think it *matters*?"

She started to pace the tiny cabin, her arms swinging from side to side. "There have been pilots who took stims, who took them with authorisation and medical supervision and all the other little niceties you chose to ignore…pilots who only took them for the recommended duration and *still* had problems afterwards. And you've been taking them for months!"

Richard took a long sip of water. It didn't make him feel any better.

Monica swung around to face him, resting her hands on her hips. "It doesn't matter how you took them," she said. "It doesn't matter *what* a Board of Inquiry has to say about it, if it thinks you were a victim of circumstance or someone who deserves to be banged up for the rest of his fucking life. What matters, right now, is that you are unfit for duty!"

"I can still function," Richard protested.

"For how long?" Monica glared him into silence. "You were starting to zone out during the briefing, weren't you? I know we're all tired, and you're not the only person who wants to sleep when he's not in the cockpit, but… what happens if you zone out during a fight? You might start shooting at us! Or simply crash into an asteroid and…"

"I'll have to be *really* out of it to crash into an asteroid," Richard said. It sounded funny, even though he knew she was deadly serious. "And the IFF gear won't *let* me shoot at friendly pilots…"

"You trust that shit now?" Monica snorted, rudely. "You know as well as I do that IFF isn't always reliable in the heat of battle. That's why they tell us to make sure of our targets before we pull the trigger."

She shook her head. "Richard, what were you thinking?"

"That I couldn't go on without them," Richard said, honestly. He knew he'd failed. He knew *why* he'd failed. But, even in hindsight, it was hard to imagine doing anything else. "I just couldn't cope any longer."

"I see," Monica said. "And…what now?"

Richard shrugged. Monica had a duty to report a superior officer who was unfit for duty. It wouldn't be easy for her, he knew, and the inevitable Board of Inquiry would ask a number of pointed questions, but it was her duty. And yet, it might harm her career. Even if she wasn't seen as a tattle-tale, even if he spoke out in her defence…there were people who wouldn't want her anywhere near them. A person who reported her senior officer for *anything*, even an open-and-shut case of corruption or abuse, wouldn't endear herself to her future superiors.

Particularly if she didn't report her suspicions at once, Richard thought, numbly. There was a point when a refusal to report something became complicity. He had a nasty feeling that Monica had already crossed that line. *And if the inquiry reveals that she was sleeping with me…*

He felt his hand start to shake as he considered the possibilities. Monica should—technically—have reported her concerns as soon as she'd had them, even though a medical check-up might have revealed that she was overreacting. Might. But she hadn't reported her concerns…either out of misplaced loyalty or a simple awareness that, if she was wrong, she would blow her relationship with her commanding officer out of the water. Now…if she reported him now, she would be asked why she hadn't reported him sooner. And there would be no good answer she could give. An inquiry wouldn't understand the realities of life on a starship. They wouldn't realise that Monica had been caught between a rock and a hard place.

Damn them, he thought. *Damn me.*

He felt a stab of bitter guilt. The stim was already starting to wear off. The urge to inject himself again was almost overpowering, even though it couldn't have been more than fifteen minutes since he'd taken the *first* stim. His body was already becoming dependent…no, Monica was right.

He *was* dependent on the stims. He was dangerously unfit for duty. He'd told himself that he could balance the stims, that he could use them without suffering any ill-effects, but he was wrong. He'd ruined his career and he was on the verge of ruining hers too.

"I will go to sickbay," he said, slowly. He forced himself to stand on wobbly knees. "I will go to sickbay and report myself unfit for duty."

Monica raised her eyebrows. "Are you sure you'll go there?"

"Yeah." Richard shrugged. "It's the only way."

He looked down at the deck, feeling another spasm of guilt. He'd tell the doctor that he'd been taking stims regularly and let her draw her own conclusions. If he was lucky, he'd either be relieved of duty and benched for the remainder of the deployment or simply sent home on the next convoy. He'd get a medical discharge and...hopefully, no one would ever know that Monica had known. It might just save her career. He tried not to think about the other possibilities. He wasn't sure he could live with himself if he destroyed her too.

And perhaps you should have thought about that before you started taking the stims, his conscience said. He felt knives of guilt piercing his heart. He'd failed in his duty. He was responsible for seventy-two pilots and he'd failed them all, both the ones who had died under his command and the ones who'd survived. *You fucked up, son, and now someone else is going to suffer alongside you.*

"They'll send me home," he said. "And you can take my place."

Monica winced. Richard didn't blame her. The appointment was a poisoned chalice at the best of times. Now, if the truth came out, there would be people who would wonder if she'd *deliberately* sabotaged Richard's career so she could take his job. It all depended, he supposed, on just how much of the story leaked out. Maybe it would be better to bring in someone new, someone utterly untainted by the scandal...someone who wouldn't *know* the pilots under his command. He laughed at himself, silently. The whole crisis had started because he'd known his pilots too well before they died.

He cursed himself under his breath. He remembered their names. He remembered their faces. Sometimes, late at night, he imagined that they were watching him from the great beyond. He'd been told that was one sign of a guilty conscience, but he hadn't killed any of them personally. They'd merely died under his command. Perhaps they would have lived if someone else had been in command...

It doesn't matter, he told himself. *They died. They will never marry, have kids, watch them grow up...*

He cleared his throat. "I don't blame you," he said. His career was over. He might as well do what he could to save hers. Perhaps that would make him look a little better, when the Board of Inquiry decided his fate. Even if it didn't...it was the right thing to do. He'd placed Monica in a horrible position. It was worth making things worse for himself if he made them better for her. "You did the right thing."

"Did I?" Monica met his eyes. "I should have gone to the XO at once, shouldn't I?"

Richard nodded, stiffly. "I'll go now," he said. "You go back to your squadron and try to look surprised when I'm relieved of duty."

Monica gave him a sharp look, but turned and headed to the hatch without saying anything. Richard was almost relieved. What *could* she say? He'd made a string of mistakes, of bad choices, and now he had to pay for them. The only thing he could do was pray that she wasn't dragged down too.

He watched the hatch close behind her, then reached for the packet of stims. The plastic felt heavy in his hand, as if the weight of the world rested in the tabs. He wanted—he *needed*—to inject himself once again, but...gritting his teeth, ignoring the little voices that said he'd need them again, he walked into the washroom and dumped the packet into the waste disposal tube. A moment later, they were gone.

And I'll be gone too, Richard thought, taking one last look around his cabin. He wouldn't be seeing it again, one way or the other. His successor would take the cabin as well as everything else. *I might not even be allowed to come back and pack.*

He paused, fighting the insane urge to do nothing. No one *liked* confessing their sins, even if they were mistakes rather than outright crimes. He'd certainly never liked admitting his misdeeds at school…and there, the consequences had been short and unpleasant rather than something that would blight the rest of his life. His lips twitched. None of his schoolmasters had ever been able to threaten his career. The nastiest punishment they'd been permitted to issue hadn't lasted beyond the end of term.

Time to go, he told himself, firmly. There was no point in putting it off any longer. He owed it to Monica to get it over with as quickly as possible. *It's time to take it like a man.*

And then the alarms began to howl.

CHAPTER TWENTY-FOUR

ALICE HAD BEEN REVIEWING the data from Margo when her terminal bleeped.

It wasn't something she had any special insight into, although she understood that one of the xenospecialists had speculated that she might have an unconscious awareness of how the virus thought...assuming, of course, that it thought at all in any way a human might recognise. The virus was planning something, she was sure, but that belief came from her tactical training rather than anything more...alien. It wasn't as if the virus could afford to sit on its arse and *let* humanity built up the force necessary to challenge it. It needed to absorb as much of humanity's territory as possible before it was too late.

She put the datapad aside and poked the terminal, wondering who'd contacted her. Major Parkinson and his subordinates were running a special exercise, one she'd been ordered to skip. Anyone else...she couldn't imagine anyone else who would deliberately seek out her company. She hadn't had any real friends on the ship outside Marine Country, even before she'd been infected. Now...she still didn't have any real friends. She keyed the pad and blinked in surprise as the message popped up in front of her. It was her father. He was onboard *Invincible*.

"What the fuck?" Alice couldn't believe it. "How the hell...?"

She sat upright, her fingers dancing over the console. Her father couldn't be on the ship, could he? It took her several moments, working her way through various databases, to work out that the master of *Vanderveken*—Captain Alan Campbell, formerly of the Royal Navy—had been invited onboard *Invincible* by Captain Shields. She felt a sudden stab of purely irrational betrayal—she *knew* it was irrational—as she probed the databases further, trying to determine why her father had been invited in the first place. A conference, apparently…the databases weren't any more informative. Her security clearance wasn't anything like high enough to find out what the conference was actually *about*.

"Damn him," she muttered. It had been easy enough to ignore his messages requesting a meeting. No one was getting any shore leave, not when the entire system was bracing itself for an attack. There was no way she could have convinced Major Parkinson to let her take a trip to *Vanderveken*. But now…Alice and her father were so close together that they were practically touching. It was a great deal harder to say no. "What now?"

She stared down at the terminal, barely seeing the words on the display. She could simply ignore the message. It would be easy enough. God knew she'd ignored the other messages from her father. But…she wanted to see him, even though she wasn't sure what she wanted to do. Hug him or kill him? Her father had been there for her, when she'd been a little girl; he'd put her on her first bike, he'd walked her to school, he'd…he'd murdered her mother, damn him. She rested her head in her hands for a long moment. It would have been easier if *all* the memories had been bad. She could have declined the message and put the whole affair out of her mind.

If you go see him now, you might be disappointed, a voice said at the back of her mind. It sounded like Major Parkinson. *But if you don't go see him, you will always wonder what would have happened if you had.*

Alice let out a sigh, then tapped a brief acknowledgement into the terminal. It wasn't easy deciding *where* to meet. She didn't want to bring her father into Marine Country, let alone her tiny cabin. But where *could* they go? The observation blister was out and there weren't *that* many other places…

her lips curved as she made up her mind. It would be interesting to see if her father realised where he was going. Perhaps it would make the bastard a little uncomfortable.

She stood, brushed down her uniform and checked her sidearm. Perhaps it would be better to leave it behind...Major Parkinson would chew her out for not carrying it, if he noticed, but she wasn't sure she wanted the temptation. There was a part of her that wanted to shoot her father dead. And yet...she told herself she was being silly. Her *body* was a weapon. She'd been trained to kill. She could hardly render herself harmless unless she donned shackles and...snorting, she holstered her sidearm and headed for the hatch. She wanted to be there before her father. Let him come to her, rather than going to him.

The compartment was empty, she noted when she arrived. Technically, anyone who wanted to use the compartment had to book, but she'd heard through the grapevine that most crewmen didn't bother. She'd never used one herself, not on *Invincible*. She opened the hatch, glanced into the wash-room to make sure it was definitely empty, then sat down on the bed. There were no distractions in the compartment, not even a terminal. She had to smile at the thought. The people who came to the compartment made their own entertainment.

She took a deep breath, forcing herself to wait patiently. Something was going to happen, but what? She could *feel* it. Boredom was good, she reminded herself; she knew she didn't really believe it. It felt like hours before there was a knock on the hatch. Alice tapped the switch with her foot, opening it. Her father stood on the far side.

Alice stood, slowly. "Come in."

Her father had been handsome, when he'd been a young man. Now... he looked old, old and gray. He reminded her of some of the retired marines she'd met, during her training; men who kept themselves in shape, but were steadily losing the battle with time. Her father was healthy enough, she supposed, but he was showing traces of life in a low-gee environment. His eyes were still sharp, yet...there was something about him that suggested he was struggling to keep himself together. But then, he *had* been through hell. Colchester, then the fires of the First Interstellar War, then being frozen… he'd been lucky to survive. Alice was sure that sort of experience would leave a mark on anyone.

"Alice," her father said. He sounded hesitant. She supposed that, to him, she'd aged twenty years in a second. "It is you, isn't it?"

"Yes," Alice said, biting down the impulse to deny everything. "It's me."

Her father looked around the compartment as the hatch hissed closed. "What *is* this place?"

Alice allowed herself a cold smile. "It is a privacy tube, father," she said, with a sweetness she didn't feel. "Crewmen come here when they want to be intimate. It is also a good place to talk."

She watched her father closely, trying to gauge his feelings. A flurry of emotions crossed his face, too quickly for her to identify any of them. She'd done her best to choose a place that would make him feel uncomfortable, although—she acknowledged privately—her father *had* been a starfighter pilot. He'd served on starships too. But then, he'd also been faithful to his wife until he'd caught her having an affair. Alice supposed it was possible that he'd never seen a privacy tube before.

And he wouldn't expect me to reserve one for our chat, she thought. *What daughter would want to bring her father here?*

"I wanted to talk to you," her father said, finally. His voice was softer than she remembered, with a trace of a Belter accent. "I tried to contact you…"

"Yes, you did." Alice crossed her arms. "I think I made it clear that I didn't *want* any further contact with you."

"I'm your father," her father said. "My flesh and blood…"

"My father killed my mother," Alice snapped. The urge to just lash out was almost overpowering. She'd learnt to control herself, but her control was starting to fray. It would feel so *good* to ram her fist into her father's throat. "I was an orphan from the day they took you away."

"I know," her father said. He sat down on the bed. "There is nothing I can do to make up for my crime. I was just so *angry*."

Alice leaned against the bulkhead. "I inherited your temper," she said. She'd been a holy terror at boarding school. She admitted that, in the privacy of her own mind. She'd come very close to being expelled, more times than she cared to admit. "But a bad temper doesn't excuse murder."

"No, it doesn't," her father said. He seemed unsure what to say. "I wanted to talk to you just once, before the end."

"You're going to die?" Alice lifted her eyebrows. She wasn't sure how she felt about *that*, not now. Once, she would have been relieved to hear that her father had passed away. "You know it?"

"This war is going to be bad," her father pointed out. "That's why I volunteered for military service, you see. *Vanderveken*...was designed to serve as a fast transport, if necessary. I crammed her hull with missiles and set out to serve the combined fleet."

"How...*patriotic*...of you," Alice said. "You don't *know* you're going to die."

Her father tapped his chest. "I was frozen for years, as you know. There wasn't any time to make the proper preparations, either. When I was unfrozen...well, the long-term effects have been...unpleasant. I'll spare you the gory details, but suffice it to say that I am probably reaching the end of my life. The doctors think I won't last another two years."

Alice scowled. "You should have been hanged."

"I know," her father said. "I was just so...*angry*."

"Angry," Alice repeated. "You were angry."

She glared at him. "You could have demanded a separation, on the spot. No one would have taken her side, not when it became clear that she was cheating on a serviceman who was on active duty. Everyone would have shunned her. You would have been granted custody, even if she fought for us. God damn it, you wouldn't have had to pay her a penny! She would have had to rebuild her life, while you and we went on..."

A wave of bitter anger cascaded through her mind. "Instead, you *killed* her. I—we—lost our father and mother at the same time. We had to go to Grandma and Granddad, who loved us both dearly but couldn't cope with two disturbed girls. I went to boarding school and…and…they taught me control. They taught me…"

But that wasn't entirely true, she knew. The schoolmistresses had had no qualms about punishing her for fighting, but it hadn't been the threat of everything from detentions and corporal punishment to outright expulsion that had deterred her. It had been the fear of ending up like her father, of destroying her entire life in a single act of madness. She'd felt her temper, she'd felt the mad urge to lash out with all her strength. And she knew, all too well, that if she didn't learn to control it, one day it would overwhelm her and her life would come crashing down in ruins.

"I know what I did," her father said. "And I'm sorry."

Alice clenched her fists. "How many times do you have to say *sorry* to bring her back to life?"

Her father flinched, as if she'd struck him. "I can't bring her back…"

"No," Alice said. "And yet you expect me to forgive you?"

"I haven't forgiven *myself*," her father said. "I don't expect you or Jeanette to forgive me either."

"The Belters seem to have forgiven you," Alice snarled. She'd never liked the Belters. She wondered, sourly, if she disliked the Belters because they'd given her father a home. "You have wives and husbands amongst the asteroids, do you not?"

"Yes," her father said. "But they haven't *all* accepted me."

"My heart bleeds," Alice said, sarcastically. "A man who murdered his wife, trying to live amongst a group of people who regard *family* as supremely important. I cannot *imagine* why they might refuse to accept you."

Her father met her eyes. "Would you like me to kill myself?"

Alice blinked. "What?"

"To kill myself?" Her father's voice was flat, as if he was too numb to feel anything. It struck her, suddenly, that she'd inherited more from her father than just a nasty temper. "To deliberately end my life?"

"Don't be stupid," Alice snarled.

"I can't undo what I did," her father said. "All I can do is try to make up for it."

Alice clenched her fists until her nails were digging into her palms. "Do you think there is *anything* you can do to make up for it?"

She cursed herself for agreeing to meet him, she cursed him for being a monster...who wasn't, in the end, very monstrous. She knew there were worse people out there. She'd taken a professional delight in ending the lives of men who ran rape camps, who exploited refugees or used women as nothing more than breeding stock to produce more fighters...she knew there were even a handful of abusers who were very close to home. There had been one girl at boarding school...if the rumours had been accurate, the girl's father had been a true monster. She shuddered at the thought. Why couldn't *her* father have been a real monster? It would have been so easy to hate him.

And no one would have blamed me if I'd killed him, she thought, numbly. *No one at all.*

"I have to try," her father said. "And if that means facing you, and your temper, then that is what I have to do."

"Yes," Alice said. "But I want nothing from you."

She forced herself to relax. It was hard, so hard, to keep her temper under control. A single punch...she could take him out of her life completely. Or she could snap his neck. Or draw her sidearm and put a bullet into his skull. She wanted to do it. Yes, she wanted to do it. He deserved to die. But it would destroy whatever remained of her career. She'd lose everything in a single moment of madness. She'd...

She'd be just like her father.

"There isn't anything you can offer me," she said. "There isn't anything you can give me that would *please* me. Even your death wouldn't make me feel any better about..."

She shook her head. She'd brought some of her troubles on herself. She could admit that, at least in the privacy of her own mind. And others had happened because no one had known what the virus could do until it was too late. But many of her problems had stemmed from her mother's death, and there was *nothing* he could do to change that. No one could change the past. All they could do was try to move on.

"I understand," her father said. "I wanted to see you, one last time, before…"

"You're not going to die," Alice said, firmly. "And I'm sure Jeanette would be a great deal more sympathetic."

"We did exchange a few messages," her father said. "And she…she isn't happy, but…"

"Her father murdered her mother," Alice mocked. "Why in the name of God Almighty would she be *unhappy*?"

Her father flinched, again. "Alice…"

Alice cut him off, ruthlessly. "You know, when I was at boarding school I slapped a girl. She'd mouthed off to me…I've forgotten what she said, now. Something bad enough to anger me to the point I slapped her to the ground. Hard. And I was punished for it, of course. They never let you get away with anything at that school.

"And you know what? Everyone was scared of me for weeks afterwards. I'd been punished—they *knew* I'd been punished—but they were still scared of me. Scared to talk, scared to open up, scared to invite me to join them… if I hadn't been sporty, I would probably have been friendless for *years*. I'd served my time and they were *still* reluctant to let me get close to them again. And *you* have the same problem. You did something unforgivable. Why do you think anyone *has* to let you in? Why should my sister and I ever trust you again when you destroyed our family?"

She took a breath. "Society punished you," she said. "But do you think that's enough to make up for what you did to *us*? Or to convince people that you won't do it again?"

"I know," her father said. "But that doesn't stop me wanting to reconnect with my children."

"I don't want to reconnect," Alice said. "I know, you're my biological father. But you destroyed all right to call yourself my father the day you destroyed my family. There's nothing you can do to fix it. The little girl who came to you for a hug when she fell off the bike and scraped her knee is *gone*."

Her father stood. "I understand," he said. "And I won't call you again. If you want to talk...you can call me instead."

"Thanks," Alice said, sourly. She wanted to kill something. "Bye."

"I am proud of you, for what it's worth," her father added. "You've done well for yourself."

He left before Alice could think of a rejoinder. Her mind was churning, a tidal wave of bitterness and resentment and a sense that—once again—she'd lost something important to her. She wanted to run after him, although she wasn't sure what she wanted to do. Hug him, or put a bullet in him. She damned him, savagely, for coming to her. She would have been happier if she'd never talked to him again...

...And then the alarms started to howl.

CHAPTER TWENTY-FIVE

ADMIRAL ZADORNOV had been in the CIC when all hell broke loose.

She had been, she had to admit, frustrated with the caution of her superior officers. The various governments on Earth were reluctant to condone raids into Margo, let alone attempts to fight her way back into Falkirk or even invade Alien-One itself. She understood their fears, but she also understood just how dangerous it was to do nothing. The cold realities of interstellar warfare meant the human race simply *couldn't* be strong everywhere. They needed to take the offensive before the virus slipped more raiders into the inner systems and started tearing the guts out of the human race.

One moment, the display had been showing the growing fleet of warships holding station near Zheng He; the next, the display was full of red icons. For a moment, Svetlana's mind refused to believe what she was seeing. It was a drill. It *had* to be a drill. There was no way that hundreds of alien warships could have slipped so close to the human ships without being detected. The MNF had deployed hundreds of scansats and recon platforms, scattering them over the inner system without—for once—the slightest hint of concern about the cost. A handful of ships might sneak through the cordon, but an entire fleet? No. It couldn't have gotten so close without being detected...

...And yet, somehow, it had.

"Alert the fleet," she snapped. It couldn't be a drill. No one would have risked carrying out a surprise drill without informing her, not when it could lead to disaster. The last thing the frail alliance needed was a deadly friendly fire incident. "Bring the ships to battlestations, send a message up the chain to Earth…"

She forced herself to think as her subordinates hurried to work. Admiral Weisskopf was technically in command, at least as long as the MNF remained at Zheng He, but he was out of touch. He'd gone on an inspection tour, if she recalled correctly. God alone knew when he'd be able to assume command, if indeed he was in a *position* to assume command. He could be on a shuttlecraft, flying through the worst of the storm. She keyed her console, informing the fleet that she was assuming command. Weisskopf could take it when—if—he reached a CIC of his own.

"Missile separation," one of her aides snapped. "I say again, *missile separation!*"

"Holy God," someone breathed.

Svetlana was inclined to agree. The enemy ships were firing thousands—no, *hundreds* of thousands—of missiles. She hadn't seen anything like it, not outside simulations where the designer had given the enemy impossible capabilities to see what the trainees would do when faced with a no-win situation. The MNF might not have enough point defence to survive the storm, no matter what it did. She knew, all too well, that the fleet *would* be damaged. The only question was how badly.

"Move the smaller ships into position to intercept the missiles," she ordered. On the display, both sides were launching starfighters. She cursed under her breath. The ready squadrons had already launched, of course, but the remaining starfighters were taking their time. Of course they were. The pilots had been asleep, or drilling, or fucking, or whatever they did when they were not flying their starfighters or waiting in the launch tubes for the command to fly. "And order the starfighters to join them in engaging the missiles."

A chill seemed to blow through the air as more enemy ships made themselves known. There were hundreds of them: battleships, carriers, cruisers… and dozens of converted freighters, spewing out missiles at a terrifying rate. How the hell had they managed to get so close? She didn't have to look at the system display to know that the enemy had pulled it off perfectly. They were not only in engagement range, although that would be bad enough; they were blocking her line of retreat to the next system. The MNF had to win the engagement or break contact, neither of which would be easy. She felt her heart sink as she watched the wall of missiles raging into her formation. Her ships had been caught with their pants down. This was going to hurt.

They used a Catapult, she realised, numbly. Why hadn't they seen it coming? They *knew* it was possible. The Second Interstellar War wouldn't have been won without a Catapult. But they also knew that Catapults were both incredibly expensive and dangerously unpredictable. It had quite simply never occurred to any of the planners that the virus would not only build *a* Catapult, but several Catapults. *We keep thinking of the virus as being limited by human economics…*

She shook her head. That was a problem for later. Right now, she had a more immediate problem.

"Admiral, the missiles are entering the outer edge of the defence perimeter," an officer reported. "We're killing hundreds of them."

And there are thousands to go, Svetlana thought, silently thanking the planners who'd insisted on constant missile defence drills. The MNF might have been caught by surprise, but its datanet was already weaving the fleet and its point defence into a single entity. Hundreds of missiles were vanishing from the display, the weapons that had killed them already moving to challenge the next target. But for every missile the point defence killed, two more seemed to take its place. *We're badly outgunned.*

She watched, grimly, as the first wave of missiles started to slam home. The virus was deliberately targeting the smaller ships, clearing the way for the second wave of missiles. Svetlana tapped commands into her console, ordering the point defence datanet to assign more weapons to cover the smaller ships although she knew it was pointless. There were too many missiles, with too many possible targets. A battleship, powering up her drives, found herself targeted by a swarm of missiles. Four lasted long enough to strike her hull, inflicting enough damage to cripple her. A fleet carrier was less lucky. Seven missiles slammed into her hull, setting off a chain reaction that blew her to hell. Svetlana cursed under her breath. The ship hadn't even managed to launch all her starfighters before she'd died...

"*Shinano* is gone, Admiral," an aide said. "*Foch* is taking heavy damage..."

"Order the fleet to cover the carriers," Svetlana ordered. The virus was going to devastate her fleet...and the hell of it was that she could barely hit back. "And signal the planet. They are to implement the emergency procedures and go underground."

"Aye, Admiral."

Svetlana nodded, forcing herself to think. The enemy starfighters had entered engagement range too, spending themselves recklessly to target the human ships. They were slashing away at her defences, weakening her before the bigger ships arrived to finish the job. She had to admire their determination, although she knew the virus's host-bodies didn't really have any sense of self-preservation. The remainder of their fleet followed, the missile freighters picking up speed...she gritted her teeth as she realised they meant to ram any targets of opportunity. The virus was spending its starfighters and ships like water, but it might just work out in its favour. Svetlana was unable to either run or fight without exposing her fleet to catastrophic damage.

"*Texas* is taking heavy damage, Admiral," another aide said. "She seems to have been singled out for special attention."

She's a battleship, Svetlana thought. *She would be a priority target whatever happened. Or...is she being targeted because she's a flagship?*

"Give her what cover you can," she ordered, shortly. The neatly-organised command groups had been shot to hell. Admiral Weisskopf's subordinates were going to be scattered, if Admiral Weisskopf was dead or out of contact. Hers wouldn't be much better. The virus was aiming to smash datanet groups and…the hell of it was that it was succeeding. That shouldn't have been possible. "And start rotating the command datanets. I do *not* want a general collapse."

"Aye, Admiral."

Svetlana forced herself to *think*. Her ships needed time, time they weren't going to get. They needed to close the range to bring their heavy weapons to bear, but…by the time they closed the range, they were going to be badly weakened. She rather suspected she'd lost control of the system. The virus was going to either drive her out or force her to stand and die…she shook her head. Thankfully, they'd evacuated most of the population. Zheng He wasn't so important that she had to die in its defence.

They can't hit us with another swarm of missiles, she told herself. *And that means there are limits to how much firepower they can bring to bear on us.*

Another carrier—a converted freighter—vanished from the display. She barely heard the aide informing her that the Belter ship was gone. The reports were an endless liturgy of disaster: ships damaged, ships destroyed, entire squadrons of starfighters wiped out…she put the dismay aside and forced herself to think clearly. She'd lost the battle, almost as soon as it had begun. She needed to save what she could.

"Undamaged capital ships are to form up on *Invincible* and prepare to retreat," she ordered, keeping her voice calm. She'd wondered, in the privacy of her own mind, how Admiral Weisskopf had lost the battle at Falkirk. She knew now. "Damaged ships are to hold the line."

A dull tremor ran through the ship. An aide looked up. "Direct hit, section seven!"

Svetlana ignored it. "Relay the orders," she said. "And inform the next in line that he may inherit command."

The display updated. Two more destroyers vanished, their icons blinking out. There would be time to remember—later—that the icons represented metal ships, crewed by flesh and blood crewmen. Sentiment had never been encouraged in the Russian Navy, but she'd always tried to remember her crewmen weren't *machines*. She cursed her weakness, a second later. She needed to make hard decisions. She couldn't do that if she became afraid to sacrifice a single life.

Hold the line, she told herself. The enemy attack had been powerful—and shocking—but it was a conventional attack now. *Hold the line and hope that they break over us.*

• • •

Richard stared at the hatch, utterly unsure what to do. He knew he should go to sickbay, like he'd promised; he knew he should report himself unfit for duty. But the alarms meant the ship was under attack, under attack in the middle of a friendly system! Nothing short of utter desperation would have prompted the captain to order his starfighters to launch immediately. And Richard's subordinates didn't *know* what had happened to him. They'd assume he was still in command...

And the confusion could get them killed, he thought. He opened the hatch and ran down the corridor, heading for the flight deck. *I have to take command, or all hell will break loose.*

He tried not to think about what he was doing as he passed through the intersection and raced on. Confusion raged all around him as the crew rushed to battlestations, some rushing supplies from one compartment to another while others took up position to repel boarders, fingering their weapons as if they expected to see the enemy at any moment. The lights brightened slightly, a grim reminder that the virus couldn't survive for long without a host-body. Richard hoped the precaution would be enough to prevent mass infection. The entire crew couldn't don spacesuits without a major drop in efficiency.

"She's ready to fly, sir," a crewman called. He gave Richard a quick thumbs-up. "Just don't crash into an asteroid."

Richard blinked in shock—Monica had said the same thing—and then dismissed it as coincidence. It had to be a coincidence. The rest of his squadron were hurrying to their fighters—he caught a brief glimpse of Monica, her short blonde hair instantly recognisable—and readying themselves for battle. He felt a pang of guilt, which he quickly suppressed. He'd have to explain himself later, when the battle was over, but until then…

"Prepare for launch," he ordered, as the starfighters were moved into the launch tubes. He checked the live feed from the ship's sensors and swore. There was a *massive* enemy fleet bearing down on the MNF. Something was wrong about the positioning, but what? It took him several seconds to realise that the fleet clearly *hadn't* come from Margo. "Give them hell…"

He glanced at the display as the catapults shot the starfighters into space. They didn't have any specific orders, not yet. Standing orders were to cover the carrier, now the former CSP had been called forward to cover the remainder of the fleet. He saw a brief twinkle of light with the naked eye, cursing it under his breath as he realised another ship had died. The MNF was taking a battering. Too many ships were already damaged or destroyed.

Monica bleeped him on the private channel. "What the hell are you doing?"

"Defending the mothership," Richard snapped. A seemingly-endless wave of alien starfighters were boring their way towards *Invincible*, targeting their torpedoes on the carrier's hull. Given a chance, they'd blow the carrier into dust. "Everything else can wait until later."

He switched channels before she could respond and started snapping orders to his squadron. They *had* to break up the alien formation before it entered attack range. He gunned his drives and lanced forward, half-expecting the remainder of the pilots to refuse his orders. If Monica had warned the others, if she'd suggested he was unfit for duty…he let out a sigh of relief as the pilots followed him. He was going to have to do a *lot* of explaining afterwards, but—for the moment—he was in command.

An alien starfighter lunged at him, guns spitting plasma death in his general direction. The targeting wasn't too accurate, but it hardly mattered. Richard fired back, blowing the alien pilot into dust and evading his wingman's fire a second before the next alien starfighter was destroyed. Four more alien craft dropped out of formation, trying to drive Richard's squadron away while the remainder of the enemy ships continued their drive towards *Invincible*. Richard gritted his teeth and ignored the provocation, choosing instead to engage the torpedo-bombers. They *couldn't* be allowed to attack *Invincible* with impunity.

If they take out a carrier, we're in trouble, he thought. A handful of carriers seemed to be missing from the display. *We can't recover fighters without a carrier...*

"Watch your back," Monica said. Her voice was very cold. He knew she'd have a lot more to say if the channel wasn't public. "You have a bogey on your six."

"I see him," Richard said. He flipped the starfighter over, firing as he brought his guns to bear. The alien starfighter exploded. "Don't let them get any closer to *Invincible*."

"There's too many of them," another pilot said. His voice rose in panic. "I..."

The voice stopped, abruptly. Richard didn't need to look at the display to know that the pilot was dead. It was almost a relief that he barely knew anything about the young man—he couldn't even remember the man's name. He'd have to think of something nice to say about the poor bastard, if he survived long enough to hold a proper ceremony...he shook his head tiredly. It was better not to think about the pilots, not to know them as people. It made it easier when they died.

Monica was right, he thought, as he chased a pair of enemy starfighters that were throwing themselves at *Invincible*. They were driving down, swinging from side to side to evade the carrier's point defence. *I really am unfit for duty.*

One enemy starfighter flipped over and came right at him. Richard yanked his starfighter to one side, flashing past the enemy before either of them could do more than fire a handful of shots in the other's direction. He ignored the starfighter behind him, trusting it would take the alien a few seconds to reverse course and bring his weapons to bear; he hurled himself at the other starfighter, the one that was starting to launch torpedoes right at *Invincible's* hull. Richard blew him away before he could unload all of his weapons, silently praying it was enough. *Invincible* was tough, but her armour wasn't quite up to spec...

But she can take more damage than any fleet carrier, he reminded himself. *Invincible* had taken a *lot* of damage since the war had begun. *Can't she?*

"Good shooting," Monica said. She still sounded wary. "Only another few thousand to go."

"We're not alone," Richard reminded her. He felt better than he had in months, although he knew it was an illusion. When the adrenaline wore off, he was going to sink back into the slump. And this time, there would be no hope of taking another stim. "We have to give them hell."

He broke through into clear space and took a handful of seconds to check the overall situation. The enemy fleet was launching another wave of starfighters – rearmed starfighters—he guessed—while struggling to bring its main guns into range. It looked as if the admiral was organising a counterattack, but the human fleet had already been badly weakened. Too many carriers were gone or crippled. The Battle of Zheng He was shaping up into another disaster.

Concentrate, he told himself, as another flight of enemy starfighters appeared. Their weapons were already blazing, filling space with deadly plasma bolts. *Concentrate on what you're doing, or die.*

CHAPTER TWENTYSIX

"ADMIRAL WEISSKOPF is confirmed dead, sir," Newcomb reported. "He was on a shuttle when the attack began and...he didn't survive."

Stephen nodded, curtly. There was no time to mourn. The battle was only minutes old and already within shouting distance of being lost. He watched, grimly, as the remaining starfighters were ejected into space, *Invincible* quivering silently as her point defence covered their launch. So far, *Invincible* didn't seem to have drawn significant enemy attention—a handful of torpedoes were not a serious threat, unless the virus got lucky—but it was only a matter of time until that changed.

"Bring us about," he ordered. He hated the idea of retreat, but the situation was rapidly becoming untenable. The fleet's forward elements were already engaging the alien battleships. "Prepare to fall back on the tramline."

He forced himself to think as two more ships dropped out of the datanet. Admiral Zadornov was still in command, but her ship was under heavy attack. Command might devolve to one of her subordinates—possibly Stephen himself—at any time. He'd already assumed command of the rear elements. He didn't want to split the fleet, giving the virus a chance to concentrate its firepower against one formation and crush it before the other could intervene, but he might not have a choice. They had to preserve as many warships as they could.

"Alien ships are approaching the planet," Morse reported. "They're already engaging the orbital facilities."

Poor bastards, Stephen thought. The majority of the facilities had been evacuated, but the planetary government had insisted on leaving caretaker crews in place. He hoped they'd have the time—and sense—to take to the escape pods before the virus blew the facilities to dust. The people on the surface would have to go underground and hope for the best. *There's nothing we can do for them now.*

He dismissed the thought as a wave of enemy starfighters crashed over *Invincible*, firing a stream of torpedoes towards her hull. A dull quiver ran through his ship as two torpedoes slammed home, alerts flashing up in front of him before fading away as it became clear the damage was minimal. He breathed a sigh of relief as repair crews hurried to the damaged sections. So far, the virus hadn't realised that parts of his armour were weaker than others. A single torpedo in the wrong place might do real damage.

"The enemy fleet is pushing us hard," Arthur reported. "Gunships inbound. I say again, gunships inbound."

"Engage them when they come into range," Stephen ordered. Gunships were larger than starfighters—and considerably easier to hit—but they could carry full-sized shipkiller missiles instead of starfighter torpedoes. They could be nasty customers if their target's point defence network had already been degraded. "And prepare to reroute the datanet if necessary."

"Aye, sir."

"Orders from the flag, Captain," Morse said. "We're to begin the retreat now."

And leave everyone else in the shit, Stephen thought. He assessed the situation quickly. It was *possible* that they'd be able to break contact and sneak through Tramline One, retreating further into human space, but unlikely. They were just too close to the enemy fleet to break contact without considerable difficulty. Admiral Zadornov would have real problems delaying the alien fleet long enough for Stephen to escape. *But what choice do we have?*

"Signal the flotilla," he ordered, shortly. "The remaining ships are to form up on us and begin the retreat."

"Aye, Captain."

Stephen winced. There was going to be a *lot* of confusion. All the carefully-negotiated command arrangements had been shot to hell in the last few minutes. A number of officers were dead or missing...there was going to be a serious argument over who should be in command, once the shooting stopped. He snorted, inwardly. They didn't have *time* to argue over who should take command. Right now, survival came first. He watched his point defence pick off a handful of alien starfighters and smiled humourlessly. They could engage in pointless arguments once the real danger was removed.

"The enemy starfighters are regrouping," Newcomb warned. "They're targeting our drive section."

"Order the CSP to move to intercept," Stephen ordered. He couldn't allow the virus a clear shot at his drives. A handful of direct hits and his ship would be dead in space—or dead. "And move our escorts to cover us."

"Aye, Captain."

• • •

"Admiral, *Invincible* is breaking formation," an aide reported. "Her flotilla is taking shape around her."

"Good," Svetlana said. Too many ships were crippled already, but...if she could get the intact ships out of the line of fire, at least *some* of the fleet would survive. "Order the crippled ships to form up around us."

The ones that can, she added, silently.

She sucked in her breath as the aliens closed the range, trying to bring their main guns into play. A line of battleships led the way, followed by a cluster of fleet carriers and a single oversized starship. Svetlana felt a flicker of cold excitement as she studied the mystery ship, contemplating what she might be. If she was a battleship, she would have taken her place in the line of battle; if she was a missile ship, she would have shot herself dry by now. And there was certainly no way she was a carrier. The only thing she seemed to be carrying was point defence.

And that suggests they want her to survive, Svetlana thought. There was no point in building a battleship-sized point defence starship. The very thought was absurd. *A command ship?*

She keyed her terminal, bringing up the live feed from the recon platforms as the battle raged on. The network had been degraded, platforms blasted out of space or simply blinded by the sheer intensity of the fighting, but they could still pick up enough to suggest that the mystery ship *was* a command ship. It certainly seemed to be heavily protected, lingering behind the battleline rather than advancing forward to deal out death and destruction to the crippled human ships. The virus, which had seemed quite happily to spend entire fleets of starships like water in order to capture relatively minor targets, was behaving oddly. And that suggested…what?

"The crippled battleships are to punch through the enemy line of battle and engage the command ship," she ordered, calmly. It was suicide, but it might buy time for the remaining ships to escape. "I want every crippled ship closing the range."

She allowed herself a tight smile. The virus was going to win the day—there was no point in disputing it—yet it had made a mistake. Her ships—the crippled ships—couldn't hope to escape, but the virus couldn't stop *its* forces from closing the range either. It had committed itself to an engagement at point-blank range, instead of standing off and blasting her ships from a safe distance. There was no way it could keep her from ramming her crippled ships right into the teeth of its formation, sacrificing her cripples to win time. It was going to cost her everything, including her life, but it didn't matter. There was no way she could surrender.

And I wouldn't surrender, even if I could, Svetlana acknowledged, privately. *There's too much at stake.*

A shudder ran through the giant carrier. "Admiral, they're targeting our flight decks…"

"Order the starfighters to prepare to break contact and fall back on *Invincible's* flotilla on my command," Svetlana said. Alerts flashed up in front of her as another shudder ran through the ship. "We're not going to be able to recover them."

"Aye, Admiral."

. . .

Richard was having a hard time keeping track of the engagement as *Invincible* and her consorts—a formation that had been thrown together at breakneck speed—slowly started to retreat. The enemy starfighters were concentrating more on crippling the retreating ships rather than trying to destroy them, forcing him to deploy his starfighters to cover the targets as they came under attack. Half the command network seemed to have been shot to ribbons, leaving him unsure just who or what was under his command. Pilots flew with whatever wingmen they could pick up, somehow continuing the fight as organised squadrons crumbled under the pressure. He didn't have any time to think about anything but killing.

He cursed under his breath as he chased a trio of alien starfighters as they flashed towards *Invincible*, veering from side to side in a series of unpredictable manoeuvres. One of them flipped over, spinning within the drive field in a manner that Richard had rarely seen outside display flying; the enemy starfighter opened fire, even as he kept flying towards the giant carrier. Richard allowed himself a flicker of admiration for the enemy pilot, although he knew that the virus's host-body was indifferent to survival. There weren't many pilots who would have dared to adjust the drive field in the middle of a combat zone. His admiration didn't keep him from blowing the alien craft into dust. There was no time to watch it die. He had to sweep on to the next one.

Invincible's stern section seemed to blossom in front of him as he zoomed closer, alerts flashing up to warn him of incoming point defence fire. At such close range, the mothership's point defence could be as dangerous to her own starfighters as it was to the enemy. IFF was often dangerously unreliable when the safety of the mothership was at stake. An enemy starfighter settled into attack position; Richard took advantage of the brief predictability to blow it away, then target its wingman. The second starfighter managed to launch two torpedoes before it died, although one of them went wide. Richard just hoped it wasn't programmed to home in on the closest target before its drive section burnt itself out. A torpedo wasn't as dangerous as a missile, but it was very definitely the fastest thing in space.

"Incoming gunships," Monica warned. "They're moving into missile range."

Richard risked a glance at his squadron display. Four pilots were dead, two more missing...probably dead. They might just have lost contact with him and been absorbed into another squadron...he shrugged. Right now, they might as well be dead. Monica's squadron wasn't much better. Technically, he should merge the two squadrons into one, but he didn't have time. All the emergency drills had left out the goddamned emergency. There wouldn't be a smooth reorganisation when they were taking incoming fire.

"Form up on me," he ordered. The gunships weren't using active sensors to target their missiles, but they didn't have to. Right now, *Invincible* and her consorts were the largest targets within range. A blind man could fire a missile in her general direction, relying on the seeker head to guide the weapon to its target. Better to take the gunships out before they could launch their missiles. "Prepare to engage."

The gunships had an ace up their sleeve, he noted coldly as the range closed sharply. Their designers had packed a handful of point defence weapons into their hulls, giving them a chance to punch through the starfighters and get into firing range. They couldn't put out anything like as much firepower as a destroyer, let alone a battleship, but it hardly mattered. A single hit would almost certainly be enough to take out a starfighter. There were stories of pilots who had survived such hits, yet only two or three of them had ever been verified.

And they have their disadvantages too, he thought, wryly. There was a reason gunships had never been popular, outside a handful of patrol and customs duties. *They can't soak up as much damage as a ship of the line, either.*

He jammed his finger on the trigger as the gunship came into view. The enemy ship staggered under his fire, then exploded. Richard smirked as two more gunships followed their leader into death, the remainder launching their missiles in a desperate bid to get their blows in before it was too late. Gunships had their advantages, but at point-blank range they were no match for starfighters. Their attack pattern was weak, too. They'd clearly wanted to get closer before they fired their missiles, trusting in their drives to rush them to their targets before the point defence could sweep them out of space.

"Got him," Monica carolled.

"What an easy target," someone jeered. Richard made no attempt to place the voice. "He was a sitting duck."

"A sitting duck who was shooting his wad at me," Monica countered. "He was hardly a defenceless *duck!*"

"Good shooting," Richard said, before the argument could get out of hand. The last of the gunships exploded, a tiny fireball flickering and dying in the endless cold of space. He glanced at his display. The enemy starfighters were falling back, but he knew better than to think it was a good sign. They needed to be rearmed before they returned to the fray. "Squadron leaders, sound off."

He listened to the reports, feeling his heart clench. Nearly half of *Invincible's* starfighters were gone. They'd picked up a number of starfighters from other ships, but it wasn't enough to fill the gaps in his roster. He reminded himself, savagely, that he probably wouldn't have to *worry* about his roster once he returned to the ship...then kicked himself, mentally, for even *having* such an unworthy fault. Monica—or whoever succeeded him— would have to sort out the mess. If, of course, the virus gave them time.

His intercom bleeped. "All starfighters are to resume CSP duties."

Richard blinked. They could take the offensive, they could give the virus a taste of its own medicine. The virus's fleet carriers were clearly visible, even if they were on the wrong side of a line of battleships. The big ships were tough targets, but they had problems of their own right now. They were too busy trading blows with humanity's battleships to worry about flights of starfighters sneaking past them and engaging the fleet carriers...

He opened his mouth to argue, then changed his mind. They didn't have time.

"Understood," he said. Orders were orders. Besides, they needed to rearm some of their starfighters too. He just hoped they could do it before they ran out of time. The virus was winning. It wasn't going to just *let* the human fleet wander off. "We're on the way."

. . .

"Admiral, *Nevada* is closing with an alien battleship. She's going to ram."

Svetlana nodded, grimly. The American starship was trading blow for blow with the alien battleship, but both ships were too heavily armoured to take *much* damage. And yet, the Americans were still closing. The virus's ship was *trying* to evade, but the battleship was too big and unwieldy to escape before it was too late. She sucked in her breath as the two starships collided, vanishing in an eye-tearing flare of light. The display updated rapidly as a gap appeared in the alien formation. They didn't have the time to alter their positions to compensate.

"Take us through the gap," she ordered. *Nevada* had died to win them time. Other ships were fighting desperately to stay alive just long enough to hurt the enemy. She was damned if she was going to allow their sacrifice to be wasted. "And point us directly at the command ship."

"Aye, Admiral."

She gritted her teeth as the enemy ships, suddenly very aware of the danger, started to pound *Brezhnev* with every weapon they could bring to bear. Svetlana watched the damage mount up, knowing it was too late. Her ship wasn't going to survive long enough to be towed back to the shipyard, even if she tried to break off. A destroyed flight deck hardly mattered when the entire warship was about to be destroyed. She watched chunks of armour shredding under the impact, enemy weapons slicing deep into her hull. It was too late.

"Impact in thirty seconds, Admiral," her aide said.

"Order the remaining starfighters to fall back on *Invincible* now," Svetlana said. "Command of the fleet is to pass to Captain Shields."

"Aye, Admiral."

"*Vanguard* is under heavy fire," another aide called. "*Tirpitz* is leaking atmosphere…she's closing with her opponent."

She'll keep the enemy ship busy, even if she doesn't manage to ram, Svetlana thought. *And she will buy us a little more time.*

"Impact in ten seconds," her aide said. He sounded very calm, for someone who was about to die. "They're engaging us with popguns."

Svetlana smiled, coldly. The enemy command ship didn't carry any heavy weapons. A mistake, one the virus would bitterly regret. She doubted she could have reached point-blank range if the command ship had been armed to the teeth. The damage was still mounting up, but…they could shoot out her drives, now, and the two ships would *still* collide. They were too close, now, for the enemy ship to escape. Two more battleships rammed themselves into enemy ships, a third trying desperately to bring the enemy fleet carriers under fire before it was too late…her fleet was dying, but it would buy time. She just hoped it would be enough. She'd underestimated the virus. She hoped her successor, whoever commanded the next MNF, learnt from her mistakes.

Shouldn't have pushed me into death ground, she thought, darkly. She might not have committed herself if she'd seen any hope of saving her cripples from certain destruction. A more careful engagement might have suited the virus better, in the long run. *I had no choice but to fight to the last. And hope my death meant something.*

She stood, ignoring the shaking as her ship was steadily torn apart. The alerts were starting to blur together into a shrill tone, heralding total destruction. She clicked it off, watching the display as the alien ship came closer. Five seconds…three seconds…one…

There was a brilliant flash of white light, then nothing.

CHAPTER TWENTYSEVEN

STEPHEN CURSED UNDER HIS BREATH as he watched *Brezhnev* die.

He knew, intellectually, that the two ships had perished in a tearing explosion. He knew that both crews were almost certainly dead, unless they'd had time to get to the lifepods before a series of explosions tore their ships apart. But it was hard to *believe* it. The display showed nothing of the force that had shattered two mighty ships. Two icons had simply merged -- and vanished.

"Captain," Newcomb said. "Command has devolved to you."

"Understood," Stephen said. He'd already assumed command of the intact ships. It was a formidable fleet, if he managed to break contact long enough to regroup, repair, and figure out a way to take the offensive or sneak back to human space. "Recall the starfighters—*all* the starfighters—and parcel them out amongst the surviving carriers."

"Aye, Captain."

Arthur looked up from his console. "Captain, the enemy command network appears to have been hit hard. Their coordination is shot to hell."

Stephen leaned forward, studying the sensor feed. Arthur was right. It *looked* as if the virus had suddenly lost its command datanet. The webbing that bound its formations into a single entity was gone, each starship fighting alone rather than coordinating its fire with its fellows. It was still a powerful fleet—Stephen would have been wary of his chances in a straight fight, even if he had had time to repair his starships and rest his people—but it was suddenly less effective. It gave him a chance to break contact and escape.

"Prepare to deploy ECM drones," he ordered. "They're to cover our retreat."

He flicked through the displays, considering the various contingency plans. There was no hope of reaching Tramline One, not without abandoning the freighters and the handful of ships that couldn't make flank speed. Tramline Two was equally pointless, particularly with another enemy fleet lurking on the far side of the tramline. He *could* play a game of cat-and-mouse within the system for hours, perhaps days, but eventually the virus would run him down and smash his fleet to atoms. He needed to break contact, and do it in a manner that would make it difficult for the virus to follow him.

And that may be impossible, he thought, stiffly. There weren't many options. *We can't abandon the freighters, or we may as well give up any hope of stopping the offensive short of Terra Nova.*

"The starfighters have been recalled," Newcomb said. "They're reorganising the squadrons now."

"Get them rearmed as quickly as possible," Stephen ordered. The virus was probably rearming its own starfighters too. It wouldn't be long before it solved its command problems and resumed the offensive. "And reinforce the CSP..."

"Captain," Lieutenant Adams said. "I'm picking up new contacts, on a least-time course from Tramline Two."

"The fleet we saw on the far side," Newcomb commented.

"And a fleet with a command ship of its own," Stephen said. He didn't presume to understand how the virus thought, but it didn't matter. He couldn't afford a close engagement with one fleet while the other was breathing down his neck. There was no way he could smash even a disoriented fleet before its reinforcements entered firing range. It would be a mistake to let the fleets combine, but…he saw no way to prevent it. "They've solved their command and control problem."

He thought, fast. "Order the fleet to set course for"—he designated a coordinate on the terminal—"Point Alpha. At Alpha, we will go into cloak and deploy drones to suggest that we're running for Tramline One."

"Yes, sir," Newcomb said. "And where *will* we be going?"

"Tramline Four," Stephen said. It would give them a breathing space, perhaps long enough to repair the ships and plan their next move. "We cannot remain in this system."

His XO didn't look convinced, but he nodded. Stephen understood, all too well. Their options were very limited. Their ships were too badly damaged to rely on the cloaking devices to hide them, if they remained in Zheng He. And the virus had no particular reason to hold the system. There was little hope of carrying out a series of raids when there was nothing to hit, save for the alien fleet itself. He'd just have to hope they'd be able to repair their ships before it was too late.

Preserve what we can, he thought. *And hope for the best.*

"Captain, Force Two is altering course," Alison reported. "She's trying to run us down."

"Figures," Stephen growled. It made sense, if one didn't care about losses. Force Two might not be able to defeat his ships, but it could weaken them enough for Force One to deliver the final blow. Or…they could simply maintain contact, making it impossible for Stephen and his ships to hide. They had to keep the range as open as possible. "Keep us on course for Point Alpha."

He glanced at the stream of automated reports flowing into his console. Too many ships were damaged, too many starfighters blown out of space… it wasn't going to be easy to repair his ships and rebuild his squadrons, not with the prospect of another engagement at any moment. His people were working hard to do what they could, but there were limits. He studied the lists for a moment, then put them out of his mind. He'd worry about them later, if there *was* a later.

The virus needs to keep us from falling back through Tramline One, he thought. It was so hard to be *sure*. It *was* basic tactics, common sense, but... did the *virus* see it that way? Or was it convinced that the battered fleet was no further threat? *It can't let us fall back on reinforcements, can it?*

He cursed under his breath. The virus knew *everything* about human space...or, at least, it *should* know everything about human space. It *should* be capable of making informed guesses of everything from production rates to if and when humanity's allies would take the field. Every goddamned security precaution had melted like snow in the face of an enemy that could turn loyal men into willing traitors. But there was no way to know how the virus would interpret the data. Or how it would react to different threats. Logically, Stephen knew he was right. But would the virus care about human logic?

I have to assume the worst, he reminded himself.

He felt the seconds ticking by as Force Two picked up speed, clearly angling to get its fleet carriers into engagement range before it was too late. Force One was moving too, carefully slipping through the remains of the once-great MNF and heading directly for Stephen's remaining ships. It was moving with an odd lack of coordination, as if the different ships no longer had a single commanding officer, but it was moving all the same. Stephen silently worked his way through the vectors, calculating possible outcomes. Force One was moving slowly. It was possible, he supposed, that some of its ships had been crippled in the engagement.

And that might be wishful thinking, he thought. *I have to assume they're undamaged.*

"Approaching Point Alpha," Arthur reported. "Our drones are ready for deployment."

"Launch on my command," Stephen said. They were too far from the alien ships for them to maintain a *close* watch on the fleet, unless they were being shadowed by a cloaked scout. If there *was* a spy out there...the whole scheme would be worse than useless. "And then take us into cloak as soon as the drones go active."

"All ships report ready, sir," Newcomb said. "They're standing by."

"Launch the drones," Stephen ordered. "Cloak us, now!"

The lights dimmed, slightly. "Cloaking devices engaged, sir," Arthur said. "We're covered."

Hopefully, Stephen thought. "Alter course, as planned."

"Aye, Captain," Sonia said. A low rumble ran through the ship as she started to alter course towards Tramline Four. "The fleet is falling into formation."

And the drones are convincing the enemy that we're still trying to sneak our way to Tramline One, Stephen thought. The virus might have its suspicions— it had seen humans use drones to advantage before—but it would have to take the threat seriously. *It should give us time to put some distance between us and both enemy fleets.*

"There's no hint they've seen through the deception," Arthur said. "Both enemy fleets are concentrating on the drones."

"Let us hope it stays that way," Stephen said. "Continue on our current course."

"Aye, Captain."

Stephen felt cold as the range steadily widened. The Book insisted on evasive courses, just to confuse any watching spies, but he didn't have time. There were too many damaged ships under his command. A single piece of electromagnetic noise might be enough to betray their location to a prowling starship. He had few illusions about just what the virus's lack of concern for economics *meant*, now it had used a Catapult—more than one Catapult—in wartime. It could fill the entire system with scansats if it wished.

And none of our beancounters would agree to do the same, he thought. *They'd never agree to spend billions of pounds on something we might never need.*

He scowled. They'd need it now.

"Captain, we will begin crossing the tramline in seven hours," Sonia said.

"Understood," Stephen said.

"They'll overrun the drones well before then, no matter how carefully they evade." Newcomb sounded frustrated. "And then they'll know we escaped."

"It can't be helped," Stephen said. "But they would still have to assume that we'd be trying to sneak through the tramline."

He glanced at Morse. "Did the Admiral manage to get a message to Earth?"

"I believe so," Morse said, after a moment. "But I'm unsure when the flicker station was destroyed. It may have been taken out before the message was relayed through the tramline."

Stephen winced. "Detach three destroyers from the fleet," he ordered. "Two of them are to remain on station near the tramline, when we arrive; the third is to sneak through the tramline and hurry up the chain to the first intact station. They are to inform Earth of what transpired here."

"Aye, sir."

. . .

Richard let out a long breath as he slowly clambered out of his cockpit and lowered himself to the deck. The flight crews ran around, trying to rearm starfighters from a dozen different carriers before they had to be pitched back into battle; Richard heard people chattering in three different languages as they swapped rumours and lies about what had happened outside the hull. He hoped they could reorganise the remaining squadrons before it was too late, whatever regs said about starfighters and their pilots being technically interchangeable. *Invincible* had only one semi-intact squadron left and he'd already ordered it to prepare for immediate launch, if the shit hit the fan...

They'll be handing out stims for real, he thought. It seemed morbidly funny, even though he *knew* it was no laughing matter. The squadron commander had already requested medical intervention. *Fuck it. Fuck it all.*

A hand caught his arm. He turned, already knowing who he'd see. Monica stood there, looking angry. Her flight suit was dank with sweat, her hair gleaming under the light…he would have smiled at her if she hadn't looked so *angry*. There was no way in hell he should have been flying and he knew it. She knew it too.

"We need to talk," Monica hissed.

"I'm coming," Richard said.

He checked his wristcom for a status update, then ordered his remaining pilots to snatch some rest. The next few hours were going to be hell for everyone, but it looked as if they might be able to have a brief rest… unless, of course, there was a *third* alien fleet out there. Richard had heard the rumours about endless enemy fleets. If the virus had millions of ships under its command…

We would have been smashed flat by now, he thought, as they walked back to his cabin. He wanted—he needed—a shower. *It wouldn't need to play games if it could just steamroller its way to Earth.*

Monica rounded on him as soon as the hatch closed. "What the fuck were you thinking?"

"I was thinking that I was needed out there." Richard jerked a thumb at the bulkhead. "And I was right."

"You could have zoned out at any minute," Monica snapped. "Did you take another…another stim?"

"I threw them down the flusher," Richard said, curtly. "It was the only way to get rid of them."

Monica glared. "You'll forgive me, of course, for not taking your word for it."

Richard felt a hot flash of anger mingled with shame. Of *course* she wouldn't take his word for it. A drug addict couldn't be trusted. He would do *anything* for his fix. Richard liked to think that he was a strong-minded bloke, but common sense suggested otherwise. A strong-minded man might not have started taking stims in the first place.

"I do." He sat down on the bed, suddenly aware of just how sweaty he was. "I have to shower and…"

"Not yet," Monica said. "Go to the doctor and tell her everything!"

"I can't," Richard said. "Right now, the ship *needs* me."

"Right." Monica rested her hands on her hips. "You expect me to believe that this ship will go straight to hell if you're not flying your starfighter? You are not irreplaceable."

"That would be true, under normal circumstances," Richard said. He stripped off his jacket and dumped it in the washing basket. "But now… we're short on everything from personnel to starfighters."

Monica took a long breath. "And…"

"And I didn't *need* stims just now," Richard added. "I flew just fine without them."

"You took one barely…what? Thirty *minutes* before we went into battle?" Monica turned away as Richard removed his trousers. "You know as well as I do that stims can be unpredictable, if you take so many of them. You were damn lucky you didn't zone out in the middle of the battle."

"I know." Richard couldn't dispute it. "But if I hadn't gone into battle, everything would have fallen apart."

"I don't think it would have been that bad," Monica said. "What now?"

"When this crisis is over, I'm going to report to sickbay and tell them everything," Richard said. He stepped into the washroom, leaving the door open. "And they can decide what to do with me."

"You're a bastard," Monica said. "One condition, then. No more stims."

"I threw them out," Richard said.

"You could get more," Monica said. She stood in the door, watching as he washed himself. "You stay with me. All the time, even when you're on the head. One *hint* that you're taking stims, just *one*, and I'll go to the XO and let the consequences fall where they may. Do you understand me?"

"Yes." Richard turned off the water and began to dry himself. "I do."

"Good." Monica's eyes were bright with unshed tears. "And if you feel unwell, or unfit for duty, for God's sake tell me before it's too late."

Richard felt a pang of guilt. "I will."

"Hah," Monica said. "If you can beat this…if…you'd still be at risk."

"I know," Richard said. "But I have to deal with it."

"Yes, you do." Monica leaned forward. Her voice was hard. "But everyone else does not, do they? You can't be a selfish prick when other people are involved."

"I suppose not," Richard said.

. . .

Stephen was tired.

He hadn't dared leave the bridge, not even after he'd convinced himself that the fleet had broken contact with the alien ships. Force One and Force Two had united, then run down the drones…it was hard to be *sure* what the virus was doing, as *Invincible* was restricted to passive sensors, but it *seemed* as if the alien ships were quartering space near Tramline One, hoping to stumble across the fleeing ships before it was too late. They were nowhere near Tramline Four, thankfully…Stephen just hoped that would continue long enough for the fleet to make its escape. If they put a little distance between themselves and the tramline, they'd be almost impossible to find…

"The fleet is ready to jump." Newcomb sounded tired, although Stephen had ordered him to take a nap during the long transit. It probably hadn't been very restful. "There's no hint of enemy presence."

And they're not trying to run us down, Stephen thought. It was what *he* would have done, if he'd been in command of the alien fleet and knew where the humans were heading. The fleet was already damaged. Running it down now would prevent its crews from repairing their ships and returning to the war. *Unless they're trying to lull us into a false sense of security.*

It wasn't a reassuring thought. His imagination offered all kinds of suggestions, worrying thoughts about what the virus might be doing. HMS *Raleigh* hadn't detected any alien ships on the far side of the tramline, but that didn't mean they weren't there. The virus might have deduced the existence of the unknown tramline chain even if it hadn't surveyed the chain itself. Or it might have been looking for a new route into the Human Sphere itself.

"Take us through the tramline as soon as possible," he ordered. His ship—his fleet—was girding itself for battle, unsure what it might find on the far side of the tramline. A deserted star system? An alien fleet? Or something in-between? "And be ready for anything."

"Aye, sir."

Five minutes later, the battered remains of the fleet vanished from Zheng He.

CHAPTER TWENTY-EIGHT

THE FLEET WAS A BATTERED RUIN.

It wasn't *that* bad, Stephen told himself. They'd saved the freighters. They'd saved the engineering crews and their equipment, allowing them to start work on repairing the damage before they went back into action. The fleet was still formidable, if it was given a chance to heal before it was too late. But they'd been soundly whipped. The roster of destroyed ships and dead lives was terrifyingly long.

He glanced at the list, noting the names at the top. Admiral Jimmy Weisskopf, USN. Admiral Svetlana Zadornov, Russian Navy. Commodore Louis Metcalfe…an endless list of names, from the highest-ranking officer in the fleet to the lowest crewman on a tiny patrol corvette. Hundreds of thousands of dead, most of whom wouldn't be memorialised in a shipboard ceremony. Stephen and the survivors simply didn't have time! They *had* to repair their ships before it was too late.

"And then we have to decide what to do next," he mused.

He sucked in his breath. Thankfully, for better or worse, he *was* the senior surviving officer amongst the fleet. There were others who'd been in naval service longer, but he was higher up the chain of command than them. They might try to unseat him…he shook his head. There was no time for a struggle over command either. His lips quirked, humourlessly.

Fleet command normally looked good on an officer's resume, but not when the fleet had taken one hell of a beating. The appointment was definitely something of a poisoned chalice. It was quite possible that several career-minded officers would be trying to come up with imaginative reasons why they *shouldn't* take command.

And it would be hard to blame them, he thought. *I'd prefer to be somewhere else, too.*

The latest set of reports from Zheng He burned on the display. Over the last four days, he'd had five destroyers constantly rotating through the system, keeping a wary eye on the virus as it searched for the remains of the human fleet. So far, the virus appeared convinced that Stephen was still trying to escape through Tramline One…it would have been a tempting opportunity for a counterattack, if there hadn't been only one real target in the system worth the risk. And he didn't have enough firepower to risk engaging the alien fleet in a straight battle. The analysts might believe that the virus had shot its missile ships dry—and Stephen would have liked to believe it—but a straight fight could still go either way.

And the virus still has reinforcements, he reminded himself. *What would it profit us to smash one fleet if it leaves us unable to stand against another?*

He studied the reports from the analysts carefully, trying to tease out an opportunity for striking back. The big starships—the *Overcompensator* moniker seemed to have stuck, as everyone was using it now—were definitely command ships. The virus had shown a significant loss of coordination when Admiral Zadornov had rammed the command ship and destroyed her. It was possible, the analysts noted, that taking out the other command ship would throw the rest of their fleet into confusion…possible, but uncertain. And impossible to prove, at least until they had a clear shot at the wretched ship. Stephen doubted it would be easy. The virus had learnt a hard lesson at Zheng He.

His intercom bleeped. "Captain," Morse said. "I've finished setting up the command conference. The other commanding officers are ready to come online."

Stephen sat back in his chair. This wasn't going to be pleasant.

"I'm ready," he lied. "Bring them online."

He watched as dozens of holoimages snapped into existence, blurring together as the holographic projectors struggled to compensate for the sheer number of participants and the limited space in the compartment. The compartment seemed to grow larger as more and more projections were pushed into a simulated rear, threatening to make his head hurt as it tried to grapple with the illusion overlaying reality. It was easy to understand, he supposed, how holographic environments could be so convincing, as long as you didn't actually try to *touch* anything. Solid-light holograms remained the stuff of far-future fiction.

And bad romance videos, he reminded himself. *And speculative nonsense.*

He cleared his throat for attention, once the last of the holograms had taken its assigned space, and kicked himself a moment later. It made him sound weak. He'd taken public speaking in school—his family had insisted on him taking the class—but he'd never been very good at it. The Navy hadn't judged him by how well he could sway an audience to his point of view.

"You've seen the reports," he said, quietly. "There is very little hope of sneaking back through Zheng He without being detected, unless we take a *very* roundabout route. If we are detected, we will be brought to battle by superior force and—probably—crushed. Do any of you have any reason to believe otherwise?"

There was a long pause. Stephen had served under captains and admirals who'd been very unreceptive to ideas from their juniors, but *he* had no qualms about borrowing a workable idea even if it came from a lowly acting midshipman. He would have been delighted if someone had proved him wrong. But no one said a word. They knew the score as well as he did. Their ships were in no condition to fight and win a battle against the virus's main fleet.

"We have two options," Stephen said, once he'd waited long enough to make it clear that he *had* given his subordinates a chance to speak. "First, we can attempt to find a tramline chain that leads back to human space. The

273

astrophysicists *believe* there should be at least one or two possible chains that go in the right direction, but—as you know—they may be wrong. We cannot *rely* on finding a usable chain. At best, it will take us weeks to get home; at worst, we will waste months searching for something that isn't there, forcing us to eventually turn back and try to sneak through Zheng He anyway."

"And in that time, the virus will have invaded Earth," an American said. The holographic caption identified him as Captain Nicolson. "We cannot afford to be out of contact for so long."

Stephen nodded in agreement. "That's one possibility," he said. There was no point in suggesting they remained in the unexplored and unnamed system, poised to threaten the virus's lines of communication. It might work, but only if they let the virus know they were there. "The other is to go on the offensive ourselves."

There was a pause. "The unexplored tramline chain leads up to Alien-One. If we sneak in through the backdoor, we might just be able to lay waste to the system—and its shipyards and supply bases—before the virus can recall its fleets to deal with us."

"I seem to recall that the system is heavily defended," a Russian pointed out. "And the full might of Home Fleet might not be enough to break through the fortifications."

"There are ways to get around the defences," Stephen countered. "If nothing else, we can hurl ballistic projectiles at the planet's facilities."

"Or hit the planet itself," Captain Nicolson said.

Stephen winced. It was rare, vanishingly rare, to deploy weapons of mass destruction against planetary targets. Theodore Smith had set the precedent of *not* hitting alien population centres, particularly ones that posed no threat to an orbiting fleet. Wholesale slaughter of civilians, even *alien* civilians, could not be condoned. And yet, would the virus notice the restraint? Would the virus even *care*? Was there any such thing as an infected civilian on an alien world?

Another officer leaned forward. "You would have us exterminate an entire planetary population?"

"The entire population is infected," Captain Nicolson said. He held up a holographic hand. "I understand—I *do* understand—the reluctance to bombard a planet back into the Stone Age. I know just how many billions we would be condemning to death. But they are all infected, they're all part of the virus now. They couldn't recover even if we purged the virus from their system!"

His voice rose. "Wouldn't you rather die than live as a mindless slave? I know I would."

"Which is the point," Stephen mused. "They were never anything but mindless slaves."

"Exactly," Nicolson said. "And they unleashed biological weapons on Earth."

Stephen made a face. Retaliation—an eye for an eye—had been common, back during the Troubles. It was the only way to make it clear that use of WMDs would not be tolerated, even if it meant slaughtering innocents. But...he liked to think they were more civilised now...he shook his head. There was no point. Nicolson was right. There were no innocent civilians in *this* war. The virus's host-bodies had to be destroyed if the virus itself was to be wiped out.

"We have authorisation to target enemy population centres, if necessary," he said, flatly. "We'll plan precisely *how* we will move on the way."

He paused. "Do any of you have any objections to moving against Alien-One?"

"One," Captain Hans said. "Assuming we get in and out as planned, we'd still be out of contact with Earth for...at least a month. Perhaps two. A lot can happen in a month."

"Yes," Stephen agreed. "But what else *can* we do?"

Captain Hans stepped forward. "I propose that we sneak back through Zheng He and return to Earth."

"That would take weeks, at best," Captain Nicolson objected.

This isn't a democracy, Stephen thought, coldly. He dismissed the thought a second later. On paper, the fleet *wasn't* a democracy. In practice, he *wasn't* an admiral and he *needed* their cooperation. And while he was sure they would follow orders when the shit hit the fan—he was morbidly sure that it *would*—they might not be so willing to do as they were told when there *wasn't* a battle going on. *They have to be convinced that they're doing the right thing.*

"The best-case scenario is that we will need at least six weeks to get home, just to make sure that we evade the prowling fleet," he said. "We can shave some time off that estimate"—he held up his hand to forestall the objections he *knew* were coming—"but the tighter the course, the greater the chance of being detected. One or two ships might sneak through, given the chance. The entire fleet?"

"Probably not," Captain Nicolson said.

"But Earth has to be warned about the Catapult," Hans insisted. "None of *us* expected it, did we?"

Stephen conceded the point. Catapults were expensive—and, as far as anyone could tell, one-shot wonders. The Catapult that had practically won the Second Interstellar War had melted down, when used for the first and last time. The boffins swore blind they would solve that problem, one day, but... the beancounters hadn't been enthusiastic about letting the navy buy more. The human race was still dependent on the tramlines for interstellar travel.

"We did send a warning back up the chain," he said. How many Catapults did the virus have? There was no way to know. Its screwed-up economy made sure of *that*. "Earth knows about the threat."

"For what good it will do them," Captain Jove muttered. The Belter crossed his arms over his ample chest. "It strikes me that we have a rare opportunity to hit the bastards where it hurts."

"Perhaps," Hans said. "We don't know how strong the virus is, or how badly it will be hurt if we incinerate Alien-One. And if we lose, we lose everything."

"The fleet is expendable, if it buys Earth more time," Nicolson countered. "I think we all knew the job was dangerous when we took it."

Hans reddened. "I don't fear death. I fear that we might lose ships that are desperately needed elsewhere."

"Ships we can't *get* elsewhere," another officer pointed out. "We're *here*, not *there*. We would have to get through an occupied system to go almost *anywhere* else, unless we gamble everything on finding a tramline that gets us home."

Stephen leaned back in his chair and listened as the argument went round and round, trying to gauge how many officers supported him. It was difficult to tell. Councils of War were rare…not, he ruefully conceded, without reason. A supportive officer from a foreign navy might be out-ranked by an officer who thought the plan was about as stupid as flying the entire fleet into the nearest star. Which way would that officer jump, if push came to shove?

"We've considered all the angles," he said, once the argument had gone on long enough. "I propose attacking Alien-One. Does anyone want to formally propose an alternative?"

He waited, curious to see what would happen. A formal challenge to his authority *might* get the officer in trouble, when the fleet returned home, or it might not…particularly if the challenge led to the fleet getting home. But…it was never easy to guess which way a Board of Inquiry might jump. Someone might argue for caution, while someone else might throw caution out the airlock and insist that the attack should have gone ahead after all.

"Very good," he said, when there was no challenge. "My engineers believe that the fleet will be ready to depart in three days. We won't be *perfect*, of course, but…they'll do the best they can without a shipyard. We'll do the remaining repairs along the way."

He paused. "I intend to take the remainder of the freighters and their supplies along with us, at least as far as Alien-One. It should keep us going long enough to carry out the attack and give the bastards a bloody nose."

"And poke the hornet's nest," Hans said, pessimistically. "They'll come after us with everything they can muster."

"Good," Stephen said. It wasn't a pleasant thought, but it did have its advantages. "The more they're throwing at us, the less they'll be throwing at Earth."

He allowed himself a tight smile. They had orders to buy time. Very well, he'd *buy* time by attacking the alien base. And if it won them enough time to get the next generation of ships and crew online, it might just be the turning point of the war. He'd sell his life and the lives of his crew if their deaths won humanity enough time to win the war.

"After that, we'll either double back down the tramline or head up the chain to Falkirk," he added. There was no point in planning *those* steps of the mission in anything but the most general terms. He had no way to know how many ships would survive the coming engagements. "And then we'll sneak back to Earth."

"If we survive," Hans said. "We might not last long enough to escape."

Stephen nodded. "If."

He tapped the terminal, bringing up a starchart. What would the virus *do*? It knew that *Invincible* and her fleet had escaped. Sooner or later, it would realise that the fleet hadn't stayed in Zheng He. What then? Would it assume that the fleet *had* managed to escape through Tramline One? Or would it deduce that Stephen had slipped through Tramline Four instead? If so…what? The files the virus had captured wouldn't show the tramline chain running up to Alien-One. It might just assume that Stephen intended to return to Zheng He—either punching his way into the system or simply sneaking through to the *next* system—or that Stephen was trying to convince it to waste time trying to run the fleet to ground. Or…did it know enough about the tramlines to guess that Stephen hadn't flown his fleet into a dead end?

There isn't a direct link from this system to Alien-One, Stephen mused. *That* would have been discovered long ago, probably before the First Interstellar War. *The virus would have to guess at the existence of multiple tramlines…*

He shook his head. There was no point in worrying about it. They'd just have to hurry to get into position before the virus started surveying the unexplored tramlines. Maybe it wouldn't be in any hurry. If it thought that humanity hadn't explored the tramlines either, it wouldn't realise that Stephen *did* have somewhere to go.

"We'll do everything in our power to give the virus a *very* bloody nose," he said, putting his thoughts to one side. They'd know the answer to *that* when—if -the virus started surveying the tramline chain. "And I expect each and every one of you to give me your all."

"Of course, sir," Nicolson said.

Stephen nodded. "We'll speak again, before we depart. Until then... dismissed."

The conference ended. Stephen let out a long breath as the holoimages vanished, then stood. There was work to do. He'd already passed command of the ship to Newcomb—he couldn't command both the ship *and* the fleet—but there were matters he had to attend to personally. And...he needed to arrange *some* kind of ceremony for the dead. The dead might not care, but the living sure as hell did. They needed to remember the dead before it was too late, before—perhaps—they went to join them. Stephen had no illusions. Alien-One was heavily defended. They were going to be pitting a damaged fleet against one of the toughest targets in known space.

And we're going to scorch a planet clean of life, Stephen reminded himself. *What is this war going to do to us?*

But, try as he might, he found no answer.

CHAPTER TWENTY-NINE

ALICE HAD BEEN TOO BUSY to notice when the fleet had started to move. The marines hadn't been involved in the battle, save for readying themselves to repel boarders who had never materialised, but they'd found themselves working hard during the aftermath. *Invincible* hadn't been badly hit, compared to the other ships, yet the marines had still had to clear corridors, assist damage control parties and generally make themselves useful. She helped the injured to Sickbay, carried bodies to the hold for storage until they could be launched into space or frozen for shipment back to Earth and a multitude of other tasks, brooding all the time. It was easy to busy herself, but hard to forget everything her father had said.

It nagged at her mind, no matter how hard she pushed herself. She knew, as much as she hated to admit it, that she and her father had a great deal in common. She knew, all too well, that *she* might have snapped if she'd been confronted with evidence of her partner's infidelity. She knew...she shook her head as the thought echoed through her head, time and time again. It didn't matter. All that mattered was that a woman was dead and her two children had been deprived of both parents. All that mattered was that Alice and her sister had been through hell because of their father.

And he has no goddamned right to demand anything from me, now, she thought, as she carried a piece of debris down to the inspection site. The alien torpedoes had done more damage than they'd realised, she'd been told, although thankfully none of it had been bad enough to threaten the ship. *Does he really think I can forgive him for everything he did?*

She dismissed the thought with a shrug as a lowly crewwoman came into view, carrying a tray of drinks. The sarcastic part of Alice's mind wondered who she'd pissed off to get *that* duty, but the rest of her was merely glad of the break. She was aching, tired and sweaty. She took the mug of sweet tea, nodded her thanks and allowed herself a sip. It was hot, threatening to burn her throat. She shrugged and drank it anyway. There wasn't much time before they had to get back to work.

Hammersmith stopped beside her. "I heard a rumour that there was an unexploded torpedo on the upper decks."

Alice shook her head. "They'd have kicked it into space by now," she said, dryly. The preliminary damage control assessment party could *hardly* have missed an unexploded alien projectile. It was rare, vanishingly rare, for a torpedo not to detonate when it hit its target. "Someone was just trying to put the wind up you."

"Looks like it," Hammersmith said. "They would have told you, wouldn't they?"

Alice shrugged. There were times when an unexploded bomb—or an emplaced IED—would be carefully disarmed and dismantled, but not in space. It was far safer to get the weapon as far from the ship as possible before its electronic brain realised that it had actually hit the target and detonated. The preliminary teams might not even have bothered to notify the crew before removing the torpedo. Unless someone had decided that the chance to dismantle an alien torpedo was worth the risk...

"Probably," she said. It was a stupid thought. She hadn't heard anything to suggest that there was any point in capturing an alien torpedo. They weren't any better, if scuttlebutt was to be believed, than humanity's own designs. "Just watch out for pieces of debris falling from high above."

"Or exploding consoles," Hammersmith joked. "That could really ruin someone's day."

They passed their mugs back to the crewwoman, then hurried back down the corridor. The entire section was starting to empty, now the bodies had been removed and the damage control teams had patched up the hull. There was no time to carry out a proper series of repairs, she'd been told. The crewmen who'd lived in the section, when they weren't on duty, had been sent elsewhere. They probably weren't very happy, Alice thought. They were competing for scarce bunkspace with crews who'd had to abandon *their* ships because they couldn't be repaired in a hurry. She would have been more sympathetic if she hadn't spent most of her career hotbunking in Marine Country.

And they should consider themselves lucky that they're alive, she thought. She'd checked, out of morbid curiosity. Her father's ship had survived the battle. Whatever else one could say about the Belters, they did good work. *Too many ships were lost before their crews could be evacuated.*

Anders met them as they reached the hatch. "The Major wants me stationed on the lower decks," he said. "There's been some grumbling amongst the guests."

"Joy," Alice said. The marines were—technically—the police force, onboard ship, but it wasn't their preferred role. "What happened?"

Anders shrugged. "Some dispute got out of hand, turned into a punch-up before anyone could do anything. Major wants to make sure it doesn't happen again. Got too many other problems to worry about it now."

"Understood," Alice said.

"You're taking over here, but keep yourself in readiness," Anders warned. "The last thing we need is a bid to take the ship."

"That's not likely to happen," Alice said. There was no reason to believe that the guests would turn mutinous. They were fleeing an overpowering alien threat. They *knew* they had to work together to survive. "Just...give them time to get used to their new circumstances."

"If we had the time." Anders shrugged, then tossed a jaunty salute. "Good luck, Alice."

"Same to you," Alice said. "You never know. They might send us somewhere *exciting* in the next few days."

"They might," Hammersmith agreed. "We're going to Alien-One, aren't we?"

"So they say." Alice shivered, despite herself. She'd been infected at Alien-One. The thought of returning bothered her more than she cared to admit. "And this time we're loaded for bear."

She kept her face expressionless as Anders headed down the corridor. The fleet—or what remained of the fleet—was powerful, but she'd seen the defences at Alien-One. The virus had no intention of allowing anything bad to happen to its core system…if, indeed, it *was* one of the virus's core systems. No one really knew just how much territory the virus controlled, let alone how many starships, shipyards and industrial nodes it possessed. A strike at Alien-One might be a war-winner…

…Or the virus might not even *notice*.

She shrugged. It didn't matter. She'd find out soon enough.

Sure, her own thoughts mocked her. *And then you'll wish you'd stayed in ignorance.*

• • •

"I'm having that *déjà vu* feeling all over again," Richard muttered, as he strode into the briefing compartment. Some of the pilots waiting for him were familiar faces, despite his best efforts; others were strangers, transferred to *Invincible* after their motherships had been crippled or destroyed during the battle. "How many times do we have to do this?"

Monica elbowed his back. "As many times as necessary."

Richard made a face. Monica had been his constant companion over the last few days, never letting him out of her sight. He ate with her, drank with her…even slept with her, although nothing had actually happened. They'd been working too hard to do more than fall into the undersized bed and go to sleep. She'd made him eat properly...God, he *wanted* a stim. He needed a stim. She didn't understand...

His hands started to shake. He clasped them behind his back as he took the stand and looked at his pilots. Some looked confident, even though they knew the fleet had been soundly thrashed; some looked pale, unable or unwilling to meet his eyes. He felt a pang of guilt for not knowing them, for not taking the time to welcome them aboard the ship. It wasn't as if he'd had time for a dinner party—the very thought was absurd, when the fleet was fleeing for its life—but he could have spent *some* time with them. They were more than just cogs in his machine.

And how many of them, he asked himself morbidly, *will be dead in the next few days?*

He cleared his throat. "Thank you all for coming," he said. "I trust that you had no problems settling in?"

There was a long pause. His squadron leaders had reported there had been *some* friction, mostly over seniority, but the problems had been rapidly smoothed out. There just wasn't *time* for a long debate over who should be in command if the shit hit the fan. Besides, *Invincible* was the host ship. Everyone else had to fit into her command structure. Which would have been fine, he noted grimly, if the command structure hadn't been shot to hell. Half of his original starfighter pilots were dead. Their squadrons were so badly damaged that they might well have been decommissioned, the survivors parcelled out to other squadrons, if they'd had the time. As it was, reconstituting them was a nightmare and a half. There just weren't enough survivors to keep the squadron traditions alive.

He allowed his eyes to wander over the pilots. "It will not be long before we are called to go back into action," he said. "By then, we have *got* to work out all the kinks. I intend to spend every waking hour in the simulators, ironing out any problems that might develop before we actually have to *fight*. The ready squadrons will remain ready"—they couldn't operate a CSP when the entire fleet was in cloak—"but the rest of you will be in the simulators. Any questions?"

There were none. Richard allowed himself a tight smile. The pilots were young, but they were no longer virgins. The poor bastards who had been rushed from the academy to fill the gaps in his roster had seen the elephant now. The ribbing and wisecracking was gone, replaced with a grim determination to survive long enough to see home again. And the older pilots had known the truth long before the fleet had been kicked out of Zheng He. The war wasn't a game. The empty bunks in Pilot Country bore mute testament to the pilots who had gone to war and never come home.

Although we didn't waste any time replacing them, Richard reminded himself. There had been no time to empty drawers and cabinets, let alone check to see what the dead wanted the living to do with their possessions. *We can't let ourselves be sentimental now.*

He sighed, inwardly, as he dismissed his pilots. He'd have to sort out everything the dead pilots had left behind, sooner rather than later. The newcomers needed the living space for themselves. But…he didn't want to do it, not when he couldn't even remember the names of the pilots who'd died under his command. He silently kicked himself for not giving the duty to the squadron leaders, although they had too much work to do themselves. It was too late now.

"That could have gone better," he said, once the pilots had hurried out of the compartment. "I need a drink."

"I imagine we all do," Monica said, tartly. "But what would Captain Shields say if someone tried to fly a starfighter while drunk off his arse?"

Richard shook his head. "How many of those young men are going to be dead in the next few days?"

"Probably too many," Monica said. "But you know what? You can give them the best possible chance by working them hard."

"I know," Richard said. He intended to drill the pilots hard, working them until they became a well-oiled team. It wasn't going to be easy, even though most navies used the same starfighter protocols. Integrating a whole squadron of foreign pilots was one thing, integrating a handful of individuals from a dozen different nations was quite another. "God alone knows what's going to go wrong."

"As long as it happens in the simulator," Monica said. "Better to chew someone out for fucking up than hold a funeral."

"Fuck," Richard agreed. They hadn't held a funeral for the dead, not yet. He understood that the ship and her crew simply didn't have time, but it still rankled. He felt as if the dead were waiting, trapped in limbo until the living said goodbye. "There are too many ways this could go wrong."

"Yeah." Monica snorted. "But you know what? We could be dead by now. We should be dead by now. And we're still alive. We might as well live while we can."

"I suppose." Richard's hand was shaking again. He wanted a stim. Or alcohol. He wasn't picky. "What now?"

Monica made a show of looking at her wristcom. "We get something to drink, then get into the simulators. And then we show the maggots how to kick alien ass."

They're not maggots, Richard thought, as they walked to the hatch. The newcomers were many things, but inexperienced was not one of them. *And that's half the problem.*

. . .

Stephen had never really *liked* the CIC, although he'd used it during emergency drills that—somewhat unrealistically—insisted that the bridge and secondary bridge had *both* been knocked out while the CIC had survived. There was something about the compartment that made it hard to believe that he was in command of a starship…even though, he had to admit, he wasn't *currently* in command. He was morbidly certain that *someone* back home was going to make a fuss about that, as *technically* Stephen had relieved *himself* of command…something that was against regulations. A captain could not lay down his command without risking a court martial.

And they'll probably say I've mutinied against myself, Stephen thought. The grown-ups in the Admiralty would understand that he couldn't command the fleet *and* his ship, not at the same time, but his family's political enemies would scent blood in the water. *They could charge me with all kinds of offences if they wished.*

He shook his head. The first two jumps had gone well—better than he'd feared—but he knew it was only a matter of time before the fleet made contact with the enemy again. It wouldn't take the virus *that* long to work out where the fleet had gone, even if it thought that Stephen had retreated into a dead end. Would it realise that there were other tramlines, including some that *might* lead into virus-controlled space? Or would it take the risk of pushing the offensive towards Earth?

Stephen let out a long sigh as he studied the display. He'd always known he would take command of a fleet—one day—but he hadn't realised just how difficult it was merely to get all the ships moving in the same direction. Seventy-five ships, from twelve different nations…normally, it would be tricky to coordinate the fleet without stepping on someone's toes and creating a diplomatic nightmare. He'd never thought that having an alien fleet on his tail, breathing down his neck, would be a *good* thing, but the prospect of the fleet being run to ground had managed to concentrate a few minds. It helped, he supposed, that most of his subordinates were *captains*. There was no one who had spent the last few years flying a desk.

Although admirals have to work harder than I thought, he acknowledged. The first exercises—simulated, thankfully—had been disasters. It had taken time for the ships to get used to the new command arrangements. They just weren't used to working together. *If they spend so much of their time being diplomatic…*

He shook his head. His fleet was getting stronger every day, as his ships were repaired and his magazines were reloaded, but he knew they weren't ready for a straight fight. Admiral Zadornov and Admiral Weisskopf had done a lot of the work, yet…all their command arrangements had been shot to hell. Stephen was leery of taking his fleet into battle. If humanity hadn't been desperate, he might have argued against invading Alien-One.

His intercom pinged. "Captain," Newcomb said. "Long-range sensors are picking up a lone alien ship. Plotting thinks she came from Tramline Two."

Stephen keyed the console, bringing up the system display. The unnamed system was barren, save for a pair of tramlines. There wasn't even a single asteroid or comet, as far as his sensors could tell. The alien ship...he cursed under his breath. The virus was clearly trying to survey the systems along the tramline chain, even if it was exploring from the wrong end. The ship on the display might not have noticed his fleet—it might not even have heard of the Battle of Zheng He—but that would change soon. And then... it wouldn't take the virus long to realise that Stephen might have taken his fleet in the direction of Alien-One.

Particularly if they know our ship managed to escape through the unexplored tramline chain and made it home, Stephen thought. *They'd* know *where we were going.*

"A survey ship," he mused. The alien ship wasn't much bigger than a destroyer...smaller than a human design, he supposed, but the virus didn't *need* big survey vessels. "And one who isn't worried about being detected."

"No, sir," Newcomb said. "We had no difficulty spotting her."

Stephen smiled, grimly. "That ship cannot be allowed to survive," he said. The sensor displays were clear. There were no hints of cloaked ships in the vicinity...cloaked alien ships, at least. The alien ship was alone, completely alone. It offered...opportunity. "Signal the fleet. We're going to take that ship."

"Aye, Captain."

CHAPTER THIRTY

I MUST HAVE BEEN COMPLETELY MAD, Alice thought, as the breaching pod glided towards the alien starship. *Why the fuck did I come up with this idea?*

She shivered, despite herself. She'd done dumber things in the past—she was sure of it—but nothing came to mind. Going into battle wearing nothing more than a halter top and a pair of shorts that barely covered her ass...she knew, with a grim certainty that defied all reason, that she looked utterly ridiculous. She'd spent hours mocking Stellar Star for showing more skin than *anyone* should in a combat situation, but now...she was wearing next to nothing herself. The logic was sound, yet...logic wouldn't protect her if the breaching pod was opened to space. A single glancing hit would be enough to kill her...

It would kill her anyway, she reminded herself. Combat armour was tough, but not *that* tough. It gave an illusion of protection, nothing more. Bullets might bounce off her armour, but plasma weapons designed to kill starfighters and burn through starship hulls would go through an armoured marine like a knife through butter. *And* it would make it impossible for her to deploy her pheromones. She shuddered again, realising—emotionally—how fragile the plan truly was. Something that had seemed perfectly logical, in the safety of Marine Country, seemed like an insane gamble once she started to put it into practice. Her imagination was suggesting all sorts of ways the plan could go wrong.

She glanced at her protective team, silently daring them to say something. She'd worked close-protection duties herself, in the past. It was easy to start mocking the poor bastard you were meant to protect, particularly when the idiot insisted on walking into danger rather than staying somewhere nice and safe. She'd heard chatter about gormless idiots…she silently asked their pardon, now *she* was the one being protected. She was going to do something so dangerous and stupid that she could easily get her protectors killed, even though they'd volunteered for the task.

It could be worse, she told herself. *I could be escorting some dumb starlet through LA.*

She put the thought aside as a dull quiver ran through the pod. In theory, the pod could reach the alien ship without being detected. There was no drive field, nothing that could be detected by a passive sensor; the hull was made of stealth materials, while the pod itself was steered by gas jets. They should be able to land on the alien ship without setting off an alarm. But she knew better than to hope that they pulled it off. A routine active sensor sweep might *just* reveal their presence, when they were too far from their target to land and too close to escape. The flight of starfighters behind them, coming in on a ballistic trajectory, might *just* be able to cover them…

Or they might not, she thought. *We might be picked off in a flash.*

She slotted her mask into place, taking a long breath as air started to move. She knew better than to risk breathing the air on an infected starship, even though the virus would think she was already infected. There was no way to know what would happen if more viral matter—*live* viral matter—got into her bloodstream. Would it go dormant, on the theory she was already a host-body, or would it bring the virus in her body back to life? She didn't know. The rest of the squad was even *more* vulnerable. There was a good chance they'd never be allowed to return to *Invincible*, even if they succeeded. They might just be infected…

It will show up in their bloodstreams, she told herself, firmly. *And any infection can be countered before it overwhelms them.*

Sweat trickled down her back as the range closed. The alien starship was small, compared to a fleet carrier or a battleship, but that didn't mean it might not be thoroughly infected. The virus might have integrated itself so thoroughly into the ship that it might as well be a single, living organism. It might react badly, the moment it realised she was there; it might throw everything it had at her, just to keep her from interfering with its control. Or it might not even notice what she was doing. Alice had plenty of experience tuning out people shouting, particularly when they weren't shouting at *her.* The virus and its host-bodies might not even realise she was trying to issue commands.

"Getting closer," Hammersmith said. He spoke quietly, his voice soft, but it felt as if he were shouting. "And we're crossing the point of no return."

Alice let out a breath. "I think we crossed that a long time ago."

She fought to control her heartbeat as the seconds rapidly ticked down to zero. This was it, the moment of truth. The moment when she would prove that she could still be useful or...she wasn't sure what she'd do if the attempt failed and she survived. Go back to the lab and play guinea pig until she died? Try to move somewhere that wouldn't think twice about accepting her? Or throw her career out the airlock and snap her father's neck? It was a tempting thought...

An alarm sounded. "Active sensor sweep," Tindal said. "They got us!"

"The starfighters are going live now," Alice said, glancing at her display. "If we're lucky..."

She felt a moment of bitter regret as the alien starship started to turn, orienting itself on the starfighters. She could have done so much with her life...if the alien ship targeted her now, she'd be dead before she knew she was under attack. And...the last seconds ticked away, a dull thump echoing through the pod as it touched down. Moments later, she heard a whine as the hull cutter went to life. New alerts flashed up in front of her as the alien gravity field pulled her down. The alien hull was steadily being opened...

"They know we're here now," Hammersmith said. He hefted a weapon as the lower hatch started to open. "Watch my back."

Alice nodded. The virus *had* to know where the pod was now. How long would it take to react? It had near-complete control of its environment. In theory, it could seal off a section within seconds. In practice...she wasn't too sure. There was no way to know. Another whine echoed through the pod as the cutter tore into the alien hull. Hammersmith waited until the hatch was open, then jumped down. Alice braced herself, hanging back despite a grim impulse to follow him. She had to know it was safe.

"Hot like a sauna, smelly like a farm," Hammersmith said. "You coming?"

Alice followed the rest of the squadron and dropped into the alien ship. Hammersmith was right. It *was* hot. She could *feel* the virus in the air, prickling against her; a dull itch started to pervade her scalp, as if she had nits or lice. She told herself, firmly, that she was imagining it as she looked around. The alien ship looked crude, unfinished. Yellow-gold liquid was leaking out of the gash in the hull, slowly changing colour as it hit the air. It took her a moment to realise that she was looking at pure viral material. The virus had *definitely* infected the entire starship.

And it might have all kinds of advantages, she mused. *Does it even need to have human-sized tubes if it can absorb monkeys or chimps into its gestalt?*

She shuddered at the thought. Xenospecialists had argued for years that primates had to be a certain size before they could develop intelligence, although she'd always had her doubts. There were plenty of humans who weren't very intelligent, even though some were bigger than her and others were smaller. And yet...it couldn't be denied that most known intelligent life forms were—on average—roughly the same size. The virus itself was the only real exception, and even *it* needed a critical mass to function. But that wouldn't stop it absorbing every life form, intelligent or not...

"I've got motion," Tindal said. "They're coming."

"Let me go first," Alice said. She moved forward, gritting her teeth. The air seemed to grow warmer, droplets of liquid splashing against her bare skin. "Don't fire unless fired upon."

"We're fucked," Tarter said.

Alice kept her thoughts to herself. Tarter was probably right. The marines were effectively trapped, unable to manoeuvre or even take cover. A pair of HE grenades would probably be enough to wipe out the whole squad, armour or no armour. She doubted the virus would be so quick to kill them—it would want to infect the intruders, surely—but there was no way to be sure. It might want to be rid of them before they could do something dangerous.

A pair of aliens rounded the corner and came into view. They'd been humanoid, once. They might have been very close to human. Now...Alice felt sick as she saw viral matter oozing around their eyes, pulsing with a weird uncanny life...she knew, with a certainty she couldn't put into words, that the virus was *looking* at her. She didn't need to glance at her biological warfare sensor to know that the level of viral matter in the air was rising sharply. She could *feel* the virus's presence pulsing through the air.

It's a distributed system, she reminded herself. *And it grows stronger and stronger with every breath.*

She braced herself as the aliens came closer. They seemed to ignore her, focusing their attention on the marines behind them. Alice allowed herself a flicker of relief at how they clearly thought she was one of them, even though she wasn't responding to the virus's commands. It had to know she wasn't part of the *gestalt*. The xenospecialists had been right, she guessed. At this level, the virus wasn't particularly bright. Faced with a contradiction—Alice was infected, yet not part of the gestalt—the virus had decided to ignore her. It made her smile, even as she gathered herself. God alone knew how many military bases had been infiltrated because someone, upon seeing a stranger, decided that someone *else* must have cleared him for entry.

"Stop," she said. She used her command voice, pushing it out as much as possible. "Stop!"

The aliens stopped dead, the viral matter clinging to them wobbling like purple-black jelly. Alice could *feel* surprise running through the gestalt, astonishment at having its orders countermanded...she wasn't sure if it was real, or if she was interpreting what she was feeling through a human filter, or even if she was just imagining it…it didn't matter. All that mattered was that it was *working*. She was giving orders, and the virus—or at least two of its host-bodies—were listening.

"You did it," Hammersmith said. "Tell them to die!"

Alice barely heard him. She could *feel* the virus shifting around her, its awareness growing stronger. Confusion reverberated through the air. It knew it was under attack, yet it couldn't see the *source* of the attack. It was a blindfolded boxer, unable even to see the enemy. It couldn't hit back and yet…given time, it would work out what had happened and counterattack. If nothing else, sooner or later it would realise that any host body that wasn't following orders had been subverted.

She concentrated as hard as she could on a single command. "Stop."

The alien shivered, then collapsed to the deck. His partner fell a second later. Alice walked forward, pushing the command as hard as she could. She could *feel* it echoing through the gestalt, *sense* dozens of host-bodies collapsing as her command pounded into her head. And yet…she could also feel the virus's mentality, trying to regain control. It might not have expected to be challenged, not in its own domain. But it wasn't helpless, either.

She looked up, sharply, as a blob of viral matter quivered into view. It looked absurd, as if a mass of jelly had decided to go walking, but she could sense the danger. Tentacles of viral matter were lashing out in all directions as the virus struggled to take back control. She wasn't sure what would happen, if one of them managed to strike her. Nothing? Or would the virus retake control of *her*? This time, there would be no escape.

"Stop," she said. "Sleep."

The blob seemed to stop, as if it was torn between contradictory demands. There were no eyes, as far as she could tell, but she was sure it was looking at her. It knew what she was, it understood what she was doing… the gestalt drove it on, even as she told it to stop and sleep…it wanted her dead. Her hand dropped to her pistol, ready to draw and fire if necessary. The blob quivered, again and again, then collapsed into a mass of liquid. A shudder ran through the ship as the gestalt fell apart. Alice smiled, even as she felt the liquid lapping against her feet. The virus had lost. The entire ship was going to sleep.

Hammersmith glanced at her, sharply. "What happened?"

"I think I won," Alice said. The marines hadn't seen the *real* contest. To them, she'd merely been speaking and staring. "The ship is shutting down."

"Let's hope it doesn't blow itself up," Tindal muttered.

Alice shrugged as she picked her way through the remains of the blob and headed down the alien corridor. There were dozens of host-bodies, all lying where they'd fallen. Liquid dripped from countless pipes, splashing and pooling on the deck. She felt droplets fall on her back, crawling down her legs like living things...she shivered, even though she knew it was harmless. The virus was asleep. The temperature seemed to be falling, although she suspected it was an illusion. A starship wouldn't cool so rapidly unless the hull was opened to space. Pulsating masses of viral material lay everywhere, quivering in a manner that reminded her of a human taking a breath. There was something so *alien* about the virus in its natural form that she felt utterly disgusted just looking at it. The virus wasn't...it wasn't *right*.

"Contact the ship," she said. "Tell them we've put the virus to sleep."

"And hope they can take control," Hammersmith said. He chuckled, suddenly. "Do you think there'll be a reward for us?"

"Probably." Alice shrugged, again. Prize money was great, if she had time to spend it. She had a feeling she wouldn't. "They'll have to see if they can take control first."

She frowned. The xenospecialists *might* be able to take control...or they might simply open the ship to vacuum, freeze the remaining viral cells and leave the ship for later recovery. If, of course, they didn't just point her at the local star and send her to fiery death. She shook her head at the thought. No, they wouldn't do that. They'd want to find a way to make use of the ship. She just had no idea how. The ship might have carried a humanoid crew, but she hadn't been designed for humanoids. The command and control system was carefully integrated with the virus.

"They're sending the specialists over now," Tindal said. "And we're being ordered to return home."

"The bastards are trying to snatch the prize money," Hammersmith joked.

"I doubt it," Alice said. Prize money went to the entire ship, not just the boarding party. *She* would get a bonus, if she lived; she didn't know about the others. "They probably just want us out of the way."

She sighed, inwardly, as they started to make their way back to the breaching pod. The plan had worked, *this* time. She'd taken control of an infected ship. But…would it work a second time? There was no hint that the gestalt had managed to send a warning before it had collapsed, there was no suggestion that there was anyone in the system to *hear* a warning, if it had been sent, but…she swallowed, hard. A little more viral matter, a slightly stronger gestalt…it might easily have gone the other way. The virus might not be able to *see* her, but it didn't have to see her to stop her. If it had vented that section of the ship, it would have thrown her into space to die.

I guess we'll find out, she thought. Going back to the ship wouldn't be pleasant, not when they'd be poked and prodded for hours before they'd be allowed to return to Marine Country, but it beat staying on the alien ship. *And then we'll know.*

Hammersmith grinned at her. "Just think! All the people who doubted you! You can look in their face and gloat as you collect the money from the wankers who bet against you!"

Alice had to laugh. She wasn't surprised to hear that people had been laying bets. People had been betting on her ever since she'd joined the navy. "The odds weren't in my favour, then?"

"I bet on you," Hammersmith said. "And I won."

"I should have bet on myself," Alice said. It was a morbid joke, but it made her laugh. "I would have got the money…and if I'd lost, I wouldn't have been *alive* to hand over the money."

"I'm sure that's cheating," Tindal said, primly.

"It's not *really* cheating," Alice assured him. They could hardly claim money off a dead body. "It's merely creatively interpreting the rules."

"Ouch," Hammersmith said. "Remind me never to gamble with you."

Alice laughed.

CHAPTER THIRTY-ONE

"YOU'RE SURE YOU CAN FLY THE SHIP?"

Commander Tomas Patel nodded, shortly. "Yes, sir. The command and control systems weren't as badly damaged as your marines feared. The biological command network is beyond repair, as far as we can tell, but the hardware is still operational. We can't get her to dance on the head of a pin, I'm afraid..."

"I see." Stephen cut him off. "And can we steer her down the tramline chain and back into Alien-One?"

"I see no reason why not," Patel assured him. "The real difficulty will be exchanging signs and countersigns when we reach our destination, but I fancy we can bluff our way through."

Stephen wasn't so sure. The virus might ignore a starship, friendly or not, prowling through the edges of an infected star system, but there was no way it would let a ship close to a major facility without asking some very pointed questions. It *knew* how easy it was to subvert an entire ship... it knew, all too well, that a ship that had the right communication codes might still not be friendly. God knew everyone had been paranoid when HMS *Raleigh* reached Zheng He. The virus might feel the same way about the captured survey ship.

"And if you're wrong?" He studied the display for a long moment. The alien ship looked undamaged, as far as he could tell, but it was difficult to say what an alien eye might see that a human would miss. "What then?"

Patel frowned. "We die."

Stephen made a face. Patel and his team had trained to take control of alien ships and operate them, but…there was a difference between flying the captured ship back home and actually taking her into the heart of enemy territory. Too much could go wrong, particularly if the virus suspected trouble. There would be no hope of getting away if—when—the shit hit the fan. Patel and his team would be killed. Or—worse—infected.

"Very well," he said, finally. "If you feel it can be done, then prepare the ship for departure."

"Yes, sir," Patel said. "We should be ready to leave in two days."

Stephen nodded. He'd already detached four destroyers, with orders to sneak up the chain to Alien-One and report back as soon as possible. *Raleigh* hadn't seen any alien settlements between Alien-One and Zheng He, but that didn't mean they didn't exist. And even if they didn't…sneaking into Alien-One wasn't going to be easy. He had no doubt they could skulk around the edge of the system until doomsday, if necessary, but that would be completely pointless. They had to do as much damage as possible to the system before the virus reacted to their presence.

"Make sure you fit a cloaking device," he said. "We don't want them to see anything until it is far too late."

"Aye, Captain," Patel said.

His image vanished. Stephen stared at the terminal, wondering if there would come a time when they didn't dare let Patel and his team back onboard. The virus might have gone to sleep, as far as anyone could tell, but that wouldn't stop it being dangerous. Everyone on the captured ship wore a hardsuit, with strict orders not to open the mask or remove *anything* wherever there was the slightest danger of infection. Stephen didn't envy them. By the time the fleet reached Alien-One, the team would be practically drowning in their own waste.

302

He put the thought to one side as he pulled up the records from Alien-One. They were out of date, but he wouldn't have any more recent data until the destroyers returned. He doubted the virus could have moved many of the facilities, even if it *did* have unmatched economic muscle…it might feel safe, he reminded himself. The sheer weight of firepower protecting Alien-One was staggering, even if most of the ships *Invincible* had seen on her last voyage had been deployed forward to Falkirk and Zheng He. Stephen knew they didn't have a hope of punching through the defences without taking heavy losses, not if they mounted a single strike. They'd have to be clever.

If only we knew what the virus would consider a serious threat, he thought, as he worked his way through a number of possibilities. *Would they react badly to a visible threat? Or would they be more alarmed by a handful of starships?*

He sighed, then tapped a command into his terminal. The tactical staff could take his handful of ideas and either turn them into a workable concept or prove they were impractical. He hoped they'd come up with *something*. Bombarding Alien-One itself with stealthed projectiles was perfectly practical, but he had the nasty feeling that it wouldn't *really* slow the virus down for long. The virus had plenty more host-bodies…

"Maybe if we use the captured ship as a Trojan Horse," he mused. "It might just work."

His doorbell bleeped. He glanced up. "Come."

The door hissed open. Newcomb stood there. "Captain," he said. "Or should I call you *Admiral* now?"

Stephen had to smile. "Perhaps we should stick with *Commodore*," he said. There could only ever be *one* captain on a ship. A captain from another ship would be given a courtesy promotion to commodore, just to avoid confusion. "But I don't suppose it matters at the moment."

"I'll try not to let the command chair get too comfy," Newcomb said. "Although it *will* be a wrench to go back to being a *mere* commander."

"You'll be a captain yourself soon, unless you fuck up." Stephen allowed his smile to grow wider. "This is wartime, Commander. Promotions are based on merit."

"I hope so," Newcomb said.

Stephen nodded. By the time they returned to Earth, Newcomb would have *real* command experience. It wouldn't matter how he'd got the job. Any irregularities would fall on Stephen, not his XO. Newcomb would be ideally positioned to be given one of the newer ships, or simply allowed to remain in command of *Invincible* if Stephen were to be promoted himself. But it wouldn't matter, if they didn't return to Earth. It was quite possible that no one would ever know what had happened to the fleet if they didn't make it home.

He put the thought to one side. "What can I do for you, *Captain*?"

"The ship is as close to ready as we'll ever be," Newcomb said. "And the foreigners have integrated well."

"That's a relief," Stephen said. "I was afraid there'd be problems."

"We solved most of them," Newcomb assured him. "And now we won a brief engagement…"

Stephen had to laugh. The alien survey ship hadn't managed to fire a shot before she'd been captured. She hadn't been *expecting* to encounter the human fleet—there was no hint that she had seen the sheer mass of firepower bearing down on her—but it hardly mattered. The engagement had been, to all intents and purposes, completely one-sided. He didn't really think it merited the term *engagement*.

"Morale is starting to climb up again," Newcomb said. "But there have been some problems, with people wanting to mourn the dead."

"I don't blame them," Stephen said. "But, right now, our priority is to get to Alien-One."

"And then…what?" Newcomb frowned. "Do you have a plan?"

"The beginnings of one," Stephen said. "I shot it to the tactical staff. They can tell me if it's workable or not."

"Make sure you run it past the others too." Newcomb leaned forward. "You can't take them for granted."

"I know," Stephen said. "But I also know that we have too much work to do."

He frowned. "Four days to Alien-One," he added. "Is that long enough to complete our preparations?"

"I think so, sir." Newcomb's lips twitched. "It would help if we knew what the plan actually *was*."

"I want to keep my options open, right now," Stephen said. "And if we have to improvise, I want as many possibilities as possible."

"Yes, sir." Newcomb stood. "I do think, though, that we should hold *some* kind of service for the dead."

"We'll arrange it for when we start moving again," Stephen said. "If we have time."

"Yes, sir," Newcomb said.

Stephen watched him go, then rubbed his eyes with frustration. He didn't blame his crew for wanting to say goodbye to the dead—or, for that matter, wanting to lay down their burdens and take a brief rest. They'd been running themselves ragged for months, even *before* the shit had hit the fan. He could *feel* the tiredness running through the entire ship, from the damaged hull to crew who were—in the end—nothing more than flesh and blood. It would be easy to go back to his cabin and take a brief nap himself, but...

He shook his head. He'd never liked the admirals who did as little as possible, or kowtowed to the politicians while making life harder for the men under their command. It had been a long time since the Royal Navy had had an admiral who didn't have genuine spacefaring experience—it was rare to have an admiral who hadn't fought in one of the interstellar wars—but an admiral's uniform sometimes seemed to do things to their minds. And now he was an admiral, to all intents and purposes, he was damned if he was forgetting what he'd been before the battle. He was *not* going to enjoy the rank without the responsibilities.

And I should know, by now, that admirals do a lot of work, he mused. *But the problem is we just don't see it.*

• • •

305

Alice dreamed.

She knew she was dreaming, even though she could neither move nor wake up. It was a dream. It *had* to be a dream. And yet, as the alien blob inched towards her, she simply couldn't move. Terror rushed through her mind, her heart beating like a drum as the alien came closer and closer. She wanted to open her mouth and scream as it loomed over her, but nothing happened. The blob fell over her…

…And she was drowning, breathing in the virus. She could feel it filling her, oozing through her skin even as it forced its way into her. It was violating her, tearing her mind to shreds as it cut through her defences one by one. She could hear it, hear thoughts slamming against her mind and body; she felt her will collapse, as if she could no longer resist.

YOU ARE MINE, the virus said. She could feel it pushing into her head. It was rape, a rape of everything she was. Nowhere was safe. *YOU ARE MINE*!

Alice snapped awake, sitting up so sharply that she nearly cracked her head against the low ceiling. Her heart was racing, her hands searching for a threat that wasn't there; she rolled over, falling out of bed and coming up in a combat crouch…the cabin was empty. There was no one there. Her fingers grabbed for the biological warfare scanner by her bed and keyed the switch. There was no trace of active alien viral matter in the air.

"Fuck," she said. She hadn't had a nightmare like that since…since *ever*. The sheets were so drenched with sweat that she thought, for a horrible moment, that she'd wet herself like a toddler. "Fuck it."

She sat on the side of the bed, trying to think. Had she been screaming? Marines normally slept deeply, but if she'd been screaming…she looked at the closed door, silently relieved that dozens of marines weren't trying to break it down. She hadn't been screaming, she told herself firmly. She'd merely been trapped in a nightmare, one that had refused to end until…

It had me, she supposed. She'd had bad dreams before—everything from trying to give a presentation naked to being chased by things with teeth—but nothing quite so *vivid*. Even the dreams of her childhood, when she had two parents and no fears for the future, weren't so unpleasant. *It had me and…*

On impulse, she picked up a blood monitor and pressed it against her bare skin. There was a brief pause, just long enough for her to start to worry, then the monitor bleeped the *all-clear*. She let out a sigh of relief as she forced herself to stand on wobbly knees. She wasn't sure what she would have done if the monitor had suggested she was infected…infected with *live* viral matter. Gone to Sickbay? Called for help? Or be forced to forget that she was infected until it was too late? The virus was designed to evolve, damn it. Was it capable of influencing her without arousing suspicions?

"Fuck it," she muttered. "How do you cope with an enemy in your own head?"

She forced herself to stand and inch towards the washroom. A private washroom was a luxury—she wouldn't blame the marines for grumbling—but for once she wasn't going to complain. Her body ached as if she hadn't slept at all. She stripped off her uniform, stepped into the shower and washed herself thoroughly. The dream was nothing more than a dream, a nightmare reminding her that the *next* time she faced the virus might be the last. She might die…

Or lose myself, she thought, as she turned off the water. *And that would be a fate worse than death.*

A dull quiver ran through the ship as she started to move again. It had been two days since she'd captured the alien ship, two days of being inspected by the doctors…who'd panicked at every little hint that one or more of the marines had been infected. None of them *appeared* to have been infected, according to the blood and sniffer tests, but…Alice didn't blame the doctors for worrying, even though it *was* annoying. She knew just how dangerous the virus was. Given a foothold in someone's body, it would eventually take over unless they received immediate and constant medical attention.

Her terminal bleeped. She tapped a switch, opening the email. There was going to be a brief ceremony for the dead, once the ship jumped through the next tramline. Dress uniform was mandatory, for those who chose to attend. Alice sighed. Attendance might be voluntary, but there were few people who wouldn't attend. The only people who would stay away were those on duty. She shook her head, then checked the time. She had enough time to knock hell out of a punching bag before she changed into her dress uniform and went to join the ceremony...

It might be me next time, she thought, morbidly. She didn't know anyone who'd died—not personally—but it didn't matter. *Or it might be someone I know.*

Putting the thought aside, she headed to the hatch.

. . .

Richard stood in the shuttlebay and watched, keeping his face as impassive as he could, as Captain Shields carried out the ceremony for the dead. The caskets in front of him were empty. No one believed there was anything in them but empty air. None of the bodies had been recovered—they *couldn't* have been recovered, even if the fleet had beaten off the attack and retained possession of Zheng He—and there was no way he could convince himself otherwise, but...he winced, inwardly. The ceremony wasn't for *him*. It was for the friends of the dead...and the navy itself, a grim reminder of how many had died to save the rest of the fleet.

He felt his hands start to shake as the squadron leaders started to recite the names of the dead. Some of them he knew, despite himself; some of them were nothing more than names, men and women who had crossed his path briefly before dying somewhere in the infinite vastness of space. Captain Shields might talk about how they would never be forgotten, how their names would be added to the Cenotaph in London, but...Richard had his doubts. He'd had ancestors who'd fought and died in the World Wars, ancestors who had been forgotten or mocked in the years leading up to the Troubles. The Cenotaph itself had survived, but other memorials had been defaced or destroyed. And now...

I don't want to know them, he thought. Another battle was looming, one that threatened to pit the fleet against a hardened enemy target. Too many people were going to die, some under his command. He didn't want to know them. It would make it harder to send them to their deaths. *And afterwards...*

He looked at Monica, her face expressionless as the recital came to an end. She'd been right about him. He'd slipped and fallen and now...the craving grew stronger, taunting him. It would be so easy to take a stim, even with her watching him. He wanted to believe it. No, the craving *wanted* him to believe it. She'd notice if he did...

Perhaps it would be for the best, he told himself. Common sense told him that it would be better, for his subordinates, if he gave himself up. *But I can't give up my duty.*

He sighed, bitterly. What *would* his ancestors—the ones who had fought and died—think of him? He'd make a mistake. He'd damaged himself... he'd *broken* himself. Whatever happened, there was no way out...not as far as he could see. Even if he beat the cravings, he would be tainted for the rest of his life. Failure—alas—was the only option.

Not yet, he thought, savagely. He stopped his hands shaking through sheer will. *It isn't over yet.*

CHAPTER THIRTY-TWO

"JUMP IN FIVE MINUTES, Commodore," Lieutenant-Commander Anisa Pettigrew said. "The live feed suggests that all systems are optimal."

Stephen nodded, grimly. He should be on the bridge. He should be on the bridge when *Invincible* returned—again—to Alien-One. He'd been very tempted to retain command of his ship, at least long enough to supervise as she inched into the hostile system. But instead...he'd forced himself to wait in the CIC. No doubt *someone* would see it as dereliction of duty.

Worry about that when you get home, he told himself, firmly. The destroyers had brought back a great deal of information, but he wanted—he needed—to see for himself. *Right now, you have to be worried about surviving the next few hours.*

"Very good," he said. "Order the fleet to hold position and wait for my command."

Stephen kept his voice under tight control. He didn't know Anisa very well. She was a young staff officer with a good record, but...*Invincible* had only three officers who were rated to man the CIC, all of whom normally had other duties. Stephen had never anticipated having to put together a fleet command staff at short notice. They'd drilled, time and time again, but it was hard to say how she'd react in a *real* engagement. They'd thought themselves prepared for the worst. The virus had taught them that their imagination wasn't anything like grim enough.

In hindsight, we should have been running fleet command drills from the very start, he thought. *But we never anticipated losing both Admirals so quickly.*

He felt an uneasy sensation in his gut as the timer ticked down to zero. It wasn't the first time he'd been to Alien-One—his ship had been the first *human* ship to enter the system—but this time…this time, they were coming in force. There were over seventy ships, just waiting for him to give the order to attack; seventy ships, pitted against the might of the virus. The destroyers had reported a significant drawdown in the number of enemy ships visible to their sensors, at least in Alien-One, but that was meaningless. The ships might not be visible, either to human eyes or starship sensors. That didn't mean they weren't *there*.

If only we knew how many systems they controlled, he thought. *We might be able to make some guesses at just how many ships they could build and support.*

He shook his head. The prize crew had spent days trying to extract something—anything—from what remained of the captured ship's data-cores, but without success. They'd drawn nothing, apart from gibberish. The techs hadn't been able to decide if the datacores were damaged, corrupted or simply beyond humanity's ability to understand. Stephen tended to believe the latter. The virus was very far from human. It had no eyes, no ears…whatever senses it had, in its natural form, were very alien. It had no obligation to store data in visual form, not when it provided an extra layer of security. The techs insisted that they would succeed, given time, but Stephen doubted it. They were human and the virus was anything but.

It wouldn't be as helpful as we might think, he reminded himself. They'd made a handful of guesses, based on the virus's demonstrated power and reach, but they couldn't say anything for certain. The virus's economy was a mess, by human standards. The researchers were doing their best, but they were hampered by very human assumptions about how a society could and should work. *The virus is just too different from us to make guesses about its true power.*

He forced himself to relax as the last seconds ticked away. The virus was strong, but it wasn't all-powerful. Humanity had given a good account of itself in the last few engagements, even though the human ships had been forced to retreat. If the odds had been even, humanity would have carried the day. Given time, Stephen promised himself, they'd build new weapons and technology and push the virus out of human space completely. They might even come up with a vaccine to remove the threat of infection once and for all. The doctors weren't hopeful, but they did have some ideas...

"Jump in five seconds," Anisa said. "Four...three..."

Stephen felt his stomach twist—again—as the display blanked. He was blind, utterly helpless...a passenger on his own ship. The display came to life again, a star and a handful of planets blinking into life. Stephen took a long breath, watching grimly as red icons and projection cones started to appear. Alien-One swarmed with life, all of it controlled by the virus. He shuddered, silently correcting himself. The virus wasn't *controlling* the population, either though force or the threat of force; it didn't manage a giant security edifice to keep the slaves in line, any more than it used implants to teleoperate the population remotely. The virus *was* the population. He could practically *feel* its presence, pulsing through space like a giant malevolent cancer. There was nothing that could be done for the races under its control. The only salvation he could offer them was a quick death.

"Jump completed," Anisa said. "Cloaking device engaged. Local space is clear."

"Hold position," Stephen said, automatically. "Launch recon probes."

"Aye, Commodore," Anisa said.

Stephen scowled inwardly. *Newcomb* had to issue those orders, not him. Newcomb was the commanding officer now...he told himself, sharply, that he'd done what he needed to do when he'd transferred command. It still felt wrong. *Invincible* was *his* ship. And he'd handed her over to his XO when he was needed elsewhere. It felt like a gross dereliction of duty.

He pushed the thought to one side as the display continued to update. The shipyard near the planet itself was a glowing mass of icons, the energy signatures so powerful that they were blurring together into a single entity. A handful of notes appeared beside them as the tactical staff crunched the data, identifying everything from slips to industrial nodes. The virus clearly hadn't learnt anything from the engagement in Alien-Five, Stephen noted. Their shipyard was still concentrated, a giant station rather than a number of facilities in close proximity. He allowed himself a cold smile. They might not have realised how the other shipyard had even been breached, let alone destroyed.

Or perhaps they put the pieces together, he thought. The shipyard was surrounded by a solid mass of active sensors, sweeping space so finely that he doubted they could slip even a powered-down recon probe into the shipyard. There was no hope of sending the marines to repeat their success in Alien-Five. *They must have worked out what we did.*

He contemplated the problem for a long moment. The virus had thrown secrecy to the winds—the shipyard was probably visible from light-years away—but it had worked out in its favour. It knew that *Invincible* had passed through Alien-One. It knew there was no point in trying to keep the shipyard's location a secret. Instead, it had set out to make the facility impregnable. Stephen had to admit that it might just have succeeded.

Watching fortresses, patrolling starfighters, hundreds of sensor platforms... they certainly crafted a tough line of defence, he thought. It was hard to believe that the different active sensor platforms weren't interfering with each other, but the virus's own nature allowed it to control the entire system as a single entity. Stephen assumed it could compensate for any confusion. There were probably also hundreds of *passive* sensor platforms scattered across space, watching for the slightest *hint* of enemy contact. *If we were planning a conventional attack, we'd need more firepower.*

His eyes sharpened as more starships came to light. A sizable flotilla—battleships, carriers, destroyers—held position between the shipyard and the planet, while thousands of starfighters and hundreds of orbital weapons platforms guarded the planet itself. Alien-One had to be important, he told himself, and not just as a source of breeding stock. The mere presence of a pair of orbital towers, their energy signatures suggesting they were worked harder than the four towers on Earth, told him the planet was *definitely* important. The virus had worked hard to turn the planet into a giant factory.

Stephen shuddered, his eyes skimming over the preliminary conclusions. Alien-One was *heavily* industrialised, with countless factories visible on the planet's surface despite the presence of an orbital industrial network. It was hard to be sure, from their distance, but it looked as if the atmosphere was badly polluted. The virus didn't seem to give a damn about the planetary environment. Stephen wondered, morbidly, what effects it had on the planetary population...and if the virus even cared. It wasn't short of host-bodies. It could simply bring in a few million from another infected system, if necessary.

Anisa cleared her throat. "Sensors are picking up starships moving from Tramline Two to Tramline One."

"From Alien-Five?" Stephen cursed under his breath. They wanted— they needed—to survey the remainder of infected space. But that would take time he didn't have. "Or from somewhere else?"

"Impossible to determine, sir," Anisa said. He caught an edge in her voice. It wasn't a question she could answer. "There are several possibilities."

It could be anything from a supply convoy to a reinforcement fleet, Stephen thought. *And normally it would be a very tempting target.*

He studied the cluster of icons for a long moment, thinking hard. He could bring a chunk of the fleet through—perhaps all of it—and smash the alien convoy...and, in doing so, alert Alien-One to his presence. He had no doubt they would win the brief engagement—he was sure his fleet outgunned the small alien formation—but it might cost them the war. And yet...he gritted his teeth in frustration. There was no way to know just *what* was being shipped to Zheng He. Taking the convoy out might prevent the virus from attacking Earth.

"Detach two drones to keep an eye on the convoy," he ordered, stiffly. The window of opportunity was already closing. "We'll have to let them go."

"Yes, sir," Anisa said.

315

Stephen nodded, feeling the full weight of command pressing down on him. It wasn't enough to have *opinions*, not now. Anyone could have an opinion, from the XO to the lowest crewman or embedded reporter. A commander had to make *decisions* and stick to them, despite knowing that the wrong decision could lead to utter disaster. If he was wrong...if he was lucky, people back home would castigate him for failure. And, if he was unlucky, there would be no one back home to castigate him. Letting the convoy go might prove to be a mistake.

But if we can take out even a handful of the virus's productive facilities, he told himself, *we'll buy time for the navy to build more ships and design more weapons.*

"My compliments to Captain Newcomb," he said. It felt odd, addressing his XO as Captain, but it was necessary. "Inform him that we can proceed with the operation as planned."

"Aye, sir," Anisa said.

Stephen felt the indecision nagging at him as *Invincible* slipped further into the infected system. No, it wasn't *indecision*. He'd made his decision before they'd even jumped into Alien-One. It was the grim awareness that he might have made a mistake, that he might have time—barely—to change his mind. His training told him it was better to make a decision quickly, even if it was the wrong one, rather than sit on his hands and wait for something else to happen, but his emotions suggested otherwise. Better to play it safe... he shook his head, angrily dismissing the doubts. They weren't fighting a genteel war, with no threat to the homeland...to the homeworld. They were fighting for their very survival.

Defeat means the end of the fucking world, he reminded himself. *And we cannot allow ourselves to hold back.*

More and more data slid into the display, the analysts overwhelmed by the sheer scale of the alien system. Stephen was grudgingly impressed. Only Earth and Tadpole Prime came close to matching what the virus had built, although he was fairly sure that the uninfected worlds were more efficient. It *looked* as though the virus had copied the Belter philosophy—there were technologies from several different eras, working side by side—but on a far greater scale. He felt numb as the true immensity—and horror—of the virus's achievement started to sink in. It had overwhelmed and infected dozens of alien races, then put its new host-bodies to work. The virus itself was nothing more than a giant hermit crab.

Then we'll crush it beneath our feet, he told himself.

He knew it wouldn't be easy. The asteroid mining stations might be primitive, by human standards, but there was nothing primitive about the defences. He didn't understand why the virus hadn't pushed through a whole series of technological upgrades; he could see plenty of places where the mining system could be improved...it didn't matter. The virus had the firepower to defend the important sections and that was *all* that mattered. It could rebuild the remainder of the system from scratch as long as it protected its industrial base.

And wiping out every last industrial miner will be a long and tricky task, he thought. The tactical staff were already picking out targets for ballistic projectiles, sorting out the timetables to ensure that the virus wasn't alerted to the threat until the main attack was launched, but there were just so *many* targets. *We may have to sterilise the entire system.*

The console bleeped a warning. "Commodore, the sensor analysts warn that we may be getting too close to the shipyard," Anisa warned. "We may be detected at any moment."

"Particularly if the system *is* filled with passive sensor platforms," Stephen mused. There were so many active sensor pulses bombarding through the system that a passive platform *might* catch wind of *Invincible*. "My compliments to Captain Newcomb, Commander; we're to pull back to the RV point at once."

He felt his lips twitch. It was astonishing to think of just *what* could be done, if the Royal Navy didn't have to worry about budgets. Fleet Carriers that were twenty or thirty kilometres from bow to stern, battleships so loaded with armour that they were practically invulnerable...endless waves of missiles, starships the size of small moons...he shook his head. The virus could have seeded the entire system with passive sensor platforms, in the certain knowledge that none of them would be detected save by sheer random chance. It wasn't as if the virus had to do battle with beancounters in the accounting department if it wanted to get anything done.

A low quiver ran through the ship. "We're pulling back now," Anisa said. "The tactical staff have completed their projections."

Stephen keyed his console, bringing up the suggestions. They hadn't changed much, although they had been updated...he accepted one of the better ideas, made a handful of tiny modifications of his own, and sent it back. The plan had too many working parts for his peace of mind—and too many concepts borrowed directly from the virus itself—but it should be workable. And, if the plan *failed* to work, he could cut his losses, lay down covering fire and break contact.

And run for our lives to the tramline, he thought. *The enemy doesn't have any bases to block our flight to friendly space.*

He gritted his teeth. The virus might not have any bases along the Raleigh Chain, as far as anyone had been able to tell, but it *did* have a flicker network. It *could* forward orders to the fleet that had taken Zheng He, instructing the ships to take up position to block Stephen's escape. And it might just succeed, too. Ten years ago, it would have been a race. Now, there was no hope of outrunning an FTL message. The flicker network had changed the face of warfare.

"Signal *Rose* and *Stanley*," he ordered. The two destroyers had remained on station near the tramline, watching from a safe distance. "They are to return to the fleet, with instructions to put Plan Alpha into effect immediately."

"Aye, Commodore," Anisa said.

Stephen allowed himself a tight smile. By the time *Invincible* reached the RV point, the bulk of the fleet would already be there. They'd be ready to launch the offensive as planned...if, of course, everything went to plan. And if it didn't...Stephen shook his head. The tactical staff had devised as many contingency plans as they could, but *some* things had to be left to chance. They'd done their best to prepare for the unexpected. Now...all they could do was begin the plan and be ready for any surprises.

He glanced at the chronometer. Ten hours, more or less, before they could begin. There would be time for the entire crew to take a nap—to rest or pray or simply grab some downtime before the shit hit the fan. And then...he wanted to pray himself, for the men and women risking their lives for their homeworld. And for the plan to succeed.

Newcomb will have to tell the crew to take a break, Stephen thought, as *Invincible* put more distance between herself and the alien shipyard. *He won't need to be prompted to do that.*

"Hand your position to your relief," he ordered Anisa. "And get some rest, before it's too late."

"Yes, sir," Anisa said.

CHAPTER THIRTY-THREE

"WE'RE READY, SIR."

Commander Tomas Patel nodded as he surveyed what remained of the alien engineering compartment. It hadn't taken him long to decide that there was nothing to be gained by trying to reactivate the alien bridge, not when half the components and control systems had been so tightly spliced into the virus that they simply couldn't be trusted. His imagination kept suggesting the viral cells would come back to life and retake control of the ship at the worst possible time, even though they'd vented the entire interior to kill the virus once and for all. Everyone knew the virus was tough, harder to eradicate than the common cold. His crew slept in their suits, breathed recycled air and ate…he didn't want to think about what they ate.

He studied the console carefully, making a final check. There were no great mysteries in the alien hardware, although the virus seemed to be rather less concerned about safety than any human designer. The starship's drives were easy to understand. The software, on the other hand, was either glitched beyond repair or completely incompatible with human technology. Tomas and his crew had wound up having to run their own command and control links into the hardware, just to get the ship moving in the right direction. It would have been a great deal easier, he told himself, if they'd simply been trying to get the ship home.

And now we're trying to fool the virus into believing that nothing is wrong, he reminded himself. *And too much really can go wrong now.*

"Here we go," he said. He wished, suddenly, for a big red button. Instead, he simply tapped the command into the keyboard. "Let's move."

A low shudder ran through the ship as her drives came to life, pushing her towards the tramline. Tomas watched, carefully monitoring the power curves. The ship *appeared* normal—and they thought they'd duplicated the IFF signal—but there was no way to be sure. Tomas was experienced enough to understand the danger of an intruder on a military base, someone wearing the same uniform and speaking the same language as the defenders, yet…it struck him as unlikely the virus would allow the captured ship *that* close to the shipyard without inspecting her thoroughly. The virus *knew* a ship could be captured and turned against her former owners. *Dezhnev* had been turned against the MNF…

We didn't think it could be done until the virus did it, Tomas thought. *The virus, on the other hand, knows what it can do.*

"The power curves are nominal," Lieutenant Fellows reported. "We're ready to jump."

Tomas nodded. "Take us through."

He sucked in his breath as the tramline came closer. He'd spent most of his adult life exploring the wonders of alien science, breaking it down to see what new insights humanity could glean from alien technology. It had been a rewarding job, even though there hadn't been *many* new discoveries since the First Interstellar War. The technological specialists had learnt a great deal from finding new ways to look at the world. They'd even gathered data from the Vesy, who'd barely discovered the wheel before learning that there were far more advanced races out there. It had definitely been an *interesting* career…

…But now it had turned deadly.

You volunteered for this job, he told himself, as his vision darkened. He felt, absurdly, as though the entire universe was going to have a sneeze. An invisible fist slammed into his stomach, hard enough to make him gag and swallow hard to keep from throwing up in the suit; he heard his team coughing and retching over the open channel. *You could have said no…*

He tasted bile in his mouth. He had to swallow twice before he could speak. "Status…status report?"

"Jump completed," Fellows said. "That bloody *hurt*."

Specialist Li muttered something in Chinese, before clearing her throat. "The jump harmonics were poor, by our standards. We all got hit pretty hard."

"Sound off," Tomas snapped. "Is anyone unable to continue?"

He waited for answers, then allowed himself a sigh of relief. The jump had hurt—clearly, the virus saw no reason to minimise the jump shock—but no one had been knocked out or otherwise crippled. He checked the status board, noting—to his amusement—there wasn't a single red light on the panel. The starship seemed to regard the rough jump as routine. Tomas suspected it didn't notice. The viral base cells might not be affected by the jump.

"Set course for Target One," he ordered. "And alert the fleet to follow us."

Another quiver ran through the ship as she picked up speed. Alerts popped up on his display, warning him the modified control routines his crew had installed didn't have perfect control of the drive field. They couldn't manoeuvre properly, no matter what they did. He considered it for a moment, then dismissed the problem. If they came under fire, the entire mission was thoroughly screwed anyway. He'd already calculated the odds of getting out alive and decided they were terrifyingly low.

"The fleet is moving into position," Lieutenant Hammond offered. "They'll be giving chase in a moment."

"Then get ready to take off the safety locks, such as they are," Tomas ordered. "We don't want the fleet to *catch* us."

"No, sir," Hammond agreed.

"I have the communications package online," Li reported. "Should I transmit?"

"No," Tomas ordered. "We don't want them smelling a rat too early."

• • •

"The captured ship is picking up speed," Anisa reported. "Force One is moving in pursuit."

Stephen nodded. The plan was simple enough, although he was all too aware that too many things could go wrong. The captured alien ship would look, to all intents and purposes, as if it were being chased by a massive human fleet. Ideally, the virus would move to block Force One while allowing the captured ship through the defences...if, of course, the planned sign and countersign worked. The planners had been unable to guarantee anything, naturally. They'd hemmed and hawed, when Stephen had pressed them, before admitting that their work was based on guesswork.

"Deploy drones," he ordered. "They're to go active on my command."

He smiled, coldly. The virus knew—now—that human ECM was far superior to theirs. He'd taught them that during the Battle of Alien-Five. But, at the same time, they couldn't allow Force One to close with their shipyard, not unless they *wanted* it blasted to atoms. He studied the display, silently running through the variables. Enemy One—the fleet holding station near the planet—would have to move to intercept. They'd have no choice.

And yet, if they ignore the threat, they actually win, Stephen thought. *Invincible* and the handful of *real* escorts surrounding her simply didn't have enough firepower to break into the shipyard and destroy it. *They just have to gamble I'm bluffing.*

He leaned forward, wishing he knew which way the virus would jump. No human admiral would want to take the risk of calling his bluff...assuming, of course, that he didn't *know* it was a bluff. The virus had scattered the system with so many sensor platforms that it was vaguely possible that one of them had picked up hints that most of Force One was nothing more than sensor ghosts...he shook his head. They'd *know*, soon enough. And then they'd give the enemy a nasty surprise.

Time passed, slowly. Stephen forced himself to move about the compartment, rather than stay in his chair and keep his eyes glued to the display. It would take hours before the shipyard—and Enemy One—knew they had incoming, hours more before Stephen knew what they were doing in response. And hours more before Stephen knew what had happened to Force Two. He silently kicked himself for agreeing to the plan, when it had been put before him. There were too many moving parts, too many places where a single failure could lead to utter disaster...

"Signal from the pods, sir," Anisa said. "The ballistics are on their way."

"Good," Stephen said. If nothing else, the virus would know that the system had been attacked. "Order them..."

The console bleeped. Red icons flickered to life. "Commodore, Enemy One is moving," Anisa said. "She's coming to meet us."

"And she's been on her way for some time," Stephen said. He felt a thrill of excitement. The tactical staff would be running projections, displaying probability cones of where the alien ships might be, but it didn't matter. He *knew* where the alien ships had to be. "Warn the fleet to be ready to execute Breakaway on my command."

"Aye, Commodore."

Stephen watched, grimly, as the range narrowed. Enemy One was circling the shipyard, rather than flying through the installation...an interesting choice, given that the odds of ramming something were incredibly low, but it hardly mattered. The virus *knew* it had to bring his fleet to battle as far from the shipyard as possible, if only to ensure the facilities weren't damaged in the crossfire. Any *normal* opponent would sacrifice Enemy One to buy time...

"They'll pass the captured ship in seventy minutes," Anisa told him. "And they'll enter engagement range of *us* in ninety."

"The fleet will execute Breakaway in sixty," Stephen said. "And signal the freighters. They are to start deploying missiles as planned."

"Aye, Commodore."

• • •

"We should have named the fucking ship," Fellows muttered, as the alien fleet converged with the captured vessel. "I *told* you it was bad luck."

"And I told you that we wouldn't be taking her home, whatever happened," Tomas countered, dryly. If the virus opened fire now, they were dead. The odds of survival were precisely zero. "I see no point in renaming the ship now."

Li let out a harsh giggle. "What would we call her, anyway?"

"The *Fuck You?*" Fellows snorted. "Or the *Finger Up Your...*"

"Enough," Tomas said, quietly but firmly. He didn't blame them for feeling tense, or for trying to deal with the tension by clowning around, but there were limits. They were staring at an alien fleet powerful enough to vaporise them with a single barrage. "Get ready to transmit the countersign..."

His breath caught in his throat as the alien ships came closer...then swept past, without even *trying* to signal the captured ship. Tomas blinked in surprise, before deciding that the alien fleet had to be focused on the human formation. They couldn't allow the human ships to get too close to the shipyard, whatever the cost. Tomas allowed himself a tight smile. They might just have made a serious mistake.

"Keep us on our current course," he ordered. "And be ready to open fire."

"Aye, Captain," Fellows said.

The alien shipyard drew closer. Tomas was unwillingly impressed by the sheer *size* of the installation, even though it looked alarmingly inefficient to him. There was too great a risk of a single hit doing immense damage, just as had happened in Alien-Five. But the virus probably hadn't had time to modify its shipyards, not if it needed to supply its fleets at the same time. He wondered, as he studied the ever-growing list of potential targets, which industrial nodes had produced the missiles that had killed his friends. Knocking them out would be a serious blow to the virus's ability to wage war.

"We're being hailed." Li's voice rose as she spoke. "I think. They're lasing us, but I can't read the message."

"Send the planned countersign," Tomas ordered. The xenospecialists had done their best, but there was no way to guarantee their work would pass muster. The virus was just too alien. They weren't even sure what they were saying, let alone that it was the right thing *to* say. "And be ready."

He took a breath. "All non-essential personnel to the shuttle."

"Aye, sir," Lieutenant Hallows said.

• • •

"Execute Breakaway," Stephen ordered. The alien fleet had roared past the captured ship, keeping their eyes firmly fixed on Force One. "All ships are to reverse course at once."

"Aye, Commodore."

Stephen nodded, gripping his command chair. This was it. This was the moment of truth. If the enemy fleet pushed hard, they'd be able to bring him to battle before his ships could pick up speed and escape. If they pushed hard…they'd have to, he told himself. The opportunity to slam their battleships right into his fleet carriers was not to be missed. They'd lose their entire fleet, at the cost of doing serious damage to *his* fleet. It would make it impossible for him to pull back and escape. And then it would be just a matter of time.

Come on, he thought. *I'm turning around and running for my life, like a bully who's just discovered that his victim has an older brother. Come and beat the shit out of me.*

"The fleet's acknowledged, sir," Anisa reported. "They're reversing course."

The range was closing sharply now. Stephen braced himself. If the virus sensed a trap, it would order its ships to reverse course too. The range would wobble, but remain open. The engagement would be inconclusive as long as Stephen stayed away from the shipyard's starfighters and fixed defences.

A human commander might have suspicions, but would he act on them? It wasn't easy to pass up an opportunity to *really* drive the boot home. The hell of it was that a human commander might fall for the trick, where the virus might decide to be careful and break off.

Particularly as it can presumably call on reinforcements from the remainder of infected space, Stephen thought. *They can tolerate us dancing around the outer edge of the system, while they summon the remainder of their fleet to crush us.*

"They're picking up speed," Anisa said. "They must be redlining their drives."

"The chance to catch us on the hop is not to be missed," Stephen said. A stern chase might be a long one, but only if the lead fleet had a chance to pick up enough speed. They might be run down before they managed to put enough distance between themselves and their opponents. "They can't let us have time to run."

He smiled, coldly, as the range closed still further. The enemy fleet might be weak in starfighters—he guessed the virus had planned to deploy starfighters from the orbital defences, rather than the mobile fleet—but it still had enough firepower to inflict serious damage. It didn't *look* as though the virus had realised—yet—most of the ships were decoys. That wouldn't last long...

"Bring the missiles online," he ordered. "Prepare to fire."

The display sparkled with red lights. The virus's ships had opened fire. Stephen snapped out a pair of orders as the missiles picked up speed. The virus had blundered...no, it hadn't blundered. It would know the decoys were nothing more than sensor ghosts as soon as the decoys failed to open fire. The lack of point defence would tell the virus everything it needed to know. And he didn't dare gamble and keep *all* of his ships from opening fire. He was short of hulls as it was.

"Fire the missiles," he ordered.

Green icons flared to life on the display. The freighters had unloaded the missiles into space, a desperation manoeuvre that would never have been considered before the virus introduced the human race to high-intensity missile duels. The sheer *cost* of so many missiles was daunting, even though twelve nations had contributed. But, for the first time, the human race was throwing a wall of missiles at an alien opponent. He thought he saw, just for a second, the alien ships flinch. Their point defence was prepped for starfighters, not missiles.

And the ECM drones probably don't help, Stephen thought. He'd fired nearly a thousand missiles, but the ECM made it look as if he'd fired *hundreds* of thousands of missiles. The virus would know that most of them were fakes, yet how could they tell the difference? The sheer weight of fire alone would guarantee that some of them would get through the point defence and strike home. *They came too close and now they don't even have time to reverse course and escape.*

"Launch starfighters," he ordered. There was no point in trying to maintain the illusion any longer. "All ships are to continue on their current course."

"Aye, Commodore."

• • •

"I don't think they believed us," Li said. Her voice was starting to shake. "They're lasing us again. I can't read the message."

"I'm getting targeting sensors," Fellows said. "They're bringing their weapons to bear on us."

Which is pretty much their way of saying 'stop or I'll shoot,' Tomas thought. *They won't let us come any closer.*

He keyed his console, authorising the missiles to launch. "Open fire," he snapped. "I say again, open fire!"

He took a breath as the first missiles blasted out of their launch tubes. "Switch to auto, then run for the shuttle," he added, sharply. The ship would keep firing until she was destroyed. "Abandon ship!"

The crew jumped and ran, hurrying down to the airlock. Tomas followed, knowing it was unlikely they'd make it out. The shuttle had been borrowed from the marines, but it wasn't *that* stealthy. Every ship and weapons platform within range would be looking for them…

A hammer smashed into the ship. The lights blinked out. Moments later, the gravity failed too.

We hurt them, Tomas thought, as he crashed against a bulkhead. The suit took most of the impact, but his arm still ached. *They know we hurt them…*

Seven missiles slammed into the captured ship's hull and exploded. There were no survivors.

CHAPTER THIRTY-FOUR

STEPHEN ALLOWED HIMSELF a cold smile as the alien fleet writhed under his fire.

It felt good, so good, to finally and unambiguously land a blow on an alien fleet. A battleship fell out of formation, streaming atmosphere and plasma as she fought for life; another seemed unhurt, a moment before she exploded with staggering force. Four destroyers mounted a valiant defence of a carrier, only to be blasted out of the way before the remaining missiles slammed into the carrier. She exploded, vanishing from the display. Stephen watched, grimly, as another battleship staggered but kept coming anyway. The virus had designed her well.

"Incoming fire," Anisa warned. "They're targeting the live ships."

"Adjust our point defence to match," Stephen ordered. The virus was distracted. If they were lucky, they could *keep* it distracted long enough to escape. Not, he supposed, that it mattered. Enemy One was no longer in a position to cover the planet. "And keep the fleet moving."

"Aye, sir," Anisa said.

Stephen tapped his console, pulling up the live feed from the recon probes near the shipyard. The captured vessel had been destroyed—it looked as if she'd gone down with all hands—but she'd done well. A dozen missiles had slammed into the shipyard and exploded, inflicting a vast amount of damage; dozens of stealth projectiles and mines had devastated the remainder of the alien facility. It hadn't been as complete a sweep as Stephen would have liked, but it would put a serious crimp in the virus's ability to resupply and rebuild its fleets. God alone knew how long it would take to recover.

A dull shudder ran through the ship as an enemy missile scored a hit. Stephen glanced at the display, then forced himself to put his concern aside. Newcomb was in command of the ship. Damage control was his responsibility, not Stephen's. The fleet was picking up speed rapidly, even as the alien ships seemed torn between continuing the pursuit and falling back on the shipyard. Stephen hoped it would take them a good, long while to decide. The more space he managed to put between their fleet and his, the better.

And Force Two should be going on the offensive right about now, he told himself, firmly. *That should make life harder for the bastards.*

• • •

Captain Danial Nicolson liked to think of himself as a simple soul. He disliked elegant plans and concepts, if only because—in his experience—there were always too many things that could go wrong. War was a democracy in the truest possible sense. The enemy—human or alien—always got a vote. Danial preferred brute force, if only because it made it harder for anyone to try any clever tricks. God was on the side of the big guns, in the long run. Most of the victories claimed by the underdogs rarely lasted long.

"Captain," his tactical officer said. "We're coming up on Point Hammer."

"Lock weapons on target," Danial grunted. Captain—no, *Commodore*—Shields had come up with a good plan, but it fell to Danial and the remainder of the battleships to carry it out. "Fire on my command."

He studied the display for a long moment, firmly convinced that an irresistible force was about to meet an immovable opponent. USS *Alaska* and her sisters had been crammed with firepower—everything from missile tubes and plasma cannons to mass drivers and railguns—but he had no illusions about their mission. Alien-One was surrounded by defences, from orbital battlestations to automated weapons platforms. Danial wouldn't have cared to try to force his way into orbit, not if he had every battleship humanity had produced under his command. Thankfully, he had a different set of orders.

The display flashed red. The tactical officer swore. "They have us!"

"As planned," Danial said. He hadn't expected to get so close before the virus noticed him and his ships. Captain Shields might have drawn the virus's mobile units away—Danial had tracked them heading for the ship-yard—but the rest of the defences would have gone on alert. "Open fire as planned. I say again, open fire as planned."

The display flared with green and blue icons as the battleships opened fire. Danial leaned forward, watching with interest as missiles and mass driver projectiles roared towards the orbital defences...and the planet under-neath. His name was going to go down in the history books, although per-haps for the wrong reasons. No one had ever bombarded a planet before, not with anything larger than a KEW projectile. The missiles and mass driver projectiles were going to inflict one hell of a lot of damage. God knew there would be protests back home when the sheer magnitude of the devastation hit the media.

"The enemy stations are launching starfighters," the tactical officer reported. "They'll be on us in five minutes."

"Point defence to full alert, engage when ready," Danial ordered. He'd kept the majority of the carriers back, pointing out that they'd just increase the odds of detection. He didn't think he'd made a mistake—starfighters were of limited value against battleships—but it was still going to cost him. "And continue firing."

"Aye, sir," the tactical officer said. "The first projectiles are impacting...now."

Danial watched, awed, as the mass driver projectiles slammed into the planet. They were little threat to a starship, which could evade incoming projectiles unless it had already been battered into a pulp, but a far more sig-nificant threat to orbital battlestations and planets. The projectiles crashed into the orbital towers, the sheer force of impact doing more damage than a dozen nuclear warheads. Danial felt his blood turn to ice as the first tower shattered, chunks of debris flying into space or crashing down to the surface. He'd watched horror movies about the fall of Earth's orbital towers, but this was *real*. Countless lives were about to be lost.

Infected lives, he reminded himself, stiffly. *We're doing them a favour.*

The devastation spread rapidly as chunk after chunk of debris hit the surface, the force of the impact throwing clouds of dust and water vapour into the planet's atmosphere. Nuclear winter was a very real possibility, threatening to kill anyone who survived the first impacts and reached safety. Danial sucked in his breath as the second tower started to crumble, the third somehow surviving a direct hit that should have sent it crashing to the ground. It was hard to grasp the *true* scale of the devastation, to realise what they'd done to the alien world. Nothing, not even the Bombardment of Earth, came close.

We might have sentenced every last living thing on the surface to death, he thought.

He pulled back as the first of the alien starfighters roared into his point defence envelope, fighting with a desperation that was almost human. The host-bodies showed no concern for their lives, or for those of their fellows; they pressed the offensive with a determination that awed him. Hundreds fell, swatted out of space; hundreds remained to fire torpedoes into his armour or simply ram themselves into his hull. The damage mounted rapidly, even though none of his ships were crippled. The alien fighters were sacrificing themselves to wear him down.

"We've hit the orbital nodes pretty hard, sir," the tactical officer said. "There isn't much left."

"It looks that way," Danial agreed. He had orders not to carry the offense too far, not when he might be caught against the planet and destroyed. But the enemy mobile units were destroyed. "Fire one last round against the survivors, then prepare to retreat."

"Aye, sir," the tactical officer said.

Danial nodded to himself, then took one last look at Alien-One. The planet was going dark, massive clouds of dust forming in the upper atmosphere. His sensors were reporting fires all over the surface, fires on a scale that dwarfed the forest fire he'd been lucky to escape as a small boy. The planet's forests were burning down, the planet's industrial base was dying... there were even hints that nuclear reactors were melting down. It was hard to believe that anything could live through the nightmare he'd unleashed. Even the virus would find it difficult to survive if all the host-bodies died out.

But this won't be the end, he thought, grimly. *And it may try and do the same to Earth—and every other human world within reach.*

"The fleet is to retreat," he ordered. It was tempting to close further, to finish the job, but they'd completed their mission. There was nothing to be gained by risking the fleet—and possibly undoing their victory—when they could pick up their winnings and go home, leaving the virus to clean up the mess. "I say again, all ships are to retreat."

"Aye, Captain."

• • •

"The alien ships are picking up speed," Anisa reported. "I think they're trying to run us down."

"It certainly looks that way," Stephen said. He didn't have a report from Nicolson yet, but his long-range sensors had picked up flashes of energy from Alien-One. It was quite likely that the planet had been hit—and hit badly. The virus could break contact, if it wished, but—perversely—it might gain something if it brought Stephen to battle. It presumably didn't want Force One and Force Two to reunite, then finish the job. "Order the starfighters to slow them down."

He sucked in his breath. "And signal Force Two. They are to alter course to assist us."

"Aye, Commodore."

Stephen nodded. If the long-range sensors were accurate, Alien-One had been bombarded heavily. The plan had certainly *called* for the planet to be bombarded, although he still had no way of knowing *precisely* what had happened. He tried not to think about just how many host-bodies had been killed in the last few minutes...maybe it wasn't genocide, by the strict legal definition, but it was close enough. Cold logic told him he'd had no choice, that they must either commit genocide or be the victims of genocide; emotion suggested otherwise. They should have been able to find another way.

We might have just blown up their homeworld, he thought, numbly. *But we may never know for sure.*

He shrugged. The xenospecialists hadn't been able to isolate the virus's homeworld, not even by comparing the virus's DNA to host-body DNA. There was no way to know, but he suspected that Alien-One was—had been—yet another infected world, bigger than most. It was hard to believe that a race would rise to master technology and spread out to explore the tramlines, all the while unaware of the threat growing beneath its feet. The world that had birthed the virus might never develop any other form of intelligent life at all. No, it was more likely that the virus—assuming it had evolved naturally—had done so in a different system altogether. And then the explorers from outer space had landed...

Poor bastards, he thought. He had no way to know what had happened, but he could imagine it. *By the time they realised the threat, it was too late. They never stood a chance.*

• • •

Richard resisted the urge to laugh out loud as he led his makeshift squadron towards the alien ship. The aliens seemed stunned by the scale of the devastation, by suddenly finding themselves smashed by a wave of missiles...by the same tactic they'd used themselves to such great effect in both Falkirk and Zheng He. The virus had to have lost *some* control over its fleets, he reasoned; the main body of the fleet was still trying to run *Invincible* and the rest of the ships down, while most of their starfighters were covering the shipyard instead of adding their weight to the battle. The timing, for once, spoke against them. He had no intention of giving them time to recover.

"Form up on me," he ordered, as flashes of plasma fire cut through space. The enemy ship was determined to keep them as far away as possible, for all the good it would do. "Concentrate your fire on the drive section."

He studied his display carefully as the alien battleship grew larger and larger. She was a monster of a ship, studded with weapons and defences that made *Invincible* look puny. A single missile had struck her amidships, blasting a hole through her armour, but there was nothing to be gained by trying to drop a torpedo into the hull. Post-battle analysis had made it clear that the alien ships had extensive layers of internal armour, as well as heavy point defence. A starfighter torpedo wouldn't do much damage unless it sparked off a chain of explosions that threatened to tear the ship apart.

But there was another target. "Lock torpedoes," he ordered, swerving from side to side as the enemy point defence grew stronger. "And fire!"

His starfighter jerked, the torpedoes lunging towards their target. The enemy point defence hastily retargeted itself, giving him a clear route away from the ship as it tried to take out the torpedoes before it was too late. The other starfighters followed suit, giving the alien point defence more and more targets to blast out of space. A handful broke through the defences and slammed into their targets. Seconds later, the enemy battleship was spinning out of control.

Crippled, Richard thought. His hands were starting to shake. He gripped the stick tightly, silently praying he'd make it back before something worse happened. *Crippled, just like me.*

"We can finish her," a pilot said, in a thick Russian accent. "We kill her now."

"Leave her," Richard said. A crippled battleship was no longer a threat. He understood the urge to finish the job, to have the right to paint a battle-ship on his starfighter, but they had to think a little more tactically. "We need to cripple as many ships as possible."

He ignored the angry mutter of protest. "Re-form on me," he said. His vision swam, just for a moment. He wanted a drink. Or a stim. He sipped water from the tube, wishing it tasted better. "And follow me to the next target."

. . .

"Update from *Alaska*," Anisa said. "She and her consorts are altering course as ordered."

"Then alter course to the RV point," Stephen ordered. The plan had worked, better than he'd had a right to expect. "And divert the drones to confuse the enemy."

"Aye, sir," Anisa said.

If that's even possible, Stephen thought, quietly. *The virus knows—now— which ships are real.*

He forced himself to relax as the range started to grow. The enemy fleet was reducing speed, reluctant to waste more time and ships trying to run *Invincible* to ground. Stephen didn't really blame them. The range had opened up too far, allowing him to use his starfighters to batter the enemy ships to rubble without putting his own in serious danger. There was no way the virus could stage its starfighters forward without carriers and all of its carriers were either gone or hopelessly out of place.

We did it, Stephen told himself. A thrill of excitement ran through him. *We bloody did it.*

He leaned back in his chair, studying the first reports from Alien-One. The analysts had warned that preliminary results were not always reliable—there were no shortage of cautionary tales of preliminary reports that were overoptimistic, mistaken or flat-out lies—but he could *see* that the virus had taken a major blow. The planet itself was effectively dead, while hundreds of industrial nodes and production facilities had been destroyed or crippled. It would take *years* for the virus to recover, even if it launched a crash-program to rebuild. He had no way to know how much they'd actually *hurt* the virus, overall, but it was hard to believe that they hadn't done a great deal of damage. They might just have bought the human race time, time it desperately needed…

An alert sounded. Stephen looked up, sharply. "Report!"

"Long-range probes have just reported a major enemy fleet entering the system through Tramline Two," Anisa said. "Projections indicate that they're heading to Tramline Four."

Stephen blinked in surprise. That didn't make sense. If the virus had summoned reinforcements…his blood ran cold. It *did* make sense. The virus had decided there was no point in trying to prevent him from destroying the remaining facilities within the system, so it was trying to block his escape instead. He ran the calculations, working his way through the vectors as quickly as possible. There was no hope of returning to the tramline and escaping before it was too late.

Another wave of red icons appeared on the display, coming from the shipyard. "Enemy starfighters," Anisa reported, sharply. "They just launched everything they have at us."

Those pilots are going to die, Stephen thought, coldly. The starfighters could not reach *Invincible,* launch their attacks and then get back to safety before their life support packs ran out. But the virus wouldn't care. *They're going to try to weaken us, to win time for their main fleet to finish the job. And that means…*

He worked his way through the possibilities, feeling a cold lump of fear forming in his stomach. Whatever he did, people were going to die. The faster ships might be able to escape, but that would mean leaving the rest of the fleet to its fate. And *that* would give the virus a chance to infect more people…hell, he couldn't even organise a last-ditch defence. The fleet was too scattered. No, he had to re-concentrate the fleet and escape. There was nothing else he could do.

"Signal the fleet," he ordered. There was only one option, only one chance left. It wasn't much, but it was all they had. "All ships are to head for Tramline One."

"Aye, sir."

CHAPTER THIRTY-FIVE

I REALLY NEED A DRINK, Richard thought.

His display was a solid mass of red light. The alien starfighters were throwing caution to the winds, attacking in a single formation that threatened to crush the remaining fleet under a tidal wave of death and destruction. Richard *knew* the alien pilots would not survive, but he also knew the virus didn't care. The pilots were host-bodies, no more important than Richard's toenails. They could be spent like water, if necessary. *His* pilots were nowhere near as expendable.

"Form up on me," he ordered. "Switch weapons to autofire"—a risk, but one they had to take—"and prepare to engage."

The range closed with terrifying speed. He'd never seen anything like it, not outside simulations. It looked as if the alien starfighters were practically flying wingtip-to-wingtip, something Richard would never have dared. The slightest mistake might set off a chain of disasters…he allowed himself to hope, just for a second, that the virus's fighters would wipe themselves out, then dismissed the thought. It wasn't going to happen.

He risked a look at the system display. Force One was pulling away, hurrying to link up with Force Two and the remaining carriers. The latter were launching all their fighters to provide cover, but they weren't going to reach *Invincible* in time. Panic bubbled up at the back of his mind, threatening to overwhelm him. His entire body felt leaden as the alien starfighters prepared to fire. He wanted—he *needed*—a stim.

You won't survive with them, a little voice said at the back of his mind. *Your career will be blown to shit and...*

You won't survive without them, another voice countered. *You're already in trouble.*

He cursed under his breath as he removed the stim tab from his belt. Monica was going to kill him. Probably literally. She hadn't thought to search his pouch. He'd told himself he could resist, he could hold himself together...that the mere fact that the stim was there would be enough to keep him from craving it. He'd told himself...he cursed again as he pressed the tab against his bare skin. It didn't matter. He'd fallen off the wagon after...after he'd only been on it for a few days.

A flush of energy shot through him, just as the alien craft came into range. His pilots didn't wait for orders before opening fire, filling space with hundreds of plasma bolts. There were so many starfighters bearing down on them that even automated targeting systems, dangerously unreliable in the midst of a dogfight, had no trouble picking off dozens of targets. The aliens opened fire at the same moment, aiming to scatter rather than wipe out the human craft. Richard had no trouble understanding their tactics. They wanted to make sure he couldn't stop them from reaching the handful of *real* ships in the fleet.

"Follow me," he snapped.

His starfighter seemed to leap under him as he pushed it forward, charging right at the enemy formation. The guns fired automatically, alerts flashing up to warn him that the plasma containment chambers were on the verge of overheating. Richard dismissed the warnings, knowing it simply didn't matter. They couldn't stop firing. There was no way they could risk letting the alien starfighters get any closer to *Invincible*.

The alien craft split into two formations, one continuing the charge towards the fleet while the other stayed and fought it out with the human starfighters. Richard gritted his teeth, snapping out orders to ignore the latter as much as possible. It wasn't easy. The alien pilots flew with suicidal intensity, tearing their way through his formations and scattering his pilots asunder. A display blinked on, silently counting the number of pilots that had been blown out of space. Richard dismissed it with a wave of his hand. He didn't want to know.

Fuck, he thought.

New alerts flashed up as the enemy starfighters closed with the fleet, firing torpedoes. Richard swallowed hard, wondering just how many of them would get through the point defence and slam into the armour...the already damaged armour. The enemy starfighters kept coming, boring in after the torpedoes...he realised, in a flash of horror, they were deliberately planning to ram the carrier. A single starfighter might not do much damage to the hull, but if they smashed themselves into the point defence weapons...

Invincible's point defence opened fire, wiping dozens of starfighters and hundreds of torpedoes out of space. Richard felt, just for a moment, a flicker of hope before the remaining torpedoes slammed home. Alerts flashed up as explosions billowed along the carrier's armour, warning him one of the flight decks had been smashed beyond easy repair. Richard picked off an alien starfighter without thinking, wondering what they'd do if both flight decks were destroyed. They'd have to land on the hull and hope they could get into the ship before their life support ran out. Their flying suits should give them some protection, but everyone knew it was just a polite fiction. Very few pilots had survived bailing out in the midst of a dogfight long enough to be rescued.

Damn you, he thought. A low buzzing sound ran through the cockpit. He ignored it as he hurled himself at another alien starfighter. *Damn you to hell.*

"Richard," Monica snapped. "You have a bastard on your tail!"

Richard glanced at the display. An alien starfighter was right on top of him...and he'd been too focused on his target to notice! The alien was already targeting him...he let out a breath, expecting to die at any second, before Monica blew the alien starfighter into dust. He cursed himself, bitterly. Monica would notice that something was wrong. She would demand...

An alien starfighter blew Monica's starfighter to bits.

For a moment, Richard couldn't believe it. Monica couldn't be dead. She was so full of life. He couldn't believe it…she'd risked her life to save his… no, she'd saved his life at the cost of her own. Bitter guilt washed through him, mingled with relief and disgust. She hadn't deserved to die. He was the only one who deserved to die…

He dragged his mind back to the present. The command and control network was an utter shambles. Too many senior pilots were dead, too many formations had been shot to hell. He forced himself to take command, to reorganise the remaining pilots on the fly. It was what she would have wanted…

But he knew, deep inside, that it should have been him who died.

. . .

Invincible shuddered as the enemy torpedoes slammed into her hull.

"Direct hits, port superstructure," Anisa said. "Heavy damage…"

Stephen barely heard her. He could calculate the damage for himself. The armour plating was warped and broken—explosions shook the ship, again and again, as enemy starfighters plunged into his ship—and the port flight deck was offline. He tried to convince himself it could be fixed, given time, but experience suggested otherwise. The internal sensors in the section were gone. That alone was enough to tell him that the damage was near-total.

"Leave the damage control teams to their work," he said. He wanted to supervise, but it wasn't his job. Not any longer. "They can't mount another offensive like that, can they?"

He studied the display. Enemy Force One—what was left of it—was falling behind, but Enemy Force Two was hard on their heels. Surprisingly, it *wasn't* redlining its drives. Stephen couldn't help finding that ominous. The virus seemed to be giving up its best chance to run the human ships down before they reunited…it bothered him. The enemy ships clearly had *something* in mind.

They know where we're going, he thought. There was no alternative, not now. He couldn't hope to break contact and escape, not with so many damaged ships under his command. *They know where we're going and they're trying to set up a surprise for us.*

He could see it, in his mind's eye. Enemy Force Two would keep its distance, shadowing the human ships as they raced down the tramline chain to Zheng He...where the ships that had driven his fleet *out* of Zheng He in the first place would be waiting for them. It was the sort of plan that a flag officer from a decade ago would have rejected out of hand, but now...the flicker network allowed fleets to be coordinated on an interstellar scale. Stephen might escape Enemy Force Two, only to run straight into *another* enemy fleet. They would sell their lives dearly—he was sure of that—but they'd still be smashed.

"The enemy starfighter force has been wiped out," Anisa said. "Our remaining starfighters are requesting permission to land and rearm."

They wiped themselves out, Stephen thought. The enemy had expended thousands of starfighters just to slow him down. They might just have succeeded. *Invincible* had lost one drive node and two more were in critical condition. Other ships were worse off. *We didn't win the engagement.*

"Granted," he said, softly. They would have time, at least, to rearm the starfighters. The pilots would even have a chance to get some rest. But it probably wouldn't matter in the long run. "And the rest of the fleet?"

Anisa looked grim. "*Gotham* was badly damaged, sir. She's lost all but one of her drive nodes."

Stephen glanced at the report, then nodded. "Order her crew to abandon ship," he said. It could take weeks to replace a drive node, if there was one on hand. He didn't even begin to have enough time to jury-rig a replacement. "As they leave, they are to rig the self-destruct to catch any alien boarders."

"Aye, Commodore," Anisa said.

The crew won't be happy at abandoning their ship, Stephen thought. *But there's no way we can get that ship out of the danger zone in time.*

He forced himself to watch as the fleet slowly crawled towards the tramline, linking up with Force Two and the remaining carriers along the way. New alerts flashed up constantly, keeping him updated. *Invincible* had been badly damaged, but at least she could still move and fight. Other ships had been far less lucky. He performed ruthless triage, abandoning ships that couldn't be saved. Their crews would have to be fitted in, somewhere. It wasn't as if he was short of berths to put them.

We'll be living out of each other's pockets for a few weeks, he thought, glumly. *Until we encounter the enemy fleet and die.*

He keyed his console, looking for other options. They didn't *have* to go through Falkirk and Zheng He, did they? But there were no tramline chains—no *known* tramline chains—that would allow them to return to friendly space, not without passing through those systems. He gritted his teeth, wondering if he dared take the risk of looking for an undiscovered chain…he knew it was too dangerous. There was no guarantee of finding anything, particularly with half his fleet battered to near uselessness. They wouldn't be able to evade the enemy either. They'd be run down and destroyed.

"Commodore," Anisa said. "We're approaching the tramline."

"Detach two destroyers to scout ahead of the fleet," Stephen ordered. If the enemy had ships in place—*if*—they would have an excellent opportunity to set an ambush. For once, they could make an excellent guess where his fleet was going to cross the tramline. "They are to jump back at once if local space is clear."

Should have done that earlier, his thoughts mocked him. *You're tired and cranky and slipping…*

He bit his lip, studying the live feed from the recon drones they'd left behind. The shipyard had clearly been badly damaged, although it hadn't been completely destroyed. He hoped the damage was extensive enough to slow down production…he shook his head in dismay. It was impossible to know for sure. The planet itself was a nightmare, the atmosphere darkening with every second…Stephen felt a twinge of guilt, mingled with the grim awareness there hadn't been any choice. Better to put the host-bodies out of their misery than give the virus a chance to rebuild. It didn't look as if the virus would be bringing the planetary facilities back online anytime soon.

We might have killed an entire planet, he thought, numbly.

The thought chilled him to the bone. Decades ago, the Belters had seriously proposed blowing up Mercury, on the grounds that the resulting asteroid field would be easier to mine. The Great Powers had—for once—been united in their condemnation. It wasn't as if the Belters were going to run out of asteroids any time soon. But…they'd drawn up plans for a planetcracker. Stephen wouldn't be surprised to hear that the Great Powers had designed their own, too. The weapons had just never been tested.

That might be about to change, he told himself. *If the only way we can exterminate the virus is to slaughter entire planets…*

"The destroyers have returned," Anisa said. "Local space is clear."

Stephen allowed himself a sigh of relief. "The fleet is to proceed through the tramline as quickly as possible, then head straight for the *next* tramline."

"Aye, Commodore."

And hope to hell we can complete some *repairs before the shit hits the fan again*, Stephen thought, grimly. The last time *Invincible* had fled down the tramline chain, there had been friendly ships at Falkirk. They'd known where they'd find safety. Now…he didn't know how far they'd have to travel before they reached human lines. *That enemy fleet is still out there, blocking our escape.*

His stomach lurched as the ship transited the tramline. He watched the display blank out, feeling his heart start to race before it came to life again. The system was empty, seemingly unsettled. The Russians had claimed it months ago—it felt like years ago—but nothing had ever been done. Its proximity to Alien-One had made sure of it. The Russians simply hadn't had time to establish a colony before it was too late. He supposed it wouldn't have mattered in the long run. It would just have given the virus a few thousand more host-bodies to play with.

"The fleet has transited, Commodore," Anisa said.

"The destroyers are to fly ahead of us and scout the next system," Stephen said. He tried to calculate where the ambush would take place, but gave up within seconds. There were just too many variables. "And then..."

He studied the fleet list for a long moment. "Detach two more destroyers, with orders to sneak down the chain," he added. "They are to avoid all contact with enemy forces. I want them to take word home. The human race has to know what we did here."

"Aye, sir," Anisa said.

"And deploy a handful of recon platforms here, near the tramline," Stephen ordered. "I want to know as soon as the enemy ships enter the system."

They won't try to be clever, he told himself, as his fleet staggered away from the tramline. *They'll just try to shadow us until we run into the rest of their ships.*

He watched, tiredly, as his crews struggled to repair their ships. It wasn't easy. There were too many repairs that couldn't be completed while the fleet was underway, too many repairs they simply couldn't perform without a shipyard...he wondered, suddenly, what had happened to the mobile shipyard in Zheng He. The ship had had standing orders to cloak and evade contact, the moment the enemy appeared, but he had no idea what had happened when the attack finally came. He made a mental note to check the records when he had a moment, then put the thought aside. The mobile shipyard wasn't with the fleet and *that* was all that mattered.

"Order the commanding officers to make sure their crews get some rest," Stephen said. He felt too tired to move. He wasn't sure just how long it had been since he'd had a rest himself. "It will be hours before we contact the enemy again."

"Aye, Commodore," Anisa said.

Stephen nodded, then checked the updates. The ship *was* badly damaged. There was no point in trying to deny it. Hundreds of crewmen remained unaccounted for, their bodies either trapped in the destroyed sections or blown into space. Or vaporised. He might never know what had happened to some of his crew. The only real consolation was that the virus probably hadn't had time to infect them. They would have died a quick death.

We hope, Stephen thought. He tried not to imagine some of his crew being blown into space, their shipsuits keeping them alive long enough for the virus to capture them. It was all too possible. The shipsuits had been designed to attract rescuers, not hide from them. *We may never know.*

He forced himself to stand. His legs felt rubbery, as if he'd aged decades in a few short hours. It would have been so much easier if he'd been on his bridge…he silently apologised to all the admirals he hadn't taken quite seriously, to all the superiors he'd dismissed as useless REMFs. In hindsight, he acknowledged, commanding a fleet wasn't easy even if one had a trained support crew to translate one's ideas into practice.

The display blinked an alert. "Commodore," Anisa said. Her voice was flat, as if she was too tired to be afraid. "The alien fleet just made transit."

Stephen nodded, unsurprised. "And now it's a race."

CHAPTER THIRTYSIX

RICHARD SAT IN HIS STARFIGHTER, shaking helplessly.

His hands were useless, trembling so hard that he couldn't trust himself to open the canopy without disaster. His entire body was itching, as if his skin was dry...he knew, all too well, that the brief period of cold turkey had only made things worse when he allowed himself to take yet another stim. He cursed himself as he heard someone outside the starfighter, fingers fumbling with the latch. Monica was going to kill him...

No. Monica was dead.

He wanted to scream in frustration, to cry like a toddler. He couldn't control himself. He hadn't felt so teary since he'd been a child, when the world had been fresh and new and dreadfully unfair. Monica shouldn't have died. It should have been *him* that had died. He was worthless, he was...the canopy came open, revealing a tired-looking face peering down at him. Richard silently accepted the proffered hand and clambered out of the starfighter, stumbling down to the deck. The flight deck was utter chaos.

"You have orders to rest," the crewman said. "The XO said so personally."

"Great," Richard said, sarcastically.

He stumbled towards the hatch, his mind spinning in circles. He could get his hands on more stims, couldn't he? Monica wasn't watching him now. He cursed himself a second later. He shouldn't be thinking like that, should he? He shouldn't be defiling her memory. She'd meant well, he knew. She hadn't been a playground tattletale. She would have reported him without a second thought if she'd wanted him gone. Hell, she *should* have reported him. She might still be alive if she'd done her goddamned job.

And I have to tell her family something, Richard thought. He'd met Monica's parents, once upon a time. They'd been good people. They didn't deserve to hear that their daughter had died saving a worthless life. *What the fuck am I going to tell them?*

He stumbled into the briefing room and keyed the terminal for a status display. The alien fleet was keeping its distance, close enough to keep tabs on the human ships while remaining well out of weapons range. He drew up plans for a starfighter assault, then shook his head. He wasn't even sure how many starfighters had survived the engagement. A brief check revealed that only fifteen pilots had returned to *Invincible*.

Fuck, he thought, numbly. How many pilots had died *this* time? He couldn't count. He was glad he didn't know their names and faces, let alone their stories. He wanted to believe that some of the starfighters had landed on other carriers, that it was just a matter of time before he saw them again, but…he knew better. It was far more likely that the rest of his subordinates were dead. *I need a fucking drink.*

He looked up as Colonel Francesca Bernardello entered the compartment, looking as shattered as he felt. She was the *only* survivor amongst his squadron leaders, his *de facto* XO. He wondered, sourly, what *she'd* do if she knew about the stims. Probably report him at once, as per regulations. She was too well-connected to suffer any adverse consequences from breaking the unwritten rules…

"Tell the surviving pilots to bed down in Compartment B," he ordered, curtly. "I have…*duties* in Compartment A."

Francesca showed no visible reaction. "Yes, sir."

She turned and left. Richard's eyes followed her, lingering on her behind. The uniform she wore was really too tight…he cursed himself a moment later, once again. He was too far out of it for anything, save for catching some sleep. The stims were calling to him, promising to keep him upright. He told himself that he was imagining it as he stumbled down the corridor and into his cabin. He was half-asleep before he hit the bed.

It felt as if he had barely rested for seconds, when he opened his eyes. His throat was killing him. He needed to drink, he needed to piss…he rolled out of bed and practically crawled into the washroom, snatching a glass of water along the way. His entire body was itching now, as if he was on the verge of jumping out of his skin. Flashes of energy were mixed with lassitude that threatened to drag him back to sleep. It was all he could do to answer the call of nature before staggering back into the cabin. He checked the terminal—there were no alerts, no calls to action—and poured himself a mug of coffee. He didn't want to go back to sleep. He wasn't sure he'd wake up.

I'm sorry, he thought, bitterly. He wasn't sure who he was apologising to. Monica…or himself. *I've been too weak.*

He forced himself to shower, then made his way down to Compartment A. It was empty. He tried not to look at all the empty berths as he stepped inside and found Monica's bunk. It hadn't been touched, not since she'd flown her final mission. She'd made it neatly before reporting for the briefing…he felt a stab of bitter guilt as he touched the sheets. She hadn't deserved to die.

She died saving your life, he reminded himself. *Show a little fucking gratitude, why don't you?*

He opened a cabinet and removed a flattened cardboard box. His fingers felt stiff, as if they didn't want to work properly. It took a moment to fold the box out, then write Monica's name and details on the top. A wave of grief threatened to overcome him as he opened Monica's locker, remembering the instructions she'd written in her will. Her personal possessions were to be sent home, when possible; everything else was to be shared amongst her squadron. Richard wondered, morbidly, if the latter set of instructions still held true. He didn't think there were more than a couple of her original squadron left alive.

"I should have done better for you," he muttered. He dug through the locker, removing three basic uniforms and a single dress uniform. He folded them on the bunk, leaving them for whoever wanted them. They wouldn't be going home. "I should have died instead."

He felt another twinge of guilt as he inspected Monica's underwear. Her bras and panties were plain white cotton, something that surprised him more than it should. Monica had never been inclined to wear fancy lingerie, not when she was on duty. She'd simply requisitioned what she needed from the supply department. He folded them neatly, then placed them on top of her uniforms. If the remaining pilots didn't want them, they'd have to be returned to the supply department. No doubt someone else would be wearing them sooner or later.

She'd probably find that amusing, he thought. Monica had concealed a packet of Mars Bars and Snickers under her clothes. They'd be shared out too. *I wonder what she was saving the chocolate for.*

He put it on the bunk, resisting the urge to take one for himself, then dug further. There was a small box at the back of the locker. Richard took it out and opened it carefully, unable to avoid feeling like a voyeur. It was her private collection, something he shouldn't be touching...there was so little privacy in the compartment that what little privacy the pilots had was practically *sacred*. A handful of photographs, a couple of souvenirs, a single golden ring and a civilian smartphone. He glanced at the smartphone and checked to make sure that it was switched off before put it in the box, then studied the ring. A wedding ring? Monica hadn't been married. He'd been the closest thing she'd had to a boyfriend. He wondered, despite himself, just what it had meant to her. Her mother's wedding ring? Or her grandmother's? A keepsake passed down from grandmother to mother to daughter? There was no way to know.

He finished emptying the locker and stood, feeling curiously empty. Monica hadn't left much behind, not here. Starfighter pilots rarely brought anything irreplaceable onboard ship, not when it might be lost at any moment, but...he sighed, dismissing the thought. Monica hadn't needed

354

much, not really. She'd known she was going to war. Better to put her goods into storage or leave them with her parents, rather than risk losing them to enemy attack.

"I'm sorry," he muttered.

He sealed the box, then sighed. He knew he should do it for every last pilot, for everyone who had been under his command—no matter how briefly—but he couldn't force himself to go through the motions. It didn't take a genius to know they weren't out of the woods yet. The fleet would need weeks to return to friendly space, even if there wasn't an enemy fleet snapping at their heels. They could be brought to battle at any moment.

And maybe someone will box up my possessions, he mused, as he picked up the box and carried it out into the corridor. It would go into storage until *Invincible* returned to Earth, if she ever did. *If I don't make it back alive...*

• • •

Who would have thought, Alice asked herself crossly, *that the old man had so much bravery in him?*

It was a misquote, she knew, but it seemed to fit. She hadn't really given much thought to what her father would be *doing* during the battle, not when she'd spent most of her time assisting the damage control teams and transporting the wounded to sickbay. She hadn't even bothered to check until the fleet had transited the second tramline, putting more distance between themselves and one alien fleet while steadily inching closer to another. In truth, she wasn't sure *why* she'd checked.

But she had. And her father had done well.

It shouldn't have surprised her, she told herself. Her father had flown *starfighters* during the First Interstellar War. Starfighter pilots weren't marines, of course, and they didn't get down and dirty with the enemy, but there was no doubting their bravery. Alice had even heard that the mortality rate amongst starfighter pilots, during wartime, was far higher than the corresponding figure for the Royal Marines. Her father had been a brave man. But then, many of the fanatics she'd killed during deployments to the Security Zone had been brave too.

And they would have done unspeakable things to me, if they'd taken me alive, Alice recalled, grimly. The skirmishes had been merciless. She'd planned to save one final bullet for herself, if the defences had fallen. *And my father did an unspeakable thing too.*

She found herself, for once, caught in a web of indecision. Her father had fought bravely and well, for all that he'd commanded a freighter rather than a battleship. The Belt Alliance had designed its ships to serve the needs of both peace and war and, while that limited them in some respects, it aided them in others. There was no way to deny that Alan Campbell, commanding officer and master of *Vanderveken*, had done well. But did it make up for his crimes?

It was a bitter thought. She knew the odds. Captain Shields—*Commodore* Shields, she reminded herself sharply—had made it clear, when he'd spoken to the crew. A powerful alien force lay in wait, somewhere ahead of them. The odds of making it home were very low. Alice was used to poor odds— she had no hope of a future, as far as she could tell—but it felt like the end. Their only real chance rested with the enemy fucking up. She didn't think anyone could realistically *count* on the enemy dropping the ball when they drew their plans. Only a moron would devise a plan that *required* the enemy to do something specific...

Neither of us might get out of this alive, Alice thought. She'd recorded a message for her sister, and a handful of others for the friends she had on Earth, but her father...she hadn't recorded anything for him. How could she? She wasn't sure what she wanted to say. She rubbed her forehead, feeling her scalp begin to itch. *What the hell do I say to him?*

She touched the terminal, requesting a private channel to *Vanderveken*. There was a long pause—the fleet's requirements came first, in wartime— before a message popped up, asking her to hold. Alice wondered, sourly, if her father was in bed, either trying to sleep or making love to one of his wives. God knew the privacy tubes had been in regular use, the last few days.

Discipline was breaking down, piece by piece. She'd even had a crewman proposition her, pointing out that they might be dead soon. She probably shouldn't have burst out laughing. He'd probably have been happier with a punch in the gut.

It felt like hours before the screen cleared. Her father's face appeared in front of her, looking tired and wan. *Vanderveken* hadn't been hit, as far as she knew, but she was in the line of battle…a place where she had no right to be. Her master had probably been ordered to send half his crew elsewhere, like just about every other commander in the fleet. *Invincible* had engineers from a dozen different ships, working desperately to patch up the armour and repair the damaged flight deck. Alice had overheard Major Parkinson bitching about the security nightmare. She thought it would be more of a problem if there wasn't a large enemy fleet breathing down their necks.

"Alice," her father said. He sounded tired, too. "What can I do for you?"

"I don't know," Alice said. Why had she called? What could she say to him? "I think…I don't forgive you, not really."

"I know." Her father showed no visible reaction, as if he was too tired to care. "I do understand."

"I do understand how you felt, back then," Alice added, after a moment. She did. That was the hell of it. She did understand how her father had felt. "But it doesn't excuse what you did."

"I know."

Alice felt her temper flare. "Is that all you can say?"

Her father looked too tired to dissemble. "What do you *want* me to say?"

"We might never see each other again," Alice said, flatly. She'd once told herself that she'd sooner die that acknowledge that she had a father. Better to let the world think she was a test-tube child than admit who'd fathered her…and what he'd done. She would have legally changed her status if it was allowed. "I'm angry at you, for what you did. But I don't hate you."

Her father smiled, very briefly. "Thank you."

"I just wanted you to know that," Alice said. She winced, inwardly. She could get rid of lovers—and friends—with ease, but she would always be her father's daughter. They might never speak again and she would *still* be his daughter. "And if we get out of this alive, perhaps we can meet again. Perhaps."

"I hope so," her father said. He smiled, more openly. "You are welcome to visit my ship, if you like."

"If I have time," Alice said. She was, technically, being held in reserve. It meant she had no assigned duties, now the immediate clean-up was done, but she doubted she'd be allowed to leave the ship. She'd spent most of the last day assisting the medical staff. "And if we make it home."

She kept her face expressionless. She'd prefer to meet her father somewhere neutral, if she couldn't meet him in her territory. But *that* wasn't going to happen until they returned home, if they ever did.

"And if I don't make it back, tell Jeanette I was thinking of her." Alice allowed herself a tight smile. "And I hope she's happy."

"Me too," her father said. "She *has* made a life for herself."

Alice shrugged. Jeanette had chosen to be *normal*, with all the advantages and disadvantages that came with having a normal life. She had a husband, she had kids...she *didn't* have any excitement in her life, she didn't know the thrill that came with risking one's life for a good cause...Alice shook her head. The virus was loose on Earth. Jeanette might find that her life had become exciting whether she liked it or not. God alone knew what world her children would inherit. The war might scoop them up in its bitter embrace.

And we were fighting over Grandpa's farm, she thought, wryly. Jeanette had wanted to sell it and keep her share of the cash. Alice hadn't been so sure. She'd wanted to retire to the farm, once upon a time. *It all seems so small now, doesn't it?*

Her intercom bleeped. Major Parkinson was summoning her.

"I have to go," she said, standing. "We'll talk again soon."

Her father raised one arm in salute. The connection broke seconds later.

Alice took a breath as she hurried through the hatch and down the corridor. She wasn't sure what had just happened. She wasn't sure...she shook her head. She wanted—she needed—to see what happened if she tried to rebuild her relationship with her father, even though she wasn't sure she *wanted* to rebuild it. Her mother had been far from perfect—Alice could admit that, at least to herself—but she hadn't deserved to die.

"Ah, Alice," Major Parkinson said. "Do you have a moment?"

"Yes, sir," Alice said. She felt a flutter of excitement. Whatever was about to happen, she was sure it would be *challenging*. And probably very dangerous. "What can I do for you?"

"We have an idea," Major Parkinson said. "And it might *just* be doable, with your help."

"Anything, sir," Alice said. "What do you have in mind?"

CHAPTER THIRTYSEVEN

STEPHEN DIDN'T RELAX, even as the hours slowly turned into days and the days turned into weeks.

He *couldn't* relax. The alien fleet was still clearly visible, well out of weapons range and yet too close for his ships to evade. Stephen had tried a handful of tactics to slow the pursuit, from mining the tramline to deploying a handful of decoys to mislead the virus's ships, but nothing had worked. The virus had too solid a lock to be evaded easily, while Stephen's collection of damaged warships and freighters simply couldn't outrun the alien fleet. He'd run through the figures, time and time again. Even reversing course and challenging the alien fleet to battle would end badly. They might win the first battle, only to lose the second.

We bought time for Earth, he told himself, time and time again. *And we gave the virus a bloody nose.*

He haunted the decks, supervising the repair work even though it wasn't—technically—his job any longer. He visited the wounded in sickbay, speaking briefly to the men and women who'd been injured in the battle; he held regular conferences with the other commanding officers, considering possible ways to win the forthcoming battle. No matter how they looked at it, the odds of survival seemed very low. They would have to close with one alien fleet with another breathing down their necks. The only upside—and he knew better than to count on it—was that the alien fleet was probably short of missiles. It had fired thousands during the engagement at Zheng He.

And we may have a way to tip the odds in our favour, he thought. *But we don't know if it will work.*

Stephen's mood didn't improve as the fleet crawled onwards, passing through Falkirk on a least-time course. The colony had been devastated, the facilities that had been built to support the MNF had been smashed beyond repair. If there were survivors, hidden amongst the asteroids, they made no attempt to contact the fleet. Stephen wasn't surprised there was no response to his hails. The virus was perfectly capable of pretending to be human, long enough to lure the survivors out of hiding. Better to remain hidden than risk a quick death or an endless servitude.

The only real surprise, he noted, was that the virus hadn't tried to fortify the system itself. It was a bottleneck, a chokepoint between Zheng He and Alien-One. But perhaps it simply hadn't had time. The gap between Second Falkirk and the Battle of Zheng He hadn't been *that* long. Stephen shuddered to think of what it might mean for humanity, if the virus continued to push the offensive. It was already far too close to the inner worlds for comfort.

And it has probably already infected the colony worlds, he thought. He didn't dare divert the fleet to check. *They'll need to be destroyed if we can't disinfect them.*

He pressed the xenospecialists as hard as he could, but even the experts in alien medicine weren't hopeful. The virus was tough, capable of adapting itself to almost anything. It might prove impossible to vaccinate the population against infection, let alone disinfect people on a planetary scale. Given time, it might even become pointless. Alice Campbell was the only known survivor, and *she'd* been lucky. The virus hadn't reached her brain. What good would it do, the xenospecialists had asked, to disinfect someone if they dropped dead immediately after? Stephen hadn't been able to think of a reply.

His black mood had only grown worse as the fleet steadily made its way towards Zheng He, preparing itself for the final engagement. He wanted to believe that the virus had sent its fleet on a wild goose chase, but he knew better. The virus hadn't chased the fleet when it had fled Zheng He, even though it would probably have won. It was either lurking in Zheng He or smashing its way towards Earth. The hell of it was that he would have preferred to encounter the fleet himself, instead of watching helplessly as it cut its way through the inner worlds. At least he'd hurt the bastard before being killed himself.

They were midway through Margo, on the verge of crossing into Zheng He itself, when the alarm finally sounded.

Stephen jerked awake, cursing under his breath. He'd only been asleep an hour.

"Report," he snapped. His steward arrived with a life-saving mug of coffee. "What happened?"

"Long-range sensors picked up the enemy fleet transiting Tramline One," Arthur reported, calmly. "There're on a least-time course to intercept us."

Stephen nodded, unsurprised. There were only two tramlines in Margo, ensuring that—this time—there would be little room for evasive manoeuvres. It would be a straight contest: ships against ships, starfighters against starfighters...with an ace in the hole that might prove either a royal flush or a bust. He hated the thought of risking everything on one throw of the dice, but he couldn't think of an alternative. The only other option was scattering...and even *that* might not work. The enemy fleet had them outnumbered as well as outgunned.

He took a sip of his coffee, feeling almost calm. There was no point in fretting any longer. One way or another, they were about to meet their destiny. And soon they would *know*.

"Very good," he said. "How long do we have?"

"Enemy Two will enter engagement range in three hours," Arthur said. "Enemy One will presumably catch up shortly afterwards. There are already hints they're redlining their drives."

In preparation for this moment, Stephen noted. One enemy fleet would play hammer, the other would play anvil. And there was nothing he could do to avoid engagement with at least *one* enemy force. The cold equations of

363

interplanetary warfare were brutally clear. There was no way he could evade contact with both fleets. Even *trying* would give the enemy a chance to bring him to battle under unfavourable conditions. *Well played, you alien bastard.*

"We'll go with Plan Omega," he said, as if there had been any other choice. "Sound battlestations at two hours, thirty minutes. There's nothing to be gained by forcing the crews to sit ready for two hours."

"Aye, Commodore," Arthur said.

Stephen nodded. "Try and get a good look at their fleet," he ordered. "Find out if they have a command ship."

"Aye, Commodore," Arthur said. "Preliminary reports suggest that they do, but we'll need to sneak a probe closer to confirm."

"Do so," Stephen ordered. "And don't worry about the beancounters."

"Yes, sir."

Stephen keyed the console, bringing up the display. The three fleets were converging at a remarkable speed, all three clearly aware that evasion was not a possibility. Force Two looked to be spreading out slightly—he reminded himself, sharply, there was still a light-speed delay—as if it intended to ensure he couldn't simply punch through its formation. He hoped he was right about the enemy being short of missiles. He'd beefed up his point defence as much as possible, but he wasn't sure they could take another heavy missile salvo.

At least they didn't use their Catapults to put a fleet right in our path, he thought, as he hurried into the shower. *That might have been too risky, even for them.*

He washed quickly, then donned his uniform and hurried down the corridor to the CIC. Anisa was already there, talking quietly to two other officers. They looked nervous, but also composed. Stephen nodded to them and took his seat, casting a quick look at the display. The range was dropping steadily. It wouldn't be long before they found out if their plan worked...

"Detach *Pinafore*," he ordered, calmly. "She is to cloak and observe the battle from a safe distance, then sneak back home whatever the outcome."

"Aye, Commodore," Anisa said.

. . .

Major Parkinson's face was calm, but Alice could tell he was concerned. "Are you sure you're ready for this?"

Alice looked back at him, evenly. "Do we have a choice?"

"Probably not," Major Parkinson said. "In all of my life, I have never sent anyone into a position where I *expected* her to die..."

"It isn't *quite* certain death," Alice said. It was true, technically. There *was* a slim chance of survival. But the odds were staggeringly against her. She'd accepted it from the moment she'd realised just much trouble the fleet was actually *in*. "I'm ready, sir."

"Your team is also ready," Major Parkinson said. "And the rest of us will provide what cover we can."

Alice nodded. "Thank you, sir," she said. "It's been an honour."

Major Parkinson met her eyes. "I had my doubts about you, right at the start. I feared that you would have entitlement issues, even after serving in the ranks. But I lost those doubts very quickly. You did have issues—yes, you did—but none of them were any worse than a *male* officer."

"Until I got infected," Alice said, quietly.

"Yes," Major Parkinson said. "And you coped well with that."

Alice nodded as she was dismissed. She knew things hadn't gone well, not since *Invincible's* first mission to Alien-One. She'd been blown off the career ladder, with no hope whatsoever of climbing back on. Her career was a mess, even though none of it was her fault. But she had shown that a woman *could* be a Royal Marine. She wondered, idly, who would follow in her footsteps. And if they'd have an easier time of it because of her.

Or a harder time, she thought, dryly. *They might have to live up to my reputation.*

The special supplies were waiting, right next to the breaching pod. She checked them automatically, feeling cold. Major Parkinson was right. The odds of survival were very low indeed. But then, she'd always known that she might meet a violent end. She wondered if her successors would be so stalwart.

It doesn't matter, she told herself, as she hoisted herself into the breaching pod. It was time to go. *I won't be alive to see them.*

• • •

Richard felt edgy as he strode into the briefing compartment, the stim burning a hole in his pouch. He'd been tempted to take it at once, the moment he'd been woken with the news the battle was about to begin, but he didn't dare take the risk. The drug was dangerously unpredictable, particularly now. He'd redesigned the command structure—once new pilots had been assigned to him—to limit the risk of him zoning out and losing control, but it was still going to be a problem. There was nothing he could do about it now.

I'll report myself as soon as we return to friendly space, he thought. He took the stand, feeling sweat prickle down his back already. The briefing room was supposed to be cool, but it felt like a sauna. *And then I'll probably be dishonourably discharged without them even bothering with a court martial.*

He surveyed the pilots, feeling a pang of guilt that—once again—he didn't know their names. There had been very little time for greetings, very little time for anything but endless simulations of prospective encounters. He was all too aware the lack of affinity was going to cost them, that some of the pilots were going to prove more dangerous to their fellows than they were to the enemy…he shook his head. *He* was probably the only real threat to his subordinates.

Apart from a few million alien starfighters bearing down on us, he reminded himself. The aliens wanted to kill them. But then, everyone knew the aliens wanted to kill them. It might not be enough. *We can do everything right and still get brutally beaten by the bad guys.*

He cleared his throat. "You've heard the briefing before," he said. "You all know what we're doing. Punch through their lines, clear a space for the marines; cover their shuttles as best as you can. And if you see a chance to take out their battleships and carriers, take it."

"We will," someone said.

"This time, we need to destroy their line of battle," Richard warned. "It isn't enough to cripple them, not now. They have to be destroyed. They must be smashed so we can get the ships past them and into the tramline."

He looked from face to face. Some were pale, some were dark, some bore the mark of the Belt while others had grown up planetside…all very different, yet very human. And they were starfighter pilots. The thing they had in common was more important than the things that kept them apart.

His voice was steady. "Forget where you come from. Forget whichever country gave you birth. Today, you fight as one. If we win, we will survive."

There was a long pause. "Get to your starfighters," he ordered. A rustle ran through the compartment. "Give the bastards hell."

The pilots hurried out. Richard braced himself, then followed them. He'd take the stim as soon as he was in the cockpit, waiting for launch. And then…he'd do whatever he had to do to win. And then…

Worry about that when you get home, he told himself. He'd been tempted to write a note for the captain, explaining what had happened, but he'd eventually decided it was pointless. If he died, no one would know the truth; if he left a note, Monica's reputation might be dragged down with him. *Right now, you have something else to worry about.*

• • •

"They're not trying to be subtle, sir," Anisa said. "They're daring us to bring our ships into engagement range."

Stephen nodded. The virus's fleet was arranged in a formation that might as well have been a mirror of his own. The battleships were at the prow, like a spear readying itself to plunge into his ships; the fleet carriers and the lone command ship were at the rear, protected by an entire *swarm* of destroyers. There didn't seem to be any converted freighters with the fleet—he hoped that meant there were no arsenal ships—but it was hard to be sure. The rear units were half-hidden by ECM.

And they have a definite advantage in battleships, he thought, grimly. *Twelve battleships to eight.*

"Retarget the missiles," he ordered, quietly. "They are to be targeted exclusively on the enemy battleships."

He saw Anisa swallow, clearly wanting to say something. The original plan called for the missiles to be targeted more widely, trying to damage or destroy the fleet carriers as well as the battleships. But spreading their fire too widely—and launching all the missiles into what might as well be a dedicated kill zone—was nothing more than throwing the missiles away. If they could weaken or damage the battleships...

Who'd want to be an admiral? The thought was funny, in a droll kind of way. *Who'd want fleet command when he'd have to make such decisions?*

"Missiles retargeted, sir," Anisa said. "The updated firing plan has been distributed."

"The datanet hasn't been disrupted, yet," Stephen said. It was a rule of thumb that *someone* wouldn't get the message, particularly once the shit hit the fan, but—for the moment—the communications network was intact. It wasn't as if they were going to be firing repeated barrages of missiles. "They'll know where to fire their first and last rounds."

He studied his display, thoughtfully. Nothing had changed in the last two hours. One fleet ahead of him, one fleet behind him; the projections, part of him noted absently, had been dead on. He made a mental note to congratulate the analysts on their success, if he lived long enough to write the commendation. It was rare—vanishingly rare—for a tactical projection to bear such a close resemblance to reality.

Although there aren't many variables here, he mused, wryly. *The whole engagement was entirely predictable from the moment we failed to break contact with the enemy and sneak into cloak. We knew they'd be mustering a force to block us.*

He keyed his terminal, opening a channel to the entire fleet. "All hands, this is Commodore Shields," he said. "We are about to meet the enemy in battle, one final time. If we win, we will break through his last line and return to safety; if we lose, we will still buy time for our homeworld to assemble new defence lines, to build new ships and produce new weapons that will even the odds. Our deaths, if we die today, will not be in vain."

It wasn't the most comforting thing he could have said, he knew, but naval crewmen knew the score. There was no point in trying to conceal the simple fact that most of them were going to die if the plan failed. They knew what they were facing. And they would have known if he'd tried to give them false hope. They would do their duty. In the end, that was all that mattered.

"Earth expects that every spacer will do his duty," he said. Nelson would have approved, he thought. The man had had his flaws, but he'd been a great hero. "And may God be with us."

He closed the channel. He'd been tempted to say so many things, from Shakespeare's famous speech to one of any number of famous parodies, but in the end he'd decided to keep it simple. The crew would understand. And besides—his lip twitched—they had too much to do to listen to him for more than a few minutes. They were about to become very busy indeed.

The display bleeped. The range had closed. It was time.

"Launch starfighters," he ordered. "Missile pods…commence firing!"

CHAPTER THIRTY-EIGHT

"THE FLEET IS FIRING MISSILES," the dispatcher said. "Try to clear the way for them."

Richard nodded. His head was buzzing. The stim had been too powerful...he pushed the growing pain aside, forcing himself to look at the display. The enemy starfighters were forming up into attack formations, readying themselves to fall on the human starships like wolves on sheep. They hadn't responded to the human missiles yet, but he knew it was just a matter of time.

"Punch through the enemy fighters," he ordered, as calmly as he could. The pain in his head grew stronger. He felt as if an elephant was tap-dancing on his skull. "And take out the battleships!"

He gritted his teeth as the starfighter lunged forward, flashes of plasma fire already lashing through space towards constantly-shifting targets. The virus's starfighters were coming forward too, readying themselves for a brief engagement before racing onwards to fall upon the human ships. Richard watched the CSP forming up behind him, ready to scatter the enemy fighters when they arrived. The CSP would keep the aliens off the motherships long enough for the attack squadrons to expend their missiles and return for rearming.

The alien starfighters opened fire. Richard jinked from side to side, feeling his starfighter threatening to spin out of control as the autofire took pot-shots at every alien starfighter that came into its sights. A handful exploded, picked off before they could return fire; others flashed past, ignoring the human craft in favour of bigger targets. Richard had to fight the impulse to reverse course and chase the bastards down. They weren't *his* targets and he knew it, but he was all too aware of just how much damage they could do. His pilots might complete their mission and return, only to discover their mothership had been blasted out of space. But then, if they *failed* to complete their mission, their mothership was doomed anyway. He didn't fancy *Invincible's* chances against a battleship's big guns.

"Follow me in," he ordered. "Don't stop for anything."

The alien battleship was growing larger on the display, a monstrous shape studded with missile tubes and point defence weapons. It was already spitting fire in all directions, blast after blast of plasma fire raking through space. Richard saw a pair of human pilots die—for a moment, he wasn't even sure if they were *his* pilots—and winced, inwardly. There was no time to mourn. He snapped his targeting sensors onto the alien drive section, cursing the sheer weight of armour the virus had rigged to defend its ships. It was not going to be easy to punch through it to hit the vitals beyond. They'd have to hope the torpedoes struck one of the handful of vulnerable sections.

Good thing they can't wrap the entire drive system in armour, Richard thought, with a flicker of amusement. *That would make the mission a damn sight harder.*

His lips twitched as he selected his targets, then launched his torpedoes. A flash of plasma fire burned past his craft, so close that only random chance had saved his life. He swore as he hurled his starfighter into a series of evasive manoeuvres, silently relieved he'd already launched his torpedoes. The virus might take him out now—if his luck failed him—but it wouldn't matter. It would be wiser to focus on the *real* threat.

His display updated rapidly as the human missiles came into view, bearing down on their targets. The virus reacted fast, targeting the missiles instead of the torpedoes. Richard nodded, unsurprised; a single shipkiller was far more dangerous to an enemy ship than a whole flight of starfighter torpedoes. He snapped orders, raking the enemy hull with plasma fire as he swept low. The more point defence weapons he took out, the greater the chance of getting a missile or two through the enemy defences. And then...

He smiled as four of the missiles detonated, bomb-pumped lasers stabbing deep into the enemy hull. The ship seemed to stagger, great explosions tearing gashes in her armour; he felt his smile grow wider as a gout of brilliant plasma blossomed up, bare meters from his starfighter. He yanked his starfighter up and away from the alien ship, the remainder of his squadron falling into place behind him. A moment later, a final series of explosions ripped the alien battleship apart. Pieces of debris shot past him as he drove his starfighter away from the wreck. The armour was so tough that parts of it had survived the starship's final moments.

"Scratch one battleship," he cheered. Monica would be proud of him. "Regroup on me..."

His heart sank as he assessed the survivors. He'd lost seven pilots from his squadron, men and women he barely knew. The other squadrons under his command weren't in any better shape. *All* of the squadrons looked to have taken heavy losses. He cursed under his breath as the command and control network updated, hastily reassigning pilots to active squadrons and deactivating squadrons that could no longer be sustained. A few squadron leaders were going to be pissed at their effective demotion, he was sure. The debriefing was going to be interesting.

Worry about that later, he told himself. *Right now, you have more important concerns.*

The fleets were closing rapidly, the battleships already exchanging long-range fire. The alien fleet had taken a battering, he noted, but it had given as good as it got. One human battleship was gone, another was struggling to hold position; it looked as if two carriers had been badly damaged. The virus might regret targeting the carriers, he thought, as he prepared himself to support the battleships. The battleships were the real threat. But then, in the long-term…

He shrugged. Right now, there was *no* long term. And if they didn't win the battle, there wouldn't *ever* be.

• • •

"The missiles did well, sir," Anisa said. "We took out two battleships and damaged three more."

Stephen nodded, coldly. He'd been right. The virus *didn't* have many missiles to throw at the human ships. But it was starting to look as though it didn't matter. He'd only had enough missiles for one giant salvo, and it hadn't been enough to shatter the alien fleet. Too many expensive missiles had been picked off, dying uselessly halfway from their motherships to their targets. He wondered, grimly, if he was looking at the future of interstellar war. Hundreds of ships firing thousands of missiles from ever-increasing range, most salvos evaporating uselessly somewhere between the two sides. It was going to be expensive…and pointless. The handful of penetration aids they'd worked into the missile barrage hadn't proved decisive.

We're going to have to find a way to cut costs, he thought. A dull rumble ran through the ship as a pair of alien torpedoes struck home. *And mass-produce missiles without breaking the bank.*

"Order the battleships to concentrate their fire on their opposite numbers," he said. "And divert the reserve squadrons to swarm the unengaged enemy battleships."

He gritted his teeth. It wasn't conventional, but conventional tactics were not going to carry the day. Doctrine called for the starfighters to support the battleships by hampering enemy ships as much as possible; there were just too many enemy ships for the tactic to prove effective. He *needed* to kill the enemy battleships quickly, before they could punch through *his* battleships and kill his carriers. The range was still closing, even though he'd reduced speed. It wouldn't be long before he was sandwiched between two fleets and crushed to a pulp.

And there's no way we can break off now, even if we wanted to, he thought. *If we tried, it would expose us to the fire of both fleets.*

He leaned forward, watching grimly as the battleships exchanged fire. The aliens were altering course, trying to bring their rear turrets to bear; *his* ships couldn't, not without reducing speed and prolonging the engagement. Giant flashes of plasma fire passed between the two fleets, followed by missiles and mass driver projectiles. The latter didn't stand a chance—there was no way they could score even a single hit—but it kept the enemy point defence occupied. He muttered an order, knowing it was unnecessary. His battleships knew to target the enemy big guns first.

We built our battleships to be tough, he reminded himself. *Invincible* was tough, but she wouldn't last more than a few minutes in the maelstrom he'd unleashed. *We designed them to soak up a great deal of fire and keep moving. And so did they.*

The range continued to close. He watched, knowing that he was no longer in control, as the battleships tore into each other. An alien battleship staggered out of line, a human battleship pounding her ruthlessly; Stephen felt a pang of sympathy for the crew, even though he knew they were nothing more than host-bodies. The alien starship disintegrated in a tearing explosion, a moment before a human battleship fell out of formation. Stephen hoped—prayed—her engineers would be able to get her drive nodes back online before it was too late. If the plan worked—if they punched through the alien fleet—they wouldn't have time to pick up survivors before they resumed running. They couldn't risk winning one battle, only to lose the next.

"Shit," Anisa said, quietly. "Sir, *Putin* is gone."

It was hardly the most professional of reports, but Stephen found it hard to blame her. A battleship had been blown out of space, lost with all hands...it didn't *look* as if there were any lifepods. He hoped that *some* of the crew had managed to get off the ship...if they did, there *might* be a chance to pick them up before it was too late. He could detail a starfighter to tow the lifepods out of the engagement zone...

"I can't see any lifepod beacons," Anisa said. "Sir..."

They're gone, Stephen thought. There might be no lifepods, no survivors. Or the survivors might be worried about being targeted—or simply captured by the virus—if they turned on their beacons. *And if they don't turn on their beacons, we won't know they're alive either. We won't be able to pick them up.*

Another shudder ran through the ship. "Multiple torpedo hits, port flight deck," Anisa reported. "They're punching missiles into our blind spot."

Reconcentrate the CSP to cover the gap, Stephen thought.

He caught himself before he could start barking orders. No, that was Newcomb's job, damn it. Stephen glanced at the display. Newcomb was already issuing orders, diverting the CSP to cover the damaged section. The repair crews had done what they could, but the flight deck was completely beyond repair. *Invincible* was going to need months in a shipyard before she could fly and fight again, if she ever got home. Another explosion ran through the ship. A torpedo had detonated inside the hull. He silently blessed the designers as the display updated. The internal armour had absorbed most of the blast.

"Enemy Battleship Four has stopped firing," Anisa said. "Sensors indicate that she's lost her main guns. She's...she's bringing herself around."

"Warn our ships to watch for kamikaze tactics," Stephen snapped. The hell of it was he would have let the alien ship go if she'd started to limp away from the battlefield. There was no point in expending weapons killing a ship that could no longer hurt his fleet. "If she brings herself to bear on one of our ships..."

He felt his heart twist as the alien battleship lunged forwards, redlining her drives as she plunged towards *North Carolina*. The American battleship struggled to alter course, to evade the sudden threat, but she was too unwieldy to change position in a hurry. Stephen watched, helplessly, as the remainder of the fleet targeted the alien ship, blowing great chunks of debris out of her hull as they tore her apart. And yet, she kept coming.

Stephen couldn't look away as she rammed into *North Carolina*. A moment later, both starships vanished in a single giant explosion.

"*North Carolina* is dead, sir," Anisa said. "I can't see any lifepods."

Stephen bit down a sharp reply. The range was still closing...and, if *all* the enemy battleships decided to ram their counterparts, his fleet was doomed. They were all doomed. His carriers would start taking fire from the big ships too, their puny weapons unable to even scratch the enemy hulls. Had he made a mistake? Would it have been better to order the fleet to scatter? Had he given orders that had doomed them all?

"Continue firing," he ordered. "Where are the marines?"

"I'm not sure," Anisa said. "They went into the haze."

"Fuck," Stephen said.

• • •

Alice heard *someone* praying quietly as the breaching pod made its slow way through the battlefield, but she ignored it. She was tempted to pray herself, even though she'd never been particularly religious. It hadn't been easy to believe in God when her religious education had consisted of Sunday School, where attendance had been mandatory and God help the girl who asked too many questions. Now...she shook her head. God would help them or not, as He wished. He knew she didn't have time to pray.

She watched the battle through the passive sensors, knowing that they might be picked off at any second. The breaching pod was supposed to be stealthy, but there were so many active sensors in close proximity that it was quite likely that *someone* would catch a sniff of their presence. And then what? They might be ignored, on the grounds they weren't posing a threat to anyone, or they might be blown out of space. It was quite possible that they'd be taken for a stealthed recon drone. Alice wouldn't have tolerated an enemy spy platform anywhere near her position and she assumed the virus would feel the same way too. A spy in the right place could guide enemy missiles directly to their target.

The enemy command ship was positioned at the rear of the formation, surrounded by starfighters and destroyers. A novice might accuse the enemy CO of being a coward, of being unwilling to risk his skin, but Alice knew better. The CO had to stay alive, even if it meant directing operations from a safe distance. And the virus wasn't remotely human. It didn't need to worry about inspiring loyalty in its subordinates. It was, in one sense, a single entity...

"We're making our approach now," she said. The enemy ship was coming closer, seemingly unaware of their presence. "And the starfighters are on their way."

· · ·

Richard gritted his teeth as the human starfighters plunged through the enemy carriers and fell on the rear formation like hawks on mice. The enemy command ship held position—she was too big to alter course in a hurry—but its escorts rapidly reoriented themselves, ready to defend their commander to the death. Richard snapped orders as a hail of ECM drones shot past, going active as they plunged into the teeth of the enemy formation. His display flickered repeatedly, translucent images of starfighters and missiles shimmering into life even though he *knew* most of them were nothing more than sensor ghosts. The virus would suddenly have more targets than it could handle.

"Break through the outer line, take the command ship," he snapped. "But don't engage her with torpedoes."

It went against the grain—they might have a clear shot at the enemy commander—but the orders had been definite. They were to distract the enemy ships, to keep them from spotting the marines, but they weren't allowed to actually *kill* the command ship unless the marines were wiped out. It struck him as the sort of plan that could go wrong very easily, and quickly too, but the commodore hadn't given him a chance to protest. If there was even the slightest chance of disrupting the enemy command and control network...

An enemy starfighter lunged at him. He blew the bastard out of space, flashing towards the command ship. It was studded with point defence weapons, all of which seemed to be trying their level best to kill him; he wondered, suddenly, why the virus hadn't bothered to give its command ship many *offensive* weapons. Perhaps it was a specialised design, or perhaps... it had simply assumed that the command ship would remain at the rear, giving orders from a safe distance while the battleships and carriers would do the work. He had to smile at the thought, even as he spotted a marine breaching pod making its way towards the target. The virus might be a little more human than he'd thought.

His head spun, again, as he picked off two more starfighters. The virus seemed to be adjusting its targeting, ignoring his starfighter even though he was in close proximity to the hull. No, it was ignoring *all* the human starfighters...he felt his blood turn to ice as he realised the marines had been spotted. A pair of breaching pods and a shuttle vanished before he could finish the thought. The marines were doomed...

His hands started to shake, helplessly. He was going to die. They were all going to die. He saw an alien starfighter swoop down on the breaching pod, weapons already spitting fire. It was only a matter of time before it scored a hit. Richard barely had time to take aim himself. The range was already closing...

...And he had a second, just a second, to realise his mistake...

...And then his starfighter smashed into the alien craft.

Darkness.

CHAPTER THIRTY-NINE

A DULL SHUDDER ECHOED through the breaching pod as it landed on the alien ship.

"Get ready," Alice snapped. The cutter was already going to work, digging into the alien hull. She checked the live feed, noting that only a handful of other pods had made it through the alien point defence. It didn't seem right to have marines die in space, unable to see their enemies…let alone fight back. She put the thought out of her head. She'd mourn the dead later, if there was a later. "Once the hatch is open, get in there."

She checked her rifle automatically, then her belt. She was practically naked…she put that thought aside too. She couldn't wear a suit of armour inside the alien ship, and anything else would be worse than useless if they ran into an alien patrol. Plasma weapons could burn through anything, short of full armour. She braced herself as the hatch opened, Hammersmith and Tindal dropping into the alien ship. The special weapon felt warm against her bare skin as she hefted it onto her back, although she *knew* she was imagining it. Just *looking* at the nuke made her skin itch. She knew she was being silly. It wasn't as if the weapon would explode if she happened to drop it on the deck.

Or if someone puts a plasma bolt through me, she thought. *It takes more than that to trigger a nuclear warhead.*

381

She slipped the control bracelet over her wrist, armed the detonation sequence and dropped down into the alien ship. The heat struck her at once, a gust of tropical air carrying with it the indefinable scent of the virus. It seemed to pervade the air, catching in her throat as she took a breath. She checked the meter automatically, one hand reaching for the mask she wore around her neck. The boffins had claimed the air was breathable—and she, at least, was in no danger of being infected—but she found it hard to believe. The virus felt clammy, touching her like an unwanted lover. She shivered at the unpleasant sensation...

...And yet, she couldn't help feeling as if she'd come home.

She could *feel* the virus pulsing through the air. It was all around her...it *was* her. She could *feel* its thoughts, moving at the very edge of her awareness. It was singular...no, it was a multitude...no, it was singular...whatever it was, it was completely beyond her comprehension. And yet, she was sure she could understand what she was hearing, if only she listened carefully enough. The thoughts were tantalisingly close.

A hand touched her arm. She jumped.

"Alice?" Hammersmith was staring at her, his eyes worried. "What's happening?"

"I can *feel* it," Alice said. She shook her head. "We have to get deeper into the ship."

She let them lead the way down the corridor, trying to ignore the thoughts and feelings rushing all around her. The virus was pulling at her, trying to absorb her...she wondered, suddenly, if she'd breathed in enough of the virus to let it take control of her. She silently cursed the boffins—and herself, for listening to them. They'd been so sure the virus would think she was already infected...they might have been right, but they hadn't really understood the virus. The host-bodies were nothing more than cells in a single giant entity. It was too large to see her properly, or to realise that she was a threat as long as it didn't focus on her, but that didn't mean it couldn't *accidentally* absorb her...

The virus is a sociopath, she thought, numbly. *To it, we're not quite real.*

The pressure grew stronger as they ran further into the ship. She could *feel* aspects of the virus slowly becoming aware of her, flashes of anger and alarm running through the biochemical network all around them. She wasn't surprised when they turned a corner and ran into an armed patrol, weapons already raised. The marines opened fire at once, blasting the host-bodies down before they could react. Others appeared, coming from doors and passage-ways…Hammersmith threw a stink bomb further down the corridor, just to see what would happen. Alice had to smile as the virus convulsed with shock. The stink bombs had been more effective than anyone had deemed possible.

"It knows we're here now," she snapped. Her instincts were screaming. "We have to get deeper into the ship."

Alice tapped her wristcom, trying to locate the other boarding parties. There was no answer. She couldn't tell if they were being jammed, or if there were *no* other boarding parties…she wondered, grimly, if those parties had been wiped out already, simply because she hadn't been with them. She hoped they'd survived. She didn't want to think about more people dying for her.

"Keep moving," she snapped. "Hurry!"

A blob oozed around the corridor, gelatinous tendrils already reaching towards them. Tindal blew it apart with a burst of plasma, only to reveal two more right behind it. Alice threw a grenade at them, watching grimly as it bathed both creatures in fire. The virus didn't seem worried, as far as she could tell. It had an endless supply of host-bodies to throw at them. A droplet of water splashed on her head…she looked up, a second before the ceiling seemed to fall on top of them. Liquid poured down, threatening to drown them. A pulsating life seemed to reach out to take her…

Shit, she thought. She could see her team thrashing around helplessly as the virus grabbed hold of them. They were dead, even though they didn't know it yet. They'd either die quickly or spend their rest of their lives as host-bodies. *Why didn't we see that coming?*

She grabbed hold of the bracelet, holding it in her hand as the virus overwhelmed her. She could *feel* it focusing on her, pushing into her...a surge of anger ran through her as she realised it was trying to *rape* her. It was slicing into her mind, pushing more and more of itself into her...it wasn't angry, she realised dully. It was trying to understand her. On some level, it thought she was still a host body. She laughed—or thought she laughed. The virus might be pervading her entire body, oozing along her bloodstream and penetrating her organs, but her thoughts were still her own.

A shock ran through her as the virus *focused* on her. It was so large, so loud...it beat down on her, battering away at her mind. She gritted her teeth, trying to keep her thoughts straight as it tried to take control. The virus was feeling *betrayed*, the same kind of betrayal *she'd* felt when her body had been unable to meet the demands she'd placed on it. It was a very personal betrayal...it was perfectly capable of multitasking on a level that humans found frankly impossible, but it was bringing more and more of its attention to bear on *her*. She laughed again as her defences started to crumble. She was so very small, and yet she had its attention.

I'm a virus inside the virus, she thought. In her dazed state, it was almost funny. *A cancer in the cells.*

She focused, snapping out commands. She wasn't sure she was actually speaking—she wasn't sure if she was actually *breathing*—but it didn't matter. The virus recoiled in shock as she told it to stop shooting, to stop fighting...the commands weren't *real*, yet they felt like real commands. She was suddenly very aware of just how the virus thought. It was more like a computer than they'd realised. She was a computer virus, issuing orders that would screw up the system...and the subunits, unable to tell the difference between real and fake orders, were trying to follow them. The virus itself could countermand her, but it took time...time it didn't have.

But it will win, she thought. Her mental defences were starting to collapse. She could feel the virus reaching into her mind. She clung to her memories—her childhood, her adolescence, her adulthood—but it wasn't enough. It was going to win. *Not unless I...*

It was hard to move, but all she had to do was press her finger against the control bracelet and *push*. There was a tiny moment of hesitation, a second in which she could pull her finger away and live, then the world went white.

• • •

"Commodore," Anisa said. "The command ship is gone!"

Stephen glanced up, sharply. The virus had been showing signs of confusion, but—whatever was going on—its electronic servants had continued to fight. "What happened?"

"I think one of the nukes must have gone off inside the ship." Anisa stopped, dead. "Sir, their entire fleet has gone mad."

Their command network must have been knocked out, Stephen thought. The virus's fleet was convulsing, as if it had taken a terrible blow. The starships were swinging out of formation, their weapons firing madly in all directions; their starfighters were spinning around, as if the intelligence controlling them had suddenly let go. A handful of enemy ships started firing at their enemies, unable to tell the difference between friend and foe. *It worked. It fucking worked.*

"Signal the fleet," he snapped. He had no idea how long the confusion would last. He needed to take advantage of it as quickly as possible. "The battleline will close with the enemy and finish him."

He snapped out orders as his fleet began to inch forward, the battleships in the lead. The survivors were badly damaged, but they could still fight. Rearmed starfighters zoomed out ahead of them, falling on enemy battleships in a desperate bid to destroy them before it was too late. The confusion that had gripped the enemy ships had even spread to their point defence. Stephen didn't need the analysts to tell him that the enemy point defence was suddenly ineffective. He just had to watch the starfighters delivering their torpedoes without hindrance.

"Order the fleet to engage with their remaining missiles and mass drivers," he said. It was just possible they'd score some hits. "And keep moving forward!"

The enemy fleet shattered. Starships and starfighters fled in all directions. Stephen couldn't tell if the confusion had driven them insane, or if it was a desperate bid to preserve as much of their fleet as possible, but it hardly mattered. His battleships raked their opposite numbers with fire, then went on to bring their guns to bear against the alien carriers. Stephen felt a surge of hope, mingled with grim determination. They could still lose, if the enemy fleet behind them caught up in time, but the virus would know it had been hurt. The remains of the MNF had avenged the defeat at Zheng He.

But the virus doesn't care about such things, Stephen thought. Humans would—it wasn't uncommon for humans to want to retaliate, in hopes of beginning negotiations from a position of strength—but the virus didn't have any pride to sting. It took no pleasure in victory, nor did it feel any despair in defeat. The only thing it cared about was survival. *It just wants to live.*

"Two carriers down," Anisa reported. "Three…"

Stephen saw a fleet carrier blow apart, then keyed his console. The probes watching Enemy Force One were reporting that the fleet had shown *some* minor disruption, but the virus had clearly managed to regain control before it was too late. There was no hope of defeating *both* forces. He wondered, grimly, just what had happened on the alien ship, during her final moments. The plan had been simple enough—and the ship's destruction had given the death blow to her fleet—but the results had been spectacular. He had a feeling he'd never know.

And all the marines who boarded her are dead, he thought, grimly. *We may never know how they died.*

"We're breaking through," Anisa said. "They can't block us any longer."

Stephen nodded. The enemy fleet was still scattering. It would save some of their ships—he didn't have the time to chase them down, not when his priority was still saving as many of *his* ships as possible—but it would also keep them from interfering with his retreat.

"Order the carriers to punch their way through the gap," he ordered. "And head straight for the tramline."

He took a long breath as the enemy starfighters started to reform, then hurl themselves on his ships. The confusion—whatever had happened—was starting to wear off. But the virus didn't have time to reorder its fleets. Too many big ships had been destroyed, or crippled; too many smaller ships simply didn't have the authority to take control. He thought he understood, now, *something* of what had happened. The command ship had been more than *just* a command ship. Losing it must have been akin to a human losing his head. It wasn't *impossible* for a headless body to survive, but it wasn't easy.

And even if it did, the intelligence guiding it would be gone, he thought. *There would be no hope of growing another head.*

He smiled at the thought, then sobered as the alien starfighters hurled themselves on his ships. Their coordination was shot to hell, but the damage started to mount anyway. They threw themselves away, dozens of starfighters ramming themselves into his hulls...he cursed under his breath as *Invincible* shuddered, again and again. The virus seemed to have targeted his ship for specific attention. Did it *know Invincible* was the command ship? Or did it merely remember *Invincible* from previous battles? It was a level of vindictiveness he would have thought beyond the virus's ken.

"Their remaining ships are forming up," Anisa said.

"Order our starfighters to rearm," Stephen ordered. A smart enemy CO would fall back until he could link up with the oncoming ships, but the virus might be too confused to try. Or it might consider the remainder of the ships expendable, if their destruction weakened the human fleet. "And prepare to launch counter-strikes."

He sucked in his breath, sharply. Two-thirds of his starfighters were gone. The remainder needed to be rearmed and reorganised before they could be sent back into battle. Nearly *every* wing commander and squadron leader had been killed...he shook his head, telling himself to worry about it later. There would be time to mourn after the battle.

"The fleet is to keep moving," he ordered. "And we're to head straight for the tramline."

He forced himself to think as his ships struggled to pick up speed. In theory, there should be nothing between them and friendly space. They'd punched their way through the only blocking force...the only force known to exist. His imagination warned the virus could easily have sent ships the long way round, trying to get reinforcements to Zheng He before he passed through the system...he put the thought out of his mind. The virus would have to survey the star systems between Alien-One and Zheng He before it could risk sending a fleet into unexplored space. Even if it knew where to go, the timing would be chancy. The plan would defy the KISS principle and suffer for it.

"We'll cross the tramline in two hours, assuming we can maintain our current speed," Anisa said. "And then we'll be home."

"We'll have to keep running," Stephen said. It was unlikely that Earth had managed to rush a relief force to Zheng He, not when the inner worlds needed to be defended. "I think..."

The display bleeped. The enemy ships were breaking off.

Stephen allowed himself a moment of relief. They would live. It wasn't perfect—he would have liked to smash the remaining ships before they could link up with their fellows and resume the offensive—but at least he'd gotten his ships out of the trap. The operation had worked, almost perfectly. Alien-One was in ruins, over a hundred alien ships had been destroyed—and more crippled—and he'd managed to get most of his ships home. Or he would, when they actually *got* home.

He sank back in his chair as the damage reports started to come in. Hardly any of the capital ships had escaped damage, even the carriers. Two of the larger fleet carriers could no longer launch or recover fighters, one of the battleships was on the verge of losing her drive nodes and falling behind. The MNF had taken one hell of a beating. And yet, they'd destroyed far more than they'd lost. They hadn't won the war, but they'd made sure it wouldn't be lost in a hurry either.

It felt like *days* before they crossed the tramline and jumped into Zheng He. Stephen waited, bracing himself for an attack. But the system was empty, at least of enemy starships. The virus had shot its bolt -- and lost. It would be months, perhaps, before it could resume the offensive. And humanity would make good use of that time. He'd seen the plans. Newer weapons, newer starships, newer tactics...the virus wouldn't know what hit it.

And our allies will have joined us by then, he told himself. *The virus will be facing three interstellar powers, not one.*

Stephen waited until he was sure the alien fleet hadn't followed them into Zheng He, then stood.

"Signal the fleet," he ordered. He felt tired, but happy. And guilty for feeling happy, knowing how many lives had been lost in the last few hours. "We're going home."

"Aye, sir."

CHAPTER FORTY

"THE FIRST SPACE LORD will see you now."

Stephen nodded, forcing himself to stand. The last month had been grim, even though the retreating ships had been lucky enough to reach friendly space—and reinforcements—before the virus had resumed the offensive. He'd been relieved of fleet command once he'd linked up with the reinforcements, then given orders to take the damaged ships home. The flight back had been uneventful, giving him time to work on his report. He had no idea if he'd be given a medal, or put in front of a firing squad. The reports from Earth had been decidedly mixed. And the orders to report to Nelson Base hadn't provided any warning of what he might be facing.

He saluted as he entered the office. "Captain Shields, reporting as ordered."

"Take a seat, Captain," Admiral Sir John Naiser said. The First Space Lord nodded to a steward, who produced two mugs of coffee. "Thank you for coming."

Stephen nodded. He hadn't really had a choice and they both knew it. The coffee was a good sign, he supposed, but he'd heard too many contradictory broadcasts from Earth to feel any assurance about his future. Or humanity's, for that matter. The human race seemed perfectly capable of fighting both itself and the virus at the same time. It made him wonder if the human race *deserved* to survive.

"First things first," the First Space Lord said. He picked up a box from his desk and passed it to Stephen. "You're a full Admiral, as of today. I tried to convince the Promotions Board to backdate it to the moment you took command of the MNF, on the grounds that that was when you proved yourself worthy of the rank, but they weren't inclined to agree. They weren't happy that…political considerations…mandated that they had to promote you so early in your career."

Stephen opened the box and blinked in surprise. An admiral's bars? He'd only been a *captain* for a couple of years. Being jumped up so quickly was almost unheard of. Even Theodore Smith had been a commodore, by time in grade if nothing else, when *he'd* been promoted to admiral. And *he* had single-handedly saved the human race.

"You've become a global hero," the First Space Lord said. "You have medals from just about every nation under the sun, all of which will be awarded at the ceremony next week. The Prime Minister *had* to promote you, particularly as you're one of the rare officers who has commanded a multinational task force in battle. There isn't a nation that will be reluctant to place its ships and men under your command."

Stephen felt a little overwhelmed. "I did what I could…"

"You saved the fleet," the First Space Lord said. "And, when you *could* have sneaked back to Earth, you went on the offensive instead. You blew hell out of an alien system, destroying its industrial base, and then—and *then*—you smashed an enemy fleet too. You deserve a reward. Everyone agrees on it."

"I lost so many people," Stephen mumbled.

"Yes, you did," the First Space Lord said, bluntly. "And it *will* weigh you down, from time to time, but…you did what you had to do. I said as much at the inquiry."

He shrugged. "There are some people who are accusing you of everything under the sun, from disobeying orders to committing genocide, but they're keeping it very quiet. They want to stay alive! No one has any tolerance for half-measures, not now. You may come across a few cranks and weirdoes who hate you, Stephen, but the vast majority of the human race sees you as a hero."

"I wish I felt that way," Stephen admitted.

"I'm glad you don't," the First Space Lord said, frankly. "And we can talk about that later, if you like. Right now…"

He leaned back in his chair. "You're off *Invincible*. She'll be in the yard for the next six months, at least. Commander Newcomb is due a promotion, as you advised; he'll either be offered *Invincible* or *Formidable*, depending on which ship is ready first. Haig was scheduled to take *Formidable*, but Captain Archer suffered severe heart problems last week and Haig has been transferred to take his place. I'm afraid you probably won't see starship command again."

Stephen looked down at the admiral's bars. "Is there no way to decline promotion?"

The First Space Lord smiled, humourlessly. "No. Everyone wants you promoted. Sorry."

"Bugger," Stephen said.

"You'll probably be given fleet command, once we put another fleet together," the First Space Lord told him. He smiled, rather thinly, at Stephen's reaction. "The Tadpole and Fox units have arrived at the front, so we can take a breath and plan our next move. Ideally, we'll go on the offensive as soon as possible, but…we have to rebuild our ships, train more crew and produce more missiles. It should be doable, if we have time. You may well have won us that time."

"At a cost," Stephen said.

"Yes," the First Space Lord agreed. "But the cost of failing, Stephen, would have been far greater."

"I know that." Stephen met his eyes. "But it doesn't help."

"We will remember the dead," the First Space Lord assured him. "And so will everyone who is only alive today because of them."

Stephen winced. He hadn't *known* most of the dead, even the ones who'd died on his ship. They had been ciphers to him. Even the ones he'd worked with, back before the fleet had been attacked, had been his subordinates. They hadn't been his friends. He knew very little about them. Wing Commander Redbird had been a good man, but what had he been like... really? And poor Alice Campbell, doomed to spend the rest of her days as a lab rat...she'd been lucky, in a way, to die. He'd already received—and ignored—a string of complaints from the biological warfare experts. They'd had plans for her future. The fact that she'd chosen to leave their clutches— twice now—meant nothing to them.

And those are the ones I know, he thought. *I didn't know anything about the others.*

"I hope so, sir," he said. "I'll do my best to make sure they don't forget."

"If we survive," the First Space Lord said. "Everyone is terrified now— and rightly so. If the virus can expend resources on Catapults, what *else* has it been building?"

"We'll find out soon enough," Stephen predicted. It shouldn't have been a surprise. But then, in hindsight, most surprises shouldn't have been anything of the sort. "Right now, though, I imagine it's adjusting its tactics and rebuilding its fleet."

"Almost certainly," the First Space Lord agreed. "Alien-One wasn't the only industrial node under its control. We're going to have to find the others."

"And then scorch a number of planets clean of life." Stephen shook his head. "Will we ever be sure that we *really* exterminated every last trace of the virus?"

"No," the First Space Lord said.

He looked Stephen in the eye. "This war is going to be different. You know that, better than I. There won't be any peace talks, no formal borders... no agreements, even, to share a handful of colony worlds. The war could drag on for years, with no possible outcome save for total victory and total defeat. It has only just started to sink in, down there"—he jabbed a finger at the deck—"that we might be entering a war that will last as long as the

Troubles, a war that will change us even if we win. The laws of war, the laws of common decency, may be thrust aside by the dictates of survival. We will not be the same."

"Yes, sir," Stephen said. "I've studied the Troubles."

"And you will do everything in your power to fight and win the war," the First Space Lord told him. "You will do *whatever* you need to do, from fleet command to a stint in the forward planning department to political hustling. You will tell people what we're facing, you will tell them the truth...you will kiss babies, if that is what you need to do to make it clear that the choice lies between victory -- or death. We cannot afford anything less than total commitment."

Stephen felt hollow. "And Amalgamation?"

"That's going to go ahead," the First Space Lord said. "Make no mistake, Stephen. We cannot win this war alone. We cannot even win as a loose alliance of human and alien powers. We *must* combine our forces. And that, Stephen, you will help with too."

"What will we lose if we do?" Stephen looked back at the First Space Lord. "What will be lost?"

"What will we lose if we don't?" The First Space Lord shrugged. "There was a story, one of the *Stellar Star* spin-offs...basically, the choice was between allying with the greatest force of human evil known to exist, at that time, or letting the human race be destroyed. The author got in trouble for stealing the concept from a far older book..."

He sighed. "It was meant to be a moral question. Do you ally with evil, or accept utter destruction? Point is, it was a cheat. There isn't a choice at all. Allying with evil might be bad, and you'll have to hold your nose, but at least you'll be alive. Someone in the future may accuse you of being a collaborator, with all the bad things that implies, yet..."

"You'll be alive," Stephen finished, quietly.

"And they'll be alive to do it," the First Space Lord agreed. "Amalgamation will go ahead because the choice is to amalgamate, or perish. And you will help."

"Yes, sir," Stephen said.

"The Board of Inquiry will probably want to speak with you at some point," the First Space Lord said. "And there will be questions from both America and Russia about their respective commanding officers...but you, personally, are in the clear. There won't be any official questions raised about your conduct."

Because it would be too embarrassing to court martial a global hero, Stephen thought, morbidly.

"You'll be assigned to the Admiralty on Earth, from tomorrow." The First Space Lord gave him a droll look. "Technically, you'll be on call; practically, you'll be on leave. Go see your family, go do whatever you like...your life will get busy again soon enough."

"And I've lost my ship," Stephen said.

"I'm afraid so," the First Space Lord said. There was nothing but sympathy in his voice. He'd been a commanding officer himself. He understood. "You can return to collect your possessions, and pass command to your XO, but otherwise..."

"I understand," Stephen said. "Thank you, sir."

"No, thank *you*," the First Space Lord said. "You did well, Stephen. And no one will forget it."

Stephen stood, saluted and walked out of the office. There was a shuttle waiting, to take him back to his ship, but...he sighed, feeling grim as he walked down the corridor to the observation blister. He'd won, but it felt as if he'd lost. He would never be a commanding officer again. He would never be sole master of his ship. He would...he would always be a guest, when he was onboard ship. He'd done well, and his reward was losing the thing that gave his life meaning.

He shook his head as he stepped into the observation blister. Earth floated below him, a blue-white orb seemingly untouched by human hands. Even the orbital tower was hard to spot, a thin thread that looked no bigger than a piece of human hair. It was hard to believe it was a true tower, home to hundreds of thousands of residents as well as the giant elevators for moving goods in and out of the gravity well. And there were four of them.

And this will be lost, if the virus wins, he thought. He hadn't needed the First Space Lord to tell him what was at stake. *Defeat means the end of the world.*

It was hard to grasp. But, perversely, it was easier to believe from orbit. Everything would be lost, from the history and culture of Britain to…to *everything.* His brother, his relatives—the ones he liked, the ones he hated— would be gone. *Everyone* he knew would be gone; their individuality stolen by the virus. They would be nothing. Less than nothing. The power struggles below would be meaningless. Human culture, good or bad, would be erased. Art and drama, literature and pulp…it would all be gone. The survivors, if there were any, would be nothing more than host-bodies. The virus had to be stopped.

And if that meant serving as an admiral, if that meant giving up his command to take up a role that no one else could do, then that was what he had to do. He would do everything in his power to stop the virus.

He took a long breath, then turned away. He had work to do. He had his duty.

And he would mourn the dead in private.

• • •

THE END
The *Ark Royal* Universe will return in:
The Lion and the Unicorn
Coming Soon!

AFTERWORD

WHEN I WROTE THE FIRST THREE TRILOGIES in the *Ark Royal* series, I deliberately intended to have the war—as seen through the main characters—start and finish within the trilogy. This time, I decided to do things differently. *Invincible* would see the start of the war, and fight a number of major actions, but she wouldn't see the end of the war. The final trilogy—provisionally entitled *The Lion and the Unicorn*—will continue the story of the Third Interstellar War.

I'm not sure—yet -when I will begin writing. My health isn't good at the moment, unfortunately, and I have a number of other projects to complete. Please bear with me a little.

And now you've read the book, I have a couple of favours to ask.

First, it's getting harder to earn a living through indie writing these days, for a number of reasons (my health is one of them, unfortunately). If you liked this book, please post a review wherever you bought it; the more reviews a book gets, the more promotion.

Second, I've attached chapter samples from books written by two of my friends. Have a read—and, if you like them, feel free to check out the complete books.

Thank you for your time.

Christopher G. Nuttall
Edinburgh, 2019

APPENDIX: GLOSSARY OF UK TERMS AND SLANG

[Author's Note: I've tried to define every incident of specifically UK slang (and a handful of military phases/acronyms) in this glossary, but I can't promise to have spotted everything. If you spot something I've missed, please let me know and it will be included.]

Aggro—slang term for aggression or trouble, as in 'I don't want any aggro.'

Beasting/Beasted—military slang for anything from a chewing out by one's commander to outright corporal punishment or hazing. The latter two are now officially banned.

Beat Feet—Run, make a hasty departure.

Binned—SAS slang for a prospective recruit being kicked from the course, then returned to unit (RTU).

Boffin—Scientist

Bootnecks—slang for Royal Marines. Loosely comparable to 'Jarhead.'

Bottle—slang for nerve, as in 'lost his bottle.'

Borstal—a school/prison for young offenders.

Combined Cadet Force (CCF)—school/youth clubs for teenagers who might be interested in joining the military when they become adults.

Compo—British army slang for improvised stews and suchlike made from rations and sauces.

CSP—Combat Space Patrol.

Donkey Wallopers—slang for the Royal Horse Artillery.

DORA—Defence of the Realm Act.

Fortnight—two weeks. (Hence the terrible pun, courtesy of the *Goon Show*, that Fort Knight cannot possibly last three weeks.)

'Get stuck into'—'start fighting.'

Head Sheds—SAS slang for senior officers.

'I should coco'—'you're damned right.'

Jobsworth—a bureaucrat who upholds petty rules even at the expense of humanity or common sense.

Kip—sleep.

Levies—native troops. The Ghurkhas are the last remnants of native troops from British India.

Lorries—trucks.

Mocktail/Mocktails—non-alcoholic cocktails.

MOD—Ministry of Defence. (The UK's Pentagon.)

Order of the Garter—the highest order of chivalry (knighthood) and the third most prestigious honour (inferior only to the Victoria Cross and George Cross) in the United Kingdom. By law, there can be only twenty-four non-royal members of the order at any single time.

Panda Cola—Coke as supplied by the British Army to the troops.

RFA—Royal Fleet Auxiliary

Rumbled—discovered/spotted.

SAS—Special Air Service.

SBS—Special Boat Service

Spotted Dick—a traditional fruity sponge pudding with suet, citrus zest and currants served in thick slices with hot custard. The name always caused a snigger.

Squaddies—slang for British soldiers.

Stag—guard duty.

STUFT—'Ships Taken Up From Trade,' civilian ships requisitioned for government use.

TAB (tab/tabbing)—Tactical Advance to Battle.

Tearaway—boisterous/badly behaved child, normally a teenager.

UKADR—United Kingdom Air Defence Region.

Walt—Poser, i.e. someone who claims to have served in the military and/or a very famous regiment. There's a joke about 22 SAS being the largest regiment in the British Army—it must be, because of all the people who claim to have served in it.

Wanker—Masturbator (jerk-off). Commonly used as an insult.

Wank/Wanking—Masturbating.

Yank/Yankee—Americans

BONUS PREVIEW

And now, take a look at Leo Champion's latest, *Warlord of New York City:*

In the twenty-second century, global civilization has moved into networks of arcology-skyscrapers that tower hundreds of stories above streets abandoned to anarchy. Inside the arkscrapers, a neo-Puritan cult of social justice rules absolutely; on the streets, feral gangs raid between feuding industrial tenements.

Diana Angela is a hereditary executive in the bureaucracy that runs the world, with a secret life as an assassin on the streets. A burned-out idealist, she's long ago given up on trying to change the world – the best intentions of the past have only led to greater misery.

And she has no reason to think precinct boss Jeff Hammer's intentions are even good. A former mercenary who may be a military genius, Hammer's narrowly taken control of a small tenement. Now he's facing vengeful exiles, aggressive neighbors, and uncertain internal politics.

Which might be the least of his problems now that he's drawn the attention of one of the city's most dangerous women...

CHAPTER FOUR

Traffic moved on the city streets at night, but carefully. Enclosed vehicles or semi-enclosed ones, modified with hand rails and running boards so that escorting troops could ride on their outsides. Sometimes they were led by advance bikes whose role it was to spot or trip any ambush; those guys tended to be twitchy with their flashguns. Foot traffic – anything that couldn't outrun a streetganger or sewerganger ambush had better be prepared to avoid or fight it – moved by stealth or in numbers.

Stealth had always been fine for Diana Angela; streetgangers were practical and eminently self-interested, and probably wouldn't bother some cloaked loner who looked like they could put up a fight but didn't look wealthy enough to justify risking death over. Her implant's thermal vision let her spot and avoid lurking groups of them anyway, because you could never be too sure. She carefully skirted around more than one potential trouble spot as she made her way through the uncontrolled country of uninhabitable high buildings south of Times Square.

As she'd surfaced she'd taken a dark silk skirt and shawl from the biggest of her pouches, cloaking herself as the crones and the crippled did. People would assume she was one, unless they scanned her or noted her boots. The dark shrouds, which would rip easily if someone grabbed them in a fight, gave her a degree of anonymity without compromising agility, and she moved swiftly through the dark streets.

Floodlights covered the approaches to Times Square, though. It was familiar enough at night, but still unsettling in her sudden vulnerability to the snipers on the wall that blocked most of Eighth Avenue immediately south of Thirty-Eighth Street. She fell in behind a three-vehicle convoy – some VIP in a black town car, guarded by two pickup trucks whose trays were loaded with musket-armed tenement soldiers who seemed relieved to have made it to safety.

Just behind her, and she hustled to get in front of them, was a convoy from some other tenement, a hundred ragged and starving tenement workers pulling five wagons loaded with refined scrap, guarded by a company of several dozen musket-toting tenement troops who seemed just as happy as the ones in the pickup trucks to have made it safely through the dark streets. The industrial slaves of the convoy who could crowded ahead to get in sooner, moving around her through the one-lane-wide gate in the wall across Eighth.

Midtown's guards wore black body armor, shined boots and black-visored riot helmets, and carried better weapons than most tenement soldiers' pipe muskets. Two of the four soldiers posted just inside the barrier had pump-action shotguns; the other grunt had a scoped rifle and the sergeant, with three gold chevrons pinned to each shoulder of his chainmail T-shirt, cradled a drum-fed submachinegun. They didn't bother to disarm the tenement soldiers riding guard on the convoy ahead of her; in fact, they didn't even bother to sneer at the convoy guards, which in the past the Association's troops had. It would go badly on the visiting guards' home tenement if there was trouble here.

Diana Angela was fairly certain that if the sergeant didn't have an explant under that riot helmet of his, he had an implant scanning for whatever metallics people had under their clothes. But her weapons were nothing special for the city, so the Midtown guards paid no mind.

Sometimes they did stop her, mostly when they realized she was a pretty young woman they could feel up. Slapping them wasn't a good idea but you could buy your way out of a search; it would just be cash she didn't appreciate having to put in some randy thug's pocket. And she had to be careful about dismissing them as randy thugs; Roman Kalashov's men had murdered the writer John Kiska four years ago, burned him screaming alive on the steps of the Public Library not far from here. They were not to be taken lightly.

But this time they either didn't notice or didn't care that she was no raff crone. She was in amongst the neon and the noise of Times Square, a party that ran twenty-four seven inside the gates of Midtown. There was the hustle of the markets to the left, through what had once been the Port Authority bus terminal between Fortieth and Forty-Second Street, the Independent Hotel rising up to her right on Forty-Second through Forty-Fifth.

From street level to tenth floor the Independent was the same garish blaze of neon and digital billboards as the rest of Times Square, some of them advertising products that had not been affordable on the streets for a century. Above that, the hotel reached a hundred and some stories, half the size of the shorter arkscrapers but connected by skyways to their network while still accessible from the street. It was the only building on Manhattan that allowed arkies and streeters to meet face to face and it was the most secure, most neutral place in the conurbation because of that.

There were occasionally arkies in this crowd, although rarely; it was easy to spot the slumming arkies because of all the personal security they had. They surrounded themselves with platoons of the bodyguards who hung out in the Independent's lobbies and charged extortionately by street standards for muscle, although to a US-15 or -18 it would be pocket change. Across from the Hotel were bars and clubs, lines in front of some of them.

Vehicle traffic passed slowly through the mobs of people, although some of the tenement bosses had footmen with batons to beat a path. Others rode sedan chairs, surrounded by guards that elbowed a way forwards. There were streetgangers with their blades peace-bonded, pushing their supermarket carts of sorted trash toward one of the Exchanges Midtown encompassed. There were ragged raff workers from across the city, pulling carts or given time off; there were bucket-shop scrip exchangers and a hundred kinds of hustler. It was eight pm but aside from a neon tint to the light it might have been eight am; this place was always in shadow anyway, but the lights made up for that.

Don't mind me, Diana Angela thought as she made her way past a group of boisterously drunk tenement high-ups in expensive suits with meaning-less – the highest tastes in street fashion had always struck her reserved, upper-class self as being *tacky*, although saying that aloud could get you killed down here – gold bling on their shoulders, aping the insignia of a world that had abandoned their ancestors more than a century ago. Just another raff chick in a hood, hiding some injury you probably don't want to look too closely at.

. . .

She remembered her first venture up to the streets, driven by curiosity after years of observing from below as she killed vermin after vermin, develop-ing her skills with every success and avenging Ian that much more. She'd found her way during the daytime into tenement bars and coffee houses in Times Square and then Greenwich Village, started to learn the ways of the city's politics.

They read Charles Dickens on the streets, and a hundred other authors banned or lost to obscurity upstairs. They read Charles Dickens and Upton Sinclair and Jack London and HG Wells and Karl Marx, and the Marx was enlightening certain young members of the streets' upper class to the fact that the raff were in chains and it was their duty, as the intellectual van-guard, to break those chains.

It had been an invigorating time, Greenwich Village in the late 2170s. The tenements' rulers were at comfortable peace, which had made them prosperous and lax. Ideas had flowed with the coffee and wine, with texts unknown in the arkscrapers and books forbidden by the authorities on the streets. Because etexts and printings of John Kiska were to be found, a bril-liant writer who had emerged from the streets themselves.

The man himself was in hiding, two million dollars on his head but still always producing new stories, which came out through underground channels of people who knew people. There were printouts and the young tenement aristocrats, younger children mostly of underbosses and senior associates whose elder siblings were soldiers, shared them with the raff. A lot of the raff had basic literacy; they could read Kiska's plain, clear, tenement language – his descriptions of squalor that every tenement worker knew in his own life, but had imagined better elsewhere. Kiska's subject matter had been tenement life, but his message had been: It's this bad everywhere, but it will get better if you make it better. The people responsible for your misery can be killed.

It had been all over the city, the spirit of the late '70s when a better world had seemed possible despite, upstairs, the purging of her visionary mentor Lucius Theron for daring to suggest radical change from above. If it would not happen from above then it could happen from below, she has believed at the time. She had fallen in love with Alex Thomson, son of an underboss but an intellectual with a fiery charisma that had convinced her of it – the world that she lived in was broken. Hundreds of millions lived in squalor on the streets, but the boot holding them down could be thrown off!

She missed the blind optimism of those days, half a decade past now. John Kiska had been killed on the steps of Midtown's Library Terrace, dragged out of a hidden basement by bounty hunters and executed by Roman Kalashov's personal soldiers. His death had been the spark that had led to the Greenwich Village Commune, which would be four years ago this May First...

She turned her mind firmly away. She was *not* going to think about the fucking Commune.

• • •

Roman Kalashov owned Times Square, but his troops with their fancy automatic weapons controlled some areas more thoroughly than others. Or, put another way as Diana Angela turned down an alley where the neon's glare was only a reflection on glass and steel in the darkness: some areas paid more vig, and got left alone.

She recognized some of the faces in doorways, whores and madams watching the street pass by. One or two of them called out to her; she made noises of recognition, as alert here as she'd been in the sewers because these alleys could be almost as dangerous.

Down a flight of stairs to a heavy steel door manned by a bouncer with a mouthpiece. She pulled the hood off and looked Nestor in the eye. The burly man gave a a slight nod and murmured something into his mouthpiece. The door slid open. The Last Stand paid Kalashov's enforcers extra vig to stay well away; it was one of the less regulated places in Times Square, and it had become her home more than home.

There were traveling mercenaries and bikers; there were hitmen and soldiers and the girls who serviced them, the girls who didn't operate in their own right. There were enough of those to make grabby hands think twice about her, and she made her way through the crowded tavern floor without much cause for concern, although she felt eyes on her.

People knew to feel her up with *only* their eyes for the most part, although every once in a while you got some idiot stranger who thought it would be fun to pat the ass or the tits of the hot blonde. Much of the time they backed off when they noticed her weapons, far more than the usual holdout pistol or blade that a lot of the call-girls had. Sometimes she had to kick the shit out of someone.

Or just dick, she thought with a smile, as a particularly handsome rider type crossed her vision, from his jacket a patched nomad biker of the Bandit Brothers. She'd come to really appreciate bikers; their code of honor was immensely appealing to a woman from as corrupt a society as the Intendancy had created. Upstairs it was impossible to be honorable, but the bikers accepted nothing less from the men, and the chicks some clubs allowed to full-patch, they rode with.

Yes. There was more than one way to scratch an itch, and killing always made her a little horny anyway. Perhaps she'd see if that biker was with anyone...or if he had friends. A wicked smile started to cross her face as she fell in behind him, a tall man with a beer in each hand.

411

"Lady D," came a soft voice behind her.

She didn't have to turn to know it was Rex, the go-to man and bodyguard for a fixer named Charles van Zanden. Not that fixers needed bodyguards in a place like here, where just about any of the place's well-armed, often-augmented patrons would be happy to do a favor for one of the guys with the information, one of the guys with the work, one of the guys who could connect you to the money.

"Not now, Rex," she said.

"Charlie wants you, Lady D."

"Charlie can wait, Rex." *I have my sights on one of those bikers.*

"Got a job for you," Rex persisted and she turned toward him. He was a big man, shaven-headed and somewhere in his forties. He wore a plain tieless suit and little pince-nez that were actually SmartContacts. The Last Stand was of course an implant-disabled zone, so like a lot of higher-level people on the streets he carried a cellphone with an earpiece and a digital wand.

"Can it wait a couple of hours?" *Just a quick fuck to get the day out of her system...*

Rex muttered something into a subvocal mouthpiece, waited a moment, and gave her back the response: "Your call, but he's been on your list over a year."

Over a year, huh?

Yeah, picking up a guy could wait. The night was young anyway.

• • •

Van Zanden sat in his corner table, a pair of private detectives on one side and the other empty. One of the detectives was big and powerfully-built in a sharp suit, the other was grossly fat, but they were familiar faces. So was van Zanden, a handsome fortyish man so clean-cut he looked out of place in a ruffians' bar like this. He was tolerated – welcomed, in fact, with his own table – in the Last Stand because of his connections, which meant work.

He was a thinning-haired blond white man in a plain tieless suit, with an electronic tablet in his hands.

"Charlie," she said.

van Zanden motioned, with a slight tip of his head, for her to sit down. She did. The detectives didn't move from across the table, but they seemed more interested in their drinks than the woman who'd just joined them. She knew that was an act – Archie and Nero were professionals, and they were paying as close attention to her as they were everything else in the place.

"You spotted one on the list, huh?" she asked without preamble.

"They did." van Zanden gestured at the two detectives.

"Which one?"

"Johnny Caustus," said van Zanden. "Need a reminder?"

The name didn't ring a bell and Diana Angela knew van Zanden had the files ready on that tablet anyway, so she grunted. "All I remember is that he's a pedo."

"Tenement underboss from Hackensack," said the fixer. "Likes young girls. Buys and sells young girls. There's a ten grand contract on his head in his capacity as a tenement underboss, we've got proof of young girls going into his apartment and…never being seen again, and he's come out of his shell to party tonight right here in Times Square."

Diana Angela smiled thinly.

"And he's been on my list since…how long?"

The fixer checked his tablet. "He first came to your attention June '83. But he was too far away, too well-protected, too hard. Until he comes waltzing in with his boss and some others, less than an hour ago. They're presently getting shitfaced at the Hux."

"I'd like to see the evidence," she said softly. Because this was too good to be true, a *prime* target right here! She noticed her tongue flickering between her lips; this would be a *good* kill indeed.

"Showing you would give its source away. It satisfies me and some of it has been independently verified," said van Zanden. "I give my word that it satisfies me."

413

Everyone in power in the tenements had done something to warrant killing, she had decided a long time ago. But it would be physically impossible to kill every tenement boss, so she focused her attentions on the particularly egregious ones. It wouldn't make a bit of difference to the big picture, but someone had to avenge those children.

Diana slowly nodded.

"Fill me in."

. . .

There were different ways to get into places, but tonight's easy prey – easy but *so* deserving – would be out clubbing, which made it both easier and harder. Places like the Hux didn't exactly allow you to stroll in with knives; she'd have to take the other approach.

Who'd taken out this contract, put down their ten grand to van Zanden, she had no idea about; that was the point of the fixer. Maybe it was some external tenement seeking to weaken this guy's; maybe it was an internal enemy, because tenement bosses and their leading families spent *all the time* scheming against each other in a constant game for status and survival.

She really didn't care; what mattered was that this fucker had killed, van Zanden swore to the best of his knowledge, and when she'd independently verified these things he had never been wrong, at least four young children. It probably hadn't been a relative of those children who'd placed the bounty – although you never knew – but she was going to be killing for Jamie, Nareendra, and Glennis; van Zanden hadn't had the name of the fourth.

"What'd this one do?" Cleopatra asked as Diana Angela came into her office. She was a tall ebony woman in a shimmering gold dress, some said the illegitimate daughter of a major Harlem OG. You could tell from the darkness of her shaved head that she was of an old gangsta family, those who had been organized crime since before the streets had been abandoned.

Diana Angela closed the door that led onto the parlor, where seven of Cleopatra's girls were waiting to be dispatched. They didn't need to hear any more than they'd already figured out.

"Pedo killer. At least four known kids, probably more," she said.

"You need an escort, a lineup, what?"

"He's in Times Square. Just a shower and then a dress, tonight. Then a cab."

. . .

Eyes turned to watch the stunning blonde woman step out of an armored yellow taxicab, alone, in front of a Times Square club named the Hux where a line of waiting hopefuls snaked thirty feet up past the doors along Seventh Avenue. Some of the eyes belonged to the place's bouncers, serious security although their guns were mostly out of sight.

The patrons, and aspiring patrons, of a club like this were likely to be the sons and daughters of powerful tenement people, to be handled lightly. But the armed force was available; clubs like the Hux drew attention from envious streetgangers too, and it wasn't unknown in places like this for fights to erupt between people from rival or warring tenements. Their soldiers settled it on the ground with their lives, the rulers got bloody noses and two-week bans from the club.

Diana Angela got to her feet under the eye of the Hux's bouncers, straightening herself up and reaching into her handbag for the clip of bills she'd need to start giving them. She was in a frilly pink slip of a party dress and white stiletto heels, bereft of anything security might conceivably interpret as a weapon.

She would have to be the weapon, but that was the fun part when it came to paedophiles. And there would soon – she kept the carnivorous grin just off her face – be one fewer of those.

The next few minutes involved a lot of bribes, simpering, and being felt up. The Hux security knew perfectly well that beautiful women did not just saunter into nightclubs unaccompanied with no angle. If she were a tenement high-up she'd be with an entourage; alone meant she was probably looking to fuck a tenement high-up. For the night, for a lifetime…it happened. It was how a girl with looks could make her way on the streets, and not something it was Diana Angela's place to judge. It was probably the course she'd have taken, if she'd been born raff, and she had nothing but sympathy, friendship, and protection for the girls in that trade.

She passed through layers of security that didn't take chances, as good as the most paranoid tenement boss because they were guarding some of those very same people. One inner-circle security team leader recognized her but said nothing, and got a crisp five-hundred discreetly slipped into his palm in appreciation. The shaven-headed ex-mercenary smiled:

"Good hunting," Logan murmured under his breath.

Not everyone on the streets was a shit. Of course, he wouldn't expedite her getaway if things turned really sour – that was up to her to work out. She was really putting her head into the lion's den here, but that was part of the thrill. Sending Johnny Caustus to hell was delicious icing, but icing on that cake. She was never going to hurt innocent people, but *God* was it fun to kill guilty ones!

The last security man on the third floor mistook the smile on her face as anticipation for a different kind of fun – that, she would have later tonight – and leered at her as he signaled to the camera to let her through. The innermost door opened.

Music, ambient house beats from an artist who'd been popular in the arkscrapers a decade ago, played at a volume low enough to allow talking without much effort. Drinks and service girls circulated; DA winked at her friend Rosa as they passed, Rosa arm in arm with a handsome black man from probably one of the Bronx or Harlem OG families, who wore a tailored purple suit and a lot of jewelry. She felt eyes on herself as she circulated, scanning the private, roped-off areas where inner-circle tenement bodyguards mixed with more of the Hux's people. It would look bad for the club for anyone to get killed on its premises, but the real high-ups insisted on at least a little of their own security while they held court.

A shame, that. There were at least six tenement bosses holding court in this room, and one of them she knew for a *fact* had a hundred thousand dollars on his head. The big beefy man with the cigar was also a happy peeler, known to enjoy flaying people alive, and she...

On target, DA. You can get Donald Larson another time.

That was the problem with this city. There were too many throats for one girl to cut no matter how hard she hustled!

· · ·

BONUS PREVIEW

And from Jason Fuesting comes *Echoes of Liberty Book 1: By Dawn's Early Light*

Eric Friedrich was supervising the last ice harvesting shift for his ship's shot-up environmental systems when they detected an anomalous ice comet drifting by. Investigating the icy tomb, Eric finds a ship that couldn't exist--a relic from a nation the Protectorate killed billions to erase from history... And will kill even more to keep secret.

When his world explodes, Eric must make allies in the unlikeliest places, and seize even the slimmest chance of survival while unraveling a conspiracy that shattered planets and set off interstellar war!

CHAPTER ONE—ICE

Space was dangerous on a good day, a day when everyone knew what to do. Improvisation only adds to the danger and so far everything had been improvisation. Nobody on the *Fortune* had a choice, or rather the choice was unsettlingly clear: ice or asphyxiation.

"Nothing's ever easy," Eric mumbled to himself as he stared at the displays projected against the inside of his helmet. *Radar is green. Ish. Links to all team members, green. Main link back to the Fortune, green. Task status, then O2 checks.*

Eric blinked, trying to ease the eyestrain from the hours of watching his men through monochrome green light enhancement. A sparkling green haze, the leftovers from the last three hours, clouded the view around him.

Hours of boredom, stuck in a suit while we pry apart an ice comet.

Eric yawned as he checked the time display.

"Team one, status," he said.

"Anchors set, connected to the tether," came the reply.

Eric glanced to his right. Barely visible above a distant ridge of ice, team one's lead gave him a thumbs up.

Good, almost done.

He glanced at his millimeter wave display and its thousands of moving contacts. A frown creased his brow as he looked at the blinking overload indicator on the display. *We really need to find upgrades for these suits. How am I supposed to warn people if my gear can't track everything?*

"Team two," he started. Flickering red on the radar display stilled his tongue. "Indy, looks like we've got another wave of stuff incoming from eleven o'clock. Take cover. Looks small, but it's going at a good clip."

"Copy that," Indy responded.

Dozens of red dots amid the sea of blue contacts winked in and out of his display as his suit's computer strained against the number of simultaneous objects it could track. Each heartbeat brought them closer. *All going the same direction. Wait. Shit.* His display lit up with a cascade of yellows following a different vector.

Eric pressed against the ice as he blurted, "All teams take cover!"

Breathing hard, he glanced in team three's direction. A huge red contact lit up the radar display. *That's almost on top of--* A large shadow streaked through the haze, sending shards of ice and rock debris billowing in its wake. *Wow, that was close. That had to be what was causing those yellow returns.*

Cautiously, Eric pushed back from the ice and spoke, "Teams, sound off!"

"Team one clear, all we got was a light peppering. No damage."

Silence.

"Team two?" Eric asked.

Digitally distorted static erupted from his headset. Eric gritted his teeth for several moments before the transmission ended. Eric sighed and pounded the side of his helmet with a fist hard enough to fritz his low-light projection with each strike.

"Say again, team two," Eric said.

"Team two clear. We got peppered pretty hard but somehow nobody's hurt. Also, anchor set and tethered."

"Team three clear. Set and tethered."

About time, we're done here.

"Roger, Indy. Prep to return to the *Fortune*. I'd like to get out of here before something else happens," Eric replied. His eyes narrowed as he looked over the status of his team. "Sokolov?"

"What?" Richard Sokolov growled.

Eric sighed.

"Stow it, Dick. Getting some odd readings over here, check your O2. Think you might have a leak."

"Hold on. Nope, gauge says I'm just fi-- *blyad!*" Static.

"What's going on?" Eric demanded. Sokolov seldom fell back into his native tongue. The ice cloud obscured the man's last known position.

"Was looking at the gauge and it just dropped half through the yellow. *Yeblya lezha pribor!* Who the hell did we loot this shit from?"

"We didn't," Indy chimed in. "Your suit's original to the ship. Probably a hundred years old."

"Great. Just great," Sokolov groused.

"Cut it, you two," Eric grunted. "Sokolov, you reading a little under ten minutes left?"

"More or less."

"Looks like my monitor is accurate. We should be back long before you're sucking vac. You good?" Sokolov grumbled. "Everyone, get back to the cable and hook on," Eric ordered before switching channels. "Desi, Friedrich. Anchors are in, we should be good. Sokolov took a strike. He's okay, but his suit is leaking. Don't take your time reeling us in."

"I can only reel in so quickly. The cradle's only rated for a certain impact," Desi's exotic accent rolled across the radio. Eric knew next to nothing about her past, other than overhearing her mention where she grew up, Orleans.

A vibration through the line from the winch signaled their trip to safety had begun and Eric eyed the haze as it drifted past them. Shifts of three teams each had worked the last eighteen hours to cut this ice comet into four fragments. One by one, each fragment had been reeled in and secured in the bay below him.

Last one. We've been lucky. Too lucky. A bead of sweat trailed down the side of his neck, just where he couldn't do anything about it in the confines of the suit. A sudden chill down his spine sent Eric checking his millimeter wave warning display again. *Nothing big, nothing fast.*

Eric relaxed as the cable pulled them clear of the debris cloud toward a stretch of what appeared empty black to the naked eye amidst the surrounding star field. Magnified many-fold by the enhancement rig grafted into his helmet, the feeble illumination from the system's distant star reflected brilliantly off the edges of a pair of bent hull plates amidships. Four square meters of steel plating sealed the rent just inside the shadow cast by the ship. He stared at a stretch of darker steel peeking from the patch. That puncture had vented Environmental Control into the void. *What is that?* Eric looked closer and then averted his eyes from the frozen smear of blood left by the doomed technician who had almost been lucky. The *Fortune* had seen better days.

"*Mon chéri*," Desi broke his reverie. "The captain ordered an orbit change once the cargo has been retrieved. Lt. Pascal will meet you in the bay."

"Roger that, Desi." *What now?*

His light amplification faded out as lights flickered on in the bay ahead. Eric and his team unhooked and kicked off the comet fragment, reorienting to land boots down. He absorbed most of the landing with bent legs and his boots jerked as the maglocks engaged. While his team of miscreants filed through the airlock, Eric watched the ice comet shard drift into the bay and strike the makeshift cradle the engineers had cobbled together.

Eric winced as vibrations from the bowing cradle shot up his legs. Cracks spidered across the fragment's surface. Smaller chunks and ice dust leapt from the fragment and bounced off the deck below. After a few unnerving seconds, both the cradle and the comet stilled.

"Guess the engineers earned their pay, eh, Friedrich?"

Eric glanced over his shoulder to find Lt. Pascal.

"I'd say so, sir. Wasn't sure if the cradle was going to collapse or if the fragment was going to shatter like the first one did."

Pascal nodded and sighed, "Yeah, what a pain in the ass."

Eric shifted his weight as he glanced about the hanger before asking, "So, LT, why are we staying out here and not going in with the others?"

"Sensors guys picked up an object nearby," Pascal replied. Eric felt vibrations through his boots and grabbed for the nearby stanchion as the *Fortune's* acceleration pulled at him. "We're matching orbits and checking it out."

"Nothing out here but ice, sir. What's worth burning fuel when we're low as it is?"

The lieutenant smiled.

Eric asked, "What?"

"You're right, Friedrich. There's supposed to be nothing out here but ice. This thing, whatever it is, has too much mass to be just ice. At least that's what Simon told the captain."

"So an honest asteroid?"

"Not likely. Our sensors are still jacked up and the cloud isn't helping. Return's unusual for an asteroid or a comet fragment at this orbital. We'll find out shortly. Should be alongside in five or six minutes, so you've got time to change out tanks."

Eric shrugged and walked over to the stowage locker to do as suggested.

Weird, but whatever. Just want to hit my rack, but I guess that's not happening any time soon.

At least Lieutenant Pascal's estimate turned out to be accurate. Eric's clock had just ticked over six minutes when he noticed an irregular arc of black occluding the starscape behind it. Lack of light and reference points made judging scale difficult, but the shadow was easily larger than the *Fortune*, possibly by several times. The lieutenant glanced back at him and the others that had filtered in over the last few minutes.

"Okay, duty nav is telling me we've matched vectors. The plan is pretty simple, go over there and find out what's special about it. Radar doesn't show any fast moving debris nearby so random strikes aren't likely anymore, but be cautious anyway, we've already lost too many people. Keep your eyes open, and stay in contact. Friedrich, you're with me."

Eric nodded and one by one the men around him disengaged their maglocks and pushed off toward the silent shadow overhead. Eric and the lieutenant were traversing the gap when the *Fortune*'s dorsal observation lights flickered to life. Only a quarter of the infrared spotlights had activated. Half of those flickered and failed, but the handful of that remained gave more than enough light to amplify. At first glance, Eric was inclined to dismiss the behemoth before them as just another dirty ice ball circling the outer reaches of a barren system, but an odd shadow lurked just below the surface.

Eric toggled his radio and said, "Hey, LT, you tracking that shadow? Our one o'clock?"

"Good eye," Lt. Pascal commented.

Eric beamed as they adjusted their approach to touch down where it seemed closest to the surface. Pascal unholstered a small pistol and fired a piton into the ice. Tethering to it, he motioned for Eric to do the same. "*Fortune*, how do you read?"

"Signal is loud and clear, Pascal," the *Fortune*'s communications officer replied.

"I've got my men covering elsewhere, but I believe we've found your artifact."

"Any ideas, lieutenant?" a rough voice cut into the channel.

"Nothing certain. Whatever it is, it's big and appears to be embedded in the ice, Captain."

"Continue your investigation, Pascal," Captain Fox replied.

"Aye, sir."

Over the next fifteen minutes, Pascal directed the others to join them as their own searches came up dry.

"*Fortune*, I believe we've located the thinnest part of the ice, but we'll need equipment to get through," Pascal transmitted.

Eric's heart beat a bit faster as he waited for the reply. *This thing is huge. What the hell is it?*

"Pascal, have your men return to the *Fortune*. We're sending Ensign Winters and a few others from engineering over. You're to remain to coordinate."

Lieutenant Pascal looked over at Eric, "Permission to keep Friedrich with me?"

Another pause.

"Granted, but he's your headache, Pascal," Captain Fox replied.

Eric rolled his eyes. The officers always acted like having him around was a chore, but they never passed up the opportunity to have him nearby.

Lieutenant Pascal glanced at him. "Before you ask, and I know you're going to, Winters spent a decade as an asteroid miner. Foreman by the time he quit, if I recall. If anyone can crack this quickly and safely, he can. There's a reason he led the planning effort for cracking that last one."

Moving shadows across the ice surface caught his eye and Eric looked up. Several vac sleds traversed one of the spotlights just forward of the aft cargo transit bay. According to his few acquaintances in maintenance, the sleds were difficult to work on and spent more time under repair than they did under operation.

"Lieutenant Pascal, Ensign Winters and engineering team on approach. I figured we could bring a few air tanks in addition to our gear so you two can top off."

"Roger that, Ensign. Good thinking," Pascal replied.

Thanks to the extra reaction mass, the sleds approached much faster than his team had and were spiked and tethered in half the time it had taken Eric's group to arrive. While his team unstrapped their equipment, Winters attached a corded black wand to his tablet and slowly waved it about while pacing a circle around Eric and Lt. Pascal.

Eric's radio crackled as Ensign Winters addressed his crew. "Tori, Spinks, set the base up over here, tether it off at least ten meters. Azarov, Church, help them set up the inductance drill when they've got the base anchored. Everybody else back off, there's a hollow chamber underneath us. It might have atmosphere, so there's a chance we'll have some decompression when we breach it."

The team carefully assembled the base, anchored it, and then mounted a large bore drill piece.

"Captain, Pascal. Winters is activating the inductance drill."

"Carry on."

The flat bit descended to the surface and slowly rotated against it for several moments before water began to climb its sides and the bit began to descend. Eric noticed most of water slipped up the surface of the drill bit into a collar instead of puffing off into space. He shot an inquiring glance at Winters.

"Hydrophilic surface coating. Draws the liquid to a chamber so it can be reclaimed. The umbilical from the drill to the sled carries more than just electricity, Friedrich," Winters explained. The ensign's eyes darted back to the drill. "Careful, slow the bit!"

Before the operators could react, the slow stream of liquid water became a jet and then shards of ice and liquid water burst forth lightning quick in all directions.

"Shit! Kill the power!" Winters yelled over the shocked voices that filled the channel. Eric flung his hands up to shield his face. Ice pinged off his visor and pelted his suit. A shadow passed overhead and more ice pelted him from behind moments later.

The chaos on the channel squelched out, overridden by the ship's command channel. "Pascal, *Fortune*. Status?"

"We had a blow-out, Captain. Pocket had atmosphere. Temp and pressure were higher than Winters expected. One minute."

One by one, the team called out their status as the ice cloud dispersed. The drill was gone, so was the sled it had been secured to. A ragged hole slightly larger than the drill base remained where their equipment had been. Checking behind him, Eric spotted the battered sled and the drill. The drill had been blown off the ice by the decompression and uprooted its tethers on the way out. Held by the umbilical and the sled's anchor, instead of shooting straight out, it had followed an arc and imbedded itself in the ice behind them.

"*Fortune*, Pascal. No injuries to the crew, though we're patching two suit leaks. The drill and the sled it was attached to might be a loss though."

Captain Fox sighed over the radio. "At least the crew's safe. Carry on."

While the team gathered at the bore, Ensign Winters smirked and said, "Now you see why I got out of ice mining, Friedrich. Too fucking dangerous."

"Hey, that thing still had the price tags on it when we pulled it out of the crate. Do you think it's still under warranty?" Church asked. His question brought several chuckles.

"*Fortune*, Pascal. Looks like the blow-out opened up a chimney of some sort, too narrow to traverse. Bends out of sight about three meters in. We'll need some time to widen it."

"Pascal, *Fortune*. You've got three hours before we need to leave."

"Acknowledged, *Fortune*," Pascal replied.

Eric stared down at the darkened hole, imagining what might lay at the other side. *Nothing's been all that dangerous so far. Could be something valuable, maybe I can get a bonus for going above and beyond? Wait, or what if there's nothing down there? We could be back home three hours sooner if I do this. Either way, that works.*

"Sir," Eric said before Lieutenant Pascal could issue orders.

"Yes, Friedrich?"

"If I ditched my propulsion pack, I think I could fit."

"You sure?"

"Yes, sir. Looks like it would be tight, but I should be able to manage."

"*Fortune*, Pascal. Spacer Friedrich has volunteered to enter the chimney while we widen it. Any objections?" Pascal asked.

"Provided he knows the risks, none," the Captain replied.

"Roger, *Fortune*. I'll keep you updated. Friedrich, give me your pack. Winters, did you bring a SAR belt on one of those sleds?"

"Standard load includes a search and rescue belt, LT. Church, grab the one from your sled," Winters said.

"Friedrich, you familiar with what's on a SAR belt?" Pascal asked.

"Part of my cross-training, sir," Eric told him.

"Good. Well, no time like the present, off you go. Stay on the radio."

Eric nodded as he handed his pack over and slid into the shaft. He passed through several meters of jagged ice before the surface suddenly smoothed out at the curve. Continuing on, the ice smoothed into a clean sheen, like it had melted and refrozen dozens of times.

Eric paused when he came to a bend and pondered what that meant a moment before toggling his radio.

"Well, Lieutenant, the shaft continues at least another eight meters after the curve. It curves again, upwards. Uh, up relative to my face. Would be straight ahead if you haven't moved since I crawled down here, I think. It's weird, LT. Ice is real slick down here. Still frozen, but it looks almost like glass."

"Got that. How's the fit?"

"Well, not too bad actually. I suppose now is a bad time to point out I'm mildly claustrophobic?" Eric commented as he pulled himself through the narrow tube.

Pause. "No, now would not be a good time for that. What else?" Pascal replied with mild amusement.

"Past the curve it starts getting narrower. Sec, I'm going to see if I can squeeze through," Eric said, looking at a particularly narrow spot.

God I hate tight spaces.

Pushing further in meant he had to crane his head to the side to get his helmet to fit through. Using fingers and toes, he scooted against the ice hugging him from every direction. And then he stopped.

Fuck.

The top of his helmet hadn't hit anything. He couldn't get any traction with his fingers and his boots only slid across the ice behind him to similar effect. He was stuck.

You've got to be shitting me. No, calm down. Calm. Down. Nobody's getting stuck out here. Help is only like ten minutes away. Breathe in. Breathe out. Fuck me. Stop panicking, asshole.

"Panic kills," Eric whispered to himself repeatedly as beads of sweat trailed down his forehead. "Panic kills, asshole. Okay, what are we going to do? We're not stuck, life just hates us. Narrow tunnel, no traction. Make ourselves smaller? How? Right."

Eric exhaled, forcing every bit of air out of his lungs that he could and tried pushing off with his boots. He moved forward a few centimeters.

429

Fuck yeah. With the ice even tighter around him, he couldn't inhale completely. *Aw fuck. Keep going, keep going, asshole.* A few more centimeters, and even tighter than before. *Maybe I should turn back. Ah shit, how?* He toggled the oxygen saturation with a chin switch, breathed what little he could, and then pushed again.

He drifted into a much wider open space, a chasm filled with ice glass, stalactite-like spikes, and frost everywhere.

"Friedrich?" Concern colored Pascal's voice.

"I'm okay," Eric panted into his radio. "Almost didn't fit, but I'm through. Far side is, ah, interesting."

"How so?"

Eric panned his light across the chamber. "Chamber, bigger. Lots bigger. There's something in here, huge. Looks like maybe the ice melted away from it. Suit's detecting radiation, alpha and beta particles mostly. There's only one area I can really get to. It's coated with frost. Give me a second, I'll try to clear some off." Eric braced himself against the ceiling of the chamber and began brushing back frost to reveal their prize. "It's--this is a hull plate."

"Say again, Friedrich. Hull plate?"

"Yeah. It looks brand new. Different from most of the plating I've seen before, shinier but more dull at the same time if that makes sense? Uh, I've found something. Looks like it might be a hatch or an airlock of some sort. Design is different from ours, but similar. I'm going to see if I can't find a way in."

"Wait a second; let me confer with Captain Fox."

"Roger," Eric replied as he brushed away more of the hoarfrost.

"Captain says you're good, but be careful, we don't know whose ship this might have been. Keep an eye on your suit's displays, no telling what sent this ship to its grave."

"Uh, sir, I found something else. There's labeling by the hatch, and a set of ensigns to the right. I'm taking pictures, but my data link isn't working."

"Describe what you see, Spacer."

"Hatch is inset to the hull, maybe a few centimeters. Yellow and black hatching along the frame. Writing in English says this is 'Aft Airlock #2'. Series of numbers separated by dashes over that. One dash one hundred forty dash eleven dash letter 'Q'."

"Relaying to *Fortune*, continue."

"Appears to be five ensigns on the hull next to the airlock. From the top, alternating white and red horizontal stripes. Upper left quadrant is dark blue, white dots. Quite a number of them. Second ensign, a bit harder to describe. Uh, red lines to the center from the sides and corners. The red is framed thinly in white; rest of the ensign is blue. Third ensign, left and right third of the ensign is red. Inside band is white with some sort of red emblem centered. Fourth ensign, blue. Upper left-hand quadrant is the second ensign. There's a set of stars off to the right, and another single star below the inset second ensign. Uh, last ensign is identical, except it doesn't have that lone star from the previous."

"Roger that, standby." Eric spent the next few seconds examining the hatch when Lieutenant Pascal broke in. "Did you copy that?"

"Uh, no, sir. Squelch didn't even break."

"*Fortune* says that numbering system sounds like a Protectorate ship, but the ensigns aren't from any known colony of theirs. You can come back if you want and let us take over, Captain doesn't want to put you in any further danger."

Eric smiled. *Nah, this is too cool.* "Negative, LT. I'm good. Haven't seen anything remotely dangerous yet. There's no power to the airlock, but I think I've found a manual override."

"Copy, proceed."

Eric engaged his maglocks and bent over the door as he pulled the electric driver from the SAR belt. *Looks to be about fifteen millimeters.* Eric fit what he hoped was an appropriate hex bit to the driver and inserted the end into the female override fitting. He slowly depressed the trigger and the resulting torque nearly pulled the driver out of his hands. Eric paused to brace himself before pulling the trigger again. The bit slipped intermittently, ever slightly too small. A puff of cold gas announced the door's opening.

"LT, hatch is coming along. Should have access in about fifteen seconds."

"Roger that. You might lose us on radio when you get inside, so don't do anything stupid. Captain says those numbers you gave gives us an idea the size of the ship embedded in this ice ball. Nearest guess is three hundred meters. Those numbers, the first identifies the deck, larger numbers being toward the belly, the second, how far from the front of the ship you are while the third is how far from the centerline."

"Door's open LT. Airlock had gas in it, so I'm going to see about sealing it behind me. Might still be atmosphere further in."

"Copy, what's the airlock look like?"

"About what you'd expect. Mostly bare. Hand-holds, another door on the inside. Wait, there's a placard here. USS Gadsden. Ship's sigil is a yellow background, some kind of coiled rope-like creature. Below that, 'Don't Tread on Me.'"

"Heh. Sounds like a privateer or maybe military, maybe the Persians. I'm pretty sure Pershing hasn't sent anything this far out though. We'd've heard about that. Proceed, Friedrich. We're probably thirty minutes or so from being able to follow. Find the bridge if you can, should be amidships and towards the top. Captain's quarters shouldn't be far from that."

A visual search of the compartment before him revealed a matching override fitting identical to the one on the hull on the inside. "Sealing her up, LT. By the way, use a fifteen millimeter on the override bolt, it'll slip like it's the wrong size, but sixteen's too big."

"Odd. Good luck."

Eric keyed his radio one last time as the outer hatch closed, "Friedrich, out."

Turning to the inner door, he realized, like its outer brother, this one was unpowered. The override fitting on this door was also much larger. *No way I've got a bit that big.*

Eric frowned and was about to turn around when he spotted a recess next to the hatch's frame labeled "Auxiliary Entry Tool, 1 pc, NSN

1820-00-C17-6436." The recess held a canted metal bar a little over a half meter long with a perpendicular hexagonal head at one end. Eric pulled the bar out of the recess, inserted the head into the override fitting, and tested which direction it wanted to turn. The fitting budged clockwise, the direction he had the least amount of travel.

"I always pick the wrong way first," Eric muttered as he pulled the head out. He dropped end of the bar almost to his knees before inserting it again. He heaved upwards and could hear the gears in the frame grind before giving way. *Of course they're stiff, they haven't seen maintenance in how long?*

Opening the inner door proved harder than he expected and doing so produced the huff of air he expected. Eric watched as the suit's sensor readout as the pressure in the room climbed. His headset crackled and hissed as his helmets external audio feeds detected air pressure. *Pressure at .2 bars. Ambient temperature, one degree Celsius. That's odd, I think? Shouldn't this place be frigid as hell? Negligible particulates. Carbon dioxide levels below the sensor's tolerance. Oxygen, too. Almost all nitrogen. Humidity bone dry. Air pressure's way too low.*

Cautiously, Eric stepped into the next compartment and surveyed the dark interior. The walls were lined with racks, each with a suit. Each suit bore the ship's yellow sigil on the breast. "Heh. Two-part airlock. Yeah, Pascal might be right, could be a privateer. Maybe not though, these look like service suits, not combat," Eric muttered to himself. He paused on his way to the hatch on the other side and stared at the thin glass display next to the door. Without power, the screen was black.

Whoever they were, they spent a lot of money on this ship. Hatch looks like an old design, too. Old, but effective.

Eric sighed. This one had another large override fitting. Eric noticed another entry bar in a similar recessed space on the other side of the hatch he'd opened.

Better leave one for Pascal.

Leaning through the opened hatch, he returned the first bar to its alcove and sealed it with the second bar from his side.

Using the second tool Eric cranked at the mechanism for the hatch leading further into the ship. The hatch resisted. He shoved. The resistance against him disappeared suddenly as the door cracked and the air pressure equalized. Eric nearly toppled over the raised section of the hatch, but caught himself.

Stupid. Of course this would be isolated from the rest of the ship. His air pressure gauge now read .98 bars. *Still cold and dry. If there was oxygen, it'd be safe enough to take off my helmet.*

Silence reigned in the hallway beyond and a few meters down the hall his flashlight illuminated a protrusion that ringed the passageway. Eric glanced back at the hatch he'd just come through. *Yeah, close this too. That rim looks like an emergency pressure door. No telling if it works without power or not. Not going to chance it.* He cranked down the last hatch and then proceeded to pan his light about as he wandered off down with the bar slung over his shoulder.

Pausing in the middle of an intersection with a side-passage, Eric noted it seemed every side passage had small plaque similar to the one over the airlock. *1-112-7-L*

Passageway.

He glanced back the way he came.

"If that was one-forty and this is one-twelve," he said to himself, doing the math in his head.

Yeah, almost two meters per number. Another hundred meters or so to go, though access up would probably be closer to the centerline.

Several passageways later, Eric caught himself humming a song and realized the constant silence bothered him. He paused momentarily by a poster depicting a man in a white uniform with a finger to his lips.

OPSEC? What the hell is OPSEC?

He shrugged and continued on. Passing through a sealed hatch he had to open with the access tool, Eric found himself in a much larger compartment the plaque called a quarterdeck. The flooring here was white tile, not pale blue sealed plastic. Stanchions connected with thick blue rope lined the walls. Something drifted through his peripheral vision startling him out of his internal monologue. He'd automatically hefted the bar back to swing before realizing the drifting form was a corpse curled into a fetal position.

Breathing heavy from the adrenaline surge, he reached out to the drifting form. His suit's Geiger counter began a slow click as he grabbed the corpse's oddly mottled green and brown uniform. What appeared to be an octagonal hat tumbled away off the corpse's head to drift across the quarterdeck aimlessly.

Not much above background radiation.

Eric rotated the body so he could get a better look. The corpse wore a white armband with large black, block letters centered on it proclaiming, "SF." Below that smaller lettering spelled out, "Security Forces." Eric squinted and froze. Two embroidered sections lined the tops of the uniform's slanted breast pockets. In dark stitching, one said, "US Marines", the other "Friedrich."

He'd seen death before, but his name on a corpse? That bothered him. He'd also seen the bodies of engineering crew when reactor containment had failed, having been on a working party that transferred them to be jettisoned. This corpse appeared the same but far more dessicated.

Shifting the corpse brought a black device that had been on a sling over the corpse's shoulder rolling towards him.

Looks like a projectile weapon, not energy.

Not wanting to disturb the corpse more than necessary, he examined the weapon and found a way to disconnect the weapon from the sling by pressing the button at the attachment points. Eric looked over the rifle.

Safe, fire, burst. Arrow on this switch is pointing to safe. Not much different from our gear at all. Forward of those engravings he found another set. *FN Manufacturing? Never heard of them. Either small enough we haven't looted anything from them yet, or really, really old.*

He pressed a button on the side to no effect followed by the button below it. A piece of the weapon rattled and drifted loose. Eric caught it. *Ah, there's the cartridges. That must be the magazine release. Good enough for me.*

Noticing what appeared to be a pistol in a holster at the corpse's hip, Eric reattached the larger weapon to the sling and carefully drew the smaller black weapon. Keeping his finger off the trigger, he examined the sleek metal weapon.

No selector, much larger bullet. Looks like a button in the palm, probably a mechanical safety. Wonder if that's a magazine release? Yep. Looks like thirteen cartridges. No clue what a M1911A3 is, but this feels serviceable.

He pressed back the slide slowly to reveal the top of a cartridge in the chamber. Eric looked up at the corpse as he let the slide return home.

"I know it's just nerves, but I'm taking this if you don't mind," he whispered and paused.

This is silly. Fuck that.

Eric laid a hand on the corpse's chest and whispered the same prayer uttered at every funeral he'd attended since the crew of the Fortune had adopted him, "Lord, receive this man into your waiting arms. He has been long from port and long from home. May he find rest and safe harbor wherever he has gone."

Prayer finished, Eric continued across the quarterdeck toward a large white hatch on the far side. He paused by a clearly ceremonial setting. The matting on the floor before him contained the ship's emblem. To either side stood rows of what might be large-bore penetrators as big around as his thigh. Colored cloth floated from the poles between the slugs. Central to the display, a stand stood at the end of the mat on the floor with several poles with colored cloth secured to them. Eric recognized several of the lengths of fabric as the ensigns by the airlock. Four of them were off to the side while the central shrine displayed the one with red and white stripes as the centerpiece. He glanced at the other four in the shrine.

POW-MIA, You are not forgotten. Must be some kind of memorial. US Navy. Not sure what that symbol is. Hmm. US Marine Corps. Nice red. USS Gadsden, ship's symbol again.

He glanced down below the hanging cloth and noticed a stand with a plaque that read, "USS Gadsden, SBBGN-X."

No clue what the BB-whatever means. Hey, is that wood? Wow, I haven't seen wood like that since I was a kid.

Eric gravitated to a display off to the side. The simple wooden stand, labeled "Chain of Command" held a number of picture frames, presumably ordered by seniority. Most of the top row was conspicuously empty.

Eric looked over the names for the slots pondering if this might have meant something. President of the United States, Vice-President, Secretary of Defense, Secretary of the Navy, all important sounding, but also all empty. The first frame in seniority to have a photo, a stern-faced older male, was labeled Chief of Naval Operations.

Admiral Mullin, huh? Yeah, not a privateer. Military warship. Eric skipped over to a photo of the commanding officer, Thomas Morneault. *Looks like he'd give Captain Fox a run for being a hard-ass. Both of them could probably chew through a bulkhead. Sounds like a name from Orleans. Desi might know.* The Gadsden's executive officer looked significantly less angry. *Well, Parsons is easier to pronounce, I guess I'd be happier too.* Eric shrugged at the last photo, Command Master Chief, and moved on. *What kind of name is Sweeting? That guy is just too happy.*

Eric opened the white hatch barring his way to the bridge, stepped through, and sealed it behind him. He ducked past several corpses in blue uniforms on the way up the ladder well, making sure he did not disturb the radiation scarred remains. He pulled himself up the ladderwell, shivering as he passed more bodies. He paused to adjust his suit's temperature upward.

Too many bodies around here, this place is a goddamn morgue.

After the first flight of steep stairs, he noticed the flooring was no longer a pale blue, but a darker blue with white flecks in it.

Heh, wonder what that means?

He continued up a number of flights before a plaque had caught his attention.

"05-75-1-C, Bridge," Eric said to himself as he fit the entry tool into the door's fitting. Eric paused, looking at the hatch on the opposite side. The plaque label, "CIC", meant little to him, but the hatch was conspicuously armored and someone had painted "Combat Information Center" on it. "Heh. Well, she's a warship for sure. I'll check the bridge first."

Aside from the half dozen corpses, the bridge was spotless, cramped, still as a crypt, and completely dark. Enough space had been left open between each of the work stations to allow the operators to get to their station and little else. Like the previous corpses, these new ones did not appear to have struggled. Eric started to poke about when a realization struck him. Five of the bodies were strapped into chairs. One sat in a chair half slewed around like he had been talking to the corpse behind him, the only corpse not secured to a chair. The ones in the seats had simple polished black boots, black belts with tarnished white buckles, possibly silver at one point, and the lettering on their coveralls was white. The odd corpse out wore what probably had been expensive looking shoes, a light brown belt with a brass buckle, and gold lettering on the name tapes.

Eric reached moved around the floating corpse, trying not to touch the stern-faced man. *US Navy. No clue what that silver insignia on the collar means. It's got wings, so maybe he's the pilot? Captain maybe? Gotta be captain.* Eric glanced down at the nametape as he checked the man's pockets. *Morneault. Yep, captain.*

"Sorry, Captain Morneault, just checking for keys. No disrespect intended." Eric fished a necklace made from linked silver metallic balls from around the corpse's neck. A set of keys and two stamped metal plates swung from the end of it. Eric read the stamped lettering on the tarnished plates. His brain refused to process the last line. *Morneault, Matthew, 210-42-3521, AB+, Christian, January 30, 1965.*

"Nineteen sixty-five? They had to be using a different calendar." Eric stuffed the chain in a belt-pouch and stepped off the bridge. *If I were the captain, where would I have my quarters?* He looked at the ladder up. *Nah, if the main airlocks are on the main level, why would I want to walk farther? Still need to be near the bridge though. No other doors on this level, let's try the next one down, shall we?*

He traced his path back down another deck and looked about at the doors near the ladderwell.

Ah, here we are, CO's stateroom.

Eric tried the door and found it locked. The key he'd taken from the Captain fit smoothly into the physical override for the electronic lock and Eric let himself in. The far wall had been covered by a large version of the red and white striped ensign with gold fringe. A simple bed filled another wall and a desk with shelves filled the other. Eric looked over the obvious computer workstation, and then pored over the small items on the desk. Finding a photo of a woman and a few children, he slowly shook his head.

I wonder if they knew what happened to their father.

His eyes were then drawn to a large poster on the wall alongside the bookshelf. The writing was warped, like someone had tried to write without lifting their pen, but readable.

"In Congress, July Fourth, Seventeen Seventy-Six," Eric chuckled to himself about the date before reading further aloud. "The unanimous Declaration of the thirteen united States of America. When in the course of human events it becomes necessary for one people to dissolve the political bands which have connected them with another, and to assume among the powers of the earth, the separate and equal station to which the Laws of Nature and of Nature's God entitle them, a decent respect to the opinions of mankind requires that they should declare the causes which impel them to the separation. Hmm. Earth, huh? Interesting."

Eric jerked, half bringing his improvised club to bear when his headset crackled, spitting only noise.

Pascal must've gotten in. I should go. He glanced at the next poster. *We the People of the United States, in Order to form a more perfect Union, establish Justice, insure domestic Tranquility, provide for the common defense, promote the general Welfare, and secure the Blessings of Liberty to ourselves and our Posterity, do ordain and establish this Constitution for the United States of America.*

Eric's radio crackled again. He could almost make out something intelligible.

Got to go.

As he turned about, he grabbed the computer tablet off the desk. His radio crackled again as he stepped out into the hall.

"...drich. Pasc...do...copy, over?"

"Pascal, this is Friedrich. I copy."

"...you broken...clear."

Eric sighed, cursed his radio, and began moving as fast as he could down to the quarterdeck where he transmitted again. "Pascal, Friedrich. Do you copy, over?"

"...rich, Pascal. Much clearer. What's...status?"

"Your signal's still breaking up, wait a second," Eric replied as he worked open the hatch back to the airlock he'd entered from. As he opened the door, his headset crackled again.

"Friedrich, Pascal, how copy, over?"

"Pascal, Friedrich, signal's clear. Mine?"

"Clear now. What's your status?"

"I found the bridge and the captain's quarters. You won't believe what's up here."

"What'd you find?"

"Well, first off, this isn't a privateer. It's a warship."

"Good, and?"

"The crew's all dead. Looks like radiation burns, but the only thing radioactive is the bodies. They're barely above background. That's not what's crazy though."

The lieutenant sighed, "What's crazy, Friedrich?"

"The captain's ident lists his birthday as nineteen sixty-five."

Pause. "Say again."

"You heard me. Nineteen sixty-five."

"That's not possible. That's--"

"I know. It's December third, 216 PE. That date has to be from before humanity came to the stars. Lieutenant, this ship's from Earth!"

"Hey, let's not get carried away. In fact, keep that to yourself until we can go talk to the captain and see what he says. I highly doubt this ship is five hundred years old, not when its design includes artificial grav. Grav plates have only been around for-- Hold on, command channel." Eric glanced back at the corpse whose pistol he'd taken as seconds ticked by. "Friedrich, get your ass down here, fast. *Fortune*'s leaving in five minutes, with or without us."

Eric nearly stumbled. "What?"

"You heard me. Beat feet, spacer. Captain thinks there's someone else out there and he's spooling up the drive."

Shit shit shit!

Eric disengaged his maglocks and launched himself down the passageway. Using the bar to correct his trajectory, Eric sailed most of the length of the corridor in a fraction of the time it had taken him to walk it. He nearly bounced off the wall at the end of the hallway, but engaged his maglocks to keep from flying off.

"Hurry up, this way," the lieutenant yelled. He stood on the inside of the airlock door. As Eric ducked through, Pascal worked the next door and waited for Friedrich to seal his door before opening the next. Working together, they managed to maintain the atmospheric integrity of the ship while moving quickly. Eric stopped to cycle the outside airlock shut, but Pascal pointed towards Eric's maneuvering pack and moved to cycle the airlock shut himself.

"We've got two minutes. We're good, Friedrich. Had them leave a sled for us," Pascal said as the airlock door slid shut.

Pascal pushed off, leaving Eric to follow him through the chimney several seconds behind.

Pascal cleared the jagged maw of the tunnel entrance and immediately spat, "Son of a bitch."

"What?" Eric asked. Pascal didn't need to answer, he saw for himself as he drifted free of the ice. The *Fortune* was moving away at speed. "Motherfucker. They left us!"

"I know, I know. Give me a second."

Eric saw a small flash out of the corner of his eye followed by an ephemeral line of violet motes that traced an almost perfect path to the *Fortune*.

Lieutenant Pascal's shoulders slumped and his helmet settled in the palm of his hand. "Fuck me."

"What was—," Eric started to ask.

"Railgun."

"Fuck."

Eric's headset blared static into his ears.

"Attention pirate vessel, this is Captain Hines of the PMV *Shrike*. By the authority granted to me by the Protectorate of Man, I order you to stand to and prepare to be boarded."

The *Fortune*'s engines flared, going to maximum burn. Flickering pinpricks of light along the hull caught Eric's eye as the *Fortune* began to veer into a sharp turn. The *Fortune*'s point defense turrets were spitting a hail of slugs toward the pirate hunter. Shock froze Eric's gut.

What do they hope to do, piss them off?

There was a brief flash as a rail slug slammed through the *Fortune*'s unarmored hull at over a hundred kilometers a second. Eric blinked as the ship he'd grown up on came apart in slow motion. Gasses escaped through ruptured plating as the ship bent in on itself and spewed a cloud of glowing dust and debris. Two engines guttered out, unbalancing forward thrust. The wreck began a lazy, twisting cartwheel. Several heartbeats later, a brilliant, blinding actinic flash replaced the blackness of space as the fusion containment dewars failed. It was horrible. It was beautiful.

Dumbstruck, Eric and Pascal could do little but watch.

"Any surviving pirate personnel activate your personal beacons if you have them or transmit in the clear. You will be afforded all legal protections set forth in the Charter by the Protectorate of Man until you can be tried for your crimes. You have fifteen minutes before we depart."

• • •